The Unwaba Revelations

Part Three of the
GameWorld Trilogy

Samit Basu

D1943094

PENGUIN BOOKS

PENGUIN BOOKS
Published by the Penguin Group
Penguin Books India Pvt. Ltd, 11 Community Centre, Panchsheel Park, New Delhi 110 017, India
Penguin Group (USA) Inc., 375 Hudson Street, New York, New York 10014, USA
Penguin Group (Canada), 90 Eglinton Avenue East, Suite 700, Toronto, Ontario, M4P 2Y3, Canada (a division of Pearson Penguin Canada Inc.)
Penguin Books Ltd, 80 Strand, London WC2R 0RL, England
Penguin Ireland, 25 St Stephen's Green, Dublin 2, Ireland (a division of Penguin Books Ltd)
Penguin Group (Australia), 250 Camberwell Road, Camberwell, Victoria 3124, Australia (a division of Pearson Australia Group Pty Ltd)
Penguin Group (NZ), 67 Apollo Drive, Rosedale, North Shore 0632, New Zealand (a division of Pearson New Zealand Ltd)
Penguin Group (South Africa) (Pty) Ltd, 24 Sturdee Avenue, Rosebank, Johannesburg 2196, South Africa

Penguin Books Ltd, Registered Offices: 80 Strand, London WC2R 0RL, England

First published by Penguin Books India 2007

Copyright © Samit Basu 2007

All rights reserved

10 9 8 7 6 5 4 3 2 1

This is a work of fiction. Names, characters, places and incidents are either the product of the author's imagination or are used fictitiously, and any resemblance to actual persons, living or dead, events, or locales is entirely coincidental.

ISBN-13: 978-0-14310-352-3 ISBN-10: 0-14310-352-3

Typeset in AGaramond by Eleven Arts, Delhi-35
Printed at Repro India Ltd., Navi Mumbai

This book is sold subject to the condition that it shall not, by way of trade or otherwise, be lent, resold, hired out, or otherwise circulated without the publisher's prior written consent in any form of binding or cover other than that in which it is published and without a similar condition including this condition being imposed on the subsequent purchaser and without limiting the rights under copyright reserved above, no part of this publication may be reproduced, stored in or introduced into a retrieval system, or transmitted in any form or by any means (electronic, mechanical, photocopying, recording or otherwise), without the prior written permission of both the copyright owner and the above-mentioned publisher of this book.

PENGUIN BOOKS
THE UNWABA REVELATIONS

Samit Basu is the author of *The Simoqin Prophecies* and *The Manticore's Secret,* the first and second parts of the *GameWorld Trilogy*. He is also a blogger, freelance journalist and scriptwriter. He currently lives and works in Delhi.

PRAISE FOR SAMIT BASU

'*The Simoqin Prophecies* is an intelligent, inventive delight. It marks the arrival of a fresh and very original voice'—*Indian Express*

'Basu draws from a vast source, only to weave it all together with amazing deftness, piecing the fragments together until they fit like a jigsaw puzzle . . . an intriguing tale, full of mystery and suspense, with generous doses of humour'—*The Telegraph*

'*Simoqin* is a romp. It is quite simply the most fun book to see in print this year. In fact this is a book that deserves only a one-word blurb—"Enjoy!"'—*The Times of India*

'A delightfully understated sense of humour that grows on you as you read on . . . playfulness is the motif of this entertaining novel' —*Business Standard*

'A host of characters and creatures inhabit the magical world [of *The Manticore's Secret*] . . . but this is also a novel guided by a sharp and informed vision of history. Basu writes as much with an eye on thrills as with an awareness of the many dimensions of his characters' —*Time Out*

Prologue

The first rays of the morning sun skimmed the westernmost treetops of Vrihataranya and ran smiling up the jagged eastern spur of Mount Batenbals, the tallest of the Grey Mountains east of Imokoi, pausing in astonishment for a moment as they beheld the slender, graceful body of Aishwarya the Duck (*Viaduci olwezasc*) crouched over a rude-shaped boulder in a perfectly executed Reverse Bakasana.

Aishwarya was no ordinary duck. A tautological statement, given that it is commonly known that there *is* no such thing as an ordinary duck, but Aishwarya was exceptional even among ducks. Aishwarya was a Famous Duck. Star of the forthcoming Bolvudis Muwi-visions *The Duck*, *The Duck II: Upon Her Damasc Beak* and *The Duck III: Daughter of the Duck*, Aishwarya was well known in the highest and most select circles. The reasons for her solitary yoga holiday in the mountains were manifold: Her last assignment, posing for the figurehead of a brand new ship commissioned by one of the most notorious pirates in the world, had unfortunately thrown her into a massive controversy over the connections between Bolvudis and the criminal underworld, and on top of that, Derozio the Dapper Drake, her partner in love and stardom, had recently publicly revealed his long-running secret affair with a peregrinating mallard named Cyrfrensis. Escape from sympathy, adulation and suspicion alike could only be found, she knew, in the mountains, and here, in the fresh air of Mount Batenbals, she hoped to restore, through meditation and exercise, the mellifluous quaver in her quack.

As she crouched on, eyes closed, enjoying the tension in her wings and the sun on her back, the harmony of her duck-chakras was suddenly ruined by the sound of heavy boots crunching over pebbles. Not more ink-footprint seekers, thought Aishwarya wearily, not *here*.

She looked downwards and saw, to her surprise, that a vaman clad in thick robes had appeared out of nowhere a little distance below her. And two more, crawling out of a hole in the mountainside that she was quite sure hadn't been there a few moments ago. The first vaman looked around warily, scanning the rocks and the forest for dangers unknown; the other two emerged fully and stood up, sunlight glinting off their heavy metallic armour.

'Kill that bird, Mod.'

'Come on. It's just a duck.'

'What is a duck doing in these parts? It could be a spy.'

'Yes, that's just what the ravians needed to acquire that deadly edge. A duck.'

Ten more vamans, emerging from under the trees, laughed loudly at this, but Aishwarya, not liking the tone of the conversation at all, retreated flapping to the safety of a nearby rock, behind which she squatted indignantly, peering out, feathers fluffed, at these bearded cads who were not only clearly devoid of Soul, but unfashionable to boot.

'Well met, Mod Vatpo,' cried a prosperous-looking vaman as the ruffianly duck-disturbers hopped briskly over rubble and rocks to join their comrades under the shadows of the trees. 'It has been many moons since we last crossed paths.'

'Indeed it has. Curse those pestilential moons,' replied Orange the shapeshifter, aiming to confuse, because he had no idea who Mod's long-lost friend was. 'But consider this; could our reunion have occurred at a more auspicious hour?'

'We are not exactly sure how auspicious the hour is, Mod,' said Reh Hanpo, president of the Rebel Union of Marginal Labour. 'I, for one, am still not happy about meeting in the open like this. Are you sure this place is safe? Will the ravians really come?'

'This is not a good time for doubt, Reh. I will tell you again, if it makes you feel any better: They promised they would meet us here, today, at dawn, when I spoke to them in Kol,' said Orange. 'Granted that was many moons ago, and the world has changed since then, but if they want to renew our alliance, they will most assuredly come.'

'You must not always worry so, Reh,' said Mod's friend, placing a comforting hand on his leader's shoulder. 'Our day is finally here. All your labours for the welfare of the Union have borne fruit. I for one have been ceaselessly amazed by your ability to keep the Union working so smoothly without a single council, a single meeting—but you must realize this day was inevitable, and an occasion for celebration, not disquiet. I, for one, have always longed to see my fellow rule-breakers face-to-face. And here we are, together, finally, ready to change the course of history, and spread the glory of vamanity across the galaxy.'

A senior politician of some kind, thought Orange.

'The secrecy was always necessary, Rash,' snapped Reh,

glaring at the Unionist leaders he'd spent years uniting. 'We could not afford another infiltration. Our scheme would have been as dead as our beloved predecessors if the king's spies had even suspected that any of us were friends. And they would have, had we not proceeded this cautiously. Do you have any idea how hard they have been looking?'

Rash. Rash Nappo, senior vaman defence minister, thought Orange. A Unionist that close to the king? He wasn't very surprised; quite a few of the other vamans were well known in their guilds. He gave the forest and the rocks another piercing gaze. Nothing. Good.

'They should have looked harder,' chuckled Rash. 'After all, we were only under their noses all along.'

'Gloat later. The king's watchdogs aren't here, good. But, look harder, and you'll notice the ravians aren't either.'

'They will be here,' said Orange firmly. 'Is everything else ready?'

'We've brought everything, Mod,' piped up Nue Tonpo, a scientist. 'Everything you thought of. Detailed drawings of the newest secret weapons. Battle plans fresh from Rash revealing positions, strengths and tactics. Reh has the scrolls that will tell the ravians the extent of our labours, and the lists, where he's named each and every vaman they can count on in their hour of need. They must be awed by this display of trust, and forgive our past weaknesses; indeed, we have been over-generous this time. We might even manage to get more than portal-secrets, if we bargain well—and who can bargain better than us?'

'We risk too much,' muttered Reh.

'Consider the stakes. The risks are acceptable.'

'I'm not surprised you think so, Mod—wasn't it your idea?' said Nue. 'Either way, that's not even all we're offering.

We're throwing in all our cards here, as you suggested, as we agreed, despite Reh's misgivings. Chak over there has maps of our own tunnels from Xi'en to Imokoi.'

'Each one of us has brought enough evidence to warrant immediate execution for treason,' said Reh.

The Unionists laughed, a little nervously.

'And you, Mod?' asked Rash. 'Have you truly obtained Kol's best-kept secrets? That, too, is a worthy prize.'

'No,' said Orange, one of Kol's best-kept secrets.

'What have you brought, then?'

'I have brought a whistle.'

Orange took out a whistle and blew it.

'Perhaps this is a good time to tell you,' he said, 'that you're all under arrest.'

Shattering the silence that followed Orange's announcement, to the north, south, east and west of the Union's conspirators, four giant armadrillos, the vamans' trusty war-beasts, burst upwards through the soil, their steel-hard snouts easily breaking through the last few yards of their golem-loosened tunnels. Earth and pebbles cascaded off their bony, plated shells in streams as with a massive, earth-shaking *thump* they landed on the ground, their silver head-shields glittering. Massive curling claws, attached to pillar-like, leathery feet, crunched into the earth, and cunning, beady eyes peeped through mask-slits in amused contempt, observing with satisfaction the drooling, slack-jawed, loosened-bowelled horror that seemed, for some reason, to affect the two-legged when multitudes of armoured, elephant-sized engines of terror materialized uninvited in their midst.

Elite vaman bombardiers of the Bhoomi Silverlode lay on their steeds' backs in leather and metal sheaths, two per armadrillo, roaring challenges as the Rebel Union's terrified leaders cowered in terror. With frightening speed, twin cannons were assembled on each armadrillo's back; one warning shot was fired, sending a large spherical ball, trailing an eerie green flame, crashing high into a tree just behind Reh. The tree exploded, filling the air with smoke and burnt, spiralling twigs and leaves, knocking most of the Unionists off their feet.

Reh and Rash, battle-axes raised, faces masks of fury, charged screaming at Orange. The shapeshifter, moving as no vaman had ever been seen to move, drew two daggers from his robes, dived between them, rolled, and knelt on one knee, his face groundwards, his hands extended and empty. Reh and Rash went down screaming, daggers embedded neatly and deeply between the armour-plates at the backs of their knees. Orange turned, smiling viciously, and drew two more daggers.

The rest gave in without a struggle. A few considered swallowing the papers they were carrying, but then they looked into the armadrillos' eyes, gulped and realized anew how sensitive their digestive systems were.

More Silverlode troopers, armed to the teeth, emerged from tunnels and searched the Unionists, their grins under their helms widening every time they came upon tokens of the extent of both the importance and the treachery of their captives. Mor Kotpo, their captain, walked smartly up to Orange and saluted him.

'We are in your debt, Gaam Vatpo,' he said. 'I owe you a personal apology, too, for having secretly doubted you. The king will be delighted—we have driven a stake through the Rebel Union's very heart, and it is all your doing.'

'Thank you, Mor,' said Orange. 'The oath I swore when I found myself granted a second chance at life, however, is not even half fulfilled. With your permission, I will take your leave. I must now enter the Great Forest, and not return until I have found the road to Asroye. Only when I have ensured the ravians' destruction will I allow myself to rest.'

'So, after having led us to victory over enemies within, you would strike out alone to destroy our greatest enemies outside. I'm afraid I cannot give you the permission you seek, my friend,' said the captain, smiling. 'You have proven yourself a master strategist, and a fine soldier, and such valour cannot go unrecognized, or unrewarded. The king desires to meet you.'

'I do not want glory, Mor. Send the king my thanks, and assure him of my loyalty. I must be on my way.'

'The king desires to meet you,' said Mor, his smile unwavering, though a few other vaman soldiers appeared as if magically behind Orange. 'He is aware of your oath, and I suspect he intends to make things a lot simpler for you. If you think about it, Gaam, you will find it will be much easier to find Asroye *with* us than to find Asroye *for* us, on your own. Come with me, now.'

Orange paused for a second, and then met the captain's eyes and nodded. If he was pleased, he did not show it. There had already been far too many smiles smiled since dawn.

A few minutes later, the last of the armadrillos dived into the earth, his ridiculously small tail waving in the air. And then the mountainside was empty again, with no sign of what had happened except a few mysterious circular spots of rubble in the ground, a few bloodstains and a sorry-looking treestump. Aishwarya the Duck emerged from behind her rock, her tail-feathers bright and bushy. The cheese-slice of her life was suddenly hole-free; the world had fallen into place, and she now knew that life wasn't *supposed* to make sense, and that her own problems weren't really that important in the greater scheme of things. Quacking joyously, she flew up, frivolous-feathered, to meet the morning sun. And she saw the future, as clearly as if it were spelt out in front of her in big shiny letters in the sky.

Duck IV.

A golem-drawn chariot sped through curling, twisting, miraculously smooth vaman tunnels. On it sat the renowned Bhoomi Silverlode captain, Mor Kotpo, the only Rainbow Council member to have anything in common with a fruit, and two other vamans of such impressive muscular development that their skins had grown completely turgid, rendering them incapable of displaying any facial expression at all. As Mor congratulated everyone on how well the ambush had been planned and executed and his men sat in stone-like silence, no doubt concealing their ecstasy with great difficulty, Orange sank back into his seat, closed his eyes and permitted himself a relaxed moment. Around him were many fabulous examples of the beauty of the underworld—myriad-hued rock-walls, sculpted stalactites, incredible water-etchings—but he showed no sign of interest as they passed by.

Orange the shapeshifter was thoroughly sick of all things subterranean. He wanted to go home.

It wasn't just that he missed the towering spires and cheery mass-murderers of Kol; there was just so much *work* to be done. A new Rainbow Council had to be created, and he didn't know if there were five shapeshifters in Kol capable of stepping up and coming even close to replacing his four best friends, or Red, the unreliable but incredibly talented girl they'd lost to the wild. And he needed to tell Violet everything he had seen in the world of vamans. So many questions would be answered, so many mysteries explained. There was just so much even the Rainbow Council didn't know.

Orange had no idea how long he'd been underground, or what had happened in the world outside. Had the ravians appeared again? Had Dark Lord Kirin succumbed to his advisers and started a war? Were Asvin, Maya and Red even alive? And where had the Civilian's invisible adviser gone? These and hundreds of other questions had haunted Orange since the day he'd stepped past the secret gates of the vaman world, as he'd lied, tricked and enchanted his way beyond veil after veil of secrecy, and entered a world whose very unexpectedness was mind-numbing, even for him. A world where precious metals were overabundant and information and ideas were currency, where there was so much to learn and discover and take back to Kol that time spent trying to dig out news of the sunworld had seemed like time wasted.

Until he'd come to Bhoomi, Orange had never realized how much living in Kol had trapped him into taking an essentially human view of the world—that other two-legged races were simply humans with special tricks attached. He'd known that only members of one particular vaman tribe were allowed to enter the sunworld, and that its customs were in all probability constructed to help sunworlders assume they knew all about vamans and what boxes they fitted in—thus making vamans less threatening. That tribe, he now understood, was the one that stuck most closely to a regressive, medieval way of life. In Bhoomi, he'd seen so many different kinds of vamans—beardless vamans, pretty, strangely elfin vamans, fair vamans, Xi'en vamans, *blue* vamans, living in what seemed like harmony in a society as complex and rich as Kol—that he'd felt shamed and small. He'd thought Gaam Vatpo was unusual, and a step forward for vamans as a people, not realizing that Gaam had just been a normal vaman who'd had more trouble than his fellow tribe members in taking several steps back. Orange knew the Chief Civilian thought vamans of tribes other than Gaam's weren't allowed to come up to the sunworld because the vaman king was afraid of his empire being corrupted by the influx of new ideas. He also knew, now, the rather frightening truth—it was far more likely that vamans didn't go up to the surface simply because humans could not be allowed to discover what they'd accomplished. Alternatively, they were all allowed to leave, but only the really backward ones wanted to.

A lot of the other things he'd discovered, though, had made him feel extremely satisfied with himself. He'd explored the vamans' vast maze of caverns filled with wonders, seen how far they'd progressed in the sciences, and realized that they'd let Kol advance by showing and selling them machines, tools and techniques that had become outdated underground—just as efficiently as the Rainbow Council had guided Kol politically for a few centuries. The Rainbow Council had often wondered why human progress in the agricultural sciences had always lagged so far behind those fields in which vamans also took an interest in—medicine, manufacture, construction, printing, transportation—when human scientists appeared to be making their own discoveries. Now Orange knew.

As the chariot made its way through the outer walls of Bhoomi, Orange sighed deeply, sat up, eyes wide, trying to absorb every possible sight, smell and sound, every cunningly created piece of this subterranean metropolis. He felt a twinge of sadness, knowing it was his last day and he would never return. Even if he did succeed in finding and helping to destroy Asroye, he would have to return to Kol and stay there. But he'd never forget his time among the vamans, and all he'd experienced. While he'd wasted no time in getting to the business of seeking out the Rebel Union's leaders and leading them into a trap, his senses could not have helped being assaulted and astounded by the wonders of Bhoomi. He'd seen strange and wonderful beasts, eaten bizarrely delicious food that had thrilled his taste-buds and ruined his stomach, gazed in awe at works of art and engineering even his mind had difficulty ingesting, seen, tried, and sensibly abandoned clothes that even Kol was not ready for yet. For a lonely, dangerous quest to save the world, he'd had a completely unreasonable amount of *fun*. But there was only so much a mind could take, even a mind like his. He'd seen the future, and it was underground. He'd seen quite enough.

After two hours of no conversation and heavy traffic, Orange found himself being marched into the inner chambers of the Core House, the gigantic, towering palace in the heart of the city that made every building in Kol look like a kennel. Flanked by a phalanx of black-clad, golden-helmeted vamans carrying fire-pipes, he walked over floors that looked like lava-flows and floors that looked like glaciers, taking in every detail; the friezes on the ceilings, the beautiful, cold-eyed palace maids, the mechanical beasts that played in the hexagonal, diamond-bordered courtyards, the sculpted war-golems that stood, massive and terrifying, at every gate. Mor Kotpo marched in front, smiling and saluting as vaman nobles of various shapes, sizes, fashions and degrees of decoration watched the procession pass, but stopping for no one.

Finally they came to a shining silver door. The palace guards stopped in unison and thumped their fire-pipes on the ground. At a signal from Mor, Orange walked forward, and followed Mor through the door, into the vaman king's hall.

And lurched forward, falling on to the floor, his mind spinning and gut churning. For it seemed to him that he had just fallen off the world. The king's hall was vast and long, and the floor, ceiling and walls were all cunningly painted to represent an exact likeness of the sky. Great pillars ran down the hall from the entrance to the vaman king's throne, but these too were painted to blend in, to make any newcomer believe that he was suspended in mid-air. Strange clouds floated through the hall, and paintings on the floor contrived with some form of magic to shift and swirl and look like a cloud-floor, with gaps even revealing a likeness of the ground far below.

'Approach, Gaam Vatpo,' called a quavery voice.

Orange sprang to his feet and looked around, at corners and pillars gradually defining themselves as his keen eyes grew accustomed to his surroundings. He walked across the hall, slowly, stopping only when his feet told him there were steps ahead, leading up to a dais where four figures sat side by side in the painted sky.

And so it was that Orange the shapeshifter was the first person not of vaman blood to cast eyes on the rulers of Bhoomi; Nor Rispo, regal, strong, formidable, clad in mail dark as obsidian, Yin Stinpula, beautiful as a katana, startlingly young, sharp-eyed, simply clad in a blue tunic, Kuin Lizpula, with her shock of purple hair and her ornate purple gown, matronly, charming, immediately loveable, and Flaad Nagpo, white-bearded, white-robed, venerable, deep blue eyes twinkling below bushy, well-combed brows.

'We are the vaman king,' said Yin. 'And we understand you deserve our thanks, Gaam Vatpo.'

Orange bowed low. 'It was my duty, your majesties. And there is much more to do.'

'Verily, noble Gaam—'

'Can we do this quickly, without the fancy nancy-boy talk? We need to decide what to do with the Slimy Ones next, and I need to go to the toilet,' said Flaad.

'What, again?' asked Kuin. Nor guffawed unpleasantly.

'Oh, all right, then,' said Yin. 'Right. Gaam. This is a magic-proof enchanted hall, right? Very strong wards all over the place. You can't do magic here. Don't bother trying.'

'I cannot use magic anywhere, your majesty. I do not know how.'

'Can we just kill him and be done with it? I really need to go,' said Flaad.

'We're not killing him, Flaad. We're killing the Slimy Ones.'

'Oh, right, right. Good. Carry on, then.'

'You should also know,' said Yin, 'that any attempt to attack us in this hall will call out big golems who can squash you like a bug before you manage to touch us. Even if you can jump very fast.'

'But I would never attack you, your majesty. I trust I have no need to prove my loyalty.'

'That is true. Poor boy just helped us catch those nasty Rebel Union types, and now you're scaring him. If you upset him further, he probably won't even tell us who he really is,' said Kuin reproachfully, smiling encouragingly at Orange.

Orange tried to teleport. He couldn't. He tried to transform into a bee. He couldn't. He considered attacking the vamans, but decided against it.

'I am Gaam Vatpo, your majesties. I do not understand why you speak in riddles.'

'Liar,' said Nor, evidently a vaman of few words and much deadliness.

'Look, we didn't get to be vaman king by being stupid, right? We know Gaam's dead. His body was found. You must have been the one who stole it in Kol,' said Yin.

'I was miraculously revived,' pleaded Orange, trying to look as earnest as possible, though he knew the game was up.

'My dear boy, don't be silly. We've watched you snooping around since you left the sunworld. We know you can change shapes. That means you're a rakshas, or a powerful spellbinder. We know you don't mean us any harm directly, because you went after the Rebel Union right away—which is why we let you live,' said Kuin.

'But now he's gotten rid of them for us, so we kill him! I knew I was right!' cried Flaad, tugging at his regal white beard in a most undignified manner.

'Stop it, Flaad,' said Yin. 'You're making him nervous.'

'Spoilsport,' said Flaad, sitting back with a smile. 'Well, Mister Magician? Who are you, and what do you want? We know you don't work for the Civilian, because we asked her and she said you didn't. And that we could kill you if we wanted—she really has enough to worry about, poor girl.'

Orange said nothing. He just looked from one of the vamans to another, dumbstruck. No one had ever made him feel *stupid* before.

'We think you're one of those secret guardians of Kol we've always suspected existed,' said Kuin. 'We think you're one of those mysterious creatures who protected the palace when the ravians attacked Kol—before the war started, I mean—and you've been looking for the ravians ever since.'

Before the war started? wondered Orange, wishing again he had some idea what was happening in the world above the ground. How long had it been?

'Why did you come here to get the Rebel Union, though? They were never that important,' said Yin.

'Revenge,' said Nor.

'For what? The attack on the palace? Or the Cravenstick Massacre?'

'Cravenstick,' said Orange, feeling naked, exposed and about six years old. His respect for the rulers of Bhoomi rose even further when he saw that none of them looked even remotely triumphant at his admission of defeat.

'My dearest friends died there,' he said. 'And I will not rest until I have driven the ravians from the face of the earth. For myself, for my friends' spirits, and for Kol.'

'What is your name?' asked Yin, her voice now low and gentle.

'I have none,' said Orange. 'I am just a servant of Kol, though the Civilian does not even know of me.'

'And I beg of you,' he said, kneeling, 'let me go. I am strong, and wise, and skilled in strategy and combat. I will be a powerful weapon against the ravians, and thus a powerful ally.'

'I'm sure you will,' said Flaad. 'But letting you go is out of the question. You see, the first rule of entering vaman territory if you're not a vaman and want to stay alive is this: you don't. There are some rules that are sacred to all vamans, even degenerates like us.'

'However, and this is a very big however,' said Kuin, 'we'll let you live, if you work for us. Answer, truthfully, all our questions about the ravians, Kol, and even the vamans, as the sunworld sees them. Stay here in Bhoomi as an honorary vaman, and lead us to Asroye and victory.'

'I wish I could,' said Orange. 'But I may only serve Kol. That is all I live for.'

'Bhoomi is Kol's greatest and most generous ally. By working for us, and helping us break the ravians, you get us what we want, and you get to keep your vows.'

'I only serve the throne of Kol.'

'But we *own* the throne of Kol,' said Yin, 'we just let humans run it because we're lovely people. Does that solve your problem?'

'Yes, it does,' said Orange. 'I am willing to swear allegiance to you, if you so choose. Your generosity has been astounding, and I apologize for my previous stubbornness.'

'And now he wants to agree with us and run off as soon as he can, telling himself his loyalty to Kol makes betraying us acceptable behaviour,' said Yin, shaking her head.

'I would not dream of doing anything of the sort,' said Orange.

'Liar,' said Nor.

'We could put him in magic-proof padlocks and keep him under constant surveillance,' suggested Yin.

'I would be powerless then, and unable to help you. And you wouldn't believe any information I gave you, because you couldn't trust me if I were an unwilling captive. The only way out of this, your majesties, is to trust me and let me go. We both want the same things, but my vows prevent my working for you.'

'You see, my friend,' said Kuin, 'if you'd come to us and confided in us before wandering around our lands, we might have put our trust in you.'

'But you didn't. And we caught you,' said Flaad.

'And it would be very bad business sense to let a resource like you slip out of our hands.'

'Kill me, then,' said Orange. 'If you think that is the right thing to do.'

'But we know it isn't. Will you help us find Asroye, at least? We really don't want to kill you, or even harm you,' said Kuin. 'Here's the new deal: you find Asroye for us, letting us keep your magical powers locked up so you don't run away. You help Kol, and you don't have to tell us any of your precious secrets.'

'You don't understand,' said Orange. 'Without my powers, I would just be another vaman. If I knew how to find Asroye, I would not be here at all. The only way I can be of assistance to you is in Kol, using my powers to help drive the ravians away. Why can't you see this? The Civilian is defenceless if I am not in Kol. The ravians have destroyed almost everyone in my order. I know the Civilian does not need to be defended against you—she keeps things the way you want them, and you could destroy Kol in a week if you wanted—but every day of my absence puts her in grave danger. Without the Civilian, Kol will fall. By keeping me prisoner, or killing me, you doom your greatest ally.'

'Still can't let you go,' said Yin. 'You've seen too much. You're too loyal to Kol. Kol gets our secrets, we lose unimaginable sums of money. I know it sounds really heartless. But you can't be *nice* if you're trying to run a kingdom.'

'I will not reveal anything I saw here, just as I would not

reveal Kol's secrets to you. I have kept secrets for centuries—it is what I do best. If you let me go, I will keep the Civilian safe, and find Asroye for you without compromising either Bhoomi or Kol, I swear it.'

'Persuasive lad, isn't he?' said Kuin. 'Should we trust him?'

'Yes,' said Yin. 'I know it breaks all the rules, but I think these are times that call for a little rule-breaking.'

'Flaad?'

'I've been wanting to kill him for a while. Still do. Bloody waste of time. Now if you'll excuse me, I need a piss.' The old vaman half-ran out through a side door.

'Nor?'

'Too risky. Sorry.'

Kuin Lizpula looked at Orange and sighed sadly.

'Are you absolutely sure you cannot agree to our terms?' she asked.

'I wish I could,' he said. 'But I know what would be best for Kol, and your terms are not. My vows are all that distinguish me from rakshases. But thank you for trying to find a solution.'

'You have still not voted, Kuin,' Yin pointed out.

Kuin said nothing. She made an almost imperceptible movement with her fingers. Mor Kotpo stepped forward, drawing his shortsword. 'Thank you for everything, sir,' he whispered in Orange's ear. 'We won't forget you.'

Orange felt a sharp pain behind his ear, and then nothing.

BOOK FIVE

1

The Dark Lord stood alone on the highest balcony in the Dark Tower, watching the shadows lengthen as the sun set over the Mountains of Shadow. His black robes, like the black-dragon-on-red banners above him, fluttered and billowed in the wind. His bare arms were striated with new scars, with his strange black dragon-skin marks meandering over his skin like drunken tattoos. Far below, columns of asurs performed battle exercises, dug trenches and built new fortifications, and snatches of lusty song floated upwards from the evening revels in the Skuan quarter. Up on Kirin's balcony, there was no sign of merriment. The wind gusting across Izakar's battlements was cold, but his face was colder.

A door creaked open, and Spikes stepped out on the balcony behind him. Kirin did not move.

'Any news from the hunt?' asked Kirin.

'Yes. The surviving Xi'en and their acolytes have been found.'

Kirin's jaw tightened. 'Where?'

'They're hiding in a valley just across the Grey Mountains. We attack at dawn.'

'Why wait till then?'

'Assembling forces. They're going to fight like wild monkeys when they realize they've been cornered.'

Kirin looked around, finally, at Spikes standing dour and menacing in the last rays of the hiding sun.

'How is she?' he asked.

'Still unconscious. Nasiviv will tell you if there's any significant change.'

'I've heard that line every day for a month now.'

'I know. It's not a particular favourite of mine either.'

'Right.' And Kirin returned to contemplating his dark domain.

They stood silently for a few minutes.

'Talk to me,' said Spikes.

'It wasn't your fault,' he said after a while.

'I'm going to push you over the railing if you don't stop being a drama queen,' he said after a while.

'What do you want me to say, Spikes? I could start whining again about my shortcomings as a Dark Lord, but we've done that. And I think I'm getting a lot better at the Dark Lord business, actually.'

'That's what I'm worried about.'

'I had to take my responsibilities seriously at some point. What happened happened because I didn't.'

'What happened was bad luck.'

'Bad *luck*?' Kirin whirled around, eyes blazing. 'Don't coddle me, Spikes. You told me yourself. I remember every word. "There's trouble at the tower. A bunch of Wu Sen monks and Pimawen assassins have turned up to kill you and take the Gauntlet back to Xi'en, and every time they've raided the tower looking for you, they've killed everyone in their way." And I did nothing.'

'You did nothing wrong. You knew you could protect yourself. You did not fear them. Rightly so, as it turned out.'

'I don't think the people who died protecting me would see it that kindly, Spikes. I was their great Leader. I had no right to return and pretend to take charge if I had no intention of looking after the safety of my followers.'

'You didn't ask them to come help you.'

'I *chose* to be Dark Lord. When I did, these people, asurs and rakshases and pashans and humans and monsters all, became *my* people. All I've done since then is try to mislead them, turn them from their ways towards what *I* thought was right, make them do what *I* wanted, what *I* thought was better for them.'

'Peace, education, brighter futures. How selfish of you.'

'No, Spikes. What gave me the right to change them? I've been guilty of the same sort of arrogance I've always despised in every chest-thumping hero in history, dragging the weak and confused towards his own stupid heroic visions of ideal futures against their will. How could I not have seen this?

'I think it's time I stopped trying to impose my wishes on my people and started trying to give them what *they* want.'

'Even if they want war and destruction? Wasn't stopping wars and saving lives the only reason you accepted your father's offer? Would you lead them into war now, just because you feel guilty about one act of carelessness?'

'I don't know.' And Kirin turned his back on Spikes again.

'Whatever you do, I trust you to know the difference between right and wrong, Kirin,' said Spikes.

Kirin said nothing.

'Don't make the mistakes your father made.'

Silence.

'I preferred the complaining to the sulking, I think,' said Spikes, and left.

Kirin gripped the railing until his hands turned white. Spikes was right, he knew. Or was he? If he'd done his duty, would *she* still be battling death in the healers' quarters? She had saved his life, and in return his weakness and indecision had almost cost her hers.

His thoughts turned again to her. To their first night in the tower . . .

She'd shut the door with one wave of her hands, and filled the air with sweet, strange scents with another. She'd walked slowly up to him, slithered into his arms and before he even knew what was happening, there they were, kissing hungrily, their clothes melting away like water. And as her warm hands sent shivers down his bare back, he'd opened his eyes, seen her face—Maya's face—and he'd broken the kiss and turned away, his heart beating frantically.

'What's wrong?' she'd whispered.

'I know you're not Maya,' he'd said.

She'd stepped back, looked down at herself, at her smooth brown skin glistening in the candlelight, and then at him, his breath tightening as their eyes met. 'I can be anyone you want me to be.'

'I want you to be *you*,' he'd said, unable to take his eyes off her. 'I don't even know you.'

'But you like me. Very much.'

'Yes.'

'That'll do.'

'No, it won't,' he said. 'Not if you look like Maya. I want to see *you*.'

And he'd watched her lines and curves swirl and harden from one flawless form to another, felt desire course through his veins anew as he feasted his eyes on an unbearably lovely warrior-woman, ebony-skinned, ruby-haired.

'Is this you?'

'This is me tonight.'

They'd stared at each other in silence for a few moments. Then Kirin had reached out for her, but she'd skipped away, laughing, and transformed herself into Spikes.

'Oh *my*,' she'd giggled, looking at him archly, tracing arabesques on the floor with a stumpy foot, 'is *that* for *me*, Kirin? All these years of faithful service, and I never knew.'

He'd just stared at her then, laughing foolishly.

'Put your clothes on,' she'd said, changing into warrior-woman form again. 'You're in love with Maya, and it turns out, to my surprise, that I'm a romantic at heart. I've been watching and waiting for you two to stop being idiots for years, and I can't do this to you now.'

'Who *are* you?' he'd asked in complete wonderment then, one part of his mind reminding him it would be polite to stop goggling at her.

'I'm not entirely sure,' she'd said. 'It might have been interesting if you'd helped me find out. But we can talk about that, and many other things, in the morning.'

'No,' he'd said. 'Don't go.'

And for the first time since he'd met her, covered with dust and sweat and blood amidst the ruins of the ravian temple in Vrihataranya, he'd seen confusion in her eyes.

And right then, as they'd looked at each other in the flickering light, each breathlessly considering drastic, immediate revisions of their lives, fifteen wildly shrieking Xi'en assassins had thrown themselves through the ceiling.

Darkness fell and stars came out over Izakar, and the moon rode out in full glory, but time had stopped for Kirin.

Kirin looks up, and sees Wu Sen monks hurtling towards him in mid-air, and Pimawen assassins running miraculously down the walls. Far too late, he remembers Spikes's warning, and realizes they are after the Gauntlet. Which is on a small table next to his bed, open and unprotected. He pulls with his mind, and it flies to his hand—he catches it just as a Wu Sen monk crashes down on the table. In his other hand, the Shadowknife lengthens and hardens into a sabre; it is thirsty. But Kirin has wasted precious seconds; the Pimawens have already hurled poison-tipped darts at him, and they almost scrape his throat as he turns them aside in mid-air, sending them crashing to the ground.

'Leave!' he shouts, wanting her to vanish, but she does not. Instead, she swings her arms in a wide arc, and a sheet of flame rushes upwards at their assailants. It burns the Pimawens, but the Wu Sen monks are unharmed. Now all fifteen are on the floor, in attack positions amidst the falling stones and rubble of the ceiling; with a flowing gesture, Kirin shatters the stones that would have crushed him, and her, an instant later. Swords are drawn. More darts are thrown and hurled aside. The door crashes open; Spikes is here. Behind him are rakshases and asur guards. A Pimawen strikes Spikes repeatedly, his fingers blurring as they perform a complicated sequence of jabs and thrusts on pressure points on his body, intending to paralyse him. Spikes raises his hands and claps, crushing his assailant's head like an eggshell.

The attackers are faster than any humans their opponents have ever seen. She throws fire and venom at them, but they are masters of close-quarters combat, and they duck and weave and skim over walls, doubling and circling and leaping, and she has nowhere to run. But an asur has thrown her a sword; she does not want to run.

Rakshases materialize. But the room is small and crowded, and they are careless; two appear hideously merged, one's arm sticking out through the other's chest. A monk shoots a streak of blue fire at them from his open palm, and they fall screaming through the window, trailing blue fire and smoke. The Dark Lord's soldiers form a circle around him, yet he is not protected; the men from Xi'en attack in no discernible formation, but the circle is never allowed to remain complete. Fresh corpses pile up on the floor—mostly asur corpses, but more asurs keep coming.

Kirin stays close to her; the Shadowknife defends them. The room is an impossible blur of blades, fists, feet and fireballs. Spikes is the only one fully in control. Blood drips from his spikes and claws; he seems not to notice sword-thrusts, and the Wu Sen's pigtails-with-blades head attacks only annoy him. He knocks two monks' heads together, ties their pigtails in a knot, and releases them; they spring apart instinctively and slice each other's throats.

Aciram arrives, laughing as he strikes, and now the attackers are fighting for their own lives. The wily rakshas has fought Xi'en warriors in small enclosures before, and under his guidance, the rakshases rally and charge. The Pimawen fight in the style of the monkey, lurching and crouching. They move faster than the rakshases, but the rakshases are stronger; the attackers are slowly herded together, their backs to the window.

A Wu Sen monk, the oldest and most skilful, leaps up on the windowsill, dodging a fireball, and takes careful aim. A dragon-shaped streak of blue light extends from his palm towards Kirin. He misses Kirin.

He hits her.

She does not burn like the others; the dragon-light seems to slither around her body, and then it dives into her mouth and is gone. She lurches forwards and Kirin catches her. She sinks to the ground in his arms. A trickle of blood rolls out of her mouth, and her pupils swim upwards.

'Healers!' roars Kirin, casting every healing spell he knows on her. Aciram vanishes. Spikes impales another monk, his claws going right through the thin, bald man's chest. More rakshases, big, young, terrifying, materialize in the room. But Kirin does not see them. She's trying to tell him something, gurgling and spitting as blood wells up in her mouth and cascades down his hands. He pulls her up, one hand behind her neck.

'They're dead,' she says, her eyes wide, astonished. 'He killed Soma and Tamasha.'

'You'll be all right,' he says. 'Rest.'

'No, Kirin, you don't understand,' she says, her voice suddenly childlike. 'If they're dead, who am I?'

He has no answer. He does not even know her name, and grief runs right through him, icy and grey.

Aciram materializes next to them, with Nasiviv the healer. Nasiviv picks her up, firmly and expertly, and Kirin rises cobra-like to return to battle. But the battle is over; the eight surviving monks and assassins leap out of the window, and as the defenders cry out in astonishment, they glide down the tower, their feet only occasionally touching its black walls. There are rakshases waiting for them at the bottom, but they never reach the bottom; shrugging off arrows and winged attackers alike, they leap over walls, jump over rooftops and are gone.

Kirin looks around in horror at the bodies littered around his bedroom. He feels as if he has murdered them all himself. Other rakshases walk over bodies, healing the wounded, but Kirin sits in a corner, staring at nothing until Spikes helps him up and leads him away.

* * *

'Kirin? May we speak?'

Aciram walked out on to the balcony, looking immensely weary. Spikes stood behind him, stone-cold in the moonlight, not meeting Kirin's eyes.

'Crow's reports are in. About fifty of them are encamped in the valley. The team for tomorrow's attack has been assembled, and is ready to leave as soon as you give the word. Flyers, teleporters and vanars. We'll be there in no time.' said Aciram.

'Consider the word given, then,' said Kirin. 'I'm surprised you took so long.'

'I would have come earlier, but Nasiviv called me to his quarters.' The massive rakshas looked uneasy.

'There is news?' Kirin's eyes lit up. 'She has recovered?'

Aciram sighed, and shook his head. 'She died one hour ago.'

'You do not have much time to grieve, I am afraid,' he said. 'There is also dark news from the east—the ravians are on the move, and you have much to do. But know this—I leave now to cross the mountains with a band of killers the like of which has never seen before, and I will personally hunt down each and every one of those Xi'en curs, and give them deaths more savage than anything you could imagine.'

The Gauntlet of Tatsu burned brightly on Kirin's hand, as brightly as his burning eyes as he summoned his dragons.

'No, Aciram. Stay here, and see to her last rites,' Kirin said. 'I will lead the attack myself.'

2

An ancient Koli philosopher who'd wanted to get rid of an annoying houseguest had once asked the question, 'If a tree falls in a forest and no one observes it, does it make a sound?' He'd gotten rid of the houseguest, but the question had lingered.

A far more difficult, though less widely known, question was this: 'If a tree falls, and is observed to fall, in a forest, but the forest itself does not exist, does it make a sound?'

This question was only asked in Ekyavan, a mysterious forest valley in Avranti, and always followed by uproarious laughter, because the seers of Ekyavan, despite possessing incredible mystic powers and impressively uncoiled inner (spiritual) serpents, had really unfortunate senses of humour.

Perhaps this was because the work they did was not funny at all.

King Aloke of Avranti had always denied the existence of the valley known (unofficially) as Ekyavan, regardless of the difficulty normally associated with completely ignoring a patch of land the size of a small city-state. It was almost certain that Ekyavan was where Avranti's awesome magical weapons were developed and tested; that there was something, or someone, hidden in the valley's woods that Avranti was desperate to hide. Some whispered it was a fallen god, expelled from the heavens, and the valley itself was a crater that owed its origin to the impact of his fall. Others spoke of star-voyagers, secret societies, beings from other worlds who visited regularly with gifts, whose teachings could explain the nature of magic and solve all the world's puzzles. The less imaginative spoke of secret treaties with vamans, captive rakshases, or reservoirs of pure magic. For the world at large, over the years, Ekyavan had become a running joke, a secret graveyard where lost household objects went to die, a palace where little green men decided the fashion trends of the future.

There were still, however, large numbers of people who took Ekyavan and its unknown denizens very seriously. Pamphlets had existed for centuries, written, circulated and read by cryptographers, treasure-hunters, swindlers and bored people, about the effects of Ekyavan on the world—hidden symbols and codes, architectural and agricultural techniques, languages, magic, art. While most of these had been proved fraudulent, aimed at parting believers from their savings, or for the sheer pleasure of displaying rudely shaped objects to large numbers of people, all Ekyavan-related apocrypha had certain aspects in common. They all involved recently unearthed ancient depictions of mysterious celestial beings descending from the skies, causing floods and animal extinctions, and settling down in Ekyavan, keeping themselves occupied right up to the present day by secretly controlling the world through unconventional means, such as carefully placed symbols, little stones embedded in people's heads, popular world religions, and strange lights and sounds.

Avrantic farmers who lived in the lands surrounding (the alleged) Ekyavan refused to discuss the valley at all with even the most persuasive strangers—mostly because they had several centuries worth of handed-down experience in identifying and being rude to lunatics, cult members and spies. Though there were other rumours, dark rumours, of what really silenced the farmers—tales of sinister, black-clad men with glowing, lidless eyes who came in the night and took away anyone suspected of speaking of Ekyavan and its secrets. The only thing there was no doubt about was this: On the fringes of (alleged) Ekyavan, the king's soldiers would stop you and ask you to return.

No one who had ventured past them had been known to return.

It was afternoon when movement on the ground caught the attention of the eagle-eyed guardians of Ekyavan. These guardians were, in fact, eagles, majestic Avrantic eagles (*Rigallig aligals*), ever-vigilant watchers with great mad eyes, sterling celestial-weapon reviewing skills and fashionable habits (such as never turning up before the last quarter of any major battle).The eagles had protected the valley for ages, making short meals of every bird, spy or civilian, that strayed into their air-space, seeing through the illusions of the stealthiest intruders, from Danh-Gem's shadowsnatcher rakshasis to shimmering, invisible Artaxerxian jinn.

To these eagles, the nine white-clad men on magnificent white steeds riding in formation down the slopes of Ekyavan valley were, therefore, about as indiscernible as an avalanche.

The sun shone bright on their beautifully woven white clothes and cloaks, their white leather boots miraculously mud-free in the sticky Avrantic afternoon. Their heads were bare, their faces stern yet pleasant, and their backs absolutely straight; these were soldiers, though no weapons were visible.

Circling above them, the eagles screamed out challenges, which the intruders responded to with cheerful salutes. Behind the riders, at the rim of the valley, the eagles saw another sight that puzzled them greatly—the border-guardians of Ekyavan, elite, battle-hardened Avrantic infantrymen, not chasing the riders but standing still, with identical reverent expressions on their curiously slack faces.

At the valley's base, in the secret ashram of the protectors of Ekyavan, Swami Amartya, first of the trinity of Avranti's greatest sages, was rudely interrupted from his meditation (which might have looked, to the untrained eye, like an afternoon nap, but there were no untrained eyes in Ekyavan) and informed that the valley was being invaded, that the eagles were restless.

Suppressing the urge to turn a few of his disciples to ashes with a fiery flash of his eyes, the sage ordered his star scholarship student and best archer, the formerly six-fingered Hrohit, to test his latest creation, the terrifying Arrow of Lightning, on their uninvited guests.

'But I cannot see them yet, Swamiji,' said Hrohit.

'Lightning can. Make your move,' replied Amartya.

Seconds later, the Arrow of Lightning streaked off Hrohit's bow and headed with deadly intent, higher than any human hand could have shot it, towards the white riders streaking steadily ashram-wards.

The riders, seeing the silver arc streaming their way and the eagles scattering hurriedly, merely rode faster. The rider in the centre raised his arm, pointing to the arrow, and seemed to mutter something.

The Arrow of Lightning, created to bring death to an entire army, to remove the need for anything to strike its targets ever again, seemed to skip and bounce in mid-air; it sputtered and twisted crazily, like a demented firework, and then streaked upwards and outwards, out of the valley. A few seconds later, a huge *boom* shook Ekyavan as the Arrow of Lightning obliterated a village outside, sending clouds of dust and earth mushrooming into the sky. Thunder-clouds appeared in the sky, hurtling towards the Arrow's landing site to heal the wounded earth with rain.

'Ravians,' said Swami Amartya grimly, as outlier clouds cracked open over Ekyavan, hurling huge, angry raindrops on the ashram. 'Set the board. Prepare a welcome, my children.'

The white riders rode into the ashram miraculously untouched by the rain, though their horses' hooves were caked with mud.

Swami Amartya stood under a banyan tree, his saffron-clad disciples, holding an array of deadly weapons, by his side.

'Lower your weapons, sages!' called a rider. 'We come in peace.'

'You bring death into our valley,' spluttered Amartya. 'A strange peace, this.'

'*We* have not killed anyone yet,' said the central rider, dismounting. 'Besides, death came to this valley many ages ago. You should know, Swami Amartya; you saw it, and so did I.' He strode confidently towards the sage.

Amartya looked keenly at the speaker as he came closer. His eyes goggled.

'Is it . . . Zibeb?' he cried. 'How are you, lad?'

The other eight riders, striding up to flank their leader, laughed aloud at this, while Zibeb and Amartya embraced.

'Your studies have preserved you well, Amartya,' said Zibeb, gazing with genuine affection at the seer, standing tall and regal, snowy beard bristling with joy, frail body emanating a cold blue aura of unfathomable power. 'I can still see, in your eyes, the young mischievous apprentice I walked these woods with in the Age of Terror.'

'And you—you look just a few years older, Zibeb Quake-vanquisher,' said Amartya. 'How have you been? Did you ever become captain, as you dreamed of being? You have an air of authority about you now.'

The tall, dark, grey-haired ravian smiled gently. 'I have done well enough for myself,' he said, as Amartya's disciples lowered their weapons. 'I am now king of the ravians.'

The ancient sage cackled, his wrinkled face glowing. 'King of the ravians! Come in, Zibeb, and your men with you. There is so much to say. Many old tales I would hear again.'

Zibeb shook his head sadly. 'I am afraid we must leave the telling for another day, Amartya,' he said.

'Perhaps, then,' and the sage smiled a most un-sage-like smile, 'a game of chess?'

The king laughed aloud then. 'Swami Amartya and I played many a hectic game of chess under these trees long ago,' he told his men. 'And I must confess, with great sorrow, that I did not win even once.'

'Lose at chess?' asked a white rider, perplexed. 'But surely you could see all his moves in advance?'

'I thus had the privilege of knowing well in advance the manner of my own defeat,' said Zibeb. 'Amartya won not because of his powers, but simply because he was better at chess.'

'I must insist on a game,' said the seer. 'I would love to see what manipulating your mighty courtiers has done for your game.'

The smile left Zibeb's face. 'I wish I could,' he said, sighing deeply, 'But we come here on pressing business. Are the Skyriders here?'

Amartya's disciples gasped, but the sage seemed unmoved. 'Yes. Exactly where you saw them two centuries ago, and remarkably well preserved.'

Relief flooded the ravians' faces.

'And you have been looking after them ever since we last met?' asked Zibeb.

'Yes. I was never very fond of travel. But why do you ask about the akashraths?'

'We need them.'

The sage's face clouded over. 'I cannot allow that,' he said.

Zibeb nodded, and stepped up close to Amartya. 'Shall we walk together, you and I, old friend?' he whispered. 'I am about to tell you secrets it is death to tell those who are not of noble ravian birth, and I do not wish to test the loyalty of my men.'

While the sage's disciples saw to the comfort of King Zibeb's riders, the king and the sage walked together through the gnarled woods of Ekyavan.

'You wanted stories, my friend,' said Zibeb. 'Here is one.

'Though we will not let it be known in Obiyalis, we are fugitives. Asroye—New Asroye, as we have now named it—

is our last and greatest seat of power. The beings that drove us from our other worlds were of the same race as those who rode the Skyrider ships in your care.

'When we first saw the Skyrider ships together, hidden in these obscure woods all those years ago, I remember we suspected their pilots were not gods, as your masters thought, but a mortal race of beings of great wisdom—like us ravians, I remember you saying. When the Skyriders and their masters came to us in our other worlds, we welcomed them with open arms, as fellow voyagers through the mysteries of space.'

'In other words, there was a war,' said Amartya.

'Yes. I apologize—I knew I could not lie to you, but a king's habits die hard. They had come to your world, this world, too quickly, we know—had they come even a few centuries before the Age, things would have been different. When they came here, they had visions of harmonious galactic civilizations, much like us ravians, and this world was a primitive one that they fell in love with, so they stayed, and taught, until they died of mysterious causes, and their teachings were corrupted. With us, they were not so benevolent. We were already mighty when they came, and too complex to see anything more in their teachings than further avenues to conquest. They would not share the secrets of their star-ships, and we would not teach them to make portals. They accused us of spreading war and strife across our worlds—'

'An extremely fair accusation.'

'Yes. We foolishly set out immediately to capture all of theirs, but their fantastic machines, that cut across the voids between worlds, were too much even for us. We lost, and lost badly. But we learnt one thing that would aid us greatly—

just before we returned to this world, we finally learnt how to pilot the Skyriders. And here, in Obiyalis, lay Skyriders we could use—that is the hope that brought us back.'

'And now you would plunge this world into a war with the beings that rode the akashraths? I will not allow it.'

'I do not wish to harm a single denizen of this world, Amartya,' said the ravian king, dripping with sincerity. 'My motives are entirely different now. We need to prepare this world for the coming of the Skyriders. If they arrive, and find this world wanting, they will destroy it, as they did ours, over and over again. We must work in harmony, humans and ravians and rakshases all, to defend this world, to preserve it. And there is not a moment to lose. I implore you, show me where they are.'

Amartya gazed at him solemnly. 'Your chessmen are very badly placed as usual, however convincing your voice,' he said. 'But what would showing you the akashraths achieve? You have seen the akashraths. You know where they are. We entered them together, tried to solve their riddles and failed. Surely you have not forgotten.'

'You have not been paying attention, old friend,' said Zibeb, his smile growing warmer every second. 'I told you we had learned how to control the Skyriders. To inspire the Skyriders to light up for us, to transform from strange vessels of metal full of secrets to sky-borne city-ships of incredible beauty, we need certain commands—which we learnt recently during our wars in other worlds—alloyed with a certain strength of pure will, which, I am afraid, only we ravians can claim to possess on this world. We are the only ones who can *fly* these airships; the symbols and levers we spent hours poring over in our youth are lower, secondary controls, that the magic of this world is better suited to than ours. *You* might pilot the star-vessels, should we train you in their ways, but there are very few others in this world who can.

'Why would I try to take the Skyriders by force? I came here to enlist your aid. Working together, we can save the world.'

'This decision is not mine to make. The akashraths . . . no, they are too deadly. The weapons I have managed to fashion down the years with just scraps of understanding from the machines are all that keep Avranti floating in this world's seas of intrigue,' said Amartya. 'As raj-guru, I cannot give them away without King Aloke's explicit command, and only unwillingly then.'

'But we must have them *now*. There is no time to lose. You must realize these regional power struggles, these Dark Lords and petty border disputes and monsters do not matter any more. I know it is strange to hear the ravian king saying this, but it is time for us to atone for our sins. This world is our last refuge, and must be defended.

'Do you have any idea of the destructive potential the Skyriders possess? Surely you have guessed much; you have studied them for years. That arrow you threw at us in welcome was an inspired creation, but nothing compared to what we could discover together. You have a scholar's mind, Amartya. Surely you are curious.'

'If Asroye controls the akashraths fully, there is no force in this world that can stand in your way.'

For the first time since he had entered Ekyavan, the ravian king frowned. 'Do you not trust me, my friend?' he said. 'After all we have been through together? Do you know how much danger I have placed myself in just by revealing these secrets to you?'

'Much has changed since we were young together under

these trees,' said Amartya. 'It is impossible to tell when ravians lie, and you are their king.'

The sage bowed his head in thought for a while. When he looked up again, at the handsome ravian regarding him coolly, his face was grim.

'You came here to play with me,' said Amartya.

'I did,' said Zibeb.

'You removed me from the board, so your riders could overpower my disciples, and take my weapons from them, thus rendering me vulnerable, and filled me with nonsense about wars between worlds to keep me distracted and confused.'

'Not all nonsense. We did encounter Skyriders, and we did learn how to pilot them. But your account is otherwise accurate. You have been outmanouevred. It was a good move, wasn't it? My riders will have found the Skyriders by now. I gave them very precise directions.'

'You intend to wage war on Imokoi with the akashraths.'

'On most of this world, actually. Beginning with Kol.'

'Why?'

'Because I want to, and that is enough.'

The sage's eyes glowed red and his body turned a bright blue. The forest shuddered.

'You were always a terrible chess player, Zibeb,' said Amartya in a voice of ice. 'You have left your king vulnerable. You should have abandoned me somewhere before declaring your intentions; it is my move now. Call your men off, or die. Do not challenge me to a contest of power.'

'I do not doubt you could kill me, Amartya. Ask yourself, though: Is it the clever thing to do? We are, after all, friends, and murder is so unfriendly.

'Let me show you some of the other pieces on the board,

now, before you burn me to little bits. Tomorrow, with or without me, the ravians will ride to Asroye to join King Aloke in an alliance. My men have the Skyriders, and know how to use them. If you kill me, Avranti will burn to the ground, and any survivors will be persuaded to enlist for our secondary armies; with the Skyriders, we need no sworn allies. If, however, you restrain yourself, Avranti and Asroye will rule this world together, as allies. And you will have your Skyriders returned to you after the war, and my finest scientists will be at your service, to help you discover whatever you do not yet know about the universe. I have lied to you today, but believe me when I say this: I have great love in my heart for you, and wish to share the future with you.

'Or you could kill me and then be torn apart by the weapons you created. My men are ready.'

Amartya shook his head in a mixture of admiration and disgust.

'You win, Zibeb.'

'It took me over two hundred years.'

'And now you will wage war on the world.'

'You used the Skyriders to create weapons of war, Amartya. And the ravians would have taken this world this time, even without the ships, even without me. There is nothing you could have done about it. Do not waste my time preaching about innocent lives lost, and do not pretend that either of us feel anything but approval for bloodshed, and war, and death.'

Amartya nodded, and cheered up immediately.

'Risking the king to save pawns!' he cried. 'You will always be terrible at chess.'

'It is fortunate for me, then,' said Zibeb, as a low rumbling sound in the distance indicated that a Skyrider's engines had come to life, 'that this is not chess.'

3

Kirin had planned the trap himself, and given how distraught and short of time he had been, had planned it very well. The Xi'en were encamped near a mountain lake, on the eastern side of the Grey Mountains, a few leagues north of Mount Batenbals. Some fifteen rakshases had placed themselves around the roughly square camp before dawn, too far away to be seen by sentries, closing the Xi'en in on three sides while the lake did the honours for the fourth. In-between the rakshases, perched impossibly high on treetops in pairs, stood lean, rangy baboon–vanar archers, experts at arboreal combat, shivering as the mountain winds raked their thick fur, looking skywards for a signal from the Dark Lord. The warriors of Imokoi stood relaxed and ready; this was the first time they were being led into combat by their ruler, and their hearts thumped slowly, proudly, in a slow drumbeat that they knew would rise to a frenzied pounding in minutes.

Far above the lake hovered three Skuan dragons, side by side, as yet unrevealed by the morning sun's fast-approaching rays. A machan had been built under the central dragon's breastplate, and on it sat Kirin, Spikes, and an Artaxerxian sorcerer named Mazouq, who was moaning gently as the freezing air bit into his bones. The dragons were too high for the sound of their wing-beats to reach their intended victims below, but Kirin was chiding them for making a racket. Of course, Kirin's state of nervousness was so advanced that he even thought the sound of his teeth tap-dancing in the cold was enough to give their position away.

'Odd place to camp,' said Spikes, surveying the Xi'en base. 'Far too exposed.'

'Not for them. They're safer in the open than hemmed in anywhere. You'll see.'

'Safe? They're outnumbered, and you've brought dragons, and rakshases. You're going to butcher them.'

'It's what they deserve.'

Spikes said nothing.

Kirin tolerated the silence for a few seconds, then spun towards the pashan. 'What?'

'You know what you're doing?'

'Of course. We drive them towards the killing ground in front of the lake, and the rakshases and vanars close in and mop up anyone running away.'

'That's not it. You've never *planned* to murder people before.'

'I have killed.'

'In self-defence. Or by mistake.'

'I intended to kill Myrdak.'

'And Bali. Did you?'

'Well, I've stopped running away now. What's your point?'

'You know you're crossing a line here.'

'It had not exactly escaped my notice, Spikes. If you don't want to be a part of this, keep your eyes closed.'

Spikes looked unpleasant.

From the far end of the machan, Mazouq the sorcerer looked at them, at the young man with his cold, burning eyes and the glowering monster whose ugliness defied description, and shuddered.

A violet glow spread in the east. On Kirin's arm, the Gauntlet of Tatsu bled an angry scarlet fire. The dragon on their left snorted impatiently.

It is time, said Kirin.

What is time? asked his dragon, confused.

It, snapped Kirin. *Move.*

The dragons nose-dived in unison, their wing-beats thundering out across the lake as they hurtled towards the forest. The machan's occupants were thrown upwards and flattened into their dragon's chest. Looking down through the rush of air in his face, Kirin heard screams below; the sentries were good. As his dragons sent sheets of flame into the treetops, he could see his prey, scattering like raindrops, swords in hand, crying out in alarm. In seconds, the camp and the trees near it were ablaze. The dragons arced out of their dives, skimming the surface of the lake. Kirin could see the Xi'en warriors clearly now, gathering together, debating whether to attack the dragons or not. He was puzzled; how did these humans intend to take on dragons?

He got his answer when four Xi'en monks ran to the lakeside, palms outstretched. Brilliant beams of light flew from their hands towards the dragons. They all found their mark; the machan shuddered as its bearer felt the impact of the light-rays, and the dragons screeched in agony, jerking and thrashing in mid-air. Kirin ordered the dragons to climb; they did, coughing and trailing fire.

Signal, said Kirin.

Three short upward flashes of fire from his dragon, and huge crashing sounds announced that the rakshases had grown to giant size, and were closing in on the Xi'en, their heads taller than the trees, their bodies parting the woods as they thundered towards the enemy. The Pimawen assassins shouted in unison and Kirin gasped in wonder as they spun their swords above their heads, until the swords, moving in a blur, seemed to turn into shield-sized spinning discuses. The Pimawen jumped on to these and flew at the rakshases, spare swords appearing as if out of nowhere in their hands; there was magic at work here, thought Kirin, and no magic he'd ever heard of before.

Kirin had expected to feel tremendous pangs of remorse the moment first blood was shed, but he found, looking down at the battleground as his dragons looped and prepared to swoop downwards again, that it all seemed unreal, like a game, and that he was quite enjoying himself. Perhaps it was his physical distance from the combat, or the magical nature of the combat, or perhaps he'd simply changed . . . He realized, sensibly, that the fight was far from over and he could ponder over these questions at some more suitable time.

The assassins skimmed through the trees on their spinning swords, cutting through branches as they charged the blue giants lumbering towards them. But the rakshases were practised magic-users too, and knew centuries' worth of tricks; some teleported, others merely charged ahead stubbornly, and others hurled fireballs. The two sides clashed, and the rakshases' superior size and strength won the day almost immediately. The assassins cut and stabbed with amazing skill, but it was only a matter of time before massive rakshas hands crashed down on their heads, crushing them like ants. Those Xi'en warriors who managed to escape from their encounters realized, immediately, that destroying these monsters was out of the question—and that running up rakshas legs in order to find more sensitive rakshas body parts merely brought them closer to rakshas hands. Escape seemed the smart option, and they dodged and weaved, running up and behind tree trunks, letting the rakshases crash on towards the lake.

The Wu Sen monks, however, were not so easily cowed. As giant bodies thrashed around them, and the air throbbed with the death-gurgles of their comrades, they drew out stringed instruments from sacks, sat by the burning lakeside, and began to play. Their intention was not, it turned out, to entertain and encourage; each note they played with their long, blurring fingers sent deadly ripples through the air. Trees shattered and fires went out as their music-darts streaked towards the rakshases; the nearest one, a magnificent blue brute the size of a small castle, found his legs ripped into ribbons. Roaring in agony, he crashed to the ground. The next few notes cut him into little shreds.

The Pimawens who'd crossed the rakshas lines and taken to the treetops found, to their dismay, that life was not as sunny as it seemed. This was because thirty vanars, also skimming through the treetops, seemed to want to stick arrows into them. The Pimawens had lost their main advantage, their incredible agility. As they leapt from treetop to treetop, the vanars kept up effortlessly, and the vanars were naturally better equipped to fight from treetops. The Pimawens realized this soon, and died.

Back at the lakeside, the rakshases were playing cat and

mouse with the Wu Sens, vanishing and reappearing, dodging the sound-darts, and appearing behind the monks to deliver crashing blows. At a signal from Kirin, the rakshases all vanished. Before the Wu Sens could understand why, the dragons swooped in again, steaming up the lakeside. The Wu Sens gave up their instruments and fled as three thick walls of fire swept down the shore. A few tried vaulting over trees like the Pimawens, and soon realized this was not a good idea—the vanars and rakshases, working smoothly together, butchered them with ease. And then there were just four Wu Sen monks left. They leapt over the walls of dragonfire into the lake, and rakshases and vanars alike gasped aloud as they jumped smoothly down on the surface, not sinking, and then ran out over the lake, striding effortlessly over the water.

Above them, as the dragons whirled and set their courses for another attack, Kirin looked at the lake closely and realized that if the monks managed to cross the lake, there would be no capturing them; it was too wide for the rakshases to teleport across. His troops had played their part. It was up to him now.

The dragons passed low over the monks at speed, turned swiftly, so they were directly ahead of the Wu Sen, and breathed fire. One Wu Sen leapt into the sky but his robes caught fire; he burned horribly in the air and fell into the water, dead. The other three, though, dived into the water a second before the flames struck them, leaving Kirin and his dragons swerving in mid-air in a cloud of steam.

In seconds, the lake's surface was calm again. The monks did not emerge.

'Drowned?' asked Spikes.

'No. They can hold their breath under water as long as they want.'

'We need altitude, then. We'll spot them, and wait.'

'No,' said Kirin. He turned to Mazouq and nodded. The sorcerer extracted a small sealskin pouch with a jade stopper from his robes. He removed the stopper, and tossed the pouch into the lake.

The lake's surface began to churn and boil. Currents emerged, the water swirled and curved into what looked like upside-down whirlpools, two spinning, twisting cones of water holding themselves above the surface. As they watched, fascinated, the cones began to take human form, transforming into standing, immensely muscular male bodies. The heads were bald, the noses long and curved. The eyes glowed white.

'Water jinn,' said Mazouq triumphantly.

The jinn dived into the water.

Minutes passed. If epic battles were being fought in the water, the lake showed no signs of it. The only sounds that could be heard were the dragons' wings beating rhythmically as they circled above the water, and the splashing sounds of rakshases scooping huge handfuls of water and putting out the fires at the ravaged Xi'en camp.

'What happened? Did they kill your jinn?' asked Kirin.

'No one kills my jinn,' said Mazouq. 'Any minute now.'

As if on cue, a jinn burst out of the water, a Wu Sen monk on his back, hanging grimly on to his neck. The monk struck the jinn with his palm, sending bolts of light into his body; the jinn seemed unperturbed by this. He turned around—he *flowed* around, his water body simply rearranging itself, so he was now facing the monk.

He then stuffed the monk into his mouth, and burped. Kirin turned his eyes away as the monk's form melted and flowed through the jinn's body into the lake.

At the far end of the lake, the two surviving Wu Sens

leaped out of the water, absurdly high, like divers going backwards. Behind them, the other jinn rose majestically out of the water, reaching out; one blue pillar grasped a monk's leg, stopping him in mid-air, but the other monk managed to leap clear of the jinn's other hand. As the jinn disappeared below the lake with his prey, Kirin spurred the dragons on with his mind, and they pursued the sole survivor over the treetops.

The Wu Sen monk was old and clearly tired, too tired to even try a palm attack on the dragons. His robes were slashed and tattered, he was bleeding from several wounds, and his leaps were growing shorter and shorter. He looked back from time to time, at the great Skuan dragons bearing down on him, and knew death would come soon.

Kirin saw the monk's face and felt his heart skip a beat; it was *him*, the monk who'd struck her.

'Let him go,' said Spikes.

'No.'

The dragons had almost caught up with their quarry when the monk tripped on a high branch, stumbled, cried out in pain, and fell into the forest, disappearing under leaves.

'Don't burn him,' said Spikes. 'You won't be able to put out the fire. I'll get out and finish him off.'

'He's mine,' said Kirin, his face colder than Spikes had ever seen before.

'What's wrong with you?'

'Come on.'

Kirin ordered the dragons to stop, and flung open the machan door, ignoring Mazouq's feeble protests. As his dragon hovered just over the tree, his Shadowknife spread over his hand, forming a gauntlet with claws, identical to the

Gauntlet of Tatsu. He leapt on to the nearest tree, and began to climb down, his claws digging into the bark. Spikes waited until Kirin reached lower, thicker branches and began springing lightly groundwards, and then simply stepped off the machan, a great stone crashing through branches, landing on his feet with a huge thud. Seconds later, Kirin joined him, and they stood back to back, scanning the forest for the Wu Sen monk.

A sudden movement to Kirin's right; he turned swiftly, Shadowknife melting into a sabre.

And then his jaw went slack, and his eyes bulged.

'*You?*' he said.

'Yes,' said Maya.

She stood there, in the morning sunlight, grinning at them, her eyes sparkling. She looked thinner and older, but some things hadn't changed; her hair was still an unruly mop, and her white robe was stained and tattered.

'And it *is* me,' she continued. 'Not the shapeshifter you found with Myrdak. Hello, Spikes.'

'It's good to see you,' said Spikes.

'Do you think Kirin's going to recover the use of his tongue at any point in the near future?'

'It seems unlikely.'

'But how . . .' said Kirin.

'How do I know all this? How did I know you'd be here? How did I get here?'

'Yes.'

'Which one?'

'Any one,' said Kirin. 'No, wait.'

He strode up to her and hugged her, hard, only letting her go when she croaked for air.

'It *is* you,' he said, a silly grin appearing on his face, threatening to split it in two. 'I can't believe it.'

'You'd better,' she said, hugging Spikes, who patted her back in a gingerly sort of way, taking care not to break her bones. 'Because the rest is going to be much harder to believe.'

'Do you still want to kill the monk?' Spikes asked Kirin.

'What monk?'

'Right.'

'You don't chase him,' said Maya. 'He gets eaten by a wild rakshas in a few days.'

'How on earth do you *know* all this?' asked Kirin, wondering whether it would be polite to hug her again, and whether she would notice if he didn't let go for a few years.

'That's one of the hard-to-believe things,' said Maya. 'I know what I know because I have an all-knowing friend.'

'All-knowing?'

'Yes. He's this chameleon who used to be a god.'

'Too much information. Tell me later. Let me just get used to you being here first.' Kirin abandoned all thoughts of politeness and hugged her again, his heart thumping crazily.

'I've missed you too. So much,' she said. 'But we'd better leave now. Say your goodbyes to your thugs, and call your chariot.'

'Say goodbye?'

'Yes. I'm afraid you can't be Dark Lord any more.'

'I can't run away from it, Maya. I *chose* to be Dark Lord, and I have responsibilities.'

'Yes, yes, very good. But I need you to help me with

something that's a little more important than your Dark Lording.'

'What?'

'The world is ending, Kirin. We have to save it.'

* * *

Aciram paced the floor in his luxurious quarters above the dungeons of Izakar, stealing glances from time to time at the exquisite body of the woman lying unconscious on his bed.

There was a knock on the door. Aciram opened it very slightly and peered out. It was Mazouq the sorcerer.

'What is it?' he asked gruffly.

'The Dark Lord sends a message,' said Mazouq.

Aciram stepped out slowly into the twisting corridor, careful not to let Mazouq see who was inside his room.

'What message?'

'His exact words were "I quit."'

Aciram considered this, and Mazouq's troubled face, for a while.

'Who else have you told?'

'No one. He told me to tell you, and only you.'

'So you've told me and Omar.'

'No,' said Mazouq indignantly. 'I haven't told Omar. Besides, Omar isn't even here. He's gone to the Free States with Bjorkun to kill spies.'

'That is true. I apologize. So I am the only one who knows?'

'Yes.'

'Good,' said Aciram. He leaned forward, almost tenderly, snapped Mazouq's neck and threw him out of a convenient window. Then he smiled a very cunning smile, changed his face to Kirin's and went back into his room.

He stood by his bed, watching her sleep. He wanted to touch her, to wake her with a kiss, but he couldn't. Not until she awoke.

He asked himself again why he'd done this; why he'd brought her here, why he'd stolen her from Kirin, risking everything. Why his life had changed the day he'd first seen her and sensed her almost infinite power.

If anyone had suggested to Aciram that he had *fallen in love*, he would have laughed long and loud before killing them for their insolence. But when he saw her eyes fluttering slowly open and her limbs come haltingly to life, and knew she was healed and they were together and somehow that made him feel happier than he'd ever felt before, he asked himself if he loved her and told himself firmly that nothing of the sort had happened, but without any conviction at all.

She sat up, holding her head, her expression curiously blank. 'My mind is a mess,' she said.

'You survived a very powerful attack,' he said. 'You need rest.'

She lay down again, and looked at him with a very strange expression. 'Everything's changed, Kirin.'

'What do you mean?'

'I remember everything. But it's all just facts and details, just information. The *people* I was have died.'

'I don't understand.'

'I feel nothing, beyond the reality of a terrible headache. In this situation, I would expect to feel relief at my recovery, happiness to see you, and a certain mixture of lust and apprehension at being in bed with you standing near me, with your stance indicating a high degree of physical excitement. But . . . no. Nothing.'

Aciram gulped. Truly there was a gap between generations, he thought.

'Your mind is numb, and that is perfectly understandable,' he said. 'Rest, and you will find all your feelings restored.'

'I do not need rest. Perhaps if you asked me deep, insightful questions, my feelings might reappear.'

Aciram smiled. 'Let's start with simple questions, questions I've been wanting to ask you since the day we met. Who are you, and what do you desire?'

'I have no name. I was called Red, once,' she said, her face still completely blank. 'And I think the last thing I remember wanting was to rule the world.'

The honesty and simplicity of her ambition, the depth of the power hidden within her, and the intoxicating beauty of her eyes pierced Aciram's crusty, ancient heart.

'And so you shall. We will take this world and rule it together, if you think that might please you,' he said. 'And while Red is a nice name, it needs a little work. I think I shall call you . . . yes, I will call you my Red Queen.'

The Red Queen, she thought. It did have a certain ring to it. If things had been otherwise, she might have felt extremely elated.

4

The light of twin Alocacti cast stark shadows over the Hall of Heroes in the Civilian's Palace. Stern Psomedean faces, frozen in marble, ravaged by time, looked through pupil-less eyes at their fellow conquerors' images, and at their puny successors, sitting on marble steps at their feet.

The Chief Civilian sat under the statue of the noble Thoseus Feeling a Little Pensive, her striking face half in shadow. Ojanus the ambhisbaena was coiled around her left leg. To her left, Mantric the spellbinder seemed lost in thought as he contemplated the armless figure of the wily Eurekus Playing Catch. The artist formerly known as the Silver Dagger paced lightly near the feet of the mighty Ossus Watching Serpents Devour his Dog, spinning a shuriken through his fingers and looking out at the night sky. Silence reigned, except for the occasional buzz of Red Phalanx vroomsticks flying by the hall, red flares sending blocks of light streaking through the high windows. Two massive Vindiciti minotaurs stood by the entrance to the Hall of

Heroes, glowering at its occupants, shooting occasional murderous glances at the statue of Thoseus.

The door creaked open, and Marshall Askesis, Chief Commander of Kol's armies, strode in, a grizzled, richly dressed, powerful-looking man with grey hair and knife-like features. He greeted Mantric and Amloki briefly, and bowed to the Civilian.

'What news from the east?' she asked.

'Grim news,' he said. 'War is upon us. All of Avranti lies in ruins, and our unknown enemies have made incursions through the land between Shantavan and Vrihataranya. Potolpur and Olivya have already been attacked. The speed of this operation is stunning. It has been just five days.'

'What of our agents, our troops, our spies?'

'All missing. I have never seen anything like it.'

'If you could describe what has happened to Mantric here,' said the Civilian, 'he might be of assistance.'

Askesis sat at the feet of the statue of wise Antikytheras Inventing a Thingie That Wasn't Used Until Two Centuries Later and heaved a weary sigh.

'Very well. A week ago, we suddenly stopped getting reports from the east. All except for one enchanted bird from Srijon the enchanter in Ektara five days ago, telling us he needed help; that magic-users were being attacked by mobs all over the city. He had, he said, barely escaped with his life. He had returned home late from a visit to his lover's house, and found his own house in flames, and a group of local youths with bows and flaming arrows making no attempt to hide. This had happened to every other magician in the city, he heard. In disguise, he had attempted to speak to people, but they had all seemed confused, as if they had no clear memory of their actions. Maharaja Aloke's palace had been burnt to the ground, and Srijon's attempts to seek shelter at our other agents' homes had failed—they had attacked him, and he had been forced to kill them to escape. We sent in some of our best secret operatives immediately to get Srijon out—but they did not return, and we have not heard from Srijon since either.'

'Ravians,' said Mantric sharply. 'Eliminating magicians from a distance to strengthen their own control over peoples' minds. But surely it is impossible on so large a scale.'

'Not at all. Consider how much our own methods of warfare have advanced in two centuries,' said the Civilian. 'Pray continue, Askesis.'

'On receiving this message, we sent messages to all our agents in Avranti immediately, but there was no response at all. We sent more envoys and messengers. None returned.

'We sent in troops from Potolpur, led by Hero school magicians. This led to startling revelations. The villages on the western fringes of Potolpur and the eastern sector of Avranti were completely deserted. No sign of man, woman or child—except for certain burnt houses or huts, which contained the corpses of magic-users—witches, ascetics, wizards, ojhas, shamans, even healers. In some cases, if they had managed to escape the siege of their homes, they were found some distance away, with arrows in their backs. But otherwise, empty villages, untended fires, howling pets. In north Shantavan, Rabin of Oodh reported that his forest realm had not been disturbed in any way, but his men had seen people, lines of villagers moving to Avranti at speed. Entire families, with strangely happy expressions on their faces. Among them had been chieftains he knew who had worked for me, but they had seemed uninterested in conversation with his men.'

'Could the ravians be using some means of mass mind control to build an army of villagers?' asked Amloki, looking as troubled as he felt. The khudran homelands were within the borders of Avranti.

'It would seem so,' said the Civilian. 'But why would they not make one attempt through diplomatic channels?'

'Kol is still recovering from their last effort at diplomacy,' said Mantric. 'Clearly they feel strong enough to not delay things further. They are ready for war. If they are indeed able to successfully control the minds of thousands of people at once, it would be silly for them to negotiate with humans.'

'What do you propose, Askesis?' asked Temat.

'Since our envoys were detained or killed, the only option left is to send in an army,' said Askesis. 'To rescue Maharaja Aloke if possible, and restore peace to Avranti. Unless you have a single hero who can somehow resolve the situation.'

'She doesn't. But it is far too delicate a business for armies,' said Amloki. 'The Silver Phalanx can get to the core of the matter far more swiftly.'

'We had at least a hundred spies all over Avranti,' said the Civilian, shooting an icy glance at Amloki. 'If they have been eliminated, I will not risk the Phalanx. The scale of this event calls for other measures. I am forced to agree with Marshall Askesis. A formidable peace-keeping force is what is needed. March to Avranti, help the Avrantics fight off plague or invasion, and return.'

'Invade Avranti and take charge, in other words,' said Mantric.

'If you wish to see it thus. If it took them five days to conquer all of Avranti, there is no time to sit and think. Have you ever seen me be unnecessarily hasty?'

Mantric knew better than to say anything.

'"Invade Avranti and take charge," indeed. Would you rather be governed by fellow humans, regardless of their allegiance, or by ravians who would treat you as a little pet?'

'I would rather be free.'

'Very well. Consider this. Would you want to send in our troops, who are at the peak of their training, to engage the enemy in the east while he is still preparing to assault us, or would you wait for him to grow strong and come to us, here in Kol, with a plan as well laid as the one he recently carried out in Avranti?'

'I would prefer to meet my enemy and persuade him to leave me in peace.'

'That is exactly what I intend to do,' said Askesis. 'Your aversion to war is both noble and well known, good Mantric; much like my own abhorrence of all things magical, of any mumbo-jumbo that makes one kind of person inherently more powerful than another. Perhaps I am blind to the brutality of my profession, and you to the injustice of yours.'

'I do not want lives to be lost unnecessarily, that's all. And they will be, if you fight ravians. As I have, in this very palace. They are very deadly, Marshall Askesis. How do you propose to defeat them?'

'We will drive the rakshases of Shantavan eastwards, and see how the ravians deal with them. Along with this, using a large number of magic-users well distributed amongst our own troops, led by the Hero School magicians and my own army warlocks, we will dispel the ravian sorcery from the minds of the Avrantics and overwhelm the ravians through our sheer numbers. This is not intended to be a battle of annihilation in any case. In the Age of Terror, the ravians were our allies—they did not use humans so. But legend has it they used entire armies of asurs against Danh-Gem's warriors, which is why rakshases were sent to fight the ravians instead, and the asurs were unleashed on humans. This time, they seek to use humans as their shields—we will respond with magic, and see how they like it. I am quite sure the number of ravians in Avranti is not overwhelmingly large. This is a new sort of warfare they are attempting; with a little luck, we will persuade them to stop.

'If we suffer large casualties, we will withdraw and rebuild. Even if we succeed, it is not as if we will have vanquished the ravians forever—they will merely abandon the humans and flee to Asroye. This conflict is merely a paving ground for diplomacy—to show the ravians that humans cannot be taken lightly.'

'Well put, Marshall Askesis. But do you have all the magic-users you need?' asked the Civilian.

'We have my army warlocks, a number of Hero School magicians among our officers, a few spellbinders formerly from Enki University, and every conjurer that the Free States and Durg can spare. But we need more, many more. How I wish I could conjure up rakshases and dragons!'

'Mantric, don't you think some students from Enki could be sent with the Commander? They wouldn't be required to fight, just dispel ravian auras,' said the Civilian, her face a mask of warm concern.

'They would be protected well,' said Askesis. 'I'm sure some would volunteer to help their city if asked.'

Mantric shook his head, his mouth a grim line. 'I thank my stars I'm not the Chancellor,' he said. 'If I were, I would have had to be the one turning both of you down, which is not a pleasant prospect. Thankfully, Ombwiri has a flowing white beard, and will have something to hold on to while telling both of you to boil your heads. Trained spellbinders may opt for the path of paid butchery, but you will not ask the children to be killers.'

Askesis's eyes narrowed to tiny slits, and the Civilian intervened.

'I will find you more magic-users, Askesis,' she said. 'A number of the city's heroes will have both training and skill sufficient to serve you. Besides, there are sorcerers in Elaken and Psomedea you have probably not counted.

'Mantric, we shall detain you no longer. I would like you to carry a message to Chancellor Ombwiri for me. Tell him I have built a secret underground library in the suburbs of Kol where every book in Enki University can be hidden if there is a war. Tell him that the responsibility of actually moving the books is his. Take Roshin with you, and see to this.'

Mantric rose, smiled uncertainly at everyone, and left quickly, followed by a smouldering glare from the Chief Commander.

After the door clanged shut behind him and the security minotaurs stomped back into position, the occupants of the room took simultaneous deep breaths and plunged back into the mire.

'Enki will always be overwhelmingly against the war, Askesis. We've always waited until afterwards to recruit spellbinders,' said Temat.

'I will still speak to Chancellor Ombwiri,' said Askesis. 'And possibly address the students later today. There must be quite a few eager to throw in their lot for their city, for their world.'

The Civilian did not comment. Askesis spoke with the air of a man who had no idea that the things Enki's spellbinders liked throwing, a lot, at army recruiters were eggs, fruits and other less nourishing but equally squishy objects.

'But what about the vamans? They're ravian-proof,' put in Amloki. 'And their armies would help tremendously.'

'The vamans have agreed to defend Kol, Amloki, not invade other countries for us,' said the Civilian. 'They do not want to display their full arsenal to the ravians at this stage. I suspect the vamans will join us in an attack only if it is on Asroye itself. It is only because the vamans are watching over us that we dare send Askesis on what might be a very dangerous campaign.'

'With or without the vamans, I am assembling the mightiest army seen on this world since the Age of Terror,' said Askesis with a certain quiet satisfaction. 'Unfortunately, it is far weaker than it could be; there are several garrisons in the Free States that must remain there, to counter the threat of Imokoi. We cannot leave the north unprotected.'

'Which brings us to the reason Amloki is here. There is good news, Marshall. At present, Imokoi is not a threat,' said the Civilian. 'The treaty has been signed. This does not, of course, mean much, but they will be far too worried about the ravian invasion themselves to consider invading Kol at this point. Tell them, Amloki.'

'When we realized the Silver Dagger's identity had been compromised, Lady Temat sent me on a diplomatic mission to Imokoi,' said Amloki.

'And *diplomatic* means, what, fewer than ten corpses?' asked Askesis.

'Twelve, but they started it.'

'We digress,' said the Civilian.

'The fault is mine,' said Askesis. 'Did you meet Dark Lord Kirin?'

'Kirin was not at the Dark Tower when I reached it, and I only stayed three days,' said Amloki. 'But I did meet several rakshas nobles, including one Aciram, who legend has it is the cousin of Danh-Gem himself. He was actually in Kirin's form when we met—when I told him I knew Kirin well, he turned back into a rakshas. Nice fellow. You look at him, you can tell he's personally killed at least a thousand people.'

'I presume you looked around for the real Kirin at some point.'

'No. Word of my other identity reached Imokoi well before I did. I was under surveillance day and night, and couldn't find out whether Kirin was at the Tower, or even alive. Spikes wasn't there, though, which indicates there's a fair chance Kirin *is* alive, and elsewhere.'

'And what were the terms of this treaty?'

'A formal truce between Kol and Imokoi, and a commitment to work together in the future for mutual economic benefit,' said the ex-Dagger. 'Essentially, if they attack us now, we help the vamans destroy them, and don't let any of them come south of Danh-Gem's wasteland ever again.'

'Imokoi agreed not to attack us? Charming. Does that *mean* anything?' asked Askesis.

'As long as the ravian threat exists, and Kirin's among those in charge, it does. Aciram seemed fairly decent too—he's been around, obviously, and knows what he's doing. The other rakshases looked like fairly predictable monsters. We'll need to take charge of them before Artaxerxia does.'

'I would like a few legions of rakshases, or any magical monsters of your choice, and I would like them right now, Amloki,' said Askesis. 'Could that not be arranged?'

'The question of military cooperation came up, but was dismissed for the present, at least until the world turns sane again. A few thousand rakshases and dragons would have been very convenient now, but they are afraid to lend them to us—what if the ravians have another army coming from the north, or over the Grey Mountains? And don't you think our troops are far from ready to fight side by side with Imokoi's prettiest for a while? Many of our soldiers will not take kindly to knowing that we are in league with the Dark Tower, and fighting the ravians and our friends in Avranti.'

'Very well,' said Askesis, standing up, 'If Imokoi is not an immediate concern, I will summon additional troops from the western Free States, Psomedea, and the centaurs. That should cover our magical needs. What of Artaxerxia? They are shielded from the ravians by Imokoi to the north and the Free States to the east. It is very unlikely that they will choose to sit demurely and watch when there's land to be had.'

'In theory, Askesis, the world is at peace with Kol now with the emergence of a rather convenient external threat,' said Temat. 'Unfortunately, the world is also aware of the beauty and nobility of our enemies, and the treachery *we* indulge in every day around teatime. What of Artaxerxia? The powers that contend for the Sultan's throne in Amurabad secretly serve either us or Imokoi. I cannot imagine that the new treaty will bring anyone in Artaxerxia joy, but such is life. The Sultan, for one, will not dare to do anything. His son Omar, who lurks about the Dark Tower, is a different matter. These equations will, of course, be further mangled by the arrival of a rebel army from Elaken, for which funds have already been allocated.'

'You have taken care of everything,' said Askesis. He bowed, and smiled. 'Thank you, Temat. We have never been friends, but, truth be told, the only reason the army has not contemplated taking over Kol these last two decades is because we would never have managed to run it as well as you do.'

'In that case, I have wasted a lot of money in bribes,' said Temat, returning his smile.

'I need a favour,' said Askesis.

'Go on,' said the Civilian, her face not betraying any sign of satisfaction.

'If it turns out to be a question of fighting unarmed villagers, children, ravians, and Avrantics, morale will be an issue, to say the least. The Free States' troops can be persuaded, but if we run with centaurs, Psomedeans and Durgans, I will need a hero.'

'We have heroes to spare,' said the Civilian. 'A whole league of them.'

'I want Arathognan.'

The Civilian sighed. 'Not Arathognan,' she said. 'If the city has to be defended, he will be needed. Choose any of the other former Champions Leaguers. Choose all.'

'There are no real *heroes* among them, no one who is known outside Kol,' sighed Askesis, waving a dismissive hand. 'We have entertainers enough among our troops. No, Temat, I need someone they can look up to.'

'Amloki is out of the question, then,' said Temat, smiling.

'Yes. While he would be of great use in any kind of fight, certainly, I do not see him leading armies into battle.'

The ex-Dagger tried, unsuccessfully, not to look offended.

'You already have Rabin of Oodh,' said Temat. Askesis

nodded. 'He will help. But I need more. It will be a very large army. Where is the Hero of Simoqin?'

'We do not know.'

'Then give me Arathognan,' said Askesis. 'It will not hurt you to have him outside the city for a while. His presence weakens your authority.'

'And so I should give him an army, and a general, and a shot at glory?' asked Temat, innocently.

'I did not come here to fence, Chief Civilian. There will be enough of that in the days to come.'

'I meant what I said about Arathognan being needed in the city, Chief Commander. Had I been worried about him, the city would have forgotten he existed by now. You want a hero? Very well. Queen Rukmini of Durg will join your army. I had persuaded her of the need to stay at home and protect her people, but this is more important.'

Askesis considered this for a while, and nodded.

There was a knock on the door; another minotaur entered, huge and eerily red in the light of a passing Red Phoenix guard's flare. The newcomer bore a scroll, which he brought to Askesis.

As Askesis pored over the scroll, his jaw tightened. 'A message from Rabin of Oodh. Shantavan is under attack,' he said. 'Villagers and civilians, unarmed—and there are children among them. Rabin will not attack unarmed innocents. He is falling back, with his men, to Durg, where he will stay until we send for him.'

'Only the ravians could treat us with such disdain,' said Temat, her face grim. 'Driving children before them to make villains of us.'

'I must go,' said Askesis, shaking his head. 'I have a war to plan, and no time to plan it in.'

'Good luck, Chief Commander. This is our greatest challenge yet, and I am sure you will prove, as ever, worthy,' said Temat.

Askesis nodded farewell to the Civilian and Amloki and strode out of the hall, his boots clattering loudly over the marble floor. Amloki watched the Marshall walk away, shoulders sagging slightly, a world resting heavily on his tired shoulders.

'Danh-Gem at his worst, or even the ravians during the Age of Terror, would never have sent human children into battle to be slaughtered,' said the Civilian.

'They really do see humans as cattle. As do the rakshases, of course. What will the rakshases of Shantavan do with the villagers?'

'I wish I knew, Amloki.'

'Only the gods can save them now,' said Amloki.

'Do not speak words of ill omen,' said Temat.

5

From the war journals of Unut the asur

So, I got a story. A werewolf I knew for a few hours, the greatest hero I'll ever meet in my life, told me that when werewolves sat around a fire and told tales, there was one simple rule for telling whether a story was good or not; if good, it would have an introduction, several bodies, and an ending.

This is a good story, then.

I'm writing this in my tent. Used to share it with Saroo, but Saroo's dead; he was in the 15th, and they're all gone. My hand's trembling, left eye's still out, bladder's melting again, but my chances of getting fixed are about as good as my chances of getting Munni and Migna to come with me, covered in oil, to the Swamp of Sticky Romance, so I better write this down while I got any hands left, before my flea-ridden tick-headed blister-sucker corporal stops pickling his pea-sized head with wormwood wine for long enough to remember to send me out on another suicide mission.

Weekend before last. I'm enjoying some well-deserved R and R, playing headball with the lads in the 15th, against the lads from the 10th, who got called back to the Tower after the 15th got wiped out by a Ventelot raid. I'd just kicked the 15th's ex-captain's skull over the defensive line into the goal, and I was looking for someone to hurt as part of my celebration when I got a call from the big ugly's tent. Unut, you horrible bastard, he says, I got a job for you. Piss off, I says, I got three weeks of leave after the last mission, by the Dark Lord's newest scheme. Insublubnation me again and I'll make you eat your ma's arm, he says. You can't, I says, my wee sister ate that already, and it's in-sub-or-din-a-tion, as you'd know if you did your reading like the Dark Lord wanted. So then he hit me, and I hit him, and he hit me again, with a club, and promoted me to under-corporal, and I volunteered for the job. If I'd known what it was going to be like, I'd have held out until they made me general.

So, five days after that, I found myself lurking, innocent like, in the woods around Castle Blagyar, waiting for my crack team of experts to show up, because I sure as hells wasn't going to storm the castle by myself.

A little history, in case you don't know what Castle Blagyar is, and many don't, unlike me, who does. Know. Many many cycles ago, there was this madman, human, Baron or Count or Some Fancy Toffness Blagyar, one of the old-fashioned centipede-eyebrows vulture-nose brigade, and he lived in this big spooky castle on top of a hill, all tall and crooked, with those upside-down cone things and those wall things that look like teeth on top and no windows and scary outlines, right in the middle of werewolf country up north. And this was proper werewolf country—big moons, empty trees, gypsies dressed up to look scared and bloody to rob people, thunder round the clock, serfs hiding in bushes howling and screaming at night for atmosphere, bats, crows, the works. Loveliest real estate you could imagine. Old Man Blagyar had one of those V names, Vlad or Viktor or Vassili and that was where the trouble began. He used to be this dashing sort, you know, adventure sports—white water rafting, dashing off to Skuanmark and ravishing shield-maidens, impaling people on huge big spikes—and everyone liked him, until he started putting white paint on his face, talking with a sock in his mouth and pretending to be a vampire. That scared people. Not funny things, vampires—they'd already been hunted out of existence, but people didn't know that back then, and here was this chap biting people and running down street corners saying Hark, The Cheeldren of the Naaiight, How They Seeng, and other such nonsense. So the humans got a nice mob together, pitchforks and torches and beer, ran around yelling, and burned down the castle, with him in it.

Blagyar didn't die. Instead, he spent some money, rebuilt the castle with even more turrets and slits in walls and things, and lived in it, hiring a few asurs as servants and not going out much. Because of what had happened to him, he became all crazy about death. Trying to conquer it, and so on—alchemists had been doing that for centuries, but old Blagyar didn't travel much. He decided he'd find a way to bring a dead man back to life. It's funny, thinking how little people knew back then—just a few weeks' journey south and he could have found as many undead as he wanted in Elaken. Instead, he stayed at home, building fancy machines to trap lightning and stick it into corpses and so forth. At some point the asurs got sick of his raving and hired an undead to come and pretend to be a corpse and wake up when he prodded it—this worked, and the old man died of shock, ending the Blagyar line.

But before he took off for hells unknown, he'd done some important things. Like, he'd built this extremely sinister castle, see, with big dungeons full of beasts he'd trapped and saved up for experiments—and remember it was werewolf country. This meant he'd also invented hundreds of different kinds of shackles and chains and things to keep things locked up for years and years, and the asurs made fortunes selling his simpler designs. The more tricksy designs they couldn't come close to understanding. He'd also written the Blagyar journals, a bunch of notes on life and death and magic and monsters and stuff, which were rumoured to be very important, but no one had ever seen them—they'd stayed hidden away somewhere in his big old spooky castle.

The werewolves took back the land after Blagyar popped it, but ravians captured the castle during the Age of Danhgem's Glory. What they did there I don't know, but the Age ended, and they left, and werewolves ruled the land again—stubborn buggers, those werewolves. The secrets of Castle Blagyar were still all locked away, and no one went after them because there were all sorts of nasty rumours flying around the place. Werewolves were too scared to go inside, saying there were twisted werewolves in there, creatures who'd been torn from the way of the wolf by Blagyar's machines, werewolves who'd lived inside the castle for generations and had no idea what the world outside was like. And when werewolves are too scared to do something, that's usually it; chances of the thing getting done are as good as my chances of getting Migna and Munni, covered in mud, to come up with me to the Mountain Cave of Interestingly Shaped Little Rocks. No one was going to risk being cursed by the ghost of Blagyar or something just to read some of his journals.

Then, about a hundred years after the Age of Danh-Gem, when the asurs were remaking our glorious empire, there were all these other stories, about a mysterious White Lady who'd come to the castle, who could be seen wandering around the battlements, singing, and doing other spooky things. How she got along with the castle's mad werewolves I don't know, and no one around Castle Blagyar was very curious either. But there was no longer any howling in the night (inside the castle, that is; they still went at it full force outside, it was werewolf country, remember) and as long as no one was bothering them, the werewolves didn't mind, and neither did the Skuans, who officially owned Blagyar's land. The werewolves kept travellers out of Blagyar land, and the White Lady kept the werewolves out of the castle. Good times. This was the story all of us grew up with—though I doubt rakshases or any of the Big Bads would have even heard it—there was an evil White Lady with an army of enchanted beasts in Blagyar, who liked luring little asurs into the castle and eating them raw. Blagyar was off the big trade roads and most asurs weren't sure whether it was a real place, or just some made-up old country from vampire stories. I knew, though, because I read my geography like the Dark Lord said.

End of history lesson. About two weeks ago the Dark Lord started getting reports of trouble in Blagyar. The werewolves who lived in the woods around the castle sent Alpha Laakon word that someone or something in the castle was making werewolves disappear, and there were howls and screams in the night, vague flashes of light and dark clouds permanently camped over Castle Blagyar. Which was all good fun, really, but Laakon didn't like the disappearing werewolves bit, and went whining to the Dark Lord.

The Dark Lord told someone to take care of it, and that someone told someone else, and so on, until there I was, waiting for my team to turn up, like I said. And turn up they did, an hour late, and said they'd all insisted the asur be asked to come an hour early. Udder-suckers, but can't blame them. Most asurs would have been late. I wouldn't have, because I've read books on punctuality, but you know how it is.

Now I've been on a lot of campaigns and important secret missions in my life. That's why I was the first choice for something like this. But in all my two and twenty years, I'd not met anything like my team that night, and if I go on a hundred other missions and live to see thirty, I doubt I'll ever do anything to compare with our raid on Castle Blagyar.

My team.

The first one to turn up was a big pashan. Granite, tough, quiet. Asked me to call him Bitnun. I'd heard of him; brain like a peahen, but good man to walk through walls with.

Then there was a sizzle in the air next to me, and I almost wet myself when I saw a pair of white eyes shining in the dark next to me, and leaves and dust hurrying along to fill out a woman's shape. An air-jinn. She said her name was Artimagnas. That was good enough for me.

But the last member of our team was the most famous of us all—the legendary Blue Wolf himself, tribeless Borjigin, who I'd thought had howled his last at least a hundred years ago. Grizzled, old, but with the most massive body I'd ever seen on a werewolf, and I'd seen a lot of werewolves. His fur was patchy, one paw dragged on the ground, but I could see why his name was still passed around. Had that thing. Commanding aura. Usually meant you were a complete gas-hole, but old Borji had a twinkle in his milky eyes as well. Call me a sap, call me a tulip-face, call me what you want, from far away if you're smart, but I liked him.

So there we were, the boys, well, the boys and jinn, chatting about this and that, exchanging notes, sizing one another up, with the great big hulking castle in front of us, some very pleasant howl-work for music, and what they call a sickle moon for light. Lovely as a jar of eyeballs.

Borji told us what we were facing. I was shocked, but the rest seemed to know. Well, Arti smiled and Bitnun grunted, which could have meant anything.

Ravians.

A bunch of ravians had sneaked into the castle, and were running Blagyar's machines or whatever was inside. We had to break in and destroy everything, which was just the kind of highly specific mission statement I like. The tickhead back at camp had given me a separate mission—I had to find the journals of Blagyar. Borji was in it for revenge, and Arti and Bits had just been told what to do. Fair enough.

Borji had arranged for a pack of local werewolves to run up the front path and cause a general ruckus, and while they were doing that, Arti sneaked us all over the walls at the back. Inside the castle grounds, we lurked around for a bit and split up; Arti and Borji, who'd be most likely to survive ravian attacks, headed into the castle, and Bits and I took the dungeons. There was a whole lot of clanging and clashing going on at the front gate, and I heard ravian voices for the first time, high and shrill and cold, like human voices with knife-edges attached to them. Scary stuff.

We were lucky, Bits and I. We only met one ravian, a fat old idiot jailer, sleeping in a guardroom. He woke up as Bits charged, but Bits squished him easily enough. We stomped his body for a bit, took the keys, giggling like crazy—well, I was, anyway—and we started setting the prisoners free.

The Blagyar dungeons were in fairly bad shape. Cobwebs, large reptiles, hordes of rats—nice enough if you like your dungeons ornamental, but far too cluttered for my taste. First few cells just had skeletons of people and werewolves who'd died in strange poses. But as we got lower and deeper into the dungeons, we found old live werewolves in cells, whimpering in fear as we opened the doors, some mad, really thin werewolves Bits had to kill, because they just attacked him without question, and bit his stone body again and again, in a frenzied sort of way, until he took their heads in his hands and popped them. Some of the scared old ones settled down after a few minutes, though, and told us what had happened.

They'd been living for years in the castle, quite peacefully, helping the White Lady with magic. Turned out she was some kind of sorceress trying to build windows between worlds; she'd talked the werewolves, Blagyar's prisoners, into working for her instead of going out and hunting in a world they didn't know, where they wouldn't be welcome. Must have taken a lot of persuasion. Anyway, the ravians had come out of nowhere, and they'd locked up the Lady and her wolves in the dungeons, and every day they'd take out a werewolf or two and take them upstairs, and then there would be one werewolf less in the dungeon.

I sent Bits off to open all the other cells, and asked the wolves to take me to the White Lady. A couple of ravians came running into the dungeons at one point, but I'd put five old and very angry werewolves at the entrance, so you can guess what happened to them.

The other old boys took me down to the very lowest level of the dungeons. I had the keys, so I opened the doors, one by one. Six cells, in a row. Single torch, which I blew out to see clearly. The first two cells were empty. The second cell had a ravian in it—he started yelling like anything when he saw us, but the old boys tore him to bits. Strange.

Fourth cell, we found the White Lady.

She was really ugly, uglier than most humans, all skinny and smooth and a little shiny. They'd beaten her up, the poor thing, she was covered with bruises and scared and half mad. But the wolves went up to her and licked her and freed her, and soon she was up on her feet, holding on to the wolves, and thanking me for being her brave saviour.

I told her to cut the flirting and tell me what was going on at Blagyar.

She told me, and that was the scariest thing I'd ever heard.

The ravians had come to Blagyar to create monsters using their own people. They'd come to make ravian werewolves.

Turns out they'd found Blagyar's journals long ago, and learned enough blood magic to ensure that the ravian werewolves, after they turned, would be loyal to ravians and not the way of the wolf. They hadn't done it back in Danh-Gem's day—must have had some shred of good sense left in them—but they were doing it now.

They had taken the first ravian prisoner upstairs three days ago. They'd come back for the second one a few hours ago.

I asked the White Lady why she was in line, was she a ravian? She said there was no time to tell the whole story, because the ravians would be here soon—and if I had any goodness in me, all I should think of was burning the castle down and killing everyone in it.

We got the two other ravians out of the cells, and then we were all sort of standing around in the dark, wondering what to do next. I said we'd wait for Bits to get back with as many werewolves as he could, then he'd lead the werewolves and ravian prisoners in a charge while the White Lady and I sneaked upstairs and swiped some journals.

The White Lady asked me a question then, a question I've been asked many times. Why me? What was I doing here with a pashan, a jinn and a bunch of werewolves? I told her why—my superiors knew I had been blessed. An old asur wise-woman had seen me when I was a wee thing, and told me mother I would never be the strongest or bravest or cleverest, but I would succeed, and I would survive. The White Lady patted my head then in a condescending sort of way, and blessed my dear sweet brave heart, and I was going to punch her in the teeth, but I didn't because she was so frail.

There was a thumping on the stairs leading up from the dungeon, stone on stone, coming closer. Bits had returned, I thought, and walked up closer to see.

Well, it was Bits, but not quite how I'd expected. It was just his head, rolling down the stairs.

I yelled a fair bit, and the werewolves charged, and a couple of ravians came running down the stairs, and there was a bit of a brawl. I'm not sure what happened, because one second I was hanging on to a ravian's ear with my teeth and the next the White Lady came up and grabbed me and the next thing I knew we were running out of the dungeons, I don't know how she did it. Not that I care. I was busy running. The White Lady led me up lots of twisty stairs, saying we were heading for the main hall, where old man Blagyar had tried bringing men back to life, where the ravians were now making monsters with his notes.

So, I won't get into big descriptions, because my right arm's really beginning to hurt now, but you know the drill. Big hall, lots of machines, chains and cobwebs all over the place. And a bunch of ravians running about in panic, because Borji and Arti had been found, and were kind of the centre of the party, and the werewolves who'd attacked the gates had broken in, and they were bounding about all over the place causing very serious property damage. But no one was breaking more stuff than Arti—she was flying around the room like a demon wind, tearing chain links, sending flame-torches flying, and dust-blasting ravians, peeling off their skins. Most of the hall was in flames, and chains were clanking and gears were grinding like there was no tomorrow. In the centre of the hall, there was this stone platform, with a ravian on it, tied down with the kind of chains they use to keep ships still. He wasn't enjoying himself, unless he normally squealed like a pig while having fun. He'd been Bitten, he was Turning. The weirdest thing was, he had these baby clothes on his face. You know, the little square things humans use to preserve baby waste? This was more perverted than anything I'd seen, and I'd seen a lot of perversion in my life, growing up where I did.

Anyway, the ravians were in a ring around him, hitting the werewolves with big flying broken metal things, but the werewolves kept coming, right up to the point where they got their heads smashed, and sometimes even then. Borji was right in the middle of it all; he was roaring like anything, and holding two big gears in his hand, swatting away everything the ravians were throwing at him. That was some sight.

Just next to the Turning ravian-werewolf, there was this wooden stand, with a book lying open on it. Blagyar's journals,

I realized, and yelled out to Arti to get it. She heard me, and flew in like a hurricane to the middle of the hall, but the ravians used all their weird mind power things to hold the book in place, and Arti was hurled back into the air. Something was wrong with her, she was wailing in pain, and then she shifted shape, turned into this spear of air, set herself on fire, and flew right into the thick of things again. But the ravians were stronger, and they all sort of pointed at her and yelled, and the spear broke and fell burning to the floor; Arti was dying, but she wasn't dying easy; she screamed and cried and turned into some kind of a flaming fountain, setting everything I could see on fire. Borji saw her fall and went berserk; he turned wolf and leaped into the air, landing right by the platform, where a lot of ravians stabbed him for all they were worth, and he went down looking like a porcupine. Beside me, the White Lady muttered something, and the journals flew out of the stand; she sent the book flying down to where Arti was fizzling out, and Arti's last dying breath set the book on fire.

Nearly everything was ablaze now; more ravians appeared, led by some kind of bigshot; he was yelling curses at the White Lady, something about how she had betrayed them, and Project Ursag could not be stopped now. She took this well, she didn't cry or anything, just picked up a sword from somewhere and started chopping ravian heads off. The Lady was one mean swordswoman.

Then there was this really terrible howl, and I know terrible—I'd heard Saroo singing in the privy for years, but he had nothing on this. The ravian werewolf had woken. He broke his chains like threads, and howled again. Two werewolves leapt on him; he caught them in mid-leap and slammed them on the floor, breaking their backs. The ceiling was falling in by now; the castle was going down in seconds, and it was time for me to leave, mission accomplished and all that, but I was rooted to the ground.

The White Lady wasn't, though; she ran right past the ravians and werewolves still going at it around the platform, jumped up beside the newborn werewolf and stuck her sword into his heart before he'd even noticed her. Then he grabbed her, and would have killed her, but Borjigin suddenly rose out of a pile of corpses, roaring blue murder, sprang at them, changed to wolf-form mid-leap, got the ravian by the neck and ripped his throat out. He dropped the White Lady, and she cut his head off. She turned to Borjigin, probably to thank him, but he was well beyond thanks now. He looked around wildly, saw me, winked, and jumped into the flames.

Everything was collapsing now; the party was over. I started running. I passed the ravian bigshot on the way to the stairs, stuck a knife into him, and kicked him in the head; it helped my case that he was trapped under a big burning beam. Still, he was defiant to the last. I told him he'd lost, and the book had been burnt, and his monster was dead. Then he said something that sort of got me; the ravians are good at these mind game things. He said it didn't matter if the new Ursag was dead; they had a spare, and the Dark Lord was as good as dead. I didn't have much time to think about what this meant, so I kicked his head again, and ran downstairs. I met him again a few seconds later; this time I was running upstairs, with flames climbing the stairs behind me. Things weren't looking good.

I ran and ran, higher and higher, until the stairs were broken and I ran into a room and met this quiet-looking wolf standing and looking calmly out of a very high window, as if nothing of any consequence was going on. I yelled at him, and he told me to get on his back. I thought we were going to do a daredevily ride through the flames, mostly hurting him, which was fine by me, but no; he just jumped out of the window. We were somewhere near the top of the castle at this point, so I was pretty annoyed; spectacular view, of course, stars twinkling and all that, but I wasn't enjoying it, because he'd killed me, and I yelled many very, very rude things at him all the way down, determined not to go out without letting the world know how I felt about stuff.

But, as you might have guessed, I didn't die. That's because the wolf just landed on the grounds, and tossed me off his shoulder. It made no sense. A very strong werewolf might have survived that fall, but he would have broken a few legs, at least. I would have thought about it more then, but bits of the castle kept landing really near me, so I staggered around a bit, being sick in a handsome sort of way, high as a kite because of the rush coming down so far at that speed.

Then the wolf looks at me, quiet like, and says, Tell your master I come for him, and then he takes off, one big leap over the castle walls and into the forest. Soon as I could walk in something like a straight line, I got the hells out of there. I turned around when I was safe, and watched Castle Blagyar crumble; it must have been a metaphor for something, but I couldn't remember what. I came home.

Now I'm here in my tent, and Migna and Munni have promised to visit and cheer me up, and I'm happy on the whole, but there are still so many questions.

Who was the White Lady? Was she a ravian of some sort? Did she live? Did they really make another ravian werewolf, or were they just bluffing? Whose baby clothes was the one we killed sniffing? Was the wolf who saved me a werewolf, or the Ursag? Was he going to attack the Dark Lord?

I'll probably never know. These questions aren't for me to ask anyway, that would be stretching the wise-woman's blessing. I succeeded, and I survived, like she said I always would, and that's the end of this story.

(*Unut's war journal ends here. Contrary to the wise-woman's prediction, he did not survive his next mission.*)

6

In a small hut in southern Avranti, the former Dark Lord and the unwaba's Prophetess kept themselves busily occupied in doing nothing. The hut was in a village that was strangely empty; Maya told Kirin this was because everyone in the land had gone to Ektara to join the army; this was some ravian scheme the unwaba had hinted at, but they were not allowed to do anything to hinder it.

Outside the hut, Spikes lumbered around by a pond, causing great distress to the local fauna. Inside, Maya slept, her face troubled; terrible dreams had haunted her for weeks. Kirin sat by her, eyes wide open, watching in concern as she tossed and turned. He was moving his fingers absent-mindedly, and cobwebs on the ceiling were rearranging themselves. Kirin did not see this, though; his mind was occupied in trying to make sense of all that he'd heard from Maya in the last few days.

The gods were playing a game with the world. This was apparently something they did from time to time, to keep themselves entertained. Only this time, the god who'd made up the game—Zivran, his name was—had decided to experiment with the game, and had placed the world and himself in great peril by doing so. He'd created a gameworld where the pieces in the game, the people of the world, were free to act as they chose, and the gods only got to watch. But he hadn't thought things through clearly. There were flaws in the game, and if they were discovered, the gods would destroy Zivran, and the game, and the world. If they were not found, the world would rebel against the game, and then the gods would destroy the world. For Kirin, who hadn't really believed in gods in the first place, this was a lot to take in.

Every significant piece in the game, Maya had explained to Kirin, was visible through a crystal to a god-player, and after initial disagreements between gods as to the relative importance of their pieces, Zivran had redesigned the board with a wave of his hand. Heroes were now randomly reassigned to gods at intervals of one day. It was of utmost importance, the unwaba had told Maya, that Kirin and Maya were off the board; the simplest way to achieve this was by doing nothing important, and not being conspicuous for a while. Both Kirin and Maya had done far too much in the last year to be removed from the playing crystals for a while, but if they kept out of trouble and adventure for long enough, other heroes would rise to replace them in the gods' crystals; the war would ensure that. Fame was a fickle thing, and apparently humanity's extremely short collective attention span was created in the image of its makers'. Kirin had argued that doing nothing was not going to save the world even if it removed them from the gods' sight. Maya had agreed, and repeated what the unwaba had told her.

'The most important thing to remember is that the gods have chosen to play the game and abide by its rules. The rules are all that constrain the gods and their powers; to cheat at the game and defeat the players you must find ways of exploiting the rules so that the gods would have to break the rules to defeat you. Of course you will have to accomplish several extremely difficult tasks before you save the world, but you cannot be the ones seen by the gods to be going on quests; that would be like dancing naked in a pit full of hungry werewolves,' the unwaba had said. 'There is no simple formula for saving the world; anything that appears to be so is a part of the game, and a trap. What you must do, instead, is to disguise yourselves; this is best done by seeming insignificant. The gods are not interested in the mundane; if they do not have high drama to sustain them, they will find something else to watch. This does not mean you can save the world by making everything uninteresting, stopping wars by force and so on; if you do, the gods will see that as rebellion and crush you.

'How do you hide from the gods and remain involved in world-changing events? You must initially appear as servants to a hero; Spikes must be with you, as your master, and we will find someone else later on if we need to; we will. Also remember, I am invisible to the gods, and have a certain amount of influence; while you are near me, you are visible to the gods, but cloudy. Your words, if you say them, which is unlikely when I am around, will seem slow and dull, and their eyes will move on. You can save the world by not being heroes. This does not mean, I repeat, that you have nothing to do. Nearly all the work in the world is done by people who are not heroes. What you have to be is people who *assist* the hero in his tasks; to overcome the players backstage, you have to fade into the background yourselves. This will be difficult for you, but the task you have undertaken was never going to be easy.'

Spikes had been extremely pleased to hear that Kirin and Maya were now his servants. 'Less backchat, then, and get me some food,' were his first words as master, and Kirin, grinning, had obeyed. The Gauntlet of Tatsu and the Shadowknife were also in Spikes's custody now. They did not make him look significantly more terrifying.

These were the facts, and Kirin was still struggling to comprehend them. *How* he and Maya were supposed to save the world they did not know, and had no chance of knowing until the unwaba woke up.

They'd spent several days regaling each other with tales of their adventures since they had last spoken in the Bleakwoods. Neither wanted in particular to bring up the time they had seen each other last, their stormy encounter on Mount Laoye in Xi'en. They had not expected things to be the same as they were in Kol, what seemed liked a lifetime ago; it was as if they were two new people, older, more guarded, better at hiding with words what they truly felt. About her time with the ravians, Maya had said nothing, except that it was painful to remember, and not something she was willing to talk about yet. By unspoken consent, they had not discussed Asvin's death even once. Kirin had accepted that without question; they had always had secrets from each other. And there was plenty to talk about; they buried themselves in comfortable discussions about the incredible places and people they'd seen in their journeys around the world. And from their days together, their walks in the barren red fields around the village and their uncertain, uncomfortable silences, Kirin had realized what the greatest difference between the present and their past life in Kol was; both of them had learned to hate.

Outside, the afternoon cast drowsy spells over empty paddy fields, and cows stared longingly at each other and chewed cud in a melancholy, passionate sort of way. Kirin looked at the little chameleon's head, poking out from a black pouch around Maya's neck. The unwaba. The Shanti-Joddha's inspiration, the true founder of Kol, the voice that had guided the world for centuries. Or so he claimed. Or so Maya said he claimed; Kirin had spoken to the unwaba just once, and they hadn't talked about history.

Kirin's first encounter with the unwaba had left him rather shaken. He'd woken up in the shadow of a tree one lazy afternoon and had sat up to see where Maya was when he'd come face-to-face with the ancient chameleon, sitting on a low-hanging branch and regarding him with a baleful stare. Kirin's yell of surprise had knocked the unwaba off his branch, but Kirin had caught him before he fell to the ground, and put him back where he was. This placatory gesture had not, however, won the unwaba's favour.

'I knew you'd do that, young Kirin,' he'd said, in his whispery voice, like sand falling through an hourglass. 'I know you know who I am, just as I know who you are, but then that was only to be expected, since I know everything, being, as I am—'

'The unwaba, oldest and wisest of chameleons,' Kirin had said, smiling. 'Good to see you awake. I don't suppose you know where Maya is?'

The unwaba had looked mightily offended at this. 'Do not be impertinent with me, young man,' he'd said stiffly.

'Your fate, and this world's, hangs by a thread, and this is not a time for levity. Maya is at present very close by, approaching us, thinking about what your presence here means for both of you, wondering what she really feels about you and reproaching herself for not mourning as much as she should for Asvin. That's good to know. Tell me more.'

Kirin had opened and shut his mouth. Maya had warned him about the unwaba's unique conversational style, but nothing could have really prepared him for the astonishing experience of having someone else say the words he was going to.

The unwaba had looked at him smugly and carried on. 'Maya is aware, of course, that you came to rescue her from Myrdak, and was displeased when she learned from me that you had left quite happily with young Red. Her name was Red? Clearly you did not waste much time talking. Red is her identity; name she has none. She is a shapeshifter, a member of a secret society of shapeshifters in Kol, and contrary to what you believe, she is alive. What? Yes. But Aciram said . . . I know what Aciram said. These are epic times, boy. No one's dead until you see the body, and sometimes not even then. We shall waste no more time on this. Your duties lie elsewhere, and so should your attention. I was speaking of Maya, the woman you love. Hang on a minute . . . Do not waste my time, Kirin. It is more precious than yours.

'Maya was somewhat mollified when she learned that your hurried shift in affections was related to the fact that Red had taken her guise, and that you saw through this deception eventually, despite Red knowing enough about both of you to impersonate Maya convincingly. You're quite a gossip for a lizard, aren't you? I don't think I want to hear any more. Nonsense. I know you do. And Maya does not know, as I know, that your own feelings for Red were considerably strong, though we shall make allowances for the considerable heat of the moment and let that pass. Do not interpret this as a signal that I have any real control over what I am saying. Just consider yourself blessed by benevolent fate.

'More importantly, I am a chameleon, not a lizard. There is a difference.

'Despite not knowing of the breach in your affections, I doubt Maya has cause to feel any fondness for Red, considering Red almost successfully seduced you, and had previously been romantically involved with Asvin, while disguised as the Durgan princess Rukmini. Now, of course, Red, in the guise of Maya, is rapidly on her way towards an intense alliance with Aciram, who she thinks is you, which is reasonable, as he wears your face. Is all this true? Consider my telling you so a fairly substantial indication, yes. It's too complicated to follow. Do you mind if I draw a little map? Yes, I do. Your intellectual limitations are your problem, not mine. Now, to continue, Maya was also extremely angry with Asvin, despite the fact that he had been under a spell when he became . . . entangled with Red. However, this did not dilute her grief at the knowledge of his death. She has not had much time to dwell on his passing, however, given the perils she has had to face in the recent past at the hands of the ravians. I don't know anything about that. Oh yes, of course, you do not know. She has decided not to tell you. I, however, know. Don't tell me. Very well. Let me tell you, then, what is to happen between you and Maya in the days to come.'

The unwaba had proceeded no further because Maya had emerged from behind his tree and her hand had come down, firmly and less gently than ever before, on his mouth. 'I think it's time I made it clear,' she'd said, her eyes blazing, 'that if you gossip about either one of us again, we will toss you off a high cliff. I do not want to hear prophecies regarding my love life or Kirin's again, and you must promise not to make them. Are we in agreement on this, Kirin?'

'Complete and utter,' Kirin had said with feeling.

Maya had let go of the unwaba's mouth and the venerable chameleon had glared at her. 'Your presumption exceeds all possible limits,' he'd said. 'Remember, I am a god.'

'Then in the name of all possible gods, stop behaving like my aunt Dimpi, who I turned into a dung-beetle when I was twelve, and tell us what we need to do to save the world.'

'Very well,' the unwaba had said, and then he'd gone back to sleep.

Having consumed all the available butterflies in the region, Spikes returned to the hut, and ordered Kirin to look snappy and clean the mud off his toes. Eyebrows rising skywards, Kirin got up, but before he could attend to the pashan's beauty needs, the unwaba wriggled out of the pouch and placed a clammy paw on Maya's neck. She woke instantly, and the unwaba said, 'I will now tell you both many important things.'

He clambered on to Maya's palm in an important sort of way, cleared his throat, sounding like a very small kitten sneezing and settled down to tell his tale.

'Once upon a time there was a chameleon named Unwaba. And when the first creation came to pass, it fell to Unwaba to inform man, greatest creation of S/He'—the unwaba was silent for a while—'that he was to be immortal. But Unwaba was lazy, and did not journey swiftly; he loitered, he slept, he ate the fruit of the great tree Ubukwebezane, and gloried in the beauties of creation, and tarried some more. And so it came to pass that S/He . . . grew impatient and sent Abantu the lizard to tell man he was to die, and Abantu, curse his insufficiently sticky feet, hurried to man's hut and told him of his mortality. And when Unwaba reached man's hut and told him he was immortal, there was no rejoicing at all, for man had already heard the words of Abantu, and thus, through the word of the lizard, death came to man. Had Unwaba been less lazy . . . had I woken up a little earlier . . .' The chameleon's voice cracked and faded. Maya patted him on the head with an encouraging finger, and he opened his eyes again.

'I was tortured and banished and forgotten. When I awoke on this world, I did not even remember who I was at first. But then, over time, I healed, and regained control over my infinite memory. If you could call it control; I became, in many ways, the supreme prophet delivering my prophecies from my own knowledge, trapped by the physical limitations of my body. I am all-knowing, but not all-saying; I know what I will say, and it is never enough.

'I have come to love this world, in my own fashion. To see it die would cause me a considerable amount of grief for a significant period of time. I have felt sympathy for mankind ever since my first mistake, and will strive until my body dies to atone for my crime. I have come to dislike the gods with surprising intensity, and will do what I can to spite their careless plans and make them pay for their callous whims. Life means nothing to those beyond it, but life is precious, and to throw it away needlessly . . . that is wrong. I'm just not convinced by this gods destroying the world thing . . .'

Maya shut the unwaba's mouth, looking with amusement at Kirin's open mouth.

'Remember the rules for conversation with me, O unwaba, oldest and wisest of chameleons? They hold for Kirin as well. Say what you were going to, Kirin,' she said.

'I'm just not convinced by this gods destroying the world thing. If they do exist as you say, don't they need us? Don't they need our faith to grow powerful, or to just survive?' asked Kirin.

'. . . vive? No,' said the unwaba. 'I don't understand. Why should they? You are their playthings. You are like ants to them. Not even ants. You are like amoebae, though science has not yet progressed enough to tell you what amoebae are. Very small things. Smaller than amoebae. I get . . .'

'I get the picture.'

'All this is fascinating in theory, unwaba, but I hope you're going to tell us what we need to do before falling asleep this time,' said Maya. 'We're not very good at just killing time when there's clearly a lot to do.'

'There is a lot you might have done to draw the gods' attention to you. For example, you, Maya, could have led the armies of the world to Asroye, using the creatures you call chubbies as your guide, and you, Kirin, could have sent your armies to attack the ravians before they reached Kol, thus saving many lives. You have also forgotten that you have actually been to Asroye before, and so has your chariot, and you could have gained immense wealth and power by telling the vamans where Asroye—New Asroye, now—is. However, you cannot do these things. You must remain hidden. You will save more lives if the world survives this ordeal.'

'But surely we can use your knowledge to somehow bring about a swift end to the war, and save even more lives,' said Kirin.

'Unfortunately, the longer the war and the bloodier it is, the greater the chances of your proceeding unobserved, and the greater your chances of saving the world. You need to keep the gods distracted. Interestingly enough, Zivran is at present doing the same thing.'

Maya nodded grimly. 'We know that, unwaba. Time, as you keep telling us, is precious. Tell us what to do now.'

'I will tell you in the present only what, in the future, I will have told you in the past. Listen closely. You are about to have the privilege of experiencing an apocalypse. What is an apocalypse?'

'The end of the world,' said Maya.

'Wrong,' said the unwaba. 'Though not wholly wrong—an apocalypse may concern the world's end; this one does. An apocalypse is a revelation of secrets, an unveiling of matters hidden to a chosen few, often a prophecy made by gods to their chosen prophets. It is usually used to describe a written account of such revelations, but I see you do not have the required materials handy. I hope you have good memories, then; it will turn out that you do.

'A proper apocalypse will contain most of the following: a discussion of the current political and social hierarchy of the dominant pantheon, a list of species, especially of the magical variety, and their abilities and stories, an explanation of the miracles of science and nature, a history of mankind, and prophecies regarding the end of the world, and what happens after. I am, of course, perfectly able to give you all this information, but because I am aware that your memories, unlike mine, are very limited, we will leave out most of these, and speak only of things you are likely to remember. If your world has a future, much of the information I would have revealed otherwise will be discovered in it. Let us, therefore, concentrate on the simpler things; the end of the world, and the role you are expected to play in it.

'What is the end of the world? The end of the world is nothing but a change. A metamorphosis from one state to another. Of course, everyone alive on an ending world usually dies, but what is death itself but metamorphosis?

'That's a nice way of looking at things,' said Kirin.

'*Divine* would be a more appropriate word.'

'What would happen to all the people in the world?'

'They will be taken off this world.'

'Where will they go?'

'Where people go when they die.'

'Where is that?'

'Somewhere else. Alternative accommodation, suitable for their altered state of being. You are supposed to be my prophet, not a housing expert. You do not need to know *where*. If you are so curious, go back to your Dark Lordly duties, and you will soon find out for yourself. As far as this world is concerned, it will die. Snakes of metal will run like rivers through the world. The armies of the undead, led by the First Pharaoh, the Scorpion Man and his Four Horsemen will ride like a tidal wave over oceans of carcasses. This world will be taken apart and put together for a new game. Before that, though, there will be many visually spectacular manifestations of divine power, which will ensure this world's people give their collective demise the attention it deserves. An endless fimbulwinter will sweep through the world; the sun and moon will be extinguished, and devoured by Tsa-Ur. Time will be broken and repaired. There will be a good deal of shuddering, with trees and mountains breaking free. Flames in the torn sky, boiling, roaring seas, great tentacled beasts will rise from the seas to walk the land, and the dead will rise again. Ships of nails, cobwebs of entrails, much blowing of horns and very interesting parties afterwards. Lots of wailing, but not as much gnashing of teeth as you have been led to believe.'

'This is the end of the world we're trying to prevent, isn't it?' asked Maya.

'Yes.'

'Why tell us about it, then? Tell us how to prevent it!'

'It is inevitable. All you can do is delay it for a while.'

'By "a while" do you mean a few thousand years at least?'

'Yes.'

'Then don't tell us. You'll ruin the surprise.'

'Hmph,' said the unwaba. 'A sad day for a former god when his apocalypse is criticized. Perhaps this world would be better off ended.'

'Since you're all-knowing—do we succeed? Do we save the world?' asked Kirin.

'Fortunately, I find I did not answer this question. Consider it logically. If I answered yes, you would grow complacent. If no, you would give up now. I know what you will do, in any case.'

'So tell us.'

'I will not tell you. As you just informed me, you like surprises.'

'Your apocalypse is very impressive, O great unwaba. But I have my own reasons for not trusting prophecies, or prophets.

And I'm not convinced I should do anything you want,' said Kirin, 'and I'll tell you why. You said you were once a god, and it turns you've lived on this world for ages, pushing people around, manipulating them. Now you're telling us you want us to save the world for you. How are you different from any of the other gods pushing pieces on a board? Why should we trust you? How do we know you aren't working with the other gods, or a different bunch of gods with essentially the same motives? And if we do save the world for you, what happens to it afterwards? Do the gods just go away? Or do you get to rule the world somehow?'

'These are reasonable questions you asked yourself before doing what you did,' said the unwaba with a sigh. 'I do not need to convince you; I already know what you chose to do.'

'Then I'm surprised you got Maya to bring me here,' said Kirin. 'Because we're leaving you here, and going away to decide our own future now.'

'No, we're not,' said Maya. 'I choose to believe him. I'd rather see a world guided by the being who created the Shanti-Joddha and Kol and helped me escape from the ravians than a world destroyed or torn apart by gods who don't care about it. Leave if you want. I'll do what's needed alone.'

'Not alone,' said Spikes. They looked at him, standing solidly at the hut's door. They'd forgotten he was even there.

'You want to go up against the gods?' asked Kirin, looking from Maya to Spikes.

'Yes, and I was hoping you'd come too,' said Maya.

'I could come for a bit,' offered Kirin. 'At least until something more interesting comes along.' The line would have been more impressive if he hadn't been smiling broadly at Maya, he thought.

'That would be nice,' said Maya. 'When our plans spring

a leak and we end up being tortured for all eternity, stuck on wheels with food just out of reach, sores all over us and vultures munching on our exposed brains, remember you volunteered.'

'Are you done?' asked the unwaba. 'So you decided to stay; how happy I would have been if this news had astonished me. I have good news for you; if you had been paying attention, you would have realized I had no intention of giving you precise instructions or lists; that would have meant setting a quest for you, which in turn would have meant visibility and disaster. You will be making all your decisions yourself; this will make you feel more secure as well. To make you feel even better, I will try whenever possible to pretend I did not know what you would do.'

'Thank you,' said Kirin. 'We'll do what we can.'

'However, since my own fate hangs in the balance, and I cannot trust you to get anything right, I will give you a few pieces of information, to do what you will with it. In a few days, the Four Horsemen of the undead will set out, to herald the coming of the undead army. This is the beginning of the end; you should try and find a way to stop them. Additionally, it is quite possible you will need, at some point, to negotiate directly with the gods. This will require actually visiting them; for this, you need at least one person in your crew who actually believes in the gods and what they stand for. The three of you are the most ungodly reprobates I have ever spent time with.'

'That's sweet,' grinned Maya. 'Where will we find these Horsemen?'

'The Bleakwood. Remember, you cannot do anything that draws attention to either of you. Spikes will have to do whatever is necessary.'

'For an un-quest, this seems remarkably like a quest,' said Kirin.

'If you look at it like that, cleaning your teeth is a quest. Yet I doubt the gods will want to watch you do it,' said the unwaba sternly, and these words of wisdom were given additional gravity by the gentle snore that followed them.

Maya put the unwaba back into her pouch and rose, her eyes sparkling. Kirin got a huge hug; he did not complain. 'We're off to save the world, and we have no idea how,' said Maya. 'I love my life.'

'Master,' said Kirin to Spikes, 'may I summon your chariot so we may, as you desired, go to the Bleakwood?'

'Yes,' said Spikes. 'And you may clean my toes on the way.'

7

Marshall Askesis's plan to invade Avranti and defeat the ravians did not work.

This was because the ravians rather uncooperatively decided to invade first.

And so it came to pass that Marshall Askesis found himself waiting with his mighty army on the silent green hills of Pataal-e-Gurh, a battleground where the earth throbbed with memories for anyone of Koli or Avrantic descent, for it was here that Prince Amrit of Avranti, founder of Kol, had fought and won several pitched battles with invaders from Ventelot and Psomedea ages ago. And today, Kol had returned to war with the mightiest army it had assembled since the Age of Terror, now as an ally of the Dark Lord, facing two of Kol's greatest former friends. Historians would call this the Fifth Battle of Gurh. Depending on which way you looked at it, Avranti or Kol had won all the previous four, and had clearly been chosen by destiny to win again.

Pataal-e-Gurh was in south Potolpur, on the Durgan border, only a few days away from Kol and far closer home than Askesis had wanted, but it was the farthest possible point where his armies could have been assembled in time—and time was short, for the Avrantic–ravian alliance had already swept past Shantavan and half of Potolpur. Most of north Shantavan had been set ablaze, and its denizens scattered. The rakshases had either died or fled to Vrihataranya, strengthening the Dark Lord's forces there. Rabin of Oodh and his archers had sought refuge in Durg, and had now marched with Queen Rukmini and her army to join Askesis at Gurh.

The banners of Kol and its allies now fluttered in the gentle morning breeze on three hills, side by side, with wide gaps between them. To the left of the hills were grasslands sloping downwards, ending in the mud-banks of the Great River Asa, grey and quiet in the morning sun, its waters preparing once again to foam red with blood after centuries of peace. To the right, the land sloped further upwards towards the hills and forests of Durg. Here, backs to their homelands, Queen Rukmini and her Durgans formed the right flank, rows upon rows of cavalry and infantry with a reserve force of forty war-elephants protecting the open ground behind them, so the Avrantics would be hard pressed to break through with their left flank and surround Askesis's army. The queen herself was on horseback, at the head of her elite company of Durgan warrior-women, their maroon and silver armour shining proudly with every movement. The woods were full of Durgans, Potolpuri pikemen and Rabin's rangers; this was an army that would not easily be taken by surprise. Already, the tribesmen of Shantavan had been tracking the Avrantic army for days from within the forest, not attacking, acting instead as silent, camouflaged scouts, ready to surge ahead and warn Askesis if the Avrantics decided to launch a major attack from within the forest.

In front of the hills were the killing fields, a great basin of flat land, of fresh green grass waving in futile defiance against the impending invasion of thousands of murderous feet. Across the basin, the enemy would emerge over a gently sloping incline leading up to a ridge. The Avrantics were not travelling down the highways through the Free States, where Askesis could have kept them occupied with smaller, more compact forces making sorties from camps in villages, wearing them down with his modern tactics and mastery of logistics; instead, they were marching southwards along the Asa riverbank through largely unpopulated lands towards Kol, in a massive wave of bodies bordered by Shantavan on one side and the river on the other. The gap between the Asa and Shantavan was too wide for any kind of ambush to be possible. This was a battle where each army would have plenty of time to soak in the other's size and magnificence.

But Askesis had vaman sapper mercenaries with him, and for vamans scale was never a problem; they were at present digging a long trench at the far end of the basin, where the gap between the forest and the river was at its narrowest. A thousand men could still walk abreast there, but it would be difficult for anyone to march across this trench. The sappers worked with digging carts that hissed with steam as giant shovels scooped out great chunks of earth; into these the sappers placed explosives that further widened the trench. Ahead of the sappers, tree-cutting chariots sank their teeth into Shantavan's bark, and coolie pashans picked up logs and carried them to the trench.

On top of each hill on the Koli side stood squads of hired vaman artillery with their wondrous calibrated ballistae and catapults, siege weapons modified into quick-rolling war-engines suited to ground combat, capable of launching huge balls of Psomedean fire across large distances with incredible accuracy. One catapult released a great rock; it arced through the air all the way across the basin and crashed into the trench. The sappers cheered hoarsely and went back to work. Below the vaman artillery, Rabin's archers lined the hills, longbows drawn, testing their range, sending arrows flying out over the troops, while men planted flags in the battlefield where their arrows fell. Koli labourers were hard at work below the archers, building rudimentary fortifications of wood and stone. At the foot of each hill stood maniples of Koli infantry, in three lines, fresh-faced novices, battle-hardened professional soldiers and elite veterans, in tried, tested and flexible formations with gaps between them to let through the reserve forces behind the hills.

On the left flank, between the left-most hill and the Asa, stood the centaurs, restless and proud, their flawless bodies painted in occult patterns, long spears and shields in their hands, tails and helmet plumes waving in the breeze. Behind the hills, in echelon formation, stood legions of Koli infantry and cavalry. Neo-Hudlumm hordes, giant blond men in studded armour bearing great axes or longswords, stood to the right of the right-most hill, jeering at the Kolis, fretting in annoyance at not being the first line of attack.

In front of the hills, at the edge of the basin, stood an Artaxerxian army, led by a hero as great as any hero Kol could have created, and a boon to Askesis in a time of dire need; the Sultan's nephew Haroun, leading thirteen thousand Artaxerxian soldiers, horse-archers with small curved bows, regiments of elite Amurabadi cavalry clad in leather and iron, bearing long scimitars and round shields, flanking columns of mixed infantry, mostly consisting of swordsmen, mercenaries from conquered lands to the west. How Lady Temat had persuaded the Sultan to empty his barracks so quickly in a time of tremendous opportunity, and what price she had paid for this assistance Askesis did not know, or want to know; he was not very good at expressing gratitude. And gratitude was due in abundance. Thousands of experienced soldiers with no objection at all to killing innocent Avrantics were a blessing, and the presence of Haroun—a young leader as brave as he was charismatic and so evidently born to be a universally loved ruler that it was amazing that the Sultan had allowed him to survive—was nothing short of a miracle.

Distributed evenly amongst all the divisions in the allied army were Koli warlocks from Askesis's legions. Normally the warlocks fought in small, roving groups protected by heavily armoured infantry and fleet-footed peltasts, moving in erratic patterns across the battlefields, isolating enemy champions and slaying them with dark sorcery, or moving into beleaguered divisions with protective wards and healing spells. But they would be fighting ravians now, and any of the soldiers not near magicians' protective auras were at risk of changing sides—spreading the warlocks so thin reduced their destructive potential, but it was the only option. Danh-Gem himself had used this technique to good effect during the Great War.

Not that any general had devised a perfect method of fighting ravians, but in a crowded battlefield ravians were less deadly than in individual combat. The overwhelming danger all around them slowed them down, and while they would still win almost any individual fight, their options were limited; they could be outnumbered and overcome, though it would always involve heavy losses.

Askesis stood on the central hill, and around him stood his Mortals, Kol's hundred finest human warriors clad in black armour, faces hidden under black helms. In front of the Mortals stood a regiment of warlocks, and disorganized companies of chroniclers, heralds, scouts and messengers, waiting for Askesis's attention. The Marshall stood in silence, looking at his Koli legions with pride, at line after line of men of every possible ethnic origin, standing together, united to face a strange and ruthless enemy, and he dreamed, as every general of his stature had dreamed before him, of a world army united under his command.

It would, of course, have been convenient for Askesis if the invaders from another world had truly united this world against them. It would have been even more convenient if the ravians had truly been strangers to the world, and not well-loved, revered heroes from times widely believed to have been simpler, a noble race inextricably associated with his world's past and present. As things stood the bonds of necessity that bound these unlikely allies together were alarmingly thin. Askesis expected, at any moment, to hear that his most powerful generals had turned against him, and towards some unspecified Path of Truth, Justice and Light. Or that the Dark Lord had broken the newborn alliance and taken the Free States, sandwiching Kol between rakshases and ravians; were not Dark Lords practically obliged to turn traitor? Psomedea, the Centaur Forests and Ventelot, too, had now been left to fend for themselves, and were ripe for plucking. Askesis's choices had been to either trust his supposed allies completely and leave Kol vulnerable or to make sure Kol was as doughtily and flexibly defended as possible, and prepare for the worst; the decision had been an easy one to make.

After the Avrantics had broken through the gap between Vrihataranya and Shantavan, they had been free to go practically anywhere they wanted, as was often the case with very large armies in undefended lands. It was not known whether some of the invaders had crossed the Asa and travelled north of the Free States. This had necessitated tactical manoeuvring as complicated as a Xi'en courtship dance. The Olivyan legions had been distributed through the northern Free States to form an initial line of defence there. The Elakish rebel army, chariots and spearmen and cavalry, had been diverted from its march on Artaxerxia after the Sultan's show of support and brought into the Free States, as had the Psomedean phalanxes, which now camped just north of Kol. This still left a huge stretch of land south of Vrihataranya and north of the Free States practically undefended; an army could pass unopposed all the way from Avranti to Danh-Gem's Wasteland. But then, Askesis reflected bitterly, that would be the Dark Lord's problem, and *he* would be ready, as Dark Lords always seemed to be.

In the east, the armies of Xi'en were on the move, and not as part of complicated courtship dances. This was the perfect opportunity for them to invade Avranti, but if they were doing so, it was part of a very devious plan indeed, because they were moving in the wrong direction. Yet another civil war had broken out in Xi'en. The clans of western Xi'en were revolting against the daimyos of the east, settling ancient scores lovingly detailed in languages Askesis had no intention of learning. Askesis wondered if the ravians had anything to do with causing that war, or whether it was the Civilian's doing. His spies did not know. What they did know, though, was that huge clouds had risen up over the Mountains of Harmony, and there had been snowstorms and avalanches for days on end. All the major passes to Avranti from Xi'en had been blocked. Askesis did not know if the ravians were somehow behind this either; he berated himself for seeing conspiracies and mysteries where none, in all probability, existed. Then again, you never really knew with ravians.

He turned his attention to his legions' generals, who had arrived on his hill desiring a final council. A mysterious company of grey-cloaked strangers had arrived on horseback from Kol, unannounced, and sought his audience. And a party of scouts had come from Shantavan with very strange reports. Askesis heard the scouts first, and immediately barked orders at his heralds; trumpets blew, mirror-bearers flashed signals across the hills, and there was a buzz of curiosity among the troops as Queen Rukmini, Rabin of Oodh, Haroun of Artaxerxia, the neo-Hudlumm chief Klevadix and White Spear, the centaur general, rode out a few minutes later, answering their commander's call.

The Mortals formed a wide ring around the top of the hill, and Askesis welcomed his generals one by one as they entered, and swiftly told them what the scouts had seen.

The Avrantic force coming to meet them could not be counted; it was simply too vast. This was because it was not just an army; the entire Avrantic army was present, but it brought up the rear. In front of the approaching army were what appeared to be thousands, perhaps millions, of Avrantic civilians; men, women, children, all apparently unarmed. In Shantavan they had attacked bearing crude weapons. The ravians had driven them into a frenzy, and they had charged into the forest heedless of the dangers that lay within. Now, however, it seemed as if they had abandoned their weapons. They came singing and dancing, playing musical instruments, bearing flowers, and had called out to the scouts to join their march for peace and love across the world. Some of the scouts had decided to join the revellers, to count how many ravians were present among them. None of these scouts had returned.

Gymros and Gerilola, the official army battlebards, coughed insistently behind Askesis until he turned around. 'We have several inspirational speeches prepared for you,' said Gerilola. 'Would you like to go through them before you address the troops, or should we pick the one we think fits the situation best?'

'It begins "Hear Ye, defenders of civilization!" and ends with you sniffing a flower meaningfully,' said Gymros. 'You'll love it.'

'Get out of my sight,' said Askesis. He turned to his generals.

'I will be frank with you; given this new information, I do not know if we can win this battle,' he said. 'Negotiation seems out of the question, as no envoy we have sent has returned. No generals in the modern age have ever fought a battle in almost complete ignorance about the enemy's strength and formation, but we must do what we can. We have decisions to make. Do we want to be responsible for the slaughter of an entire nation whose people do not rule their own minds?'

'If only they were not human,' said Rabin. 'I do not know how I will ask my men to shoot civilians.'

'They're attacking us. We have a superb army. They are untrained in battle. I do not see where the problem lies,' said Klevadix. 'Let them come! We will break their spirits in a day, and they will slink back to the east.'

'We cannot affect their morale in any way if their spirits are held in leashes by ravians, who must be hidden among them. An untrained civilian militia is one thing—unworthy opponents, but opponents bearing weapons, intending to harm us, giving us reason to defend ourselves,' said Askesis, 'If they bear arms and invade us, their lack of strength is their problem. Considering their numbers, their threat to us would have been one of attrition, because we simply do not have the resources to kill everyone in Avranti and then deal with the army following them. But we could have blocked their path, as planned, and filled the basin with bodies and retreated without significant loss, and done it again. Our reserve forces could have swept across the Asa in a week and engaged their army in the rear, and we could have driven the remaining civilians unharmed back to Avranti. *Could have*, however, does not work here. If they are unarmed, and believe they are marching for peace, then killing them earns us eternal infamy.'

'We are soldiers,' said Klevadix. 'We do not fight to be popular, but because we are ordered to.'

'Unfortunately, the world cannot be won by arms alone, noble Klevadix,' said Haroun. 'The ravians are masters of distorting information, and if we start a massacre here today, within a week all alliances between humans will be broken, and all our nations will be cast into bloody civil war.'

'If we attack them, our alliances will be broken long before that,' said Rukmini. 'I will not slaughter unarmed Avrantics.'

'My views on this matter are already known,' said Rabin.

'If I order them to shoot defenceless civilians, my archers leave the field.'

'What do you suggest then?' asked Klevadix, mouth twisted. 'We surrender? Pack our bags and go home? This is a ravian ploy to drive us back to Kol. They test our strength of character. We must not wilt.'

'And where will we stop? The ravians will lose nothing here. How many will you butcher before our troops revolt?' asked Rukmini.

'Speak for yourself. My army knows what discipline and honour are. What are your views, White Spear? You have been silent.'

'Only because you discuss human concerns, which do not apply to us,' said White Spear. 'I will abide by whatever decision Marshall Askesis arrives at.'

'Haroun and Rukmini are right,' said Askesis. 'We must find another solution.'

'Send in your magicians first,' said Haroun. 'Let them mingle with the crowds, dispelling the ravian auras, and seek out the ravians and destroy them. Once the Avrantics' minds are freed, they will scatter and flee. We can drive them back and then meet their army, if it decides to stay.'

'An excellent suggestion, in theory,' said Arunava, general of the warlocks, 'but difficult to implement. Mingling with their civilians would involve yielding too much ground. If the peace march suddenly turns into a mob, we will have a riot on our hands, and we will lose more lives if they are close to us. Besides, I am not sure we are strong enough to physically defeat the ravians with magic alone. And if we are lost, it is just a matter of time before your soldiers change allegiances. I am confident we will be able to protect our troops. But sending us out as the first line of attack may prove to be disastrous.'

'With your permission, Marshall Askesis,' said a voice from the ring of Mortals, 'I might suggest a solution.'

The generals turned in surprise to see who had dared interrupt them, and found it was a man from the grey-cloaked company who'd arrived at the same time as the scouts. He was unarmed, and had handsome features and long hair tied behind his head. His face looked strangely familiar.

'Who are you, and on what grounds do you presume to interrupt this council?' asked Askesis sharply.

'I have no name,' said the newcomer, striding into the circle, 'but my face does. It is the face of Icelosis of the Seven Heroes, defender of Kol. The last name I used was Bekrom—call me that, if you will.'

'And the men you lead—do they have names?'

'No,' said ex-Bekrom, 'and they are not all men, though today we have all decided to wear the same face. We come from Kol, though the Civilian has not sent us; indeed, she is not sure we even exist. May I approach? I have counsel that is best heard by as few as possible.'

'And how do we know you are not a ravian or an assassin?' asked Haroun.

The stranger looked at Haroun and smiled. His features shifted, and transformed into Haroun's, and everyone who saw the change gasped.

'I may yet be an assassin,' said the shapeshifter. 'But I would be a very poor assassin indeed, to choose to strike in full view of the most powerful human army ever assembled.'

'Tell us what you have to say, and quickly,' said Askesis, looking out over the field, his eyes drawn by movement. In the distance another party of scouts rode out of the forest. The sappers, their work finished, drove their carts back along the riverbank. The trench was now full of logs. The pashan coolies lumbered behind the vaman carts as they began to cross the battlefield.

The generals moved closer together and the shapeshifter spoke in hushed tones.

'We are shapeshifters from Kol, descended from the half-rakshases of old. What we do and why I cannot reveal at this point. Suffice to say that our leaders have almost all been slain by ravians, and we have decided not to wait in Kol for the ravians to come and finish us off. We have been in Avranti, and have seen the ravians gather the army that now comes to meet you. There are ravians among the humans who approach, maintaining some kind of web of control over humans around them. We will break that web for you, moving among them; we have leaders to avenge, and ravians to kill. Our vows forbid us from waging war against humans—we may only defend Kol, and that defence can only prove successful if it is carried out in secret. So we cannot help you defeat the Avrantic army that follows the civilians. This I am sure you will achieve on your own. Until it is safe to attack, do whatever you can to hold the Avrantic army beyond the trench. We will remove the civilians and help you return them unharmed to Avranti. In return, we ask only this: you ask us no questions afterwards, and tell no one you ever saw us. You will never see us again.'

'Are you a gift from the gods?' asked Rukmini, awe written plainly on her face.

'If we are, we were not informed of it. Well, Marshall Askesis? Will you put your trust in us?'

Askesis nodded gravely. 'What must we do?'

The shapeshifter told them.

The council on the hilltop lasted for two more hours as Askesis and his generals added their military expertise to the shapeshifter's ideas and Gerilola and Gymros listened intently, taking notes for background; they would make up far more interesting tactics later on. When the generals were done, the battlefield of Pataal-e-Gurh suddenly exploded into activity. The shapeshifters, who numbered around two hundred, were given fresh horses. They rode them to the left flank, where they joined the centaurs. Then the allied armies were treated to a magnificent sight; the centaur army at full gallop tearing down the riverbank, crossing the Artaxerxians, and then racing towards the Durgan forces on the right. Queen Rukmini and the Durgan cavalry accompanied half the centaurs and the shapeshifters into the shadows of Shantavan, and the other half of the centaur army took their places on the right flank. A Koli legion on the rear echelon moved forward to replace the centaurs on the left flank, the thunderous sounds of thousands of boots marching in unison reverberating around the hills.

As Askesis stood on his hill, orchestrating the movement of his troops, listening to the sound of music float in from the far end of the battlefield and herald the arrival of the enemy, he wondered for a very brief moment what his soldiers were thinking. The bards would say their hearts were filled with pride and fear, but Askesis's own memories of his days in the ranks were different—in the silence that preceded the many battles in his past, he'd thought of the little things, of the witty retorts that came too late to fire at his corporal, of what he'd eaten for breakfast, and how there was a slight pain in his right ankle and how lucky he'd be if he still noticed it at the end of the day. And he'd thought about some of the too-big-to-handle things, how time would soon slow down until every clump of grass and chunk of brain would seem to float in the air, how elsewhere in the world people were eating and sleeping and playing football, and how lucky he was to be alive, and how unlucky he was to be born in a time of war. He'd asked his tent-mate what he thought about while marching to battle, and had received the enigmatic and possibly enlightenment-inspiring reply 'Squirrels' and realized that everyone in the army thought of different things, which made sense. Because even if they'd only appear in the epics as brave, valiant props who went 'ooh' when heroes spoke and followed them endlessly to their unfortunate deaths, or receive less honourable mentions in lists of countless casualties, each soldier was a different person. Askesis had learned that lesson early, and had always felt a degree of regret as he watched its importance recede further and further in his mind as he rose through the ranks. Now, as he watched thousands move at his command, he felt a sudden thrill of power. It did not matter, really, what his soldiers thought and felt; for now they were pieces on a chessboard, and he was playing. If asked, he would have said he loved them all equally.

It was well past noon when the Avrantics crossed the ridge and caught their first glimpse of their official welcome to the Free States. And across the wide plain of Pataal-e-Gurh, Askesis's army saw the people they had come here to fight, men and women and children, entire families, villages, cities, and provinces walking or dancing towards them, intoxicated by ravian spells and their own music. Hundreds walked abreast with wide, fixed smiles on their faces, singing songs of harmony and brotherhood, holding hands in an endless chain of joyous humanity. They'd made great banners bearing messages of peace, wore garlands of wild flowers and threw fistfuls of petals and coloured powder in the air.

The ravians danced along with the humans, hidden, as Askesis knew they would be. They weren't controlling the Avrantics like puppets, but simply pushing their emotions in one direction—the happiness the Avrantics felt was mostly of their own creation. They were delighted to be there, on this day, to be able to tell their children how they changed the world. They were marching to save all humanity, to shame armies into submission, to show those cruel and twisted politicians and warriors that a little love and a little music were all you needed, that every soul in the universe could be brought together if only someone would make the first move.

'The enemy's forces are savage and numerous; giant men with cruel faces who ride on hideous beasts whose like has never been seen before. Their approach shakes the earth, and my heart trembles; what hideous sights will I see today? But the soldiers of Kol, battle-hardened and brave, merely laugh in their faces. Tonight, they will feast in their tents, they say; the enemy will dine in hell,' wrote Gymros. 'Even from his hill, Askesis can smell the enemy's stench. It suffocates him but he, too, laughs contemptuously as he gazes upon the invaders. They bear fearsome weapons, crafted underground by demons. Their ugly, towering forms roll over the clean earth like—'

'What are those things that you have many of, Gerilola?'

'Fingers?'

'No. They couldn't roll like a finger. Pay attention.'

'Fingers can roll.'

'You're thinking of fingers that have been cut off. Not epic enough.'

'Oh yes. Sorry about that.'

Askesis knew that it would take the ravians mere minutes to change the mood of this sea of people completely, from enthusiastic, warm, hopeful friendliness to a frenzy of undirected emotion to savage fury and back again. It burned his heart to see humans driven thus, like drugged cattle. Part of his warrior's mind toyed with the idea of letting the Artaxerxians loose—he could almost taste their impatience from afar. He imagined the sky darkened by hissing clouds of arrows, raining steel and death on the unarmed fools across the battlefield, and then the thunder of hooves as the cavalry drove into them like a single spear. He shuddered.

The peace march rolled forward. Many people were not dancing any more, but walking in long strides, peaceful and resolute, as their moods altered. Now they had visions of dying to show the world the horrors of war, of teaching the savages with their swords and bows the value of life. They would die in thousands, in fields of corpses harvested by brutes, but they would die proudly, and drown the spirits of war with their own blood in full view of the gods above.

Askesis waited until the first line of the approaching crowd had almost reached the sappers' trench.

Then he raised his right hand, and the war officially began.

On each hill, warlocks cast spells on great boulders doused in Psomedean fire, which lit up in eerie green flames. The vaman catapults hurled these high into the sky and Askesis's entire army let out a huge roar as the giant fireballs grew smaller and smaller, hurtling towards the Avrantics in impossibly great arcs. Wood from the logs in the trench splintered and flew about as the fireballs landed with uncanny accuracy on the trench, which lit up in seconds, creating a wall of green eldritch flame that rose twenty feet in the air, but let out no smoke. The warlocks had set powerful enchantments on the fire; it radiated not heat but magical ward spells, a wave of magic that rolled over everyone near it, lapping at their senses, driving away the clouds in their fuzzily happy minds. The leaders of the surging tide of humanity halted and stumbled, their passion and resolve suddenly dissolving, and they looked around wildly, trying to understand how they had reached where they were, and why it had previously seemed such a good idea to challenge the armies of Kol. Children wailed and wept, and the march faltered. Sheer momentum kept it moving ahead, though, as thousands more jostled their way over the ridge, pushing the craven forward. A few Avrantics were pushed into the flames and died instantly. The sight of their bodies burning horribly did nothing to encourage those who replaced them at the head of the mob.

As the march ground to a halt, the ravians considered their next move. They could not move into the forest; the spirit of the defenders could only be broken if they saw the Avrantics being slaughtered in full daylight, not in the secrecy of the forest.

As the ravians loosened their grip on the humans for a few moments to discuss their next step through mindspeech, the shapeshifters teleported into the crowd. Their arrival weakened the ravian spell further, and moving swiftly through the throng, changing shapes often, they began to free the minds of the Avrantics through their very presence. Songs faltered and were replaced by angry, confused shouting. Flowers and musical instruments were thrown away, and fights broke out. And then the shapeshifters found their first ravian; in the middle of a change, a shapeshifter found a tall man charging at him. He yelled in alarm, and instantly five other shapeshifters teleported to his aid. The ravian fought well, but was overcome. The first strand of the web had been cut. Other ravians spotted shapeshifters and incited nearby humans to attack them. The shapeshifters merely teleported out of brawls and continued their hunt. Their guess that the ravians were evenly spaced proved correct; this gave them a fairly good idea as to where more ravians were, whereas the ravians had no idea where their attackers would come from, as the humans, panicking all around them, provided excellent cover for their wily foes. The ravians saw enemies where there were only innocents, and lashed out wildly, driving the humans to attack one another. And the shapeshifters moved ever deeper into the crowd. Another ravian was found, and then another, and another, and each one in turn was swiftly overcome, trapped in a whirl of bodies, unable to dodge or strike efficiently, predicting with their ravian senses where the death-blow would come from, but unable to do anything about it. As the army waited patiently across the battlefield and increasingly large numbers of extremely confused Avrantics milled about helplessly, the ravians grew rash, and incited the Avrantics to a frenzy. Waves of people ran screaming into the trench, trying to smother the flames. They failed and burned, and more ravians were discovered.

And then a new danger emerged, causing ripples of fear all over the crowd. Great horned demons, with flaming whips and long, curling claws, began to appear near the river, and vanish again, starting what was almost a stampede into the forest. The ravians broke formation and charged; the demons vanished, and other shapeshifters arrived to battle the ravians who'd exposed themselves. With an arsenal of tricks up their shifting sleeves, the shapeshifters drove the humans they'd freed into the forest, where the Durgans and the centaurs were waiting for them. Whispers rippled through the crowd; they had been prisoners of the ravians, but now they were free, and the soldiers would take them home. The news travelled faster than ravians or shapeshifters, and slowly the flood of humanity turned into a trickle, until the whole march slowly stopped. The ravians were still trying in vain to form some kind of formation against their elusive attackers, and their holds over the mob's mind weakened further every minute as they strove to locate the shapeshifters. Several shapeshifters lost their lives in the process, but they were wearing down the ravians. The humans as a whole were now pushing back, away from the battlefield; far behind them, the Avrantic army began to retreat to make way for a river of people that had suddenly reversed direction.

In the forest, supervised by Queen Rukmini, soldiers began the delicate process of moving hordes of extremely frightened and confused people into manageable lines. Flanked by centaur and Durgan guards, the peace march began the long walk home.

Several hours later, as the sun began to set, the ravians attempted a charge; a score of them working together managed to lift up several burning logs from the trench and toss them into the river. But they had now lost any semblance of control over the Avrantic civilians, who were now walking into the forest of their own accord, angry, disillusioned, terrified of the great army waiting across the battlefield. The web had been snapped, unravelled; the ravians began to retreat through the masses they had brought to be slaughtered, drawing together to defend themselves more effectively against shapeshifter sorties.

The shapeshifters had undertaken a task of truly mammoth proportions. It took them two whole days to remove the civilians from between the opposing armies. The Avrantic army, aware of the thousands of Durgan and centaurs moving in the forest, retreated further and strengthened its left flank, widening as far as possible the gap between its forces and the forest.

On the morning of the third day, Askesis received news from the north that confirmed what he already suspected; the ravians had not sent their main force to this battle, just enough to keep the humans under control and keep his army occupied and away from their main army, which was marching along the southern border of Vrihataranya towards Imokoi. The advantage lay squarely with Askesis now; he'd saved the lives of untold thousands, and made arrangements for their safe escort to Avranti, thus achieving a massive moral victory. Tactically, too, he had the upper hand; Shantavan was his now, and any attempt to even enter the forest would result in massive losses for the Avrantics. Besides, his troops were fresh and raring to fight, and though the Avrantic army was mighty, second only to Xi'en in terms of size, its logistical systems had always been inferior to Kol's. Far more importantly, the ravians had removed the Avrantics' greatest strength. What made most armies very eager to avoid conflict with Avrantic troops was Avranti's magical weapons. A few Avrantic nobles armed with these weapons, rumoured to be celestial in origin, could end a battle within hours. But there were no magical weapons, and no powerful enchanters on the Avrantic side at Pataal-e-Gurh, for they would have weakened the ravians' grasp over the minds of the army's generals. And since the ravians had not sent their greatest heroes to this battle, the mighty warriors of legend who could crack the earth and kill entire war-bands on their own, they too could be overcome by sheer numbers. The Koli army, on the other hand, now had more magic-users than it needed, even without the shapeshifters, who had blended in with the returning Avrantic civilians and, true to their word, were never seen again by anyone present that day at Pataal-e-Gurh.

When the last of the civilians had walked into the forest, and news had come from the right flank that all was well, that Queen Rukmini and her warrior-women were safely on their way towards Avranti, Askesis sent envoys to the Avrantic general seeking their surrender; a surrender he fully expected, given, he thought, that the ravians had already achieved as much as they could. This time the envoys did not disappear like the others. Instead, they were sent back headless, tied to horses. Askesis's legions prepared once again for battle. The magic fire on the great trench had burnt out by then, but Askesis made no move to renew it; he wanted the enemy to come forward and meet him, he was itching to begin the battle. So were the Avrantics; they speedily and efficiently organized their forces behind the ridge, great battalions of infantry, lines of elite troops on chariots, a token cavalry and an awe-inspiring force of war-elephants.

The battle began at dawn on the fourth day.

The Avrantics advanced, filling the slope between the ridge and the filled-up trench with surprising speed. Their army was divided as it had been since ancient times into chaturangas: elephants, chariots, infantry and cavalry. Their left flank had been reinforced to face attacks from Shantavan; several lines of archers and heavily armed infantry, and cohorts of horse-archers to deal with moving sorties. The light infantry had been split up in two, one half in front, the other at the rear, and between them the chariots led the war-elephants to the field. Cavalry dominated the right flank by the river. Avranti's generals rode on chariots in the centre. As Askesis watched them swell into the basin of Gurh, he realized the well-shielded centre was where the ravians must have assembled. This was a well-trained military force, the ravians did not need to physically be present among the troops to influence the soldiers—they just needed to be near the generals so the soldiers received the orders the ravians desired.

'The air is thick with anticipation,' wrote Gerilola. 'The mighty warriors of Kol ache to sink their clean steel into the cowardly, wavering enemy's black heart, but not for nothing has Askesis been called the Grey Fox; he is the ultimate master of tactics, and still he holds them back. The enemy approaches with broad swords and cruel grimaces. Today will be a day of days.'

'Can we move to behind that tent?' asked Gymros. 'We are too near Askesis. What if they have those terrible arrows and decide to use one on this hill? We are too important to place ourselves at risk thus; an entire nation depends on us.'

'Yes,' said Gerilola, rising hurriedly. 'I think the hill on the right has a better view, anyway. And we can capture the emotions of the reserve troops better from there.'

The Avrantic infantry marched over the trench into the basin of Pataal-e-Gurh. On the right flank, the centaurs fretted and fumed, but no signal came from Askesis. In the forest, archers on horses or on trees, bows taut and ready, waited for an Avrantic charge into the forest; none came. Messengers raced to all the Koli divisions, bearing scrolls from Askesis. In front of the Artaxerxian lines, Haroun read his scroll, threw it away, and turned to his troops.

'The ravians will drive the Avrantics forward recklessly,' he said. 'They do not care about losing soldiers; as you have seen, human lives no longer mean anything to them. Marshall Askesis and I came here hoping to avoid a battle, but as you can plainly see, that looks unlikely. Today, as we stand here at our rightful place, in front of all others, I say this to you: You are the pride of all Artaxerxia. For years they have thrown us at their mightiest enemies, waiting for us to be vanquished. But time and time again, we have defeated the hordes of the west and south, and the puppet-masters of Amurabad. Today, as we face Avranti, an enemy we have all longed to fight since the day we entered the army, I thank you once again, my brothers. Our time has come again. We will shed blood, and if we die, one day we will ride together again in the gardens of paradise. Ours is the first charge. Make me proud.'

The Avrantic infantry spread out over the battlefield, and Askesis realized his troops were outnumbered. This did not seem to cause him any degree of concern.

On the right flank, Klevadix tore open his scroll and turned, smiling, to his men.

'Kill them all, you horrible bastards,' he said, and the neo-Hudlumms roared in joy.

The first of the chariots crossed the trench.

'Catapults,' said Askesis.

Flags flew up, and the vamans released five huge balls of fire that streaked over the charging Avrantics like comets. The infantry charge did not falter; they were almost within bowshot.

As the fireballs sped towards the chariots, the ravians made their move. The fireballs skipped and turned in mid-air as their trajectories altered. Two arced leftwards to splash and sizzle into the river, three others skipped over the lines of chariots, and into the elephants, killing two instantly in thunder-bursts of blood and bone and wounding several others. A line of elephants teetered and stumbled, trumpeting in rage and bewilderment, and men fell screaming off their backs.

The elephants went berserk, forcing an all-out charge, The chariots sped forward, ahead of the stampeding behemoths, and the cavalry on the Avrantic right charged alongside them. The vamans adjusted their catapults and ballistae and fired again; more elephants died, and huge siege arrows cunningly filled with explosives crashed amidst the cavalry. Horses and their riders were thrown into the air in clouds of flesh and metal. Some landed in the river, and others were trampled by the elephants.

The infantry were in range. At Askesis's command, the archers on the hills filled the sky with arrows; hundreds of Avrantic infantrymen lost their lives in that deadly rain as shafts pierced armour, shields and skin alike. More vaman missiles broke the war-elephant lines, and hundreds of infantrymen perished in the next volley of arrows. But the Avrantic lines did not falter; soldiers ran over the bodies of their fallen comrades to fill in the gaps, desperation bringing out the valour that their ravian masters could not inspire.

The Artaxerxians charged. Magnificent brown horses streaked forwards, archers with shortbows firing swiftly and accurately into the chests of the approaching infantry. Spears and shields rose up to meet the cavalry. Scimitars and lances flashed in the sun as the lines met, and the earth shook with the impact. A whirlwind of earth and dust and bone rose in the air, heads shattered, shields splintered, horses fell to earth taking their riders with them. The Avrantic line was broken, and those left wounded as the cavalry barrelled through their ranks lived on for mere minutes before Artaxerxian infantrymen reached the battlefront. The Artaxerxian horsemen were slowed down eventually by the sheer mass of the bodies they bore down on; bows were thrust aside and swords pulled out as men stabbed, swung pushed and died in frenzied, throbbing swarms of limbs.

'The Artaxerxians prove themselves second only to Kol in valour and skill on the battlefield,' wrote Gymros, observing through a telescope a young Avrantic stagger blindly on an empty patch of ground, holding his intestines in his hands, before a glancing blow from a horseman took off half his face. 'War is so beautiful, so poetic, such a metaphor for love, life and everything worth dreaming of! How I wish I were not compelled to sit here with a pen while the true heroes dazzle even the sun with their strength and swordplay!'

On the left flank, the Koli legion strode forward to meet the Avrantic cavalry. On the right, the neo-Hudlumms were released; they ran like wolves, swinging their broad blades above their heads, hungry for blood. The centaurs could not be restrained any longer; they flowed like a torrent towards the Avrantic left flank, and drove right through them, smashing bone and flesh, fighting and killing even as horse-archers poured arrows into their bodies. The Avrantic chariots wheeled around in the empty spaces on the right, letting the elephants pass and falling in line behind them. The Avrantics commanded most of the space on the battlefield, but Askesis's troops held the advantage; the magicians now came into play, weaving spells of death and deceit, beguiling their enemies with illusions, burning them with magic fire and confusing them with horrific visions.

The legions of Kol too lost many men as the Avrantic cavalry charged, but their superior numbers and mixed formation won the day; the warlocks attacked the horses with mind-turning spells, and they cannoned into one another. Most of the Avrantic cavalrymen drowned in the Asa as their maddened mounts took flight. Passing by the chariots and elephants, the Koli legions advanced down the left flank and attacked the reserve Avrantic infantry, and as they outflanked the enemy and drove them forward to the centre of the battlefield, vaman artillery pounded into the heart of the swarming Avrantic ranks, each missile taking out scores of advancing infantrymen, each burning boulder rolling in a trail of destruction over flattened corpses.

'The centaur charge is led by a young centaur stallion named Purple Heart,' wrote Gerilola, improvising wildly, 'the son of a shaman and a blacksmith, who'd abandoned his vow of non-violence when a cruel ravian hunter had eaten his wife. East he rides, like a woodland god, and none can stand before him. Watch, as he leaps on a chariot, crushing its rider beneath his vengeful hooves! Against insurmountable odds, in hellish conditions, the army of Askesis proves, again, indomitable. But surely the ravians have some hellish sorcery plotted; will Askesis and Purple Heart survive their nefarious scheme?' And if that was not the kind of war report that would justify his lucrative pay-per-word contract, he thought, he didn't know what was.

The war-elephants trundled on towards the hills. Archers on platforms on their backs shot wildly into the melee, slaying friends and foes alike. Behind the elephants, the centaurs ran in to do battle with the charioteers. A deadly dance began in the heart of the basin, as the man-horses and chariots whirled and swerved in intricate formations, centaur arrows and spears missing their marks, vaman artillery crashing harmlessly around them. The ravians did not miss, though; their arrows swerved with their targets and brought them down. The humans on chariots did not fare so well; in most cases, the centaurs outmanouevred them, separated them from the ravians, herded them together and finished them off with their deadly spears; thus died most of Avranti's generals, abandoned by their troops and their new masters, and the last sounds they heard were the ululating war-whoops of the fierce-eyed man-horses of the Centaur Forests.

The Avrantic left flank rallied, finding the centaurs otherwise occupied, but their plans came to naught, for Askesis finally gave the signal, and the Durgans and centaurs waiting anxiously in Shantavan rushed out with wild yells behind the rear infantry, peppering the Avrantics with arrows and driving them further inwards. On the right, the neo-Hudlumms entered the fray, cutting down dismounted cavalrymen with great, sweeping axe-strokes.

The Avrantic army was now surrounded. Another Koli legion rushed in to aid the Artaxerxians. On the hills, Rabin's archers were now shooting slowly, taking careful aim. The circle was closing from the rear, as the Avrantic reserve infantry crumbled under the fury of the Koli left flank, and warlocks dealt death with abandon, and cackling vamans sent a relentless stream of comets of death crashing into their midst. The Durgans and centaurs streaming in from Shantavan shattered the Avrantic left flank, and screaming wood-spirits summoned by the centaur shamans tore into the heavy infantry, breaking any attempt to make a stand. The war-elephants' charge had almost been halted. At least a hundred elephants lay dead in the field, mostly shattered by the missiles from the vaman ballistae. But some twenty elephants survived, and achieved what the rest of the army could not; they broke the circle. The Artaxerxian lines fell apart as the maddened war-elephants trampled over Artaxerxians and Avrantics and headed for the hills.

But Haroun of the Artaxerxians would not stomach this; he rode in pursuit of the elephants with a few of his bodyguards, sending arrows into their legs. Haroun himself caught hold of a rope that held a platform up, and swung acrobatically up on the elephant's back. He slew every man on the platform as onlookers cheered, fending off arrows with his sword, his skill and balance unbelievable. He then raced forward on the lumbering beast's back and stuck two long swords into the base of its skull. As the elephant stumbled and fell, the Artaxerxian hero slid smoothly down its trunk, and landed gently on the field, striking a dashing pose amidst much applause a feet away from the fallen elephant. The applause died a sudden death, and so did the elephant, which chose unfortunately to roll over the heroic Haroun in the process of doing so.

Rabin's archers picked off the men on the elephants' backs as the beasts reached the bottom of the hills. The archers then watched in amazement as the Kolis broke formation and fled instead of stepping up to fight the elephants, but they were only following orders; the elephants charged on in straight lines between the hills, and the Koli legions still waiting behind the hills, moved aside politely and let them pass, and then surged forward and closed the gap in the circle.

The very centre of the circle, though, belonged to the ravians, who had abandoned any thoughts of mind control and other subtle arts, and were fighting for survival. Here in the battlefield among soldiers, they were at an advantage;

they kept moving, killing with every thrust, deflecting arrows and catapult bolts on to their enemies. But as their opponents swelled in number, undeterred by the hills of corpses they felled around them, things became less clear; they were facing opponents fighting on instinct, hacking and stabbing blindly. Technique was no longer a factor, and no ravian danger-sense could predict slipping on freshly liberated intestines, or being hit in the eye by random splinters of bone; even ravians grew tired eventually. Warlocks circled them like vultures, sending blasts of death magic across the circle. The ravians dodged most, but could not dodge all. There were only about a hundred ravians left, trapped in the centre of the field, when Askesis ordered the Durgan war-elephants to enter the killing grounds. The battle was won. In the rear, Durgan cavalry and centaurs raced across the ground, picking off survivors. The Koli infantry and the neo-Hudlumms swept across the field, adding their numbers to pockets of resistance. The defenders around the hills broke ranks, eager for a taste of the battle, and chased down the last of the shattered Avrantic left flank; some horsemen managed to fight their way out of the tightening ring of Koli warriors and break into Shantavan; they were not pursued as they fled from the battlefield.

On the central hill, Askesis watched the great basin of Pataal-e-Gurh, littered with the bodies of innumerable corpses and smiled grimly. He'd not expected a battle of annihilation. All that remained was to snuff out the remaining ravians; this would take a few hours, but they would be done by sundown.

It was then that Arunava the warlock cried out in alarm and pointed to the east, at dark clouds blotting out the sky, travelling against the wind towards the battlefield. Tendrils of smoke streaked across the sky like tentacles, and massive swirling torrents of impenetrable darkness followed them. On the battlefield, the ravians cried out fierce challenges, and made a savage charge; they broke through the circle of attackers, hacking and slashing without mercy, and trod lightly over the carcasses of the fallen as they fled.

Shadows enveloped the battlefield, eating away the sun's face in the west, bringing near-darkness and confusion in their wake. The ravians dealt death mercilessly, felling muddled, blinking soldiers like wheatstalks. Warlocks lit flares and sent them flying at the ravians, revealing their positions, but they pressed on regardless, in desperate hurry. They seemed unconcerned about the arrows and fireballs that followed them; many died in the process, but others, at least forty in number, found horses and galloped off into the darkness, and after a while they broke through the line of Koli infantry that held the trench, and disappeared into the forest. The clouds moved further westward, until the entire army was in shadow. Light could be seen in every direction, far away across the horizon; but above Gurh there was only darkness, solid, thick and inky. Flares were lit on each hill, and warlocks in every maniple lit torches with enchanted fire. The surviving generals rushed to Askesis, wondering what sorcery they were about to face next; Askesis had no answers. The legions closed their ranks. Their superb training showing as they assembled swiftly and efficiently in the centre of the battlefield and stood poised and ready in the smothering dark, flushed with pride at their recent magnificent victory, waiting for whatever new enemy was about to reveal itself. As the thunder of hooves and the men's shouting died down, a new sound could be heard—a dull droning, as of distant thunder, yet with a metallic, harsh edge.

And then the darkness melted, the clouds dissolving around them like ink thrown in a river, and within seconds it was as if the ominous clouds had never existed. The droning sound in the sky was louder now, and harsher. Askesis's armies looked up, and their eyes widened, their jaws dropped. Hardened veterans cried out in wonder like children as their minds slowly absorbed the wonder in the sky.

Six ships of metal, shining silver and gold, floated above the battlefield in a huge hexagon. Huge, smooth, mind-numbing marvels of construction, one shaped like a turtle, others like a swan, a whale, a jellyfish, and the remaining two like strange animals never seen on this world. Each was the size of a palace, and was adorned with strange symbols and scripts. Massive tubes ran across their bellies and their sides were lined with portholes and studded with metallic constructs that shone like rubies and emeralds. The prows of these ships were constructed in the shape of animal heads, looking downwards, coldly surveying the ground below.

Askesis looked up, blinked, and looked again, but the airships were still there; they were very real, floating islands in the sky, trailing smoke and vapour. On the ground, many men kneeled and prayed, for surely the marvels in the sky were the chariots of the gods themselves, come to bless them in their hour of glory. They felt small, insignificant; all they had achieved on this day paled in comparison with magnificence on this scale.

With a strange, clicking, buzzing sound, trapdoors began to open under the ships, and large metal barrels emerged, protruding from the animals' bellies, and Kol's troops watched on, fascinated; perhaps these were stairs of some sort, perhaps the gods themselves would walk down and speak to Marshall Askesis, grant him boons to win this war for humanity, crushing ravians and monsters alike. The droning noise of the airships turned to a high-pitched whine, and the air throbbed with anticipation.

Six pillars of light suddenly appeared on the battlefield, one under each ship, each pillar covering an area the size of a small gladiatorial arena, and cries of amazement echoed all over Gurh and turned a second later into shrieks of horror. In a flash, everything the light touched burned to cinders. Centaurs and men were transformed into frozen, black corpses in the blink of an eye, and even the Durgan war-elephants were instantly turned to mountains of ash. Concentric circles of fire spread out over the battlefield, burning everything in their path. Hundreds of soldiers died in seconds. The rest stared blindly, unable to comprehend the enormity of what they had just witnessed.

The ships began to move, circling the battlefield slowly, and the pillars moved with them, incinerating everything they touched. Entire legions were decimated in a minute. Most of those who were far enough from the first attack to have enough time to will their limbs into action were consumed by the widening circles of flame. A few managed to leap into the river and were saved. The sound of thunder rolled over the plains. Up in the sky, there were flashes of light stabbing out from rows of cannons that had emerged from the sides of the airships, blue and red and green thrusts of light, and for each flash, on the ground there were thundering explosions, sending fountains of smoke and chunks of bodies spiralling high into the sky. Some soldiers ran blindly from one moving tower of burning light only to be caught under another; some bought themselves a few minutes of life by huddling together helplessly in the very centre of the battlefield, and watched helplessly as walls of flame surrounded them, until one of the ships ended their misery; it rolled slowly across the killing field, its light-beam devouring everything in its path, and the soldiers died instantly under its fiery gaze.

Askesis stood on his hill, unable to move, and watched his army burn. And as he looked in the brilliant light at the corpses of young boys who had died at his command, his thoughts were filled with regret. Where was the glory in their death? What had they died for? How would their families survive? Had they been prepared for the horrors they had seen in their last minutes, the gaping wounds, the dying screams, the befouled earth, the shattered, charred faces of men who might have been their friends? How had he brought them to this accursed place? Askesis was a man of logic; he saw clearly that there could be no victory against the powers he faced now. The order of things had changed, the world where humans held sway had ended. Kol would fall, and so would Imokoi, their colours and shadows succumbing to this all-devouring white light. The vamans would hide in their holes while they could; their fate did not concern him. He would not run back to Kol and wait for the inevitable. He would not struggle like a cockroach on its back while the gods watched and laughed. His only alternative was total surrender. But he would not make his men burn with him. He looked behind the hill, and was touched to find that his reserve troops still maintained perfect discipline as they stood in columns, waiting for death, waiting for orders. He commanded his trumpeters to sound the despairing notes of defeat and dispersal, and watched his troops break ranks and flee, noting with pride how men dragged other men on to their horses before they scattered, fleeing desperately from the great fingers of light and fire that spelled out the world's doom on the bloodstained fields of Gurh. He looked up; two ships approached, but many of the men would outrun them. His Mortals still stood with him, though the vamans and the warlocks had fled. He ordered his Mortals to ride back to Kol, and save it if they could; they begged him to come with them, but he refused. On the battlefield, horses with flaming manes and whimpering riders on their backs hurdled walls of fire and lanced through clouds of dust and ash. In Shantavan, centaurs and Durgans sped southwards through falling flaming branches. To Askesis's left, explosions consumed Rabin and his archers as they fled downhill. To his right, burning neo-Hudlumms raced uphill singing death-songs as the light overtook them and their bodies were consumed, and the vaman catapults crackled and splintered. The soul-stirring war-reports of Gymros and Gerilola turned to ashes seconds before their authors. Above Askesis, a ship slowly wove its way towards his hill. He planted his sword in the earth and waited for it, his stern features showing no trace of the storms raging in his mind. He turned and watched his soldiers fleeing homewards, and they looked back at him as their horses sped away, alone on his hill, face brilliantly lit as the blinding light-tower closed in on him, and then he was gone.

* * *

And far above the killing fields of Gurh, around the table that was the map that was the game that was the world, there was much rejoicing, and laughter, and drawing of deep breaths, and derivations of significance and meaning, and bad poetry, and slapping of backs, and stroking of tentacles, and promises of payment of rash private wagers. Zivran's Game, the Players said, was a masterpiece—how exquisite its design! How quaint its pieces! He was to be congratulated. And he was congratulated, effusively, and he muttered gratefully into his beard and cast shy glances at the radiant Players. They were entranced, and some were already pleasantly drunk. They huddled closer to the game, and looked towards their crystals as new pieces were assigned to them.

* * *

On the akashraths, the ravians moved great wheels with their minds. White-cloaked captains set their courses towards the south-west, towards the magnificent, impudent, doomed human city of Kol.

8

Inside the Pyramid of the First Pharaoh, in lost subterranean halls of heroes, a great humming and chanting filled the air at the Scorpion Man's bidding. A tapping, rustling sound swelled into a wall-shaking roar as millions of spirit scarabs crawled over ancient, dusty walls, tracing out ever-shifting mandalas, amassing as great swarms to push aside tablets of stone, open caskets, and stir great boiling tanks and cauldrons of slime and brine. The pyramid echoed with creaks and groans as the heroes of the past woke again, freed themselves of their diverse confinements and strode down lost corridors on unsteady feet, their minds abuzz with their pale master's words, their heads still held high in remembrance of their former glory.

The hanging stairways of the Great Pyramid echoed with the sound of zombies and ooze-dripping ghouls and ghoulehs marching up the step-labyrinth from the bottomless depths below, zigzagging lines of dead soldiers in single file, an ever-moving never-ending ant-farm preparing for the harvest.

The hall of Erkila, queen of the damned, was now occupied by the tailors of the undead, Marichellis from the haunted Volstone hills in Olivya. As the giant cat-woman statues watched with their burning eyes, a line of skeletal warriors dragged barrows full of limbs towards Erkila's sarcophagus, in front of which the Marichellis sat at their creaking spinning-wheels and stitched and stuffed their grotesque dolls, strange amalgamations of human and animal body parts and materials that had never known life, held together with gut-threads, nails, wires and incantations; crocodile-headed men, human torsos on giant spider bodies, dogs with spiked chariot wheels for legs, lance-horned giant bulls and hundreds of other twisted chimaeric creatures that were then taken to necromancers for reanimation.

In the innermost sanctums of the Great Pyramid, surrounded on every side by labyrinths full of deathly traps and ancient curses, and guarded ceaselessly by nameless monsters that had lain brooding in ravenous hunger since the dawn of time, lay the hearts of Erkila's generals, the lych-lords. The lych-hearts, keys to their masters' destruction, were in many forms; some beating in iron chests, others pouring back and forth through hour-glasses, yet others flitting ceaselessly within their confined rooms in the forms of emerald spiders or bats. The heart of the greatest lych-lord of all, Izogul the Deathless, was placed in the eye of a needle, inside a stone egg, inside a scarab, inside a canoptic jar that lay in the Pharaoh's chamber. The Pharaoh slept still, but the hieroglyphs on his walls had started moving on their own, farmers and hunters in the pictures changing positions, shifting into new places to tell a new story, the tale of the death of the world.

Around the Pyramid of the First Pharoah, the Ayinhara desert in south Elaken was teeming with lifelessness. Under the pale light of the rising moon, the sand shone white and cold, and in a pale swirling mist the legions of the undead stood, feeling their bodies erode away as they awaited the call to end the world. The dry desert air throbbed with menace and anticipation, despite the fact that many thousands among the whispering host had been waiting for centuries.

On the lower steps of the pyramid stood necromancers with their curling horn-helms and robes of black and purple, skull-masks stained with ichor spirits they drank from cups of bone, gloating as mounds of corpses were dragged in great carts towards the pyramid. The necromancers' ram-headed staffs cast forth pale green clouds, summoning spirits from rows of jars embedded in the sand, releasing hungry Avrantic pretas and Elakish moumras who chuckled and gurgled in eerie glee as they sank their fangs into their new bodies, which jerked and twitched awkwardly before standing up, pulled by invisible ropes, dragged into bitter un-life by the puppeteers that danced within them, slavering hungrily at stiffening tissue-strings, pouring cold fingers of venomous spirit through still, sluggish veins.

On great dune-hillocks to the south of the pyramid danced hungans, voudon priests with entrails tied in their wild dreadlocked hair, commanding cohorts of slowly swaying zombies, whose hulking bodies were in advanced states of decay, flesh and muscle and innards rotting and flapping. Riding loas lurked silently in each zombie's head, ready to dance their death-dances at the hungans' command. Jakyinis hummed shrill incantations, damballas hissed with long forked serpent-tongues lolling over their gaping open chests and exposed snake-egg hearts. The armies of the zombies and the skeletal undead stretched as far as the horizon in every direction; and behind their ever-swelling battalions stood the Legions of the Void, unnumbered ranks of roaming martial spirits, long-dead nations of fierce martial races, now gaps in reality filled in with swirling sand to form the shapes of the human armies they had once been, great kings and proud heroes, chariots, camels, even elephants, each a raging sandstorm trapped in a memory of a shape, bright swords and spears glittering once more in the moonlight.

The undead army had been assembling since the day the Great Pyramid had been sealed, long ago, but as world's end approached, the dead began to dream in every land, their still synpapses pulsing with visions of the Scorpion Man, and in their homes in the dead of night the living shuddered, their spines tingling with sudden cold as troops of corpses travelled by. The lych-lords issued forth from the Great Pyramid and spread out across the world, raising undead and recruiting spirits. Graveyards were robbed and crypts plundered, necropolises emptied and cremation sites enchanted, as the dead gathered around invisible banners, answering the Scorpion Man's call, waiting for their lych-guides to lead them to the Pyramid of the First Pharaoh. The dead walked through hidden paths, and sailed to Elaken on secret ships, and those among the living that did not hide as they passed, or were brave enough to challenge them, were soon added to their numbers. In the Free States, mercenaries were recruited to transport mysterious voyagers to the west, and were simply added to their cargo when curiosity got the better of them. Seafaring necromancers killed more pirates than the navies of the southern nations combined. The armada of the dead sailed relentlessly across the southern seas, calling up the spirits of drowned sailors. In the north, the size-shifting, flesh-eating draugr left their treasure-mounds, where they had lain restless for ages, cheated of the afterlife they had dreamed of, tricked into endless servitude by bloated, corpulent valkyries who had snatched their spirits from battlefields with false promises of eternal feasts in the heavens.

Behind the zombies, under murky suspended swamps of un-leaves stood the slimy, decaying trunks of the Karloflora, hordes of roving tree-spirits overflowing with mildew and hatred. On their dripping branches, Avrantic vetals hung upside down, cackling maliciously. Revenants from Ventelot, torn from their graves by lych-whispers and unfulfilled quests, stood stiff-upper-lipped near the dark woods, looking disapprovingly at thousands of nomadic jiangshi, terrifying essence-absorbers from Xi'en, hopping comically as they shuffled their ranks. Aswangs from far lands to the south-east, mild-mannered, weary-eyed human farmers or butchers by day and ravenous corpse-stealers by night, scurried between the battalions of the undead, carrying their messenger familiars, the tiktiks, bearing messages from the pyramid to the leaders of the hordes.

Two troops of skeletal warriors trudged from the west towards the Great Pyramid, drawing good-natured jeers from the undead already assembled because of their stork-like marching. They couldn't help it, of course—it was difficult, wading through sand with feet of bone.

As the companies merged forces, their leaders shook sand out of their eye-sockets in disbelief—they realized, through the instinctive phrenological skills of skeletal undead, that they were brothers, reunited after a hundred years. They broke ranks and clasped each other with joyous cries, rattled their ribs together and hissed, with their spirit-tongues, the traditional 'How's life, zombie?'

Most of the living called all undead people zombies, which was inaccurate, given that the zombies were a specific kind of undead, from the islands south of Elaken. *Undead* was, of course, the only polite and politically correct term, but among the undead, *zombie* had become a perfectly acceptable substitute, in a somewhat complex in-joke about the ignorance of the living. The nickname used among the undead to describe the living was, of course, *dinner*. These enchanting social customs would have been more widely known among the living if more undead had been more inclined to leave social acquaintances among the living alive, or, indeed, if more undead had been capable of saying things more complex than 'Hrooorrrrrghhhhargharghargharrrghhh.'

The lych-lords were not just masters of the dead; they had thousands of willing servants among the living, and they called to their followers in their hour of need. Mad world's-end cultists drew out the empty-headed and eccentric; vetals possessed them and drove them westwards. Religious evangelists summoned vast crowds of people with empty lives, seeking salvation in empty words, to great gatherings, where they joined the lych-lords in prayer and sacrificed their own lives. Priests of darkness poisoned their own followers or drove them into devout frenzy, and wherever the living lost their way, the dead found greater strength. Leading the way in all matters of life–death transitions were the lych-lords' greatest practical joke on the world, the sacred missionary order of Demonic Possessions Anonymous; thousands of people flocked to their ziggurats, believing that the priests who ran the order *removed* demons from people.

As the last of the skeleton-men fell into position and the Great Pyramid was completely surrounded by the teeming armies of the undead, a shrill screech was heard. At the apex of the pyramid, a small, glowing white figure appeared. It was Erkila, in vulture form, and she grew in size until all could see her, and then she flapped her wings thrice and screeched again, and the undead fell silent. Below Erkila, on the pyramid's southern side, a massive slab of stone moved aside with a grating sound. A square passage opened, a tunnel to another dimension, a window into infinite darkness. Hordes of undead shuffled aside, creating a path for whatever would come out.

There was a sound like a trumpet-blast, and the undead armies cheered as one, hoarse growls and shrill screeches, clatters and clangs, storms of whispers, agonized moans mingling and creating an unholy crescendo. This, then, was the beginning of the End. The First Pharaoh would not come out tonight, to burn the seas and melt the air, but his heralds would. The Four Horsemen, chosen by Erkila herself, would ride their steeds out to the lands of the living to announce the coming of the last day. Having delivered their final message, they would return, and then the reaping would begin.

Horns brayed dully, and the breathless host fell silent. There was a clatter of hooves, and the First Rider emerged, riding slowly down the slope of the pyramid. Even in the moonlight, the horse and rider appeared red, dark, bloody red and gold. Tzimem was his name, and he was once an emperor in the south-western lands now lost under the wave that made the Vertical Sea. His square mask shone gold, and his horse, an undead Marichelli creation, had a narwhal horn on its forehead and was the colour of terracotta. In his right hand he held a crude, broad-bladed sword, and in his left a beating human heart.

No sooner had Tzimem's mount dug its heels in the sand than there was a great rolling of human-skin drums, and the Second Rider emerged, a diminutive, sinister grey man who went by the name of the Muratorian. In life he had been a great Hudlumm general, a short, stocky, charismatic leader of a horde that had terrorized the far north. Now he wore a thin crown and carried a longbow, and looked rather uncomfortable on his magnificent white charger, possibly because it was a horse skeleton, always a pain in the buttocks to ride, especially if, as in the case of the Muratorian, an aversion to new technology meant the rider refused to use a saddle.

The Third Horseman, or Horseperson, sat on a magnificent black steed, a living Artaxerxian stallion of exceptional size, whose hugeness made its rider look even smaller. The Third Rider looked like a human girl, about six years old, except that she had big, pretty blue eyes with no pupils and pale green skin. In her time, long ago, for she had been one of the very first humans, she had been the most dreaded witch in the world, or at least the known world, which at that time had consisted of a few caves in the Grey Mountains, and a little pond. She had abandoned her ancient bearskin and skull for more modern attire; now she was dressed in a frilly frock made of fish scales, and wore a pointy hat of great magnificence. She was called The Unnamed, mostly because of her habit of making her head spin like a top and vomiting in every direction when asked what her name was. With her rode her were-cat, Manslaughter.

The drums sounded again, and the Fourth Rider rode out, a splendid figure, a grim-eyed, broad-shouldered, frighteningly handsome man in black armour, bearing a massive scythe as long as a lance, riding on a pale grey horse with flaming red eyes. This was the Cold Prince, the Scorpion Man's champion, a mighty warrior from the east. His face was pale and stern, and still bore the colour of human flesh. He was now known officially, in the rewritten Book of the Dead, as Pralay the Destroyer, but whispers of his great deeds in his lifetime, recently unnaturally cut short by divine error, still rode before him, and drowned out his new name, and told the armies of the dead his true name: Asvin.

Side by side, amidst great cheering and howling, the Four Horsemen rode out through the path the undead cleared for them, past fields of dead faces, forests of rotting feet shuffling in the moonlight, shifting hissing oceans of sand. Their steeds' hooves kicked up clouds of white sand that rose around them and enveloped them. They stopped and turned on a high dune-hill, and watched the massed legions of the dead and the Great Pyramid standing like a mountain-top amidst clouds of ill omen. They waited until the cheers died down, and a tidal wave of silence rolled through the desert, infinite sorrow, anger, and yearning in its wake; then they spurred their mighty horses westward and were gone.

* * *

'And the Fourth Rider shall ride a pale horse, and he will be grim, and his scythe will be found suitable for a great reaping, but you will not know him by the name that would logically be obtained by bringing these diverse elements together under one umbrella of reason,' said the unwaba.

'And this is why we're stuck in the Bleakwood? To meet

the heralds of the end of the world? What do we do with them?' asked Kirin.

'I will not tell you what to do, since you have such an aversion to being manipulated by evil conspirators like myself, and because telling you would be the equivalent of handing you a quest. In any case, these Riders will be closely watched by the gods, so you cannot meet them,' said the unwaba, sounding smug, or at least as smug as it is possible to sound while whispering through a chameleon's throat.

'Thanks, then. We like knowing these things. Next time there's a contest at the Underbelly, we could win a candlestick for general knowledge or something,' said Kirin.

'Unfortunately, the Fragrant Underbelly will be destroyed when the ravians destroy Kol,' said the unwaba, 'so the chances of your winning any contest there are somewhat slim.'

Kirin and Maya both sat up, aghast. 'When the ravians what? Destroy Kol? How do we stop them?' gasped Maya.

'You cannot stop them, since an act of that magnitude will undoubtedly draw the attention of the gods,' said the unwaba.

'But they'll all be watching the war, or the Riders! There's a chance they won't notice us!'

'I said what I said. I know what I know. You will do what you will do.'

'I'm not going to sit by and hide while Kol is destroyed,' said Kirin.

'This is a test of your will, son of Danh-Gem,' said the unwaba. 'Defeating gods is never easy, and you will have to make several sacrifices before you succeed—this is but the first. You know the rules. Remember, if by your actions your rebellion is revealed and thus thwarted, and your plan to save the world fails, Kol is doomed along with everything else.'

Kirin sank down on the ground, considered clasping his head dramatically and decided against it. 'The ravian airships will destroy Kol, and you tell us this in advance, and expect us not to be affected by it?'

'Be as affected as you desire. I expect you not to do anything rash. Too much is at stake.'

'I'm not going to let Kol go, just like that. It's the only home that means anything to me.'

'That is truly touching. I must point out, though, that your megalomania, as evident from your belief that saving your own home means more than saving the world, shows that you believe you are a hero despite your protestations, which should cause your companions much anguish, because it reveals how unsuitable you are for this important an undertaking. You must let Kol be destroyed, because you cannot afford to take the chance that the gods are looking elsewhere. Do not gamble against the gods any more than is absolutely necessary. You will now apologize for making it necessary to explain things clearly and slowly to the meanest intelligence, which in this case, let me clarify, is yours, and waste my precious time.'

'I'm sorry. But when Kol falls, what will prevent the ravians from destroying Imokoi, and the rest of the world?' he asked.

'That we will see,' said the unwaba.

'Between the ravian airships and the dead, what's going to be left to save? What's the point of lurking around and saving the board when all the pieces are dead?' asked Maya.

'When I say *save the world*, you must not take me too

literally,' said the unwaba. 'If you must know, *this* world cannot be saved. The game will go on until it ends.'

Kirin and Maya looked at him in shock. 'We *can't* save the world?' said Maya. 'What are we doing here, then?'

'You cannot save *this* world,' said the unwaba. 'But if you meet the gods, and ask them nicely, and have a few convincing arguments up your sleeves, they might make you another one.'

'You're going to fall asleep now, aren't you?'

'Yes,' said the unwaba, and did.

9

The sense of dull foreboding that had enveloped Kol since the year of the Simoqin Prophecies had now sharpened into mass hysteria. The once thriving sale of amulets and talismans had stopped; no one had any to spare any more, and even the ones known to be fake were kept—just in case. Kol had never been a city whose inhabitants greeted you with a smile and a wave, at least unless they were trying to take away all your money, but now general hostility had reached epic proportions. Not without reason; *everyone* was a potential enemy. The ravians could be anywhere, twisting, whispering, scheming; no one was safe. Magic-users travelled in groups, fearing attacks. Other citizens lived in dread and avoided strangers, especially tall and attractive ones. Thick blankets of fear covered the city like a fog. Avranti had fallen, and was lost to the world. The survivors of Pataal-e-Gurh had nearly all deserted the army, and lurked about on the streets, ashen-faced, wild-eyed, telling their stories of the battle, of the day the age of the humans ended. All hope was lost. They had seen the beginning of a new world, where humans would have to learn their place. The ravians were coming, like avenging gods, bringing death from the heavens, and against them there could be no victory.

Angry rumours roamed like feral dogs through the city, biting and snarling; the Civilian, they growled, was responsible for all this. She had turned Kol away from the ravian way of light and embraced the darkness of Imokoi. In the last Age, the asurs and rakshases had been punished for their hubris; this time, it was humanity's turn. The official pronouncement that the ravians had not responded to any overtures of friendship or peace was, the mob decided, a lie, for surely the ravians were friends and heroes, and by stabbing them in the back the Civilian had doomed them all. The deserters had, of course, mentioned that all Askesis's attempts at negotiations had been met with silence, but that was a mere detail.

It was the perfect time for a revolution, but the revolution never happened; this was because all the Civilian's political rivals, and all the money that would have raised them to replace her, were busy getting out of Kol. A lot of people had woken up one day to find they no longer ran the world, and this inspired in them a sudden desire to visit the great outdoors and get in touch with their inner selves.

If this was the heart of an empire, its arteries were now clogged. The streets of Kol were lined with great wagons and vaman-made landbarges, and ever-swelling crowds milled about them, jostling, cursing and shouting. Thousands of Kolis were fleeing the city, returning to their villages, seeking refuge with relatives elsewhere, desperate to flee the fiery death that rolled sky-borne from the east. Others sought refuge underground; the vamans had created vast tunnels and halls underneath the foundations of the city, to act as storehouses and shelters in dark times. Endless lines of people thronged at tube-worm stations, waiting for the great hollowed annelida to transport them through newer, deeper tunnels to the burrows of war. Fights started frequently; the citizens of Kol, previously unacquainted with the threat of actual annihilation, found new ways to divide themselves every day, and long-forgotten barriers racial, regional, religious and social were discovered anew; the city guards had their hands full trying to keep riots from breaking out all over the city. The Civilian's counter-propaganda squads were fighting a losing battle; their assurances that the otherworldly invaders would be vanquished before they reached Kol by the world itself, by little things like the common cold and the malarial mosquito, usually ended in scenes of mob violence.

The Chief Civilian stood on the balcony of her palace, watching carpets flit about between towers and spires, flies buzzing around the rotting Big Mango. Ojanus was half asleep around her shoulders; she patted his sleeping head absent-mindedly. With her, staring gravely at her unreadable face, stood Mantric, Chancellor Ombwiri, and Amloki the khudran. Three Kaos butterflies, gifts from the centaur shamans, sat on Ombwiri's arm, their wings flapping in slow, rhythmic beats, sending howling winds and thunderstorms to slow down the invaders. On the eastern side of the balcony, Arathognan, the heir to Kol's long-empty throne, stood alone, looking outwards and upwards, searching the sky for specks of gold, for the beast-shaped celestial airships of the ravians.

A solitary figure on a speeding vroomstick streaked down to the balcony and landed gently. It was Roshin of the Red Phoenix. She carried a small wooden box under her arm.

'It is done,' she said.

The Civilian took the box and opened it. Within it lay Kol's greatest treasure, the Heart of Magic, the ruby within a gold mesh that kept Kol's magic field stable and its carpets and vroomsticks in the air. Temat handed the box to Amloki.

'Keep it safe and airborne when the time comes,' she said. 'I need not tell you how important this is.' Amloki nodded, covered the box with his black cloak, and cast Roshin a smouldering look out of habit.

'All significant artefacts have been transferred to vaman vaults,' said Roshin. 'The objects you wanted removed from the palace have been given to Mati for safekeeping.'

'Good,' said the Civilian. 'And is there any news from Imokoi?'

'Yes. They will do nothing to help us, as they are busy preparing their own defences. Ravian armies have been sighted in Vrihataranya and the northern Free States,' said Roshin. 'But I doubt there is anything they could do; our agents inform us that the Dark Lord no longer wears the Gauntlet of Tatsu, and it is believed that the dragons no longer serve him. The Dark Lord, has, however, sent an invitation, for you and for Mantric, though he will not consider it rude if either of you refuse. He is aware you are awaiting guests.'

'Kind of him,' said Temat. 'What was the invitation for?'

'The Dark Lord's wedding,' said Roshin. 'He's marrying Maya.'

Everyone on the balcony suddenly became very preoccupied with their sleeves.

'This would seem to indicate that she is alive,' said Temat. 'Has she made no attempt to send messages to Kol?'

'No. She has not made any public appearances yet, but

one of our spies has seen her, walking on the battlements of Imokoi with Kirin.'

'I could make arrangements for you to visit Imokoi, Mantric,' said the Civilian. 'There is a lot Maya must know that would do us no harm to learn. And if she is being held prisoner in Imokoi, she must be rescued.'

'Rescue Maya? She would be most offended,' said Mantric. 'She's alive, and that is wonderful news. You can stop looking at your fingers, Amloki, I'm not going to burst into tears. I was never a very good father.'

'Kirin wouldn't hold Maya prisoner. Not the Kirin I knew, at least, but I clearly didn't know him very well. What worries me is her silence,' said Amloki. 'There's a mystery here that needs to be solved immediately.'

'If she hasn't bothered to write, it might be because she takes after me. I suppose I should be glad she remembered to invite me. How time whooshes. Maya married. Good for her,' said Mantric.

'I suppose this means Asvin's dead,' said Amloki. 'Roshin, are you *sure* it's Maya? What happened to the sorceress who left Kol with Asvin pretending to be Rukmini?'

'This will take time to unravel, and time is a luxury at the moment. We will not make any assumptions until we know more,' said the Civilian. 'If it is Maya, we will resolve the mystery swiftly; for now, I might remind you that we still have a city to defend. Chancellor?'

'Enki's libraries are emptied,' said Ombwiri. 'And all my spellbinders have volunteered to help the city's defence in any way they can.'

'Today is a day full of surprises,' said Temat.

'Flight is not an option for magic-users. The ravians will not enslave us if they win; we will all be hunted down and killed,' said Ombwiri. 'If Enki survives, I will be remembered as the Chancellor who took his students to war.'

'The city guards have also arrested several hundred people on various charges, mostly fabricated,' said Roshin. 'Some of them are important community leaders who were vocal in their criticism of the way you were running things. Their friends and followers are demanding justice.'

'Ask the city guards to make them see reason in any way they choose.'

'It will be done.'

The Civilian looked around the balcony, at the guarded faces of Ombwiri and Amloki and the openly upset ones of Mantric and Arathognan.

'I wish to hear no speeches about civil liberties and the real casualties of wartime. Tell me, instead, what we can do to save our city,' she said.

Around the palace, and every other building of strategic importance in Kol, the vamans toiled away, adapting their defences quickly to deal with the new threat. Incredibly tall skeletons of scaffolding, of beams and great wheels with pulleys and ropes and platforms sprung up overnight. Bulky catapults and ballistae were being hoisted to rest on rooftops and bridges, pulled up by ropes made from the webs of giant underground spiders. Armadas of flying carpets tied together tugged lighter machines and ammunition from tower to tower. The problem was one of scale. Kol was well-equipped enough to face a dragon onslaught with some degree of confidence, but would the vaman artillery be able to destroy the air-fleet before it burned the defenders to cinders? The catapults had been designed for speed and flexibility, with finely tuned calibrations that allowed their handlers to cope with the aerial acrobatics of swift-flying, looping dragons. There was no time to build the bulkier projectile-hurling machines that might be needed to penetrate the armour of the celestial chariots. Had there been more time to prepare, or had more been known about the nature of these strange and wondrous machines, the vamans could have built larger, slower, catapults, but there had been no need until now; an aerial assault on this scale could not have been anticipated. Given the size of the airships, the massive vaman machines would look like toys, but as the story of Disegno and Brotozoan showed, a carefully placed, well-hurled missile could fell the mightiest giant (in the children's version, Disegno's stone had hit the giant Brotozoan on the *forehead*).

The sky above the city was full of vroomsticks and carpets manned by guards, soldiers and civilian volunteers, wave after wave of human locusts going through carefully planned military drills; if the airships were close enough, spellbinders and archers could inflict deadly damage through hit-and-fly raids. Nearly every carpet and vroomstick in the city had been confiscated for this. Many of the chariots were piloted by firefighters with compact cauldrons of strange chemicals—foams that strangled fire, and boxes of powders that starved it. Those of the Champion's League heroes who were not helping civilians leave the city peacefully led groups of air-raiders through their manouevres, and Kolis with any spirit left cheered as they passed; the noble figures of Reinforced Iron Man, Mr Seik, the Hex Men, the Sadori Sisters and many others inspired nothing but confidence. Not as inspiring, but very valuable additions to the war effort given their natural aptitude for both flight and violence, were the leather-clad vroomer gangs, who'd surprised everyone by volunteering to help defend Kol, and had even taught the city guards a few new moves, crazy air-slaloms, brain-churning diagonal rolls and crow-swoops they'd perfected through decades of dedicated air-street crime. But if there was one man who made the citizens of Kol take heart and resolve to stay in the city, it was Arathognan, whose tireless efforts to rally his fellow Kolis had led to levels of popularity that would have had him assassinated at any other point in the city's history.

Messages came to the Civilian at regular intervals regarding the progress of the ravian fleet. Vaman troops had been trailing the ships secretly since they had crossed Dorkinge, a former outpost of the ancient empire of Ventelot that now stood on the south-western border of Potolpur. The vaman commanders had explained to the Civilian that the best time to attack the airships was when they landed to renew their supplies; unless they drew their sustenance from the air, there would surely be something they needed from the ground they were so eager to conquer, and on the ground, the combined might of the vamans and what was left of Askesis's army could surely crush them.

But the airships had not landed, and the vamans had waited in vain. Still, the only plausible strategy for the Civilian to follow was to somehow keep the city standing until the ravians retreated to tend their sky-chariots, and then destroy them the moment they descended. What plagued the Civilian most was her almost complete ignorance about the capabilities of her opponents: If the ravian light-pillars were as large and incredibly destructive as Pataal-e-Gurh's survivors had described, would they not destroy all resistance in minutes? And with fires raging on that scale, what could the firefighters do? How long would their chemicals manage to keep things under control before all of Kol was buried in flames? What if the ravian ships did not need to come down to earth at all? Kol's defence was based on the assumption that whoever attacked the richest of human cities would seek to occupy and control it; there were thousands of ways in which a ground invasion of Kol could be defeated, and enemies made to pay dearly for every street of the city they conquered. But what could the defenders do if the invaders wanted to utterly *destroy* Kol, and everyone in it? If the ravians continued to make no effort at diplomacy, thought the Civilian, it was probably because they now planned to reduce humans to the same state they had almost succeeded in driving the asurs to at the end of the last Age; a primitive people, hiding in hills and caves, or toiling in fields as indentured slaves while their feudal overlords pursued higher concerns. And if the ravians actually had the resources to carry out such an outrageous plan, what could be done to stop them?

The Civilian did have a second plan, as her nature demanded, but while the second line of defence was mighty, it was also most unreliable. The Kaos butterflies could, if they desired, fill the skies above Kol with thunderclouds and torrential rain, which would handle the threat of fire. But it would also mean the removal of all airborne defence, and cripple the vaman artillery; besides, there was the risk of flooding the underground shelters. If the airships could rise above the clouds, they would be safe and hidden. After that, it was a waiting game. Perhaps the intensity of the light-pillars could make the rain-clouds disappear in mountains of steam. And the Kaos butterflies were not born to follow commands—uncertainty was the very essence of their being. Using centaur shaman spells to control them shortened their life spans dramatically, and thus a sustained defence based on weather control had been deemed too risky. All the answers would come once the fires began; but by then, it would probably be too late for Kol.

That evening, the airships reached the outer suburbs of north-east Kol. There were no clouds to cover their approach this time; they wanted to be seen and feared. The last rays of the setting sun illuminated them in violet, pink, and orange as they floated in the sky, weird, beautiful animal-shaped palaces of marvels, their bejewelled bellies glittering, their ominous drones reverberating to the heavens. In central Kol, the vamans shouted orders and tuned their war-machines; above Enki University, standing tall on a fluttering carpet, Arathognan raised his sword in the air in a gesture as noble as it was futile, raising half-hearted cheers all over the city. In the palace, the Civilian waited and watched her enemies in silence, Mantric toying idly with protective wards by her side. In the labyrinth under the palace, Violet the shapeshifter teleported back and forth with secret scrolls, weeping as she remembered the rest of the Rainbow Council.

The akashraths floated on towards the heart of the city, towards Kol's tallest buildings and strongest centres of defence. The Civilian had left most of the city undefended—she had guessed, correctly, that the carnage would begin at the most potent symbols of Kol's dominance, at buildings which represented everything Kol stood for—power, wealth, knowledge, diversity. They would break Kol's heart before burning its body.

A blackout had been ordered in Kol, and as daylight faded, the city that never slept hid its dazzling lights for the very first time in its history. Pale clouds that had followed the airships into the city blotted out the moon and stars. But there was still light in the sky; the symbols on the bellies of the akashraths glowed phosphor-green in the dark, spelling out messages of doom in alien tongues. The defenders looked up in wonder, expecting at any moment to see white light-rivers shining brighter than the sun, but the akashraths did not attack. The Civilian had predicted that the ravians would wait until the full extent of the damage they unleashed on Kol could be seen. Once again, she was right.

At midnight, a small swarm of black-clad figures on silent blackened vroomsticks, invisible in the night, swept towards the akashraths. The Silver Phalanx was on the hunt, hoping to storm the airships in secret and break and kill anything they could find. But the swarm dispersed and returned, frustrated; the akashraths were too high. The magic field was unstable, and their vroomsticks jerked and faltered. The Silver Dagger considered leading a raid and taking the Heart of Magic with him, but abandoned the plan almost immediately. If he were slain and the golden mesh destroyed, all would be lost.

The Hex Men tried their luck next, but even their spellbinding powers could not keep their vroomsticks stable. Messages were tapped from tower to tower; it was the vamans' turn.

The tower-tops of central Kol were suddenly awash with sound, as the missiles of the vamans were loaded into catapults and ballistae. Hundreds of fireballs lit up and an instant later, there was a fountain in the sky, as massive chunks of metal, wall-piercing siege arrows and chunks of masonry, all glowing with sorcerous fire, arced their way towards the ravian airships. Several found their mark, exploding with ear-splitting booms on the metal sides of the floating palaces; the air was full of smoke and the loud sound of metal screeching against metal, and the rooftops echoed to the roars of exultant Kolis and vamans. Lights were lit inside the air-chariots, stabbing out of the rows of portholes on their sides, and the droning altered in pitch; now there were dull, hammering sounds, high-pitched whines and the screech of great gears grinding. The vamans sent another round of missiles into the sky, and hurt the akashraths again, but they did not fall. Instead, they began to rise higher, taking barrage after barrage of siege arrows and explosives, but not retaliating, focusing their energies on moving out of range, until, an hour later, even missiles from the most powerful vaman catapults came hurtling back into the city, exploding in the streets, keeping the firefighters busy. The airships had escaped, but they had taken the pall of gloom that hung over Kol with them as they rose; hope had returned to Kol's faithful. Surely the akashraths were too high to attack the city now, many said. After all, even dragons had to fly fairly low to burn cities or their flames would vanish in smoke; what were these airships but dragons of metal? Kol had won the first round. They would hurl these invaders back into the heavens every time they ventured low enough to cause any damage, and wear them down until they tired, and descended to rest and die.

At dawn they saw the airships again, and realized they had not done as much damage in the darkness as they had hoped. The akashraths had all been hit; their bellies were dented, scratched and burned, but their armour had not, as yet, been breached. Some internal damage had been done, though; four of the six airships were trailing clouds of black smoke, and one seemed to quiver as it flew. They flew slowly and deliberately over the towers of Kol, finding their targets and hovering above them, ignoring the vaman missiles streaking harmlessly through the sky beneath them. The swan-shaped airship now cast its shadow over the Civilian's palace, the fish over Enki. Others hung humming over Ossus Square, Hero School, the business district and the Ziggurat of All Religions. The Chief Civilian, flying with her Red Phoenix bodyguards towards the government headquarters in south Kol, did not look back; no one, not even the immortals who'd lived secretly in the city since its birth, loved Kol more than she did, and she could not bear to watch its greatest edifices crumble.

Hatches opened on the ships' sides, and gleaming barrels emerged. All of Kol looked up. The droning stopped.

Pillars of white light and fire appeared out of nothing, lances of destruction boring into Kol. Enki University blazed in defiance, residual magic swirling and collecting into a huge explosion that shattered the buildings around it as it collapsed, Kol's tallest spire sinking slowly into a mountain of rubble. The Civilian's palace and its beautiful gardens burned, and the bridges between awe-inspiring interconnected towers in the business district snapped like matchsticks. Torrents of fire and smoke drew street-maps visible from the heavens as they raced their way through Kol's empty boulevards. Hero School melted away. But the image that burned deepest in the eyes of the watching Kolis, the one that would haunt them until they died, was in Ossus Square, where the great statue of the hero Ossus, looking sadly southwards, stood proudly in the blaze, lit up like a god, until huge cracks crawled up his body, and he bathed in light, dead once again, his mournful face looking up at the sky reproachfully as it shattered into a million pieces.

The akashraths began to move, sweeping slowly across central Kol, burning up the vaman artillery within seconds as they passed over them. Several heroes died there, trying to save their brethren from the flames. The survivors fled on vroomsticks to pre-assigned points of assembly, but they were merely going through the motions now, and many considered escaping while they still could, before the gusts of flame that were sweeping from rooftop to rooftop, crackling insolently in the faces of the feeble efforts of the firefighters, engulfed them all. They had seen the world change, and knew better than to hope for salvation. Kol was broken. The end was near.

10

Maya sat in the shadows of a gnarled, blackened tree in the Bleakwood, watching Kirin sleep and itching to send a few fireballs into the air out of sheer boredom. She wished she had her long-abandoned diary with her; the endless hours of inactivity might have actually made it possible for her to catch up with the present.

A thumping sound made her rise and spin around, but it was only Spikes. The pashan stomped up to the tree and looked down at Kirin.

'I thought I'd come and see if he was up. I'm not sure our plan is a good one.'

'Well, he's not. And the unwaba did say you'd have to do all the talking.'

'True. I will meet the Horsemen on the bridge where we met the knight, Sir Cyr, the last time we were here.'

'Do you want me to come with you? I could hide behind a tree or something, and not get in the way. They might be a bit more than even you can handle.'

'If they are supposed to end the world, I don't think

your presence would change things dramatically. I will do what I can.'

'Good luck.'

'If I do not return, please take care of Kirin.'

'Coming from you, that's the most sentimental speech I've ever heard. Now go, and come back soon.'

Spikes squatted, and patted Kirin's head very carefully. Maya hugged him, and after an awkward grunt, he walked off westwards, soon breaking into a run. Maya watched him gather speed until he was a grey blur, hunched, splayfooted, faster than a horse, and she wondered yet again what madness had taken them all.

They had wandered around the Bleakwood for several days in a vague sort of way. The unwaba had told them to stop the Four Horsemen, but had not mentioned where they could be found—*the Bleakwood* was not really useful, as directions went. There was also the question of adding another member to their team, someone who truly believed in gods, but that could presumably wait until the Four Horsemen had been deterred. The unwaba had also neglected to mention, despite his infinite wisdom, exactly *how* the Four Horsemen could be stopped, assuming they would not just stop if politely asked to do so.

Kirin had not helped matters much by falling ill five days ago. He'd been restless all day, that day, not talking much, looking deeply troubled. Maya had woken in the middle of the night to find herself alone in the Bleakwood. At first she'd thought Kirin had left again, but Spikes was still there, and an hour later they'd found Kirin, huddled up under a tree, wearing the Shadowknife and the Gauntlet, unconscious. He looked as if he'd seen something terrible, but there was no sign of any enemy. Maya and Spikes had decided at the time that he must have seen the Horsemen and tried to stop them on his own to save his friends, which, Spikes had pointed out, was just the kind of behaviour the unwaba would have disapproved of. Kirin had not explained himself even after Maya had cast a dozen healing spells on him. This was because he had not woken up yet. Spikes had decided that carrying Kirin around in circles in the Bleakwood was a bad idea, especially if any gods were watching, so Maya had spent five days sitting and waiting for either Kirin or the unwaba to wake up, while Spikes stalked through the forest on his own, listening for the sound of hooves.

Then their luck had turned, further reinforcing Maya's faith in the unwaba. In the clearing where they had met Tlotlot and his band of displaced highwaymen and fought the nundu what seemed like decades ago, Spikes had met Tlotlot again, riding, riding southwards, with two ragged, elderly accomplices, and found, in their terrified blubbering, the answers to one of the questions that had plagued him and Maya since the unwaba's last speech. Tlotlot and his bandits had encountered the Four Horsemen two days ago, and had asked them to choose between their money and their lives. The Horsemen had turned out to possess neither, which the bandits had accepted in good grace. But the Horsemen had then very ungraciously attacked the bandits, killing all except the three now fleeing desperately in the general direction of anywhere else. As far as Tlotlot and his very depressed men knew, the Horsemen would arrive at the clearing in about a day, if they proceeded in their current course at their current speed—the bandits had certainly done nothing to change either. Spikes had tried to get Tlotlot to describe the Horsemen in detail, but all he'd got were streams of words, mostly 'bone', 'vomit', 'blood', 'sword', and also, for some strange reason, 'fish', which didn't really add up to anything coherent. Spikes had let the bandits move on, and had watched with cold amusement as Tlotlot's henchmen swore revenge and painted 'Rob Zombi' on their leather vests.

Now Spikes had gone to meet the destroyers of the world on his own, and Maya, already half sick with apprehension and frustration, lay back on the parched, grey ground next to Kirin, looked at him and wondered: If the Horsemen had been far away, what had Kirin seen? What new danger stalked them through the woods?

The Four Horsemen, or, technically speaking, Three Horsemen and One Horsegirl and One Werecat, rode steadily through the twisted, claw-branched trees of the Bleakwood. The Unnamed rode last, by mutual, unspoken consent; it was a question of hygiene. Tzimem and the Muratorian rode ahead of her, Tzimem's war-charger snorting impatiently and the Muratorian letting out little groans of pain at every bump. Fear and decay rode with them; they were the end of all hope. The Cold Prince, who had journeyed through these lands most recently, rode ahead. When they had ridden in the dark green woods of eastern Elaken, everything they passed had withered and rotted; trees died, earth cracked, streams dried up and flowers faded. In the Bleakwood, however, their passing effected no change; others had killed the land long ago, and the trees seemed to look at them and shrug indifferently. The Horsemen were quite pleased, therefore, when the Cold Prince led them to a small and fully functional stream that ran through the scorched land as if in a great hurry to reach the sea. As the Horsemen approached the stream, its waters began to boil and hiss, and then seemed to slow down, and the Horsemen nodded in appreciation, relieved that something in this godforsaken part of the world was showing them the respect they deserved.

But the Horsemen were not particularly pleased when they reached a narrow bridge they intended to cross, and saw a spectacularly ugly pashan standing in the middle of it, looking at them without displaying any sign of panic. Even when they reached the bridge, and the Cold Prince's red-eyed grey charger stepped on its frayed wooden planks, the pashan did not turn and run; instead, he looked closely at the Cold Prince, and blinked his yellow-green eyes' vertical lids.

'Asvin?' said Spikes. 'Is that you?'

The Cold Prince's shoulders seemed to sag a little.

'I was Asvin once,' said Asvin slowly. 'I wish I could say I was happy to see you . . . Spikes.'

Spikes seemed unmoved by this lack of affection. He took a step forward and stared insolently at Asvin. 'Damn. Connecting pieces. Does this mean . . . yes, it must. You're always conspicuous, leading the way. And you believe in the gods, too.'

The Cold Prince struck a noble pose, looking heavenwards, and the gash in his throat spread unpleasantly. 'I do. Earlier, I believed in them as a child believes in his father; now, I believe in them as a burned child believes in fire.'

'So this is his idea of a surprise, the sneaky little bugger. They won't be happy, not at all. They don't like being played.' Spikes seemed uninterested in the other Horsemen now; it was as if he could only see Asvin.

The Cold Prince drew himself up in his saddle, and the stream stopped flowing altogether. 'In this life, if it is life, or in the last, you and I are not friends, pashan. Cease your babbling. Your dark schemes, whatever they are, do not concern us. Now stand aside and let us pass, lest I be forced to make you taste my scythe.'

Asvin raised his mighty blade threateningly, thus regaining the pashan's attention.

'You'll do,' said Spikes. 'I don't like this any more than you do, but you're clearly the one I need.'

Tzimem snorted impatiently and spurred his horse forward. 'End this,' he growled. 'We must be on our way.'

'Stop me if you've heard this before,' said Spikes, 'but None Shall Pass.'

He clenched his fists, and mighty claws slid out. There was a series of clicking noises, and all his spikes emerged, jutting out of his back. The Unnamed screamed in horror, and the Muratorian's horse reared up, with unfortunate consequences; a second later, the Muratorian was sitting on top of a heap of bones. He looked extremely annoyed.

'Whatever you are, and whatever your purpose,' said Spikes, 'you do not scare me.'

Tzimem roared in anger, and urged his steed forward, but his red horse would not budge. The Horsemen looked at the bridge, and realized why; since the moment Asvin's horse had set its foot on the bridge, the ancient timber had started rotting. It would collapse if they tried to ride over it.

'I intend to speak with you, and I will,' said Spikes. 'You do have a choice, though; you could choose to remain dry. The stream is pleasantly cool, but as far as I remember, moisture will make you all rot faster.'

'Who *are* you?' asked the Muratorian, getting up stiffly, as his horse slowly reconstructed itself. 'Why should we listen to a lowly pashan?'

'I am the Dark Lord's right hand,' said Spikes. 'Easily the most important living being you'll meet in this quarter of the known world. Is that worth a few minutes of your time?'

'Say what you have to say, Spikes,' said Asvin. 'We are in a hurry.'

Spikes retracted his claws. 'That is what I want to discuss,' he said. 'You are in a hurry. The Four Horsemen, heralds of the end of the world. Very grand. But do you have any idea exactly what it is that you intend to do, if I may be so bold as to ask? Where are you going?'

Tzimem snorted, laughing behind his gold mask. 'We will not share our secrets with one as lowly as you.'

'In other words, you don't know.'

Tzimem would have charged across the bridge then, but Asvin raised a placatory arm.

'We are here to announce the end of the world,' he said.

'Why are you in one of the emptiest places in the world, then?'

'We must ride across the world like a wind of ill fortune, as a symbol of its end, and then we will return to the Great Pyramid and lead the armies of the First Pharaoh in a tide of destruction.'

'That makes no sense,' said Spikes, tapping his chin with a stubby finger. 'Your commanders clearly don't know what they're doing. I face the same problem with the Dark Lord sometimes. Heads so high that clouds obstruct their vision.'

'Explain yourself,' said the Muratorian, walking up between Asvin and Tzimem.

'First of all,' said Spikes, 'do you have any idea how long it will take you to ride across the world? And does the world include islands, and undiscovered land masses? What about sea creatures? It's their world too.'

Three of the Horsemen regarded him in stunned silence. Behind them, the Unnamed killed time by turning her head around and trying to vomit on her frolicking werecat.

'It does not matter how long it takes,' said Asvin bravely. 'When it is done, we will return.'

'Fair enough,' said Spikes. 'But won't the armies of the First Pharoah feel silly when you come back after your round-the-world vacation while they stand around, no doubt with bits falling off, and then there's nothing left to destroy?'

'There's always something left to destroy,' said Tzimem, but the other Horsemen seemed less satisfied. 'Why would that happen?' asked Asvin.

'Well, since you're all dead, I can't blame you for not staying in touch with current events,' said Spikes. 'But if you want to end the world, you'd better hurry. You've got competition.'

'Competition?' roared Tzimem.

'Yes. While you were busy being dead, the world entered the Age of the Market Economy, and any important job always has several contenders now. Things aren't as simple as they used to be in the good old days. While you consider the possibilities, allow me a minute's rest. I have never spoken so much before in my whole life.'

The Horsemen of the Scorpion Man and the heir of Katar regarded each other in silence for a minute.

Spikes cleared his throat loudly and began. 'The ravians are advancing on human cities, in unstoppable all-conquering airships. They'll have killed most of the world's city-dwellers before you even reach the ruins of Kol. And then there's the world itself, which is rebelling against unwelcome intrusions and other forces that seek to control it. I have been told there are great beasts underground that are ripping up the earth from within, causing earthquakes, floods, and killing a lot of pesky vamans. And all this despite the fact that the dragons have been busy fighting them. If they defeat the dragons, they could probably destroy the world in a day.'

'But . . . *we* are supposed to end the world,' gasped the Muratorian.

'My sympathies,' said Spikes. 'Do enjoy your vacation. You may ride on now, if you so wish. I will not obstruct you.'

Asvin turned to the others. 'What should we do, my lords?'

'We ride on,' said Tzimem. 'Our orders are clear.'

'But they aren't,' said Asvin. 'What if we were only supposed to wander around the world *symbolically*? Perhaps we could go back now, if we wanted.'

'Or,' said Spikes, 'you could consider the fact that the world needn't end at all, if you decide not to go back to the Great Pyramid. Do you really want to end the world? It's a nice world. Not this bit, perhaps, but a lot of the rest of it.'

Asvin looked delighted at this idea, but Tzimem snorted contemptuously.

'No, the world must end,' said the Muratorian. 'Our task is sacred. It is why we exist.'

'Fine. I would like to point out, then, that you will probably cease to exist after you end the world, so if you like existing, you should take the bit about visiting everyone in the world and telling them about the end very seriously.'

'But by the time we have finished, a lot of new people would have been born, so we would have to start again,' said Asvin.

'Death has improved your mind,' said Spikes. 'Is it the lack of romance?'

'I wouldn't say that,' chuckled Tzimem. 'The new boy's been seeing a *lot* of Erkila.'

Asvin cast a reproachful glance at him, and perhaps Tzimem looked penitent, but it was impossible to tell under his mask. 'Come on, lad,' he said. 'It's all right to tell *him*. He's just a mortal, and this is another country, and besides, we're all dead.'

'Speaking of mortality,' said Spikes, making up for a lifetime of taciturnity in one fell swoop, 'why is it that you have old immortals and young immortals? Do you also have really old immortals that are so old that they can't do anything, and then they're killed off? I only ask because I suspect you'd know about this, and I've always wondered.'

The Muratorian's horse had now rebuilt itself, and the Muratorian straddled it, wincing. 'Enough of this prattle,' he said. 'What do we do, my brothers?'

'We kill this nice young lad and carry on with our mission,' said Tzimem.

'I want to go home, and so does Manslaughter. And I'm not your brother,' said the Unnamed.

'I do not know,' said Asvin, looking noble and sad.

'Do what you will,' said Spikes. 'If you want to stop existing, destroy the world. If you carry on as you are now, and if the world gets destroyed by underground monsters or ravians or gods or anyone else, I'll tell them you lot said hello.'

'If I might make a suggestion,' said a rich, deep voice. They all looked in surprise at the Unnamed's werecat.

'Perhaps we should return to the Pyramid and lead our armies against the competition first,' said Manslaughter. 'Once they are eliminated, we can destroy the world whenever you see fit.'

The Horsemen looked at one another, slightly sheepishly, like the kind of sheep that people counted in nightmares.

'What is your vote, Muratorian?' asked Asvin.

'Would you like to know my vote?' inquired Spikes.

'No,' they said, almost in chorus.

The Muratorian sat in thought for several minutes, and then raised his head. 'We will destroy our rivals first,' he said. 'I have not waited so long only to have my final hour of glory snatched away from me.'

Tzimem turned his horse around and Asvin was about to do the same, when Spikes said, 'There is just one more thing.'

The Horsemen groaned. 'Have you not done enough damage for one day?' asked the Muratorian. 'What do you want now?'

'Asvin,' said Spikes. 'Let him carry out your original mission while you lead your armies to destroy the monsters of the underworld. It will save you time.'

'No,' said Asvin.

'Yes,' said the Muratorian. 'Go with the mortal, Cold Prince. It will temper the Scorpion Man's anger if our new plan turns out to be a mistake. Besides, you know the modern world, and will probably achieve our goal faster than we would have together.'

'How will I know when my task is done?' asked Asvin, lost.

'It is done when you decide it is done,' said Tzimem. 'Now let us part. I have just realized that the new plan means we start fighting sooner. That is good. I am tired of showing off in front of woodland creatures.'

'I will not travel with a pashan. Let the Unnamed go,' said Asvin.

'I'm going back,' said the Unnamed firmly.

'Come with me for a day, Asvin,' said Spikes. 'If you change your mind, you can always catch up with them.'

'Yes. Don't be a baby,' said the Unnamed, who was clearly either too young or too ancient or too undead to find Asvin charming.

After several minutes of heated debate, Tzimem, the Muratorian, the Unnamed and Manslaughter thundered off westwards towards Elaken, leaving Asvin and Spikes eyeing each other uncertainly across the rapidly rotting bridge.

'What do you really want, Spikes?' asked Asvin. 'Is this some scheme of Kirin's? Where is he? Where is Maya?'

'Before you say anything more,' said Spikes, 'hear me out, because I've rehearsed this speech many times, and it's very good. I have chosen you to be my companion not at anyone else's bidding, but because I think you might be the right person for the job. I will not enjoy travelling with you any more than you will with me. But we must journey together, you and I, because . . . because your quest is important. There is a lot more to say, but not here. There is a safe place close by, hidden from all eyes, where we can speak more freely. But before I take you there, there is something I must ask you. You have died, Asvin, but have you grown up? This is the story of your life; Avranti birthed you and betrayed you, Kol trained you and forgot you, and the gods favoured you and wronged you. Yet now you seem to have placed your faith in yet another power, another shot at permanent glory, though ironically you seek to gain eternal glory by ending human history. Did your life teach you anything? Do you have a mind of your own, and are you willing to use it? Do you feel that life—or whatever you have now—has treated you unfairly, and do you want revenge? If your answer to any of these questions is no, let us go our separate ways, and good luck; if not, follow me.'

Asvin thundered across the bridge, and then looked westwards, at the bridge crumbling behind him, at the lands of the dead he'd left behind. Ahead of him lay uncertainty, and certain danger, and the hope of answers. Apart from the gash in his throat and the ugly monster breaking into a run in front of him, it would make a deeply meaningful painting, he thought.

Kirin awoke to find Maya sitting next to him, running a hand gently through his hair. He'd always been fascinated by Maya's hands; now they were rougher, and her fingers had grown even longer, possibly because of overuse of magic. He lay there quietly, feeling the sunshine on his skin, feeling her fingertips, leaving little trails of magic tingling in his scalp without her even being aware of it. He wanted to turn slightly and kiss her fingers, to tell her this was the way he'd like to wake up every time, if she'd be so kind as to make the necessary arrangements.

'Has the unwaba said anything since I left?' he asked instead.

'No,' she said. 'Are you feeling all right? What happened to you?'

He began to tell her, and stopped when he noticed she wasn't paying attention. She was looking up, with wide, stunned eyes. He turned and groaned loudly inside his head.

Spikes was walking towards them, and next to him, tall and broad and handsome, and undead, walked Asvin, carrying a long and dangerous-looking scythe.

Kirin looked at Maya's face, and wished he hadn't woken up.

Asvin, on the other hand, wished he hadn't died, which, even Kirin would have acknowledged, gave him more claim to sympathy.

She ran up to him, still unable to believe it was him, and he swept her up in his arms and would have kissed her, but at the last instant he let her go, because he had seen the sudden look of revulsion in her eyes when their skins had first touched, when she had felt how cold and clammy he was now, felt how differently his muscles moved. They stood facing each other uncertainly, smiling, and he found himself wondering whether he smelled terrible, and whether she was afraid of him. She was crying, and he would have cried too, but his eyes were dead and dry, and he suddenly felt *dead*, somehow more dead than he had felt before, because she stood in front of him, and no one had ever made him feel as alive as she had. She clasped his hands, trying to ignore the stiffness of his fingers, and then she held him close to her, ignoring the shivers running down her spine, ignoring the churning in her stomach, because dead or alive, he was Asvin, and she had missed him. And because she had so much to say to him, but her mouth had dried up, and her head was spinning wildly.

After what seemed, to Kirin at least, like an eternity, Asvin released Maya, walked up to Kirin and shook his hand gravely. 'It turns out I picked the wrong side when we last met; I would have apologized, but I feel I have been punished enough for my error,' he said. 'I understand we will be working together, and I want a chance to redeem myself.'

Kirin made a noise halfway between a gurgle and a mumble. Trust the Hero to sound gracious even while smelling like last year's garbage heap. Asvin had come between him and Maya when he was alive, and when he was dead. But coming between them while *undead* was simply rude. There should have been rules about this sort of thing. He looked at Maya, observing him with a hint of reproach in her eyes.

'I'm, um, glad you're back,' he said. It was the best he could do, given that his primary desire at that moment was to strangle either Spikes or the unwaba. He could almost hear the chameleon's voice in his head, stealing his lines: 'Why didn't you tell me Asvin would be here? Oh, but I thought you liked surprises.'

'We've got to save the world, Asvin,' said Maya.

'Until a few minutes ago, I thought I was going to end it,' said Asvin. 'But clearly I have just changed sides. This is not a difficult proposition for someone of royal blood, though mine seems rather sluggish of late. What must I do?'

11

Arathognan was tired, so tired he was afraid he would collapse any moment, but no one could have guessed it as he strode into the Chief Civilian's temporary headquarters in south Kol. Red Phoenix guards led him underground, through a vast and musty wine-cellar to a secret chamber where the Civilian and Ombwiri waited with Shohm Muppo, the newly-appointed commander of the surviving vamans in Kol. They rose as Thog entered, shaking rainwater out of his tied grey hair, trailing water as he sank gratefully into an empty chair. Thog blinked, his eyes adjusting to the light of wet Alocacti, to the grim expressions of the room's other occupants. The muffled sound of a great roaring could be heard through the ceiling; outside, great sheets of rain lashed all over Kol, and gale-like winds howled dirges for the burnt city.

'I visited the shelters. The tunnels are safe for the moment,' said Thog. 'But water is seeping through; the shelters are not as well sealed as the vamans promised.'

'Only the newer ones, which were built in a hurry,' said Shohm. 'No one was ready for *this*. But even the weakest shelters will hold for a few days.'

'They will not have to last that long,' said the Civilian. 'I do not think the rain will last the night.'

'Let the rain last as long as the gods will,' said Thog. 'It keeps Koli spirits high. In every shelter, they sing the praises of the gods, for showing us mercy in our darkest hour. Truly, it is a miracle, a sign. Kol will survive.'

The others looked at him blankly. No one had the heart to tell Arathognan, after all he'd been through, that the rain that had held off the invaders for two days had very little to do with the gods; that Kol's fate was in their hands, and they had run out of ideas.

After the ravian attack had devastated central Kol, when it was clear that the city's defences did not stand a chance against the light-pillars of the akashraths, Ombwiri had asked the Kaos butterflies to give Kol rain, and lots of it. All through the day and night, endless clouds, dark and pregnant, had swarmed over Kol, pouring out their hearts, covering the city in hissing forests of steam. The Asa had swelled and overflowed; merry, gurgling tributaries now ran down the streets of Kol. Great fires had sizzled in fury as they were extinguished, revealed the charred bones of Kol's greatest towers. Most of central Kol was in ruins, but thousands of lives had been saved. The akashraths had tried to burn through the clouds, but had failed; while the beams of light were strong enough to pierce the clouds and destroy all they touched with their sheer intensity, no fire could be lit in the torrents of water that enveloped Kol. The butterflies had rested at night, and had flapped their wings at Ombwiri's command again the next day at dawn; all through the night, Koli warriors had flown desperately through mazes of bridges and fallen buildings, seeking out and aiding wounded citizens, trying not to look up at the eerie phosphorescent symbols on the airships that hung in the air above them.

But as dawn came and clouds gathered again, one Kaos butterfly, too exhausted to push the elements any more, had stiffened and fallen off Ombwiri's arm; yet another had died at sunset. Now only one Kaos butterfly remained, sitting on Ombwiri's shoulder, its wings beating slowly and rhythmically as Ombwiri egged it on with a variety of healing and invigorating spells. The Civilian had spent hours watching the last butterfly and waiting for inspiration to strike. Outside, it would soon grow dark above the rainclouds. What would happen when the skies cleared? Could the airships fly forever? What would happen when Kol dried up by dawn and rose at first light, fresh and sparkling, waiting to be engulfed in flames?

Roshin arrived with fresh news. Mantric had created strong ward spells that could be attached to vroomsticks, allowing them to fly steadily in the rain. Most of Enki's spellbinders were zooming all around the city, trying to create illusions of tall towers in the city's parks to confuse and distract the ravians. Pashans were wading through the streets, dragging massive land-barges full of corpses, dragging away great chunks of masonry, and trying to repair anything that had not been burnt completely. Yarni and his pashans, now conscripted city guardsmen, had spent most of the day being extremely and creatively violent to opportunistic looters who'd seen the battle as an opportunity to visit the houses of the rich and absent. And the vamans had opened more of their tunnels to the people of Kol; many tube-worms, fat and engorged by fresh sludge were already carrying people to exits outside the city.

'Is there anything the vaman king can do for us tomorrow, Shohm?' asked the Civilian.

'We have already assembled heavy catapults underneath the city,' said Shohm. 'But it will take at least a day to raise them to the rooftops. And if the ravians are given a day, there might be no rooftops.'

'Then we have nothing,' said the Civilian. 'We will have to abandon the city.'

'They will come down one day, soon. When they do, we will be waiting. The vaman king sends you his word. We will vanquish the ravians and rebuild Kol for you.'

'Should I order the defenders to leave their posts?' asked Roshin.

'Yes. If they object, tell them they will have all the battles they want in the days to come.'

'Very well. When will you leave? I will ensure all arrangements are made.'

'I will not be leaving,' said the Civilian, her face covered in shadow, her voice flat and even.

'Neither will I,' said Arathognan. 'We will find some way to fight them if the rain-gods abandon us.'

'I could go ask the men outside to flee,' said Roshin. 'But I suspect it would be a waste of time.'

'Don't bother asking the spellbinders,' said Ombwiri. 'It was hard enough to get them to join.'

'And it is not in the nature of vamans to leave problems unsolved,' said Shohm.

'That's quite enough solidarity for one evening,' said the Civilian. 'In case any of you have plans of standing in a circle and joining hands one by one, abandon them. Instead, let us spend the few hours we have left devising a plan to destroy those airships.'

At sunset, the last butterfly was allowed to rest. The stars came out again, and so did swarms of carpets and vroomsticks, wheeling and circling angrily under the hovering metal animals' vast bellies. On rooftops and bridges in the soggy, smouldering heart of Kol, artillerymen looked up at the clear sky and prayed that the night would never end. And far outside Kol, streams of humans, asurs and pashans trudged out of freshly dug tunnels, looked back at their city, charred and broken, and wept. Innumerable words of love and compassion, of regret, longing and forgiveness were spoken in Kol that night, and even in the gloom there was an all-pervading calm; Kol had accepted that its time had ended, and was preparing itself for a quick, dignified death. The Chapter of Chroniclers was formally declared closed, and its records smuggled out of the city. In the ruins of the Fragrant Underbelly, Triog sat alone, mixing himself drinks and toasting his lost patrons with tuneless songs. And when dawn came, and tendrils of light snaked their way across the sky, skirting wisps of cloud, gently melting the darkness, and the last Kaos butterfly fell off Ombwiri's arm and spiralled slowly downwards like an autumn leaf, Kol was ready. Kol was silent. Silent save for the droning of the akashraths, as their hatches opened, as metal panels slid aside, and mighty light-throwing cannons hummed their way to incandescence.

And then there was a new sound, a throbbing sound like a great heart beating in the distance, and Kol looked up in wonder, and found new hope.

The sky was full of dragons.

A great brood of Skuan dragons, green, red, black and

blue, studded the horizon to the north and west, speeding towards Kol's tower on swift leathery wings beating in unison, thumping out the rhythm of the world's heart. From the south came gigantic slow-flying huracans with winds of destruction in their wake, and the earth shook with every beat of their wings. And from the east, trailing cloud-streams, the snake-like dragons of Xi'en slithered across the sky, their usual calm and majesty abandoned in the incredible fury of their approach. From every direction they bore down on the akashraths, and as they flew over Kol's suburbs, hurtling towards the towers of central Kol and the airships, Kolis forgot all caution, poured out of shelters and took to the streets, their cheers dying quickly, their blossoming awe at the sheer scale of the spectacle before their eyes overcoming their joy.

The akashraths blazed forth in all their deadly glory, and an avalanche of screams rushed through Kol as columns of white light bore once again into the city, crushing stone, melting tar, flesh and bone, sending waves of flame running again through Kol's streets. Vaman catapults and their controllers flew through the air like twigs. Carpets and vroomsticks disappeared forever into impenetrable walls of smoke. And then, as suddenly as they had appeared, the light-pillars vanished. The airships sealed themselves and waited for the dragons.

The first onslaught came in a torrent of fire, as the Skuan dragons looped and circled in swarms, each sending thick streams of flame scurrying along the golden bodies of the akashraths. The dragons attacked from every angle at once, sometimes hovering, flapping their wings, sometimes streaking along the surfaces of the ships, seeking weaknesses in their armour. The Xi'en dragons joined in the onslaught, their horned heads stabbing forward, spitting out comets of fire that exploded into the sides of the airships. The first attack was disorganized, driven by rage; the roars of the dragons were often interrupted by harsh cries of pain as massive bodies slammed into one another with unimaginable force, and several magnificent Skuan drakes were injured by stray claws and fangs as they retreated to bring order into their ranks. Within minutes, the air around the akashraths was empty again, and massive reptile shapes sped upwards and away, falling effortlessly into lines, synchronizing their wing-beats and fiery snouts, their leaders throwing messages from mind to ageless mind as their shadows rippled over the rooftops.

On the streets, Kolis cried out in dismay; the ravian airships seemed unharmed. Their surfaces, and the air around them, shimmered slightly in the sunlight, but their movements were, as always, measured and unhurried, as they too rearranged their ranks, moving away from one another, each seeking a different altitude.

The Skuan dragons attacked again. Sleek, deadly saurian bodies arced upwards and steered into low, flat dives, skimming over the airships two by two, engulfing them in flame, and shooting past, only to waver, circle and rise again. But still the akashraths held firm; whatever the wondrous metal they were wrought of was, it was impervious to fire. Or perhaps there was some magic in the symbols carved on their undersides, which now glowed fiery red instead of pale green as they awaited the next wave of dragons.

The Xi'en dragons, realizing that fire was not the answer, chose, instead, to try sheer force. As the last of the fire-drakes hurtled away from the airships, the lords of the eastern skies descended on the giant metallic animals, raking them with their horns, claws and fangs, curling and slithering across their smooth bodies, slamming into every curve, every carving, every possible weakness in the metal hides. The akashraths began to sway and stutter; soon great dents and furrows began to appear on their skins. Nearly every inch of the akashraths was covered with slithering, jostling, hammering dragons. It could only be a matter of time before one broke through.

There was a series of clicks and hums, and flaps opened on the sides of the akashraths, revealing rows upon rows of barrels. Finding the openings they sought, the dragons slid towards the barrels, intent upon burning up the airships' innards.

With flashes of red, blue and green, the barrels spat explosives, and tore the Xi'en dragonbrood to shreds. Wide, gaping holes appeared in the dragons' bodies; dragonhides bulged and split apart as explosions rippled through one Xi'en sky-snake after another. Immense bodies, torn to ribbons, fell away from the airships and plummeted down on the city, shattering buildings, snapping bridges, starting fires. The airships, still firing, began to move, shedding dragons on the way in a rain of burning flesh. Vast fire-serpents uncoiled limply and fell; the survivors, against all reason, did not retreat. The akashraths met the next Skuan charge with flashes and fire, bringing down dragon after dragon, and on the ground people cried out in sorrow as shape after graceful shape halted in mid-air, caught by the ravians, jerking and thrashing in position, and then hurtled downwards, crushing Kol with their spine-shattering descent.

The dragons seemed undaunted by this; it was as if a great power was driving them onwards, renewing their fire and fury. The huracans, volcano-born earthquake-bringers from the southwestern islands, had reached the airships now, but they did not rush in like the others; instead, they soared higher and higher above the akashraths until, from the streets, they were just tiny specks impossibly high in the sky. At a signal from the huracan leader, the Skuan and Xi'en dragons surrounding and snapping at the akashraths fell back. And then the huracans folded their wings and fell like stones in unison, crashing down on the tops of the akashraths, smashing their massive quake-bringing tails, with their giant spiked clubs at the ends, into the gleaming metal.

The airships' shells rippled, dented, groaned, and finally cracked. Metal screamed, plates burst out, gaps appeared in the ships' armours, displaying their innards, showing ravians scurrying about amidst great rooms full of sophisticated machines.

Driven to a frenzy, the Xi'en and Skuan dragons attacked again. Ignoring the deadly light-bursts, pushing their dying comrades' bodies in front of them as shields, they swarmed around the airships, while the huracans spat lava into the ships through the cracks on the roofs. Gripping the shattered bodies of their brethren in their cruel talons, the dragons swiftly blocked the explosive-hurling barrels long enough for the huracans to take off, ponderously, and move to a safe distance high above the battle. And then every dragon that still survived, every dragon that had flown for a week to be part of the greatest mustering of dragons this world had ever seen, snorted, puffed, and filled the gaps in the akashraths' armours with fire. The airships kept up their relentless barrage, and the sky above Kol was a mind-churning melee of broken, falling bodies, ripped metal plates, sparks, showers of blood and cries of pain. But the dragons would not be defeated, and time and time again they rallied and pounced, using fire, claws and talons, ripping and burning, twisting and dodging, opening new breaches for their comrades to attack through, and as the ravians died inside the airships, and burned along with the dials and levers they were using, the akashraths stopped spitting fire, and their flame-volleys spluttered, crackled and died.

The dragons roasted the airships for several minutes. When they were satisfied that everyone in them had been properly cooked, they fell back, rose high into the sky and screamed in savage triumph, streams of fire streaking up towards the heavens as yells of joy and gratitude rose in the streets far below. There were no words, no meeting between the people of Kol and their sky-warrior saviours, no thanks given nor asked for; the dragons had shown no sign that they had even noticed Kol's defenders all along. Nor did they descend to mourn their fallen brethren; they had died in combat and returned to the earth they cherished and guarded, and for dragons, that was enough. With great thumping wing-beats, they turned towards their homes, in the mountains and islands, and went their separate ways, their mission fulfilled, their numbers drastically diminished.

The akashraths continued to float above Kol for the rest of the day, charred, twisted, belching smoke and sparks, their humming and grinding now turned to dying screeches and moans. But they were losing power; the few defenders left on Kol's rooftops did not know whether the ships ran themselves, or whether some ravians survived still, but the akashraths were slowly descending on the city. An hour before sunset, they were low enough for the vaman artillery to attack. And as the vamans pounded the husks of the akashraths with enchanted projectiles, loaded with spells of attack by Mantric and the spellbinders, the airships exploded, one by one, and their ruins fell spectacularly over the wasteland of broken buildings and dead dragons that was Kol, bare-boned, smoking, shattered.

As the sun set over Kol, lights were lit all over the city, as shelters were emptied and people trickled out, trying to convince themselves of the enormity of what had happened.

The Chief Civilian hovered on a carpet above the ruins of her palace. The swan-shaped akashrath had fallen there, and its head, still undamaged, seemed to mock her as it lay, resplendent, powerful, broken, on the centre of her power, its neck trailing off into thick metal cables, twisted and still spitting sparks. She looked skywards, at the vroomsticks rushing through the air above the devastated city, at the surviving Champions League heroes, led by Arathognan, treating themselves to a well-deserved victory lap, at the slow-moving land-barges of the freshly dead and the spellbinders scurrying about, healing the wounded.

She turned to Amloki and Roshin, on vroomsticks by her side.

'Well done,' said the Civilian. She smiled. 'Now have this mess cleaned up.'

12

Kirin awoke to find himself high above the earth, floating effortlessly above snow-capped peaks. Other people might have found this mildly disturbing, but Kirin merely smiled, and looked at himself. He was in human form. He hadn't gone to sleep wearing the Gauntlet, so this came as no surprise either; it merely meant he was dreaming.

He looked above him and flinched slightly. The sight of a gigantic black dragon, shining snake-like body looped casually across clouds, looking down at one with liquid white eyes each the size of an adult elephant, was bound to produce at least an involuntary muscular reaction.

Qianzai, Mother of Darkness, guardian of the world, had summoned him.

Kirin looked at his friend and protector and exulted in the feeling that being near her always gave him; that there were so many things great and beautiful in the world, that his own trials did not really matter that much. That in some way, everything was all right, or at least not all wrong.

But Qianzai's eyes were full of tears.

It's so good to see you, said Kirin.

Qianzai said nothing. A huge puff of smoke escaped her nostrils and floated between their faces for some time before drifting away, and Kirin saw tears running down the great dragon's leathery muzzle.

What's the matter, Qianzai? asked Kirin. *Why are you crying?*

I was thinking of your father, she said. *And how sad he would be to see his son now.*

I tried to be Dark Lord, Qianzai, said Kirin. *I failed. I tried to stop the war, but then I learned that it could not be prevented—that the powers that created it were beyond me. I have not abandoned Imokoi. The task that now lies before me is greater than Imokoi, greater than anything my father attempted. I have been forced to walk a different road. Had my father been here, I think he would have done exactly the same.*

Qianzai snorted, and anger bubbled and swirled in her eyes. *This is what you always do, is it not, Kirin? You blame others for your failures. You are merely a victim of circumstances. Every single time! I wish I had seen it before. I was blinded by my love for your father. Just as he was blinded by a father's guilt. If he had known what you were truly like, I do not think he would have let you take his place.*

Kirin almost woke up in shock. *What do you mean?* he asked.

Do not feign innocence, Kirin, or I will burst out of the ground beneath you and eat you.

But I really don't know what you're talking about, Qianzai, said Kirin. *What have I done?*

What have you done? Qianzai's eyes burned in rage. Who *summoned every dragon in the world to fly to Kol's aid? It was not* me.

The ravian airships needed to be destroyed.

So the Dark Lord sent his strongest slaves to do it.

I never saw the dragons as slaves. They were simply the only ones capable of fighting the airships.

Were you not aware that we were already fighting a war with the creatures of the underworld?

Yes. And if I had not called the dragons, Kol would have been destroyed, and in a few days, every other city in the world.

Did you consider the consequences of this? Do you know that two vaman strongholds have been destroyed because the dragons were not present to fight their destroyers? That the dragons whose lives you threw away in your blindness could have protected the world and its creatures for centuries more? More importantly, do you have any idea how much damage has been dealt to the earth itself because of your war-games?

It was no game, Qianzai, snapped Kirin. *Kol was my home. I did what I had to do to defend it. As Danh-Gem himself would have.*

Qianzai's eyes softened, fury yielding place to sorrow.

How little you know, she said. *The failure is mine as well. I did not see how thoughtless and foolish you are.*

Enlighten me, then, said Kirin, his voice as cold as the snow below him.

Your father had many flaws, but the dragons loved him nevertheless, said Qianzai. *Unlike you, he understood what being a dragon meant. Why did the dragons prefer the rakshases to the ravians in the Great War? It was because the ravians saw us as powerful beasts, creatures to use and exploit, monsters to slay. The rakshases, on the other hand, respected us and honoured us. Their king, your father, wore the Gauntlet that bound all dragons save me to his command; I could have killed him and destroyed it had I wanted to, but I did not. We were lords of the earth and sky who had pledged our service to him, not his slaves.*

That's very convenient, said Kirin. *Suddenly, history changes, and the dragons turn out not to have served Danh-Gem at all. I don't suppose the dragons had anything to do with killing untold numbers of people in the Great War. The dragons did not help create the Bleakwood, or Danh-Gem's Wasteland. All dragons are but noble gardeners of the living earth. Tell me more.*

I hope for your sake that your words are born out of your ignorance, said Qianzai. *How dare you presume that all dragons are one, that they are driven by the same desires? Many dragons are warlike; most of the Skuan clans have always been, and they were happy to burn and destroy at Danh-Gem's call. Several of my brood obeyed his commands with joy, and scorched the earth with no regret while fighting his battles for him, but only when they* chose *to. There were several occasions when his wishes were not acceptable to us. He never forced us to obey him then, even when doing so would have won greater victories for him. If the dragons had unleashed the full extent of their power and executed Danh-Gem's commands without question, do you think the ravians would have won the war? But Danh-Gem was not the monster that drove my peace-loving, earth-tending children to their deaths. That monster is* you.

Qianzai looked away, and pain filled her gentle white eyes. Kirin could think of nothing to say; he hung his head and waited until Qianzai spoke again, her voice trembling.

Perhaps Danh-Gem's respect for the dragons proved to be his undoing. Perhaps if we had served him better, we would not have spent two hundred years imprisoned in spirit-cages, enduring unimaginable pain side by side with the rakshases, waiting for magic to grow again and break our bonds. If we had simply annihilated the ravians as he had asked, the world would have been different. Without dragons present to guard the balance, the earth itself grew rebellious, and the strange beasts that seek to kill it from within were born. The dragons might have prevented that. Or perhaps not. I do not know.

What I do know is this—even in his darkest hour, on the edge of madness, your father did not treat us as you did. He did not use us as pawns, as expendable lives that existed only to serve his whims, as pieces that could be sacrificed at will. He did not stop us from performing our most sacred duties to squabble over buildings. I do not know why you did what you did, Kirin. But in doing so, you have failed. You have betrayed us. And the love that I felt for you is now dead.

But they would have destroyed Kol, said Kirin. *I could not let them. I only did what I thought was right.*

And it burns me to think that I helped you do it—that the power of my blood, that flows through your veins, strengthened your ability to command my kin. In one night, you proved yourself greater than your father, and in the same breath, worse than he ever was. What powers you wield, Kirin! What a great emperor you would make, with your ability to rule, the strength of your will! The monks who made the Gauntlet did so out of fear, hoping to protect their monasteries from warlike dragons, never even dreaming of influencing more than one at a time. They did not know what they created, and most killed themselves when the Xi'en emperor took it from them, and when it then fell in the hands of the greatest power this world has ever known. But even in his greatest hour, Danh-Gem could never have brought every dragon in the whole world to heel as you did. Or perhaps he could have—perhaps he chose not to. Perhaps it is your ravian blood that gives you this ability, and fills you with disdain for those you command. Your father knew how it felt to be considered inferior. Perhaps it was this that made him greater than you.

She looked at Kirin, at his shocked, helpless face, sighed, and looked away.

What should I do now? asked Kirin.

Do not look to me for advice, said Qianzai. *Forget I exist. Understand it is only the promise I made to your father that holds me back from seeking you out and killing you now. Use the Gauntlet as you will, but know this: you have already released me from my vows. And while I loved your father, I love my own kind more.*

Kirin's jaw hardened. *Very well,* he said. *There are some things you should know, in that case. If I ever told you my mistakes were not of my own making, it was because I thought you were a friend, and I thought you would understand. Since we are friends no longer, I have no hesitation at all in accepting full responsibility for all my deeds. I respect and admire the dragons and their pride, and I accept I wronged them by forcing them to carry out my commands—but I did not have time to be polite.*

Kol is more important to me than these nameless beasts you fight. Were I a hero, I would need a home to return victorious to; even though I am not, Kol is the only place I could call my own. I belong neither to my father's tower, nor to my mother's secret city, and I felt I needed to do whatever I could to save the only place I truly love. Does that satisfy you?

No, said Qianzai. *It only shows how petty you are. Kol is not your home, and will never be. You will never belong anywhere, in this world or any other. I thought your existence, your mixed blood, was proof the world could live in harmony. I believed your past had taught you to think of matters larger than your own desires. That faith cost me my children, and put the world itself in greater peril.*

Tell me if there is anything I can do to earn forgiveness, said Kirin. *I will do it, whatever it is.*

I did not come to ask anything of you. Some wounds will never heal, said Qianzai. *But the next time you throw away the lives of my children, we will meet again, and I will ensure that you torment dragonkind no more. Remember that, and be prepared. There is nothing more to say.*

And Kirin woke up, sweating and trembling, and sat in silence, watching Asvin flit silently from tree to tree as he patrolled the camp, until dawn filled the Bleakwood with a pale, grey light. He woke Spikes, and asked for the Gauntlet of Tatsu. He looked at the red clawed hand, which still called out in his mind, a shrill, harsh voice echoing across mountains far away, asking him to face his destiny, seize the sky and fill the earth with the ashes of his enemies. He cradled the Gauntlet close to his heart, and put it on, shuddering slightly as power coursed through him, red-hot fingers of fire tingling in his veins as dragons all over the world hissed in welcome and awaited his command.

Then Kirin pulled the Gauntlet off and returned it to Spikes, and leaned forward and whispered in his ear.

'Why?' asked Spikes.

Do it, said Kirin.

'I hate it when you do that,' said Spikes. 'Are you sure? It seems like a very bad idea to me.'

I think this is something the gods might notice. And I'm not sure I have the strength to do what needs to be done.

Spikes looked at him closely, and then shrugged. He carried the Gauntlet to a nearby clearing and laid it on the ground.

And then he pounded it with his stone fists until it broke.

A red light seemed to pulse through the sky when the Gauntlet cracked, and an angry, hot wind blew through the Bleakwood, snapping dead branches, and Kirin was afraid; had the dragons found him already? Were they attacking?

The Gauntlet burst into flames and slowly blackened and crumbled. The wind gusted for a few seconds, and then all was still again.

Spikes strode calmly across the clearing, his arms stained black and red. If he felt any pain, he hid it well. 'You're going to regret this,' he said.

We will not forget you, said a dragon's voice in Kirin's head, but what that meant Kirin did not know.

The day had clearly not started well; it showed no signs of getting any better. They were travelling eastwards, heading towards the Kol–Ajaxis highway that connected Kol and the Free States to Psomedea. Asvin walked ahead, his head held high, his feet dragging only slightly. His horse walked by his side, carrying his scythe. Spikes followed, trying to look inconspicuous and, as always, failing spectacularly. Kirin and Maya, covered in the kind of attire that would have caused even the most gullible man in the world to regard them with deep suspicion—giant hoods and cloaks that they had removed from some over-ambitious bandits—shuffled along behind them in sullen silence.

After several days of waiting in the Bleakwood for the unwaba to wake up, Asvin had announced that he was going to carry on with his task, alone if necessary. When the others had pointed out that it would be difficult to find people in the Bleakwood, because of which it would be difficult to inform the masses of the world's impending doom right then, Asvin had decided to set out at once and keep going until they were no longer in the Bleakwood, thus cunningly solving the problem. Kirin had offered Asvin the use of his chariot; Asvin had refused to abandon his horse, and had taken great offence when Maya had pointed out that the horse was dead. It had taken a great deal of coaxing before Asvin had agreed to carry on, and it was only after he had been mollified that the others had remembered that they would have preferred not to have gone in the first place. Very little had been said since then. The only people who now knew about the end of the world were some formerly cloaked and hooded bandits, who'd listened politely when Asvin had made his little speech, but had thought he'd been talking about Spikes.

But they were in open country now; the road to Kol was just a few hours ahead, and fresh green leaves on healthy young trees around them tried their best to lift their spirits. But it was a losing battle; as Asvin passed, the leaves turned yellow and floated to the ground.

Maya looked at her fellow companions, and wished she were anywhere else. Kirin had barely spoken to her since Asvin's arrival, and she could not blame him. Actually, she could, she thought defiantly. The unwaba had already told her more than she wanted to know about the way Kirin felt about her; she'd stopped him several times, because it was unfair to everyone concerned, but the little chameleon was both stubborn and irrepressible. If he were to be believed, Kirin had loved her since they'd met; in which case, all this was *his* fault. This whole Asvin situation wouldn't have arisen at all if Kirin had only summoned up the nerve to tell her how he really felt at any point during the five long years when everyone they knew in Kol had assumed they were a couple. If Kirin had come with them to Bolvudis instead of running away to meet vanars and leaving her alone with Asvin. If he would only say something *now*, instead of avoiding her eyes.

She wished she could tell him how happy she had been when they had met in Vrihataranya; how time had rolled back for an instant and it was as if they were still in Kol, when the most dangerous quest in their lives had been getting Kirin into Enki University's library unobserved. And she had seen the look in his eyes when he had realized it was really her, and had felt nothing but joy in knowing he loved her still; it was as if everything in the world had fallen in place for him.

Or it might have been a trick of the light, she thought. Blindly believing everything the unwaba had said would not do at all.

She wished she could convince herself that she had never really been in love with Asvin.

It would have been more convenient, she thought, if she had done this while Asvin was alive. And now, she was already thinking about Kirin. And if that was not enough cause for guilt, Asvin was right *there*, all the time, looking noble and sad and reproachful, and ridiculously attractive for a zombie. She looked at the unwaba, sleeping peacefully in his pouch, and wondered yet again whether all this was some elaborate deception, whether somewhere, the gods were watching the three of them and laughing their heads off.

She reminded herself that Asvin had been unfaithful to her, that she was just one of the many women he had loved, that she would have left him if he had been alive. But he had died while trying to find her, and even his tryst in Shantavan with Red had occured while under a spell; *The Hero Always Had an Excuse*. But had she been the love of his life?

The unintended cruelty of the question took her breath away. This was no time to think of romance, she told herself severely. There was work to be done. There was a world to be saved, and given the tangle their personal lives were in, saving the world was probably a relatively easy task that could be finished off first.

The sun was high in the sky when they reached the road, and encountered several large wagons heading towards the Centaur Forests, loaded with salted meat and sour-looking Olivyan farmers. Asvin informed the occupants of these wagons that the end was nigh; they ignored him and rolled serenely southwards. Asvin was enraged, and wanted to chase them and cut them down to size with his mighty scythe, but Spikes intervened.

'Since you are clearly looking for something useful to do,' said Spikes, 'let us discuss our plans.' He nodded and winked, pointing upwards as he said this; a truly gruesome sight.

'Are you sure we should do that out in the open like this?' asked Asvin. 'Did not your all-knowing lizard, whom I have not had the privilege of meeting yet, instruct you to keep everything secret?'

'He said his presence gives us a certain degree of protection; while he's with us, the gods will not notice Maya and me, and will find you and Spikes uninteresting,' said Kirin. 'We could invent a really complicated code of whistles and hand gestures if you want, but if the gods are really watching us, I don't think that would help much.'

'That will do,' said Asvin. 'Well, I hate saying this, but Spikes was right. I accept that the order I set out to obey—

telling everyone of the world's end—was clearly not one the Scorpion Man meant us to take literally. And I would like to visit the gods—they owe me many answers. Explaining *this* would be a start.' He ran his hand across the open gash that ran across his throat. 'When does your lizard wake up and tell us what to do?'

'I don't think he intends to,' said Kirin. 'He said he wouldn't send us on quests; he would just give us the information we needed at the right time. We will probably have to make our plans ourselves. Which brings us to an interesting question. How are we supposed to go meet the gods? Does anyone know?'

'Well, depending on what you believe in, the gods are either sitting on top of a high mountain, or underground, or under the sea, or in the heavens, above the sky,' said Maya, 'but in general, they're in places that have been inaccessible at the times the legends were written. Mortals who reached them usually did so after dying, and in any case, stories about gods and mortals are always meant to be interpreted, not used to make travel plans. When civilization expands, gods probably move further away to avoid the traffic.'

'The unwaba said the gods sit around the world, using it as a board to play their game,' said Kirin. 'I don't think we can reach them physically; in any case, we can't just turn up there, we would be seen. We need to speak to Zivran alone and in secret; how can we threaten him otherwise?'

'There must be a path, even if it's not a material one,' said Maya. 'Some form of trance or dream-state that lets people see gods and speak to them, or a secret portal somewhere. That must be why we need someone who truly believes in the gods; maybe only a true believer can find this path and reach them through his prayers. Asvin?'

'Yes?'

'Pray,' said Maya, smiling at Asvin. 'Very hard.'

'I have,' he replied. 'All my life. I don't think that works.'

'All right,' said Kirin, 'trances, then. Shamans do that when they speak to the gods, right?'

'Yes, but most shamans speak to elemental spirits and so on; there are just so many powers that roam the earth; we don't want to end up at the wrong house. We'd end up smoking something that would knock us out for days, and we'd see a lot of things, fun, but would they be gods? I don't know,' said Maya.

'A lot of the undead masquerade as gods as well,' said Asvin. 'I've seen them, in the Great Pyramid, wearing fancy head-dresses and wooden masks, making fools of shamans.'

'The unwaba will have to tell us what works, and how to do it,' said Kirin firmly. 'We can't wander around the world trying out every culture's most exotic drug. It would be interesting, but no.'

Maya frowned. 'But that would be setting us a quest, wouldn't it?'

'Not if it were the wrong quest,' said Spikes.

He looked around, observing their blank faces without comment.

'Is that it?' asked Kirin.

'No,' said Spikes. 'What I mean is, if the gods think Asvin is on a quest to meet them and ask them why he died, and then Asvin pretends to fail that quest, but in the process gets what you need to speak to the gods, then it should work. The unwaba could tell Asvin what he needs to do.'

'That's either really brilliant, or really silly,' said Kirin. 'I've reached the stage where I can't tell the difference.'

'In other words,' said the unwaba, sticking his head out of his pouch, 'you have reached the stage where you must seek the infinite wisdom of a higher power.'

His head flicked from side to side, and when he spoke again, his whisper was saturated with smugness. Even former gods are entitled to derive satisfaction from a well-timed entrance.

'First of all, let me welcome Asvin to this little conspiracy. Asvin, looking at you brings me happiness, because it shows me yet again how far the gods have strayed. Allowing a hero like you to die before he achieved anything significant? A terrible, callous crime. Zivran must pay. I must also encourage you on your self-control even in your current state. Killing Maya would have made things very inconvenient for everyone.'

'*What?*' gasped Maya. Kirin reached for his Shadowknife, and felt silly, because it was, of course, with Spikes.

Asvin stared at the unwaba, his mouth open. His features arranged themselves slowly until they expressed the amazement he felt.

'Calm yourselves. You are no longer in danger. Asvin had toyed with the idea of killing Maya to turn her undead with the Scorpion Man's aid, and thereby resume their great romance. However, displaying the propensity towards sacrifice and self-denial that the gods have always enjoyed in the finest Avrantic heroes, he decided not to. In doing so, he proved he was still Asvin, and not Pralay, the Cold Prince. Furthermore—'

Maya closed the unwaba's mouth swiftly.

'You can't tell us what's happening inside our heads,' she said. 'It's wrong. We've talked about this before.'

'I thought those restrictions applied only to yourself and Kirin,' said the unwaba when she let go.

'Any of us,' said Maya, gritting her teeth. 'Is that clear?'

'All right,' said the unwaba. 'Let us, then, talk about what must be done.'

He gave them a few seconds to finish shaking their heads and shooting furious glances at him, and then spoke again.

'The rest of you are unaware that Kirin, in blatant defiance of my clearly expressed orders, summoned all the dragons in the world to rescue Kol and defeat the ravian airships. They succeeded, at no small cost. And you almost lost me, your only chance of survival. I was angry, and the anger of the unwaba, oldest and wisest of chameleons, is a terrible thing. However, seeing how dismal you were, how hopeless, how lost, I decided to forgive you and carry on. Kirin has learned not to defy me again. You have been fortunate; the gods did not observe his little rebellion, choosing to believe, instead, that it was Aciram, who rules the Dark Tower wearing Kirin's face, who sent his dragons to Kol's aid.'

'Thank you,' said Maya, grasping Kirin's arm. 'I wish you'd told me.'

'Pay attention,' said the unwaba. 'Kirin's foolishness has, however, placed us all in great danger. If the dragons had not destroyed the airships, they would have swept over the Free States, destroying every human city in their path, and then moved on to Artaxerxia. There would have been prolonged battles; the vamans would have responded to the threat from the skies, jinns and rakshases would have joined the battle, and the dragons, too, would have responded in time, giving the gods enough entertainment to satisfy them for months, and giving us enough time to save the world at leisure. However, Kirin's misplaced loyalty to Kol has ended this battle prematurely. I knew, of course, that he would do what he did. I also know I would not stop him, that he needed to learn on his own how terrible the cost of defying me is.

'Now you have an additional responsibility. The gods need more to keep them satisfied; you cut short one enjoyable segment of the game, and you, therefore, must arrange something else to ensure they stay entertained. If you do not, they will look at the rest of the world even more closely, and they will find you and destroy you.'

'Are you saying I ended the war?' asked Kirin.

The unwaba laughed, or perhaps he coughed. The sound, whatever it was, was dry. 'You ended nothing,' he said. 'A great ravian army still approaches Imokoi. The dragons still fight nameless beasts under the surface of the earth. The undead army still chafes restlessly, waiting to sweep across the world in a tide of destruction. Besides all this, there are innumerable suitably touching personal stories all over the world for the more sentimental gods to take an interest in. But even all this is not enough. You must make sure the gods have something to observe that is so intriguing that they will be sufficiently distracted to not notice your dark, secret deeds. You cannot, of course, provide this distraction yourself—that would be seen as a great quest—but you must, while staying unobserved, make sure the gods are looking elsewhere.'

'How?' asked Kirin.

'If I could allow myself to tell you,' said the unwaba, 'I would have. I will now take a short nap, and wake up when you have thought of something.'

His eyes closed, and his head nodded slowly as he snuggled into Maya's shoulder. She looked at the others, aghast, and found no comfort in their faces, which were as helpless as her own.

'Well?' said the unwaba.

'Muwi-vision,' said Kirin. 'Where is Mantric?'

'A truly excellent suggestion, and I was happy knowing you would make it. Mantric is in Kol, and more specific directions are pointless, as he will have moved by the time you reach the city. Remember, though, that no one else must see you—no one at all. What you do in Kol must remain hidden from all eyes. In fact, it is better if Mantric meets only Asvin; he cares too deeply about Maya, and will tell the Civilian if you or Spikes ask him for anything. Think carefully before you decide what to say to him; he is eccentric, and will not follow instructions. Do not reveal my presence to him; he is even less trusting than you are, and will not understand the danger as well as you do, being old and set in his ways. Without my presence to protect you, Asvin, you must remember that the gods might be watching you, and listening to anything you tell Mantric. They will be slow to suspect you of deceit; already, the judges of the Game feel nothing but guilt when they see you. Use this opportunity well; you will not have much time, and you will need to be very convincing. Is that understood?'

'Yes,' said Asvin, reaching new levels of confusion every second.

'Good. What else do you want to know? Oh yes, you want to know how to reach the gods, and you have already realized this must be done using a combination of some trance-inducing magical object, and Asvin's faith. Well done; if I had had to tell you, the significance of the quest would have rendered us visible. Remember to ask Mantric what, in known chemistry or unverified myth, causes the most powerful visions; once you know this, I will be able to give you the more mundane but necessary instructions you will require to catch the bird.'

'The bird?' asked Kirin, now convinced they were all mad.

'The bird,' said the unwaba, and fell asleep.

That night, Kirin awoke with a start as something cold and wet touched his ear.

'Thanks to this timely warning, you will not make a noise indicating how startled you are and wake up the others,' said the unwaba. 'I have some things to say that are for your ears alone.'

Kirin rubbed his eyes and yawned.

'About the bird?' he asked.

'About the bird? Listen to yourself. You sound ridiculous. No, I will now tell you something that you, and only you, need to know. From our previous conversation, you might have guessed that I am displeased with you,' said the unwaba.

'You know, I thought you weren't being as loving as usual,' said Kirin. 'But it's all right. A lot of people aren't very happy with me at the moment. We can cuddle and make up, if you like.'

'There is something you should know before you go any further, young Kirin,' said the unwaba. 'As your recent encounter with Qianzai taught you, decisions of a certain magnitude inevitably invite consequences. And now you journey to Kol, to learn how to face the gods. And though you are disguised as a servant, in the gods' eyes, if you are found out, you will be regarded as the leader of this little enterprise. Tales from this world's past have demonstrated time and time again that when the earthborn and the gods meet, there is always a price to pay.'

'I thought we were going to seek a favour.'

'There is always a price.'

'Which is why we're resorting to blackmail, right? Make us another world, Zivran, or we tell the other gods you're cheating, and if we die, we take you with us. Sounds like a fun plan.'

The unwaba blinked solemnly. 'Even if your plan is successful, you will have made an enemy in the heavens. Mortals have tricked the gods before, but they have never escaped vengeance. And gods can wait a very, very long time.'

'So even if we save the world, we're all going to die?'

'Not all of us.' The unwaba looked away.

Kirin smiled in the darkness. 'Just me?'

'There is a price to pay for defeating the gods. It is the way things are. If this mad scheme succeeds, you may save the world—but you will not live to enjoy the fruits of your victory. This is the sacrifice you must make. I did not think it fair that you should be unaware of this. On the bright side, you will be undertaking a glorious task, and the gods will honour you as they take your life.'

'That's nice to know,' said Kirin. He stood up swiftly.

'What are you doing?' asked the unwaba, clinging on to Kirin's hair.

'I'm waking the others, and then we're getting out of here,' said Kirin, 'I've really had enough of you. You're clearly mad, and we don't know what we're doing, and we could be spending our time far better fighting for the things we care about. There's a war going on, and I could have made a significant difference already instead of listening to you and your idiotic prophecies.'

'Maya is committed to carrying out this task,' said the unwaba with a certain degree of malice, 'and you will find the others are too. You were the only one who doubted me—which is why I took it upon myself to tell you of your impending death, so you could leave if you wanted to. I am trying to give you the illusion of choice. You should be grateful.'

'Tell me, then, all-knowing one,' said Kirin, 'what happens if I leave? Do the others succeed? Does the world survive?'

'I am not a teller of alternate futures,' said the unwaba. 'So I will not lie to you. I will merely point out that in the event of your departure, Maya's chances of surviving this venture diminish considerably. There are still gods to deceive, and there is still a price for such an endeavour. If the gods could actually be *defeated*, beyond all question, by their creations, without any appropriate retribution, the universe itself might collapse. That cannot be allowed.'

'If we win, for now at least, and I die, does Maya survive?'

'I cannot promise that.'

'I thought you knew everything. Answer my question, or I will do something that ensures the gods see us—and you. If we succeed, and the world is saved, and the gods discover they have been deceived—does Maya survive if I stay and take the blame?'

'Yes.'

'Then you know I'm going to stay.'

'Yes. But I could pretend to be surprised. I could tell you I had expected you to leave, since going ahead meant not only death, but spending several of your remaining days watching the poignant, touching romance involving the woman you love and the heroic zombie.'

'But did you really expect me to leave without seeing how it all ended?'

'No.'

'So it was all for the sheer enjoyment of telling me terrible news, and thus punishing me for my disobedience.'

'Not at all. I do sympathize, you know. Hearing all this so soon after you lost the dragons cannot have been pleasant. You must have lost any semblance of self-belief.'

'Why wake me up just to tell me I'm going to die, then?'

'*I* was awake,' said the unwaba, curling up in Kirin's hand. 'Revelations of great importance were inevitable.'

13

King Amrit's Park, named after the first king of Kol, had always been a place of great historical relevance. Down the centuries, its shady green avenues had seen many of the world's most important people quarrel, conspire, gossip, make love or simply sit and think; even today, with much of Kol reduced to rubble, its trees offered calm and solitude.

King Amrit's Park had not survived the ravian onslaught unscathed; large sections of what had been beautiful green gardens were now charred wastelands. Even Streaker's Corner, where Kolis who found the weight of the world oppressive could take off their clothes and rail about their sorrows to large and encouraging audiences, was empty and denuded. Streaker's Corner had been the only place in the city at ground level where, if one turned around in circles (as was frequently the case), one could see all of Kol's greatest towers silhouetted against the horizon. Now, sadly, all one could see from Streaker's Corner was skeletal, incredibly tall vaman scaffolding that cast long, striped shadows across the scattered remains of the Big Mango.

The vamans had been reconstructing central Kol for two weeks now, and while work had progressed at a phenomenal rate, it would be a long time before Kol's spires, arches and domes would stand proudly again in the sunshine. Not that anyone was present at Streaker's Corner to mourn the demise of Kol's towers; King Amrit's Park was closed to the public for the day. The sky above the park was full of vroomsticks, Red Phoenix guards spiralling above the trees in lazy circles, and on the ground shadows flitted from tree to tree; the Silver Phalanx was in charge of making sure no concealed assassin disturbed the gathering that was taking place in a secluded grove in the park.

The Chief Civilian of Kol was meeting ambassadors from all over the world, assuring them that Kol still stood; that Kol was still strong despite its broken heart. The armies of the Free States, reorganized and strengthened by Artaxerxian forces loyal to the Sultan, now held the lands to the south of the Great Forest. The ravian army that had been marching westwards on the southern fringes of Vrihataranya had retreated and disappeared into the forest; Kol claimed this as a victory, though the new ambassador from Imokoi, a jackal-headed shabtic demon named Duamu whose very presence was causing most of the humans present to break into cold sweats, said the ravian army had moved inwards to ward off an attack from the rakshases of Vrihataranya. Either way, the Free States and the lands to the west appeared to be safe for the moment. Imokoi, Duamu said, was more than ready for the ravians; it was licking its fangs in anticipation. Dark Lord Kirin had asked the Civilian to send a force of humans and vamans to Danh-Gem's Wasteland, south of Imokoi, not because he needed help but to share in that glorious bloodbath; that scarred plain would echo once again to the sound of war-drums and death-screams. But the Civilian could not agree to this; though she would be eternally grateful, she said, for Imokoi's help at a time when Kol was in dire need (Duamu might have looked a little confused at this, but being jackal-headed helped him conceal his surprise), Kol would have to keep its forces nearby, since Avranti was still cut off from the world, and danger could issue forth from the east at any time.

Shohm Muppo, the vaman ambassador, refused in turn to petition his king to send an army to Imokoi. The vamans were under attack, he said; strange monsters had arisen from the depths of the earth and were ravaging their tunnels. Bhoomi would aid Kol with everything it had, but could not send an army to help the rakshases.

Negotiations continued for several hours, amidst lavish meals and occasional entertainment, and as the sun began to set over King Amrit's Park, setting the leaves alight with orange fire, the Civilian was pleased with herself; everything had gone as she had predicted it would. She was about to call an end to the day's discussion, when there was a sudden consternation at the entrance to the grove. But it was only Mantric, arguing with Roshin, demanding to be allowed to address the council.

The Civilian was surprised; not only was this unplanned, but Mantric had always made it a point to avoid, with an almost religious fervour, anything that stank of politics. She waved her consent, and Mantric stepped into the grove, into the centre of the circle where the ambassadors were assembled, and cleared his throat.

'I'm really sorry to have interrupted your very important

council,' he said, 'but there's something I have to tell the Civilian that you should all know.'

'Mantric is Kol's greatest spellbinder, and a close friend,' said the Civilian. 'Mantric, we are almost finished here. Whatever it is can surely wait; I will be at your service very soon.'

At any other time, with any other person, this gentle speech from the Civilian would have sent the interloper running for his life. But this was Mantric. He cleared his throat again and spoke, louder and more clearly.

'I'm afraid not; they should all know, and so should their rulers,' he said. 'I've just learned that the world is about to end.'

Several of the ambassadors laughed uncertainly. The Civilian's eyes narrowed and they fell silent.

'Tell us more,' she said.

'An army of undead creatures is about to sweep across the world, ending all life,' said Mantric. 'It's the end of the world, just like all the legends predict, and only the gods can save us.'

He looked around at the assembled ambassadors, whose expressions ranged from annoyance to amusement.

'And what should we do with this news?' asked Shohm Muppo.

'Do what you can. But fear not,' said Mantric, striking a dramatic pose, 'for I will save you all. That is all I had to say.' And with that, he turned around and stalked away, followed by several sympathetic glances of the sort that clever people give harmless lunatics.

'What on earth were you doing?' Amloki asked Mantric several hours later in the Civilian's south Kol headquarters.

'That is what I would like to know as well,' said Lady Temat, entering the room. 'Have you lost your mind?'

'I met Asvin,' said Mantric. He waited for this to sink in, and as questions rose in their throats and almost boiled over, he raised his hand for silence.

'He's dead. But he's not done. He's one of the Scorpion Man's Four Horsemen, and he's been sent out of the Great Pyramid to tell the world of its impending doom. When he goes back to Elaken, the dead will destroy the world and everything in it.'

'How did he die?' asked the Civilian after a few stunned seconds.

'The ravian who abducted Maya killed him. But he didn't seem to want to talk about that much,' said Mantric. 'I tried to get him to meet you, but he refused to see anyone else; he said the world could still be saved, and I was the only one who could do it.'

'How?' asked Amloki, feeling left out. *He* should have been the only one who could have done it. That was the problem with being so good-looking; it caused jealousy.

'He said I have to undertake a perilous journey to win the gods' favour—only they can protect the world now, or give us the means to do it. I have to give them a gift, something that will please them so much that they will grant me some kind of boon in return, or give me divine weapons that will let us stop the armies of the dead and let this world survive. Don't look at me like that.'

'Mantric,' said the Civilian, 'you're joking, aren't you?'

'I can scarcely believe the words coming out of my mouth,' said Mantric. 'The joke, if there is one, is on me—I had never even believed in the gods, until now. And now, strangely enough, I must go find them.'

'I need to see Asvin. If there is really an army of the dead, and he leads it, it could strengthen our position greatly.'

'He's gone,' said Mantric. 'I did ask him to meet you, but he didn't want to.'

'What else did he tell you?'

'Not very much, really. He did ask me what created the strongest trances, but didn't seem to want to know much else.'

'What creates the strongest trances?' The Civilian was now completely lost.

'That's what I said,' said Mantric equably. 'The answer, of course, is the safat.'

'What, in the name of everything sacred, is a safat?'

'You know. Legend. Bird. Flies around all the time, can't perch anywhere. Lays eggs in the air, the chicks hatch and fly off before the eggs fall to the ground. All seems quite pointless, but the eggshells cause stronger visions than anything else in the world.'

'Did Asvin feed you a safat's egg?'

'No, why should he? He didn't even know what it was. He did look a little hungry, though. But he didn't want any food. I offered him a biscuit, but he said he didn't need to eat any more. Makes sense, since he's undead.'

'Please concentrate, Mantric. Why did Asvin ask about the safat?'

'How should I know? I assumed the question was born out of academic interest. Maybe he's had visions, or wants to have them. Little chance of him catching a safat, though, since no one's even sure they exist. In fact, if you remember, Kristo Nalegamo bought a stuffed bird that a pirate sold him, which he thought was a safat, but it turned out to be a pelican.'

'Mantric. Please. Stop rambling. Did Asvin tell you what he planned to do next, or how he might be found?'

'No. You don't think he was planning to actually catch a safat and eat its eggs, do you? I don't see how he'd manage, but you never know with Asvin.' Mantric looked a little guilty. 'I didn't think of that. I should have warned him.'

'Warned him of what?'

'Well, eating safat's eggs and seeing the visions as a result can only end in madness. Permanent madness. Or at least the legends say so. Hmm. I should have mentioned that.'

'Is he trying to save the world too?'

'No. He's supposed to end it.'

'Then why is he asking you to save it, if he wants it ended?'

'How would I know? The ways of heroes are a mystery to me. Besides, he'd just asked me to go and find the gods. I was a little overwhelmed.'

The Civilian laughed, and buried her head in her hands. 'We're all mad. *Where* will you find the gods?' she asked.

'Asvin said I would find them at the edge of the Vertical Sea,' said Mantric. 'Where he came by this information he didn't say. It's an interesting theory—you know, it's possible that the magic level, as we crudely call it, is merely a function of distance from the gods, if the gods are what generates the magic in the—'

'Stop,' said the Civilian. 'Something is clearly wrong with you. I understand—we've all been through a difficult time. What you need is rest.'

'What I need is money,' said Mantric. 'Lots of it. And ships. I need the navy.'

'I'm afraid I don't have ships to spare,' said Temat icily. 'You might not have noticed it, but there is a war going on, and every ship is needed if the south is to be protected; the pirate armadas are now openly entering Kol's territorial waters, and there is always the risk of a Xi'en invasion. More importantly, Kol is being rebuilt. You are needed here, Mantric. If you have conceived some sort of wild plan of disappearing again, abandon it, or I will have you thrown into the dungeons.'

'But what about Asvin and this news? Don't you think we should take it seriously?'

'If Asvin is indeed undead, he no longer controls his own mind. Don't you remember how the ravians sent undead puppets to the city? This is some ravian trick.'

'I don't think so,' said Mantric, unperturbed. 'He was wearing several powerful magical totems. No ravian could have controlled him. I wish you'd been there. He was very persuasive. Said a lot of inspiring things that I've forgotten.'

'You really intend to go?' asked Amloki, his eyes shining.

'Of course,' said Mantric. 'Asvin did say it would be the greatest quest ever undertaken. Imagine—sailing to the edge of the world, and meeting the gods, and saving the world. It will be a research trip like no other.'

'I'm going with you,' said Amloki.

'Of course you are,' said Mantric. 'You're coming, and so is Arathognan. We will need a hero.'

'I remember a time when I used to rule this city, and my word was law,' sighed the Civilian. 'Neither of you is going anywhere. Is that clear?'

Mantric and the ex-Dagger looked like spanked schoolboys.

'I'm of no use to you in Kol any more,' said Amloki. 'If you need Mantric to stay, let me go instead. I wouldn't need the navy.'

'How would you get to the edge of the world?' asked Mantric.

'I have my methods,' said Amloki, seizing the opportunity to look suave.

'Ah, but what gift would you give the gods even if you found them?'

The ex-Dagger considered several very good replies, but, seeing Temat's thunderous face, decided wisely to restrict himself to an elegant shrug.

'In all seriousness, Temat,' said Mantric, 'I must go. I have no doubt at all that Asvin meant what he said; it could not have happened at a worse time, and I know it is hard to believe, and that an enterprise of this nature requires months, even years, of planning. But if the world does, indeed, need to be saved, and you are too busy running the city to save it yourself, who would you rather send to do it?'

'Us, that's who. After all,' said the ex-Dagger, 'saving the world is not something that should be left to children.'

In the long silence that followed, there was a lot Lady Temat could have said, but something broke inside her, and when she looked up at her only friends again, her face was calm and a smile twisted lazily across her thin lips.

'Go if you must. Both of you. Kol and I will be fine,' said the Civilian, her eyes suddenly bright. 'Two boys off to have an adventure. I wish I could come too.'

'We'll pick up Thog, and leave right away,' said Amloki.

Temat shook her head. 'The city needs him more than you do.'

'That's fine,' said Mantric, wisely deciding not to push his luck. 'It's not as if we can rush off immediately, of course—I will need several things brought here from Bolvudis. Keep Thog, and keep your navy.'

'But we're still going to need a lot of money,' said Amloki, grinning widely. If they were truly travelling southwards by sea, to places where no one knew him, it was time to retrieve something he'd tucked away in an old drawer in his room. Something that the south needed to meet if it wanted to think, later on, that it had lived a full life.

A silver dagger.

14

Most people believe that gods exist. Many do not; this does not trouble the gods, who know that if gods, in turn, were to not believe that people exist, people would actually cease to exist. Mortal belief does make gods stronger; it inflates their egos, which is always good for the metabolism. Some gods, in fact, chose long ago to *sustain* themselves on belief, to survive on the prayers of their followers. These gods are, alas, now dead. The creations of the gods are made in their image, give or take a few heads; like their gods, they are fickle.

But even those people who believe most fervently in the gods, not caring that their faith means nothing in particular to the omnipotent beings that rule their lives, acknowledge that their gods are a little . . . eccentric. The gods know this, and it does not trouble them. The real problem, they would say, if they cared enough to explain, is that their tiny creations are small-minded. It is not their fault; creatures so tiny cannot be expected to see the big picture. They are not supposed to perceive that the gods' allegedly whimsical behaviour is in fact all part of the mostly benevolent divine plan, which is rumoured to be about to exist as soon as the gods get around to it. Gods cannot be expected to look into the details all the time. This is why they have a large supporting cast; familiars, naguals, angels, apsaras and the like, who get the dirty work done, while the gods make love, war, games, babies, interesting works of art and puns that would have been terrible if made by beings less powerful.

The gods would, of course, be the first to acknowledge that the system is not perfect. Whenever work of a certain scale is executed quickly—as most divine work is, because most gods are not renowned for their patience—there is scope for error. The strange and wonderful bird known as the safat is one such error.

Gods are beings of quicksilver, of dreams and half-thoughts and portents; their servants, usually talented local artisans, are the ones who actually push the elements around, and millennia of working for gods have not yet succeeded in eradicating their regrettable tendencies towards literalness. When Zivran the Creator had asked Sambo, his nagual, to create birds, a set of beings with wings, that would live in the sky, Sambo had, after much research on flight dynamics, aerial vectors and hollow bones (all of which he'd had to invent first in order to study better) produced the safat, a triumph of semi-divine engineering, a born master of the air. Unfortunately, Zivran had said nothing about this bird ever needing to touch the ground, so the safat had no legs and was doomed to fly all through its life; a similar mistake had left sharks incapable of sleep and permanently bad-tempered. Its inability to perch and nest or, indeed, ever stop flying had made the safat's family life somewhat difficult, as it had to make close friends and subsequently lay its eggs in mid-air.

That whole business of egg-laying and incubation was also something Zivran had never really gotten his head around. The phoenix, another example of faulty, over-literal avian engineering, was unable to actually lay eggs; its only means of warming its eggs enough to hatch them was by flying into fires; an inspiring image for poets and magicians, but not an experience hugely enjoyed by the phoenix.

The safat, however, had overcome the deficiencies in its design and developed an ingenious method of ensuring the survival of the next generation. Safat chicks could only live if they managed to escape their shells and learn to fly before the shells hit the ground. This meant mother safats had to lay their eggs at very high altitudes in regions where the air was extremely hot, so the eggs would fall longer and crack faster, and the newly hatched infants could spread their wings and use warm air currents to glide upwards to safety. While safats had successfully hatched their young in deserts and above volcanoes, the discerning safat's maternity destination of choice was in the far north, north of Avranti, near the stork nesting grounds in north Vrihataranya, in the uninhabited mud-plain that housed one of the world's most spectacular natural wonders—the Ciliole Geysers.

In a large basin of streaked yellow-brown mud, surrounded by ugly, bubbling mud puddles, lay about two hundred mounds of sinter, cones and craters scattered at random, periodically spitting out steam and water, at least three geyser-fountains spewing forth at any point of time. Some of the fountains were mere inches high; others rose higher than the trees to the south, and the earth trembled as their jets emerged.

In the centre of the basin was the mightiest geyser of all—a massive cone-geyser known as the Young Incorrigible, that sent angry fountains of steam up to dizzying heights at regular intervals about an hour apart.

Sitting on the spout of the Young Incorrigible, apparently unmoved by the great danger he was placing himself in, was Spikes.

Asvin stood a little distance away from Spikes, trying unsuccessfully to avoid getting wet; even though he hadn't got caught by a geyser yet, there was a fine spray in the air, and all over Asvin. He was trying to convince himself that it was this exposure to moisture that was responsible for his terrible mood, but the true reason for Asvin's dissatisfaction was Spikes, who had told him several days ago that he was no longer allowed to talk to Maya. Asvin must have been under the gods' eyes in Kol, and it would just not do to throw Maya in that sort of danger, Spikes had said. Asvin had had to accept that most of his conversations would be with Spikes henceforth; Spikes seemed to be looking forward to this.

Outside the Ciliole Geyser basin were the beautiful woodlands of north-east Vrihataranya. Kirin and Maya were lurking efficiently under a tree near the basin. Kirin had been afraid they ran the risk of discovery by being so near Asvin and Spikes, but Maya had told him not to worry; the unwaba was with them, and besides, since they were only two supposed attendants, they could easily be classified by any god watching as acceptable retinue. She had told him a story she'd learned from Mantric in Kol—the true story behind the well-known legend of Eukantseus, the Psomedean musician who'd gone to the gods to reclaim the spirit of his dead wife. Down the ages, people had been told that Eukantseus had been told to walk away from the heavens without looking back, and that he'd been unable to resist checking whether his wife was following him or not—he'd looked back, and lost her. What had really happened, said Maya, was that his wife had joined him back on earth, but he'd looked back to see whether his servants, who'd followed him to the heavens and had been carrying his comfortable sandals, had survived the trip. The gods, irritated, had taken his wife away, but had given Eukantseus what they had thought was a reward for effort—for the rest of Eukantseus's sadly brief life, drunk women had found him irresistible.

Flying in excited loops far above Spikes were two storks. Their names were S. G. Madhavan and H. P. Bhuthalingam; no one else was very sure how Spikes had summoned them, and Spikes refused to tell. The stork–pashan contract, he had said loftily, was sacred. Madhavan and Bhuthalingam were almost fainting and falling with excitement; even though the services required of them were unorthodox, to say the least, they were working with the most famous pashan in the world—the Oathbreaker's Egg pashan, no less, and they were willing to do almost anything for him. The prospect of going back to the great stork-nest and regaling their neighbours with tales of what would surely be a great adventure was already making them dizzy.

As Spikes sat on the geyser-mound and the others waited impatiently, they all privately shuddered to think how slim the odds of this mad plan succeeding were. Getting the safat's egg would require incredibly precise timing. The unwaba had told them, on the way, that chewing the safat's eggshells would send them into a deep and swirling trance, and that Asvin's prayers could then be used to send Kirin and Maya to visit the gods in secret, while Asvin and Spikes kept the gods entertained. Asvin had been very upset at this; he'd wanted to meet the gods himself, but he had accepted, after much persuasion, that it would be impossible for him to go anywhere in secret at present, since the gods were already watching him.

The unwaba had instructed them to come to the Ciliole Geysers. They'd waited, in hiding, in Kol for several days until he'd told them the time was right; that a safat was approaching Ciliole and planned to lay her egg there. They had wanted to know more about safats, but this had annoyed the unwaba for some reason. 'It does not matter how many safats there are in the world, how many spots they have on their bellies, or what they like their friends to give them on their birthdays,' he had spluttered. 'What matters is that there is one safat heading to Ciliole to lay an egg, and you have to decide how to get your hands on the shell before it disappears into the mud. You cannot afford to simply wait for the safat to lay her egg when she chooses to, and let the shell fall just anywhere; you will lost it if so. Thanks to Kirin's stupidity, you cannot even capture the safat with a dragon. You cannot wound or kill her—that would make it difficult for her to lay her egg. You cannot bring her down on the ground—that would kill her. You cannot let the shells land on a geyser, or in the mud. You have a lot of thinking to do, and this is not the time for discovering fifty interesting facts about the safat. That is all.'

They had realized, too late, that the unwaba's annoyance was owing to the fact that he could not tell them exactly where the eggshell would fall, or exactly when the safat would lay her egg; this was because he simply did not know. There were too many factors to take into consideration, and the unwaba's predictions, while stunningly accurate at all times, could not take into account the actions of the unwaba's mortal enemies, the Kaos butterflies, and the alterations in the safat's flight that weather changes might cause. The discovery that there were things the unwaba didn't know had affected them in various ways; Asvin had been stricken with doubt, and Kirin and Maya had been pleased, albeit maliciously. Spikes's reaction, however, been easy to predict. He'd said 'Hmph.'

'I see the safat,' said Madhavan. 'Should we start?'

'Yes,' called Asvin. 'Guide her towards us, but do not hurt her. When I give the signal, make sure she is directly above Spikes. If she shows signs of laying her egg before you manage to bring her above Spikes—and I'm sure you will be far more likely to know than I what the symptoms of potential egg-laying are—then you will have to find some way to distract her.'

'I can't hear you,' said Bhuthalingam. 'Are there any new instructions?'

'No,' yelled Asvin. 'Just what Spikes told you before.'

The storks flew westwards, where a tiny shape could be seen far above, approaching the geysers.

'Well, the safat is here, good Spikes,' said Asvin. 'Are you ready?'

'No,' said Spikes. 'I'm just sitting on top of a boiling geyser because it helps me think.'

Asvin smiled. 'And so it begins.'

He shook his fist at the sky.

'Let the heavens shake and tremble!' he cried. 'For I, Asvin, Prince of Avranti, The Chosen One, Hero of Simoqin, Prophesied Saviour, Pride of the East—'

'Get on with it,' murmured Spikes. 'The bird's almost here.'

'—Wielder of the Bow of Fire, the Sword of Raka, the Armour of the Scorpion Man, the Ring of Akarat and Many Other Important Objects, snatched from life before my time!'

'Forgot where you were going with that sentence, didn't you? You, Asvin, lengthy introduction, then what?'

'I demand justice!' cried Asvin, unperturbed. 'For I am become Pralay, Cold Prince, Rider of the End, Dealer of Doom and Death, not the Preserver and Renewer, not the Hero it was my destiny to be! The gods have betrayed me! I demand answers!'

He raised his great scythe with one arm in an eerie display of undead strength, and waved it about, sending arcs of blue fire gusting into the air.

The safat could be seen clearly now. She was a great gaunt bird, with incredibly large scarlet wings, and a bald turquoise head. She looked like an ancient vulture, a thin, forgotten creature from another time, come to a primitive land to visit her past.

The storks were flying with the safat and troubling her greatly. Nudging, shoving and crowding, they were slowly steering her towards the centre of the Ciliole basin.

'I really don't see how she can lay an egg now,' said Asvin. 'Should we try something else? Birds need to feel comfortable before egg-laying. Trust me, I know.'

'Get ready to give the signal,' said Spikes, looking at the ground, where a faint rumbling sound was beginning to rise from the depths of the earth, a great beast growling underground.

'This isn't going to work!' Maya whispered frantically in the woods. 'Get Spikes away! It's too dangerous!'

The rumbling reached a crescendo.

'Time. Signal,' said Spikes.

Asvin waved his scythe in the air, and the storks pushed the safat forward, until she was right above Spikes. She screeched indignantly, snapping at the storks.

The Young Incorrigible geyser hissed like a dragon and opened, and Spikes shot up in the air as if hurled by a catapult, on top of a fountain of steam. He had also started leaping when the steam picked him up; now even when the geyser reached its full height, Spikes soared upwards, the world's first flying pashan. One final push from Madhavan, and the safat was in position; Spikes seemed to hang in the air in front of her. Their eyes met. The safat flinched.

'Boo,' said Spikes.

The safat stopped in mid-air, flapping her wings furiously, squawking in shock and indignation. Looking at Spikes on the ground was bad enough, but having Spikes appear out of nowhere in the middle of the sky was just *unfair*. She knew, then, what she had to do.

Her eyes bulged. Her tail-feathers rose and spread. She looked angry, then curious and then faintly pleased.

With a soft plop, a bright blue egg emerged from the safat's nether regions and hurtled groundwards, and Spikes, succumbing to gravity, fell with it. Madhavan and Bhuthalingam flattened their wings and arced into dives as well. The safat, resolving never to seek romance again, flapped away, glad that not being able to sleep meant she would never have nightmares about Spikes.

Egg and stone-man plummeted on, and on the ground Kirin and Maya looked away, dreading the moment of impact. For Spikes, the blue egg was all that existed in the world just then; everything else was a grey streak and a dull roar. But about sixty feet above the ground, the egg wobbled in mid-air as a gush of steam below them sent hot air billowing about them. The storks rolled out of their dives smoothly into wide circles, keeping the egg between them.

The egg cracked. It jumped in mid-air and broke in half.

A bright head emerged, and a second later, scarlet wings, surprisingly large, stretched outwards, and the safat chick screeched harshly and instinctively rode the current of hot air pushing it upwards,

The skies reverberated to a thunderous crash as Spikes and earth collided, creating a large Spikes-shaped crater in the heart of the Ciliole Geyser basin. Mud and rock billowed and spattered upwards and three geyser-vents opened up beneath the pashan; they were small geysers, but Spikes disappeared in a cloud of steam and smoke.

The safat chick soared away, shaking its wings gingerly and screeching, no doubt towards a troubled life. The eggshell pieces, meanwhile, fell lightly until they disappeared into the cloud of steam around Spikes. Madhavan and Bhuthalingam landed on a convenient rock and looked on nervously. All was silent, except for the gentle hissing of a few minor geysers at the edge of the basin.

Maya was about to run into the basin, but Kirin held her back. Asvin walked gingerly over to Spikes's crater.

'Spikes?' he called. 'You alive?'

The steam-cloud cleared, revealing Spikes, kneeling calmly in the middle of the crater surrounded by wisps of steam in a haze of spray, holding a piece of the eggshell in one stony hand. The rest of the eggshell had disappeared in the mud, but they had what they had come for.

'Yes, I'm alive,' Spikes said. 'You?'

Asvin halted, and for a moment it seemed as if he would attack Spikes. But duty won over impulse, and he shook his head sadly and took the eggshell from Spikes.

'I hope the gods are ready for me,' he cried, 'for here I come!'

Without further ado, he put the eggshell in his mouth, and Kirin and Maya gasped; this was not part of the plan. The same thought charged into their minds simultaneously; had Asvin decided to abandon their plan? Had he gone alone to ask the gods why they'd allowed him to die?

But then Asvin took several cracked shell fragments out of his mouth and cast them, carefully, on a patch of dry mud.

'Woe is me,' he said, looking skywards. 'Of course I cannot eat the eggshell! All this was for nothing, and the gods mock my despair! How could I think that I could achieve anything by trying to eat? How could I forget I am undead? My quest has failed, and all hope is lost! Oh, cruel Fate!' He sank to his knees and clutched his still heart. He was either acting very badly, or simply stating what he felt; even though he could not cry any more, it seemed to the others that the ghosts of tears ran down his gaunt cheeks, and real ones filled Maya's eyes.

Spikes patted Asvin's back, very carefully.

'It's all right,' he said gruffly. 'We'll think of something else. Let's go.'

'I have a few more things to say,' said Asvin tremulously. 'There are so many questions; let me ask them. Even if I am not in their midst, I am sure they will hear me, and find a way to explain why they have treated me thus. I know they are watching. I cannot have done all this for nothing.'

'Even if they were listening when you started, they would have fallen asleep by now,' said Spikes.

'Why do you hate me so, Spikes?' asked Asvin, his voice breaking.

Spikes rubbed his nose in what might have been a contrite gesture or an attempt to remove some of the mud that caked him from head to foot, making him look like a two-legged rhinoceros.

'Boot. Wrong foot. And I don't hate you. Just trying to make up for centuries of people like you killing people like me. Pointless, and I'll stop,' said Spikes. He took Asvin's arm, and guided him through geysers towards the woods that lay southwards.

'Should we go get the shell now?' whispered Maya.

'Not yet,' said Kirin. His lips moved, and Spikes looked at him sharply and nodded. The pashan called out to the storks, and thanked them with what, for Spikes, was a long and elegant speech. Madhavan and Bhuthalingam made unambiguously long speeches in turn before soaring off homewards, their breast-feathers fluffy with pride. They were thrilled to have served the heir of Katar, and were eager to let their nest-brethren know the Oathbreaker clan could stop giving themselves airs now; they had failed, and the Oathbreaker's Egg's pashan walked the earth.

Spikes then took Asvin's arm again and led him firmly into the shadows of the Great Forest. Kirin and Maya waited until Spikes and Asvin were no longer visible, drew their hoods over their heads and then ran out to pick up the shell.

'What next?' asked Maya, examining a bright blue shell fragment in her hand. 'Wait for the unwaba to tell us what to do?'

'That would be nice, but who knows when he'll wake up next? We should lie low for a few days and then just eat the shells and see what happens,' said Kirin. 'It feels strange to even say this, Maya, but we're really going to meet the gods. What next? It might be a good idea to decide what we're going to say.'

15

The Silver Dagger led Mantric swiftly through a maze of narrow streets lined by lime-white, low houses glowing ghost-like under the moon. They were in the port district of Ajaxis, the capital of Psomedea. The streets were mostly empty; a flotilla of ships full of undead from Xi'en had been swept into Ajaxis's harbour by a storm of ill fortune, and the undead had decided to stay awhile and sample some of that famed Psomedean cuisine. The city was under curfew at night and would remain so until the army was sure it had exterminated all the flesh-eating monsters that now stalked its streets, hungry and eager for exercise after many days cramped up in the holds of junks. Mantric and the Dagger had not met any undead yet; given the Dagger's newfound exuberance, this was a good thing for the undead. In the distance, the clatter of centaur hooves and the occasional groans of the undead could be heard, but as the Dagger pulled Mantric into a dark alley and knocked on a window, the loudest sound Mantric could hear was the wheezing of his own tired lungs.

The window slid open and a bald, bearded man stuck his head out.

'What happens when an irresistible force meets an immovable object?' he asked.

'A big bang,' said the Dagger, shaking his head.

'Good. The following statement is true. The preceding statement is false. How is this possible?'

'Ignore my answer.'

'Perfect. Why did the dish run away alone?'

'Because there was no spoon.'

'Welcome to the mansion of Al-Qatras,' said the man, and shut the window.

Nothing moved in the street for several minutes.

'What happens now?' asked Mantric, whispering for no particular reason.

'They'll be a while,' said the Dagger.

'This would be a good time to tell me where we are and why,' said Mantric. 'I thought we were going to meet a pirate.'

'We are. But good pirates don't lie around in pirate bars. Too many blood feuds.'

'So this is some kind of secret elite pirate headquarters?'

'Not at all. In fact, no pirates are known to come here.'

'And that's why we're here looking for one.' Mantric seemed satisfied by this.

The Dagger sighed. 'I wish you hadn't come,' he said. 'This isn't a place you will like.'

'This is my big quest,' said Mantric. 'I'm going everywhere.'

'It could get dangerous.'

'Oh dear. I wish I had magical powers I could use to defend myself.'

The Dagger grinned. 'All right, then,' he said. 'We're going to a slave auction.'

'I don't want a slave.'

'That's good, because you're not getting one. We're here for our pirate.'

'We have to rescue our pirate from slave-traders?'

'No. Our pirate's coming here to buy a slave, and will be very surprised to find me.'

'We will have to find a different pirate,' said Mantric. 'I'm not travelling with slave-owners.'

'You'll travel with this one, and like it. This pirate buys slaves to set them free.'

'Sounds like a silly sort of pirate.'

'This pirate makes a living out of plundering from other pirates. Nothing illegal at all.'

'Can't be very popular in pirate circles, then. How did you get to meet him?'

The Dagger looked around and sighed. 'It's a bit of a long story.'

'You said they'd take a while.'

The Dagger smiled, and shuffled his feet in an embarrassed sort of way. 'I'm taking this end of the world business very seriously, you know,' he said. 'Far too seriously. I keep wanting to start writing down all my stories, all my adventures. In case I die. Which is funny, because I've been ready to die since the day I started out in this profession. If I died during a mission, the Phalanx would remember me. But it would be rather pointless if the whole world ended, wouldn't it? There would be no one left. The stories would die with us.'

'That doesn't make the stories any less interesting. I have time.'

Amloki listened keenly for a while, half hoping to hear noises from inside the house. Nothing. He stepped away from the window and paced about the alley.

'I suppose I might as well tell you. This was about twelve years ago, when I was a relative innocent. There was this fearsome old pirate called Greenbeard. Killed hundreds of people, sank ships, robbed, plundered, pillaged, was generally unpleasant. You know the type.'

'Why was his beard green?'

'It wasn't. But the other colours were taken. Anyway, he'd been carving up Koli merchant ships, and the Civilian sent me to get rid of him after the navy failed. So I got on a ship, got myself captured and enslaved, and cut my way out of the galleys using a piece of string and a few fishbones. I could have killed old Greenbeard the day I broke out, but there was a problem. I fell in love with his daughter.'

'Why was his daughter on board? Don't pirates think it's bad luck to have a woman on board?'

'Yes. But she was there nevertheless, and it was bad luck for me. I decided to wait for a few days, woo Orpi—that was her name, and still is, of course—and see if I could try and persuade Greenbeard to change his ways and save his life. And get a khudran son-in-law in the bargain.'

'You wanted to marry this Orpi?'

'Young. Foolish. So, I started skulking around the ship, pushing off pirates and pursuing Orpi.'

'And you succeeded. So is it Greenbeard that we are here to meet?'

'Don't interrupt me. I spent several days wooing Orpi, but—this will shock you—she did not succumb to my considerable charms. I was not, of course, as skilled in the technicalities of romance as I am now—I need not be modest with you, old friend—but I admit I was very surprised when I saw my affections left Orpi cold. One reason for this, of course, was that she was far too young for me—only sixteen, but I did not know that, and I was not as adept in guessing human ages as I am now. But the reason for my failure was not my youth—it was that I had a rival. Orpi's heart belonged to another.

'There was a young stowaway on board, a boy who called himself Fujen. A pretty lad, not more than fifteen years old; what he was doing on board the *Guffin*, Greenbeard's ship, he would not tell me. I met him while prowling around the decks, and we became friends instantly, for he, like me, had the soul of a true adventurer. My friend Fujen, I discovered, was my rival, and Orpi's betrothed; I was incensed, as any true lover would be. I toyed with the idea of revealing his presence to Greenbeard, but that would have been dishonourable. I considered challenging Jen—Fujen—to a duel, but that, too, would have been unfair; I could, of course, have killed him in about two seconds, and this stayed my hand.'

'But you won the girl eventually, and lost interest at once.'

'No,' said the Dagger. 'And when I found out the truth about Fujen, I was only too happy to yield. I have never been able to stand in the path of true love. Greenbeard found out too, and would have killed them both, which was a story ending I found unacceptable. I killed Greenbeard and completed my mission, Orpi and Jen took over the ship and released all the slaves, and a lot of blood was spilled, mostly by me. Jen and Orpi are still together—Jen is the pirate we are here to meet—and every year, on Orpi's birthday, Jen comes to Ajaxis, finds a particularly valuable slave and sets her free.'

'And what was this truth you found out about Fujen?'

The Dagger raised a warning hand as bolts were drawn inside the house. The door creaked open, and a gigantic minotaur lumbered out and back in again without a word. Mantric and the Dagger followed him inside. The room was full of broken furniture and was completely uninteresting, except for a trapdoor in the middle of the floor. They walked down through it, and followed the minotaur through a maze towards the sound of stringed instruments playing deeper underground.

Al-Qatras Mansion was centuries old; it had been founded by a wealthy Artaxerxian slave-merchant back in the age when Psomedea's phalanxes ruled the known world, and its triremes shattered the navies of any nation that challenged its dominion over the seas. But there was nothing distinctively Artaxerxian about it any more, apart from a few half-hearted attempts at exotic decoration. The businessmen who now ran Al-Qatras were as diverse as the slaves sold there. And Al-Qatras was where the finest slaves were sold, where true connoisseurs of subjugation gathered to find interesting new people to own. It was not the principal slave-market of Ajaxis; that was in the heart of the city, where citizens gathered to inspect the latest living merchandise from all over the world, and on every weekend you could go there with your friends and prod and poke other human beings to test their suppleness, firmness and strength. There you could find your everyday soldiers and craftsmen, labourers, servants and concubines of every colour, size and shape that civilization knew; there you went shopping for your commonplace dancers and farmers, soldiers, mamluks, zanji and saqalib, mothers and children. But in Al-Qatras you got the very best, taken off slaving ships and caravans long before they reached the market. The slaves in Ajaxis's market were nearly all human; the asurs ran their own slaving trade routes elsewhere, and selling a centaur as a slave had once sparked off a war. But in Al-Qatras, you could find strange creatures captured out of legends; unique monsters that could be yours for a price, grotesque beings you could never buy anywhere else in the world.

All ancient cities had thriving slave markets, of course; even Kol had one, though the Civilian had recently banished slavery and the slave market had to pretend to be a matrimonial agency. The Civilian knew she had no real hope of truly eradicating slavery; slavery had many forms, and many disguises, and would last as long as inequalities of power existed. But modern-day rulers who had to wrestle with things like democracy made it a point to give slaves at least the illusion of some rights, and try to win their support; it was good politics.

Mantric and the Dagger sat down on huge, soft cushions and stared appreciatively at scantily-clad slave-girls carrying large trays of fruits and sweetmeats from one auction room to another. Al-Qatras was huge, well lit and decorated with tremendous enthusiasm and incredibly bad taste; ugly animal figures, vulgar statues and overpowering smells of incense filled the mansion's ornate, gaudy chambers. The auction galleries had several wings, each with inspiring names like Harem Heaven, Boy Toys, Smouldering Soldiers and Little Delights; they were in the smallest hall, where only really big spenders went, a hall called Trouble Time. Jugglers, sword-swallowers and belly-dancers entertained them as they waited; in about an hour, the hall was full. Mantric saw, to his astonishment, that smooth-faced men carrying the insignia of several well-known Koli nobles were among those present. They all looked slightly surprised when they saw Amloki and Mantric, but bowed and exchanged half-smiles, no doubt thinking of the rewards they would receive for telling their masters that the Chief Civilian, too, wanted slaves from Al-Qatras.

The slave auction began, and the Dagger grew impatient; there was no sign of Jen. A two-headed ogre from Ventelot was sold to a plump Artaxerxian. A crocodile-headed gharian from Avranti went for a high price to a famous hunter from Elaken. Strange half-humans came and went; woeful-looking creatures, far from home, dressed up to appear fearsome, their bodies bearing the marks of captivity and torture. Lost amidst unnatural, bland-faced predators, they accepted their new owners without comment, and lowered their heads, and were led away in chains to a corner of the hall, where they stood in a huddle, waiting for the auction to end and their new lives in servitude to begin.

The Silver Dagger looked at Mantric. He'd expected the spellbinder to have created some sort of disturbance by now; he'd even half hoped for it, hoped that his old friend would start trouble which he could help finish, to try and overcome the guilt that enveloped him every time his adventures led him to Al-Qatras. But Mantric seemed to have lost interest; he was not even looking at the slaves as they were led around the hall. Perhaps his mind was already far away, tussling with some obscure paradox, balancing some irrelevant equation. But then there was a raucous whistle at the entrance to the hall, and the Dagger forgot all about Mantric. Jen had arrived. He nudged Mantric and whispered, 'The pirate's here.'

Mantric looked up and around, slightly puzzled; there was no one in the hall who even remotely resembled his idea of a pirate. The Dagger seemed to be looking at a striking young woman in a white gown, who'd just walked in, a big, green, villainous-looking parrot on her shoulder. Not that Mantric blamed Amloki for staring at the newcomer; even to his mostly uninterested eye, she was terribly attractive; she had the friendliest face he'd ever seen, though at present she was trying hard to mould her features into a cold mask. Tall, athletic, graceful, she walked calmly across the room, ignoring the servants bobbing and bowing in front of her, and sat on the edge of a cushion. It was only then that she met Amloki's eye. Her face broke into a wide, happy grin, for an instant; she quickly turned away, clearly trying hard not to laugh.

'Is that Jen?' asked Mantric.

'Yes,' said Amloki, his face a study in innocence.

'She's a woman.'

'Yes.'

'But you said . . .'

'Yes.'

'The stowaway was a boy, you said.'

'I discovered the truth later.'

'Oh.'

Mantric turned to look at Jen with renewed interest. And flinched as he encountered the steely gaze of her parrot, who clearly did not like old men who stared at his mistress.

'And that,' said the Dagger, 'is Pollux.'

There was a sudden hush in the hall as the star exhibit of the auction was brought forward. Three minotaurs, holding thick chains, let in a mountain yeti. She was shaped like a large pashan, but appeared much larger, because she was covered in shaggy white fur as thick as a yak's, fur that was streaked with dirt and blood. There was a collective gasp as she raised her arms, shook her chains and growled thunderously, shaking bits of plaster off lurid friezes on the ceiling. On her fur were drawn strange symbols in black; letters not unlike the Xi'en script but somehow more primitive and powerful, secret marks written in the language of yetis. The majesty of her form, even in captivity, was breathtaking; very few of the people in the hall had ever seen a yeti before, and even they were overcome with awe; there was no such thing as an ordinary yeti, but even among yetis, this was clearly a leader. Her eyes, almost covered by thick, shaggy brows, shone with sorrow and wisdom. The Dagger looked at Jen, who appeared transfixed; this was what she had come for.

'This is wrong,' said Mantric. 'I know your friend intends to set the yeti free, but that's not enough. No one has the right to put a yeti in chains.'

'Calm down,' said the Dagger, hoping Mantric wouldn't.

The chief auctioneer, a prim-faced Elakish nobleman, announced to the hall that the creature that now stood before them was called Telu-Yeti, and was known in the Mountains of Harmony as a death-sister, a healer of unparalleled skills.

'This charming beast will keep you free of all illnesses, break the ice at parties, and make a lovely carpet in the fullness of time. Do I hear any bids?' he said. Several prospective buyers raised their hands, Jen among them, but before they could start clamouring for Telu-Yeti's ownership, Mantric jumped to his feet and dragged the room's attention away from the yeti. He achieved this by the simple process of shooting a large blue fireball at the auctioneer, causing the gentleman to run off yelping, covered in flames.

'Carpet? *Carpet?*' spluttered Mantric. 'That's it! The auction is cancelled. You're free.'

He waved his hand, and the chains binding the slaves turned into silken threads. In two seconds, the hall turned into the scene of what, in the Fragrant Underbelly, would have been called a Level Eight brawl; the ogre and the gharian led the other slaves into battle, ripping throats, slashing bellies and tearing off heads; guards ran in, armed to the teeth, and had their teeth knocked out. The minotaurs didn't help their employers at all; they charged at the slaves, but their utter lack of manoeuvrability resulted in their cannoning through walls, or into the guests they were supposed to protect and one another; in their confusion, the guests of Al-Qatras drew weapons, and in a few moments the madness spread, and plunged the whole mansion into utter mayhem. In the epicentre of the carnage stood Mantric, eerily calm, casting illusion-spells; giant spiders suddenly appeared in the room, weaving shining, hypnotic webs, and strong men cast down their arms and cried. Walls crumbled, and torrents of spellbinder flame lashed through the mansion; monsters sprang out of nightmares and stalked through ruined corridors.

Jen leaned elegantly against a statue of a plump, naked Psomedean goddess and watched the proceedings with a jaded eye. There was a tap on her elbow; she looked down, and winked.

'Hello, Jen. It's wonderful to see you,' said the Silver Dagger.

She picked him up and kissed him.

'For my part, I confess to feeling a slight elevation of the spirit, but nothing so violent as to necessitate serious introspection,' said Pollux.

'It's all right, you stupid bird,' said Amloki. 'I've missed you too.'

Pollux turned about on Jen's shoulder, thrilled. He noticed a Skuan merchant, running through falling rubble, staring at him in horror. 'Squarrawk,' he said unconvincingly.

Jen side-stepped to avoid a shower of crystal shards as one of Mantric's fireballs shattered an ugly chandelier.

'Who's your friend?' she asked.

'Mantric. Spellbinder.'

'Why is he upset?'

'He doesn't like the idea of slavery.'

'So I see.'

A few guards ran by them, screaming, followed by a basilisk illusion.

'We need your help,' said the Dagger.

'Anything for you, and he seems like a charmer as well. I'm in. What do you need?'

'You. Your crew. We're off on the greatest quest mortals have ever undertaken.'

'So we are. Where are we going?'

'We're going to save the world,' said the Dagger.

Jen considered this gravely.

'It's going to be expensive,' she said, as an arrow shuddered into the wall a few inches from her.

'Excuse me,' said the Dagger, and killed two guards who were attempting, in their foolishness, to attack them. 'Don't worry about money,' he continued. 'We've been on the job for a while; we'll be ready to leave in a few days, after a few friends of ours get here. When can you start?'

'Well, I'm going to need a new ship; I've had trouble with undead frigates,' said Jen. 'This year, I wanted to give

Orpi a special birthday present; a ship named after my nickname for her. I've already had the figurehead built. If you buy me a ship to go with it, consider me hired.'

'Done. What do you plan to call this ship?'

'The *Baby Duck*.' Jen looked embarrassed, but only slightly.

'We're going to need to work on the name a little bit,' said the Dagger.

Mantric came rushing towards them, his clothes burnt and torn. Behind him, his monstrous illusions faded, flickered and vanished.

'I think I've made my point,' he said breathlessly. 'I would like to leave now.'

'But you've changed all the minotaur guides into slugs,' the Dagger pointed out.

'Come on, Amloki,' said Jen with a smile. 'We both know the way.'

She surveyed the carnage around them and shook Mantric's hand gravely. 'You will make an excellent pirate,' she said.

The wall at the far end of the hall disappeared in a cloud of rubble and dust, revealing about fifty minotaurs, heads down, ready to charge.

'May I take the liberty of suggesting a rather speedy departure?' inquired Pollux.

'Come, Telu-Yeti!' called Jen. The yeti, who had been hiding rather ineffectively behind a tiny brass vase, shuffled towards them, delicately crushing the skulls of all who lay in her way. For a creature of her bulk and shagginess, she moved at an astonishing pace; within seconds, she had crossed them and charged out of the hall. They raced after her, dodging spears and arrows, until they reached the labyrinth. Mantric sent fireballs flying behind in several directions, and they stopped for a few seconds to watch Al-Qatras burn.

'Mmfm!' said Telu-Yeti.

'I think she speaks for us all,' said Mantric solemnly, and he gathered up his robes and sprinted into the labyrinth's tunnels in an enthusiastic and undignified manner.

16

Maya and Kirin walked into a small cave that Spikes had recently found and evacuated. The cave was still full of domestic smells left behind by a family of bears, its former inhabitants, who were now wandering through Vrihataranya with throbbing behinds and newly-acquired lifelong aversions to pashans. It was midnight, and Vrihataranya was awake to the sound of chirping insects and distant screams as predators rose and went to work. Outside the cave, Spikes and Asvin sat by a crackling fire and told each other unpleasant stories. Inside, Maya and Kirin sat face-to-face on a thick blanket of leaves, watching each other in the light of a hovering fireball, fragments of bright blue safat eggshell in their hands.

'Should we?' asked Kirin.

'You first,' said Maya.

Kirin tossed the shell fragment into his mouth, chewed on it solemnly, grimaced and swallowed. Maya watched breathlessly as his eyes closed and he slowly toppled sideways, his face loosening into a wide, stupid grin. She gulped down her own piece of shell, and the world slowly faded away around her as she sank into blissful slumber.

When Maya awoke, it was still dark outside, though she felt as if she had slept for years. She looked up and sensed, in the faint light from the cave's mouth, Kirin standing over her. She stood up and raised her hand to cast a light spell, but Kirin said, 'Don't. Wait till we're outside the cave.'

'What's wrong?' she whispered.

'Nothing,' he said. 'Just—don't.'

Her curiosity piqued, Maya lit a fireball. Kirin stood in front of her, but something was different; the light from her fireball seemed to pass through him, and he cast no shadow on the cave wall. This in itself was no particular cause for concern, but at Kirin's feet lay Kirin, or at least his body, exactly as he'd lain when he'd fallen over after eating the safat's egg. With one significant difference; his body was naked. The projection, or spirit, or whatever it was, of Kirin that stood in front of her was, fortunately, decently covered. Maya laughed aloud and turned towards Kirin, expecting him to be cringing in embarrassment; instead, he was staring at her feet, very studiously. It took a second for the pieces to assemble themselves in Maya's brain, another one for her to look down, to see her own body stretched out in full glory, and yet another to snuff her fireball out.

As she recovered from the surprise and tried to keep completely unnecessary thoughts about Kirin out of her head, Maya realized that the eggshell had had other effects on her mind as well. She felt light, as if she were floating; she reminded herself that she was no longer attached to her body and its limitations and then she found, to her amazement, that she was rising, that she could fly if she wanted to. And as she adjusted to her new eyes, to the *idea* of new eyes, she looked around again and realized that every living object in the cave now emitted a strange, dark glow, a fingerprint, a heartbeat, sufficient to make her aware of the presence of every tree-root, every lichen, every insect around her. Even the rocks and the earth announced their presence, their shapes and silences drawing maps in her mind. Strange ethereal shapes that had nothing to do with any object in the cave floated at the borders of her vision, and the cave-mouth seemed to pulsate as she looked at it, at wisps of life-force drifting in from the forest outside.

'How long have you been awake?' she asked, watching soundless words leave her mouth and wash over Kirin's face.

'You had your clothes on until you got up. Don't worry. Should we leave?'

'And leave ourselves lying here like this?'

'Spikes and Asvin won't come in, or let anyone else in. We have more important problems to deal with.'

'What are we supposed to do now? Where are the gods?'

'The unwaba said they were sitting around the world, on a circular table, playing their game.'

'But how do we get there? And how do we find Zivran without the other gods seeing us?'

'Getting out of this cave would be a start,' said Kirin. 'Remember, none of this is real in the physical sense; this is a trance we're sharing. I don't think there are any rules; if there were, the unwaba would have told us.'

'How can you be so calm? Aren't you seeing what I am?'

'Probably. But I've done this sort of thing before, with the Gauntlet of Tatsu. Let's move.'

They walked out of the cave into the forest and stood still, swaying a little, as waves of sensation pounded into them and drowned them; millions and millions of life-patterns, lights in the darkness and impossibly clear sounds from far away. Maya reached out for Kirin, and recoiled, horrified: a large, fierce-looking wombat stood where Kirin had been a second ago. She blinked, instinctively conjuring up a fireball, and in its light she saw Kirin, staring at her, stunned.

'Something's wrong,' he said. 'You're changing shape.'

'So were you,' said Maya. 'What now?'

'Imagine you're somewhere in the heavens, somewhere secret, near the gods, and we'll start from there.'

'How is that going to work?' Maya felt fingers of panic tugging at her spine, small, insistent, impossible to ignore. She looked over her shoulder and saw them, little blue jointed worm-like things wriggling all over her back

'I don't know. It's an idea. Do you have any?' Kirin asked, finding it difficult to address a penguin without laughing.

'I can't just imagine a place like that, Kirin. I don't know what the heavens look like. This is insane. We need to wait for the unwaba to wake up again.'

'We've eaten the safat's egg. It has to be now. Just hold on to me, close your eyes, and think of something.'

Kirin held out his hand, but Maya ignored it, and buried her face in his shoulder. 'If this doesn't scare you, I can't imagine what you've been through,' she said. 'I wish I'd been there.'

'So do I. But it's my fault you weren't, so let it go. And I'm as completely out of my depth as you are, but now I'm used to it; the trick is not to let anyone else know what you're feeling. Now don't open your eyes until I tell you to.'

'Are we there yet?' asked Maya after a while.

'No. Are you having divine visions of any sort?'

'No. I just had an interesting idea about illusion spells, but no gods. I'm sorry.'

'Don't be. It was probably a silly idea in the first place,' said Kirin. 'This is ridiculous. We're two adults, standing in the middle of a forest, trying to imagine heavens we've never believed in. You're right. We'll wait for the unwaba to wake up, tell us he knew this was going to happen, talk about how wise he is and tell us other ways to look like idiots.'

Maya let go of Kirin and returned his rueful grin. 'So we're not meeting the gods?'

'Doesn't look like it.'

'This was fun, though. Should I go back into the cave first and change?'

They heard a soft, wet sound and the world vanished into utter darkness.

'Later, then,' said Maya.

And then there was light. Millions of stars lit up above them, burning in colours they could not name. They turned this way and that; trying to make sense of what they were seeing and failing entirely; they were *inside* something, they were some*where*, a place of constant change, of movement faster than thought, an ocean of energy and dreams in which they groped blindly for familiar scraps. There were fleeting instants of comprehension, recognizable shapes and ideas—mountains and palaces and forests and deserts flickered in and out of vision, and rivers of liquid music drifted through the air. With every movement, worlds appeared and disappeared; galaxies turned, oceans swelled and dried, walls of light and smell rose and fell. They stood on what seemed to be a floor of white marble, but it turned into a soft cloud the next instant, and a grassy meadow the next. Kirin and Maya stood in silence, watching this spectacle unfold, and they knew then, as they had never known before, how small they were, how insignificant; they struggled to understand the wonders around them, trap what they saw and felt with words and thoughts, cage their sensations and conquer them, and they failed again.

'Look at me,' said Kirin. 'Shut this out. We'll both lose our minds, if we haven't already.'

'How?'

'Just stop thinking about it. Stop looking. Nothing here exists, and we don't have to understand it. We need to concentrate on what we need to do, or we'll drown.'

'How do you know that?'

'I don't. I'm making it up. You have to pretend with me.'

The heavens cleared. Now they were standing, floating, in emptiness, in silence, drifting specks in a vast, unfathomable void. Far away, they could see the world, its swirling oceans and misty lands, and they gazed in wonder as they watched the gods gathered around it, shining, powerful, massive beings of every imaginable form, and some beyond description. Other worlds could be seen too, barren and empty, sullen masses drifting, as they were, in Zivran's garden.

'What now?' asked Maya.

'Now we wait until brilliant ideas suddenly strike us,' said Kirin. 'Or until someone notices us and hopefully listens to us, or until the trance passes and we either return to our bodies or float around hopefully forever.'

'I see you've considered all our options.'

'I try.'

'I have another option,' said Maya. 'We walk up to Zivran and talk to him. Though he might think we were bugs—if the gods are so big from where we're looking, imagine how huge they'll be when we get nearer. If we can't get Zivran to notice us, we'll find his ear and whisper ideas into his head. That technique seemed to have worked for the unwaba.'

'Do you have any idea how far away they are? It might take us months—years—to reach them. Stay here. Something's bound to happen.'

A discreet cough behind them broke the silence, making them realize that Kirin had been right; something was happening, as predicted. Some*one* had appeared; as they turned and looked up, higher and higher until their necks hurt, they saw a being the size of a mountain, a creature with hundreds of arms and heads; his body a bizarre tapestry of feather, bone, hide, skin, membrane, shell and scale, on which heads rose like warts on a toad's back, some human, some monstrous, several animal-like, with beaks or compound eyes or tusks. And all the heads that they could see were staring at them fiercely. Kirin and Maya goggled back at the newcomer in awe as he loomed over them, wings and arms and pincers folded defensively; and even as their eyes grew slightly accustomed to the madness of his body, they realized he was constantly changing shape as well; heads popped in and out of his body, city-sized patches of skin molted and coalesced. They looked down, their necks hurting, and saw that scores of legs supported his mostly spherical central body, anchoring him to a plane that could not be seen, a road below them paved with stars, that ran through the void towards the world where the gods played and made merry.

'Do you think he can see us?' asked Maya. 'Aren't we too small?'

'Who. You?' said Sambo, the words coming from two adjacent heads in the middle of his chest. 'Where. From?'

One of the voices was a loud roar, the other a shrill squeak; in other circumstances, they would have found this amusing.

'We're from that neighbourhood,' said Kirin, pointing at the world, 'and you must not interrupt, because we're terribly important people on a mission of incredible significance.'

'You. Not. On. List,' said Sambo, this time speaking in four new voices, through bird heads that huddled together in an armpit.

Maya smiled her most charming smile. 'Sambo, right?'

Sambo nodded like a wave. 'I. Am. Nagual.'

'Delighted to meet you,' said Maya. 'For some reason, I'd thought you'd be small and look very worried.'

'I. Large.'

'We need to see Zivran,' said Kirin, blinking, because safat-egg-induced visions had, for a second, made Sambo look like a very large tomato.

Sambo extended a head and examined them closely. 'Wait. Minute,' he said. 'You. Mortals! How. Get. Here? Not. Supposed. Be. Here!'

He extended arms in every direction, hiding them completely, and looked in every direction in space-time for a while. When he was sure no one had noticed them, he turned on them angrily.

'Not. Allowed. Go. Away.'

'That's not good enough,' said Kirin. 'We've come a long way, and we're not going without seeing Zivran. We know what's going on here.'

'Be nice to the chicken,' whispered Maya, wondering why Sambo had turned into a chicken. She closed her eyes and opened them again, and found he hadn't.

'What. Chicken?' thundered Sambo, waving threatening tentacles. 'Be. Gone!'

'Look,' said Kirin, shaking his head and clearing his eyes, 'Mortals have met gods before, right? You know the stories. In each case, the gods' minions tried to stop them. Made nuisances of themselves, just like you're doing now. And you know what happened to them. They died, or looked really stupid. So just help us, and spare yourself the trouble. We like you.'

'Why. Want. Meet. Zivran?'

'We can't tell you. You're just a lowly underthing,' said Kirin. He regretted this impudence immediately, as several of Sambo's heads changed shape and started displaying interesting variations along the general lines of many teeth.

'Lowly underthings being, of course, the only sort of things that people are interested in nowadays,' added Maya, floating forward, surreptitiously pinching Kirin very hard. She would have added more words calculated to soothe and charm, but she became distracted at this point by little fairy lights floating around her head, and giggled.

Sambo considered the puny creatures in front of him and felt a tremor of fear run through his motley body, gently tickling his many spines. They were clearly insane, and he regretted, for the first time, giving his creations the power to carry diseases. If the little bags of dirt bit him, who knew what might happen? And they looked perfectly capable of it, too. It was their glazed eyes that scared him, more than anything else. But his duty, as always, came first.

'No,' he rumbled. 'Be. Gone.'

'Why?' inquired Maya.

'Read. Sign.'

He raised a few arms triumphantly, and they saw, floating behind him, a large, hurriedly painted wooden sign the size of a tower, covered with scribbles and signs in billions of languages, innumerable words that flowed and circled, swarmed and buzzed like bees, until they came together, and the sign read 'No Mortals'.

'We're not mortals,' Kirin pointed out. 'We're substance-induced astral projections. Now bring Zivran to us.'

'Return. Later. Game. Now. Zivran. Busy,' said Sambo, shivering inside, asking himself why he did this work without any form of payment. Unending lists of germs he had crafted by hand were running through his brains.

'There's no point coming back when the world's destroyed and we're dead, is there?' said Maya.

'How. Know? Secret!'

'We know a lot of secrets,' said Maya. 'For example, we know that you were the one who created our world, and Zivran just took all the credit.'

'How. Know?' All Sambo's faces look worried.

'We have friends in high places. We also know that you are Zivran's most loyal servant, and impossible to corrupt.'

'All. True. Thank. You,' said Sambo, slowly bringing two of his least favourite arms into position. He would swat them quickly and forget them, he decided.

'Tell me, Sambo,' said Maya, 'was not Zivran afraid that a being as mighty as you might challenge his master?'

'Bred. For. Obedience,' said Sambo, postponing the squashing for a moment to see if they were going somewhere with this train of thought.

'So you were created to follow orders? But wasn't Zivran afraid that some other god might order you to destroy him?' asked Maya.

'No. God. But. Zivran. Command. Nagual,' said Sambo with pride. His arms began to move together, very slowly.

'That's very interesting,' said Maya. 'Because, you see, *we* are not gods, but substance-induced astral projections. Kirin, when you asked Sambo to bring Zivran to us, did you use your ravian mind-control powers?'

'No,' said Kirin, breaking into a smile.

All Sambo's eyes widened in shock. Mountaineous muscles contracted, and his arms jerked into motion, converging on the intruders' bodies with frightening speed.

'Well, Kirin?' yelled Maya. 'Would you like to try again?'

Stop, said Kirin.

And Sambo froze, two hands mere feet away from their bodies.

'You. Cannot. Control. Nagual. Mind!' he growled.

'Of course not,' said Kirin. *Now put your arms away. You don't want to hurt us.*

'You. Try. Control. Nagual?' roared Sambo, his arms falling limply by his side.

'Wouldn't dream of it,' said Kirin. 'The very idea! Sambo, can you make us another world? A world just like the one we had, which your master is about to destroy? We would like that very much.'

'No,' said Sambo, 'Need. Direct. Zivran. Order.'

No, you don't, said Kirin. *Zivran's orders no longer apply. You answer only to me now.*

'Need. Zivran. Direct. Order,' said Sambo unhappily.

Make us another world, Sambo.

Sambo's faces contorted in pain, and three of his heads exploded. He clutched their stumps and groaned. Kirin and Maya felt their bodies vibrating, and would have run, but Sambo looked up again a moment later and they saw that new heads were already beginning to grow out of the stumps.

'Stop teasing him, Kirin. Sambo, dear, can you steal this world away from the Game and hide it from the gods?' asked Maya.

'No. Need. Zivran. Direct. Order. You. Try. Control. Nagual? Tell. Truth.'

'It amazes and shocks me to think you could even suggest such a thing,' said Kirin. *Bring Zivran to us. Now.*

'Zivran. Glory. Burn. You. Zivran. Too. Powerful. You. Face,' said Sambo smugly.

'All right, then,' said Kirin. *Tell him to conceal his powers when he comes to us—keeping us alive will help him get out of this mess unscathed. And if you won't make us a world, make us a safe place to meet him. And tell him to hurry. We don't have much time.*

Sambo gave up, and nodded, heads swaying in unison.

He spoke a Word, and then there was a hut. Kirin and Maya walked into it, into a small earthen room, empty except for a wooden table and two chairs. They sat. Glasses of mead appeared before them. They drank, and spat; it tasted terrible. They looked at each other, and smiled nervously.

'We should do this more often,' said Maya. 'We're a good team. I can't think of anyone who I'd rather rush in with when facing infinitely powerful beings with absolutely no idea what to do.'

'You were amazing. I thought I was supposed to be the one unmoved by all this,' said Kirin. 'Of course, all we've done so far is outwit the servant, I wonder what we'll do when the master gets here.'

'If you're thinking what I'm thinking,' said Maya, 'you have absolutely no idea.'

And then her face froze and her eyes clouded over, and her hands rose stiffly and placed themselves on the table.

Kirin was naturally surprised by this, and would have commented, but he could not, because he no longer had any control over his spirit-body, and his hands, too, were placed on the table, palms downward; his face mirrored Maya's in its terrified immobility.

Kirin and Maya spoke in unison, their mouths moving jerkily, their eyes unseeing.

'ZIVRAN IS HERE,' they said.

And then they slumped back in their chairs, as their minds returned, and gulped non-air in greedy breaths for seconds, clutching their heaving chests. And their eyes clouded over again, as their forms stiffened; they spoke.

'TRULY HAS IT BEEN SAID AND SUNG THAT THE ALL-KNOWING ONES, THE STAR-BRINGERS, THE TORCH-BEARERS, THE CHILDREN OF S/HE . . . ARE THEMSELVES, IN THEIR INFINITE POWER AND COMPASSION, THE GUARDIANS OF THE VOID AND THE TEMPLARS OF THE HIDDEN FLAME, THE UNKNOWING, GRASPING DARKNESS, AND THE WALLS OF THEIR OWN INFINITE SOUL-CITADELS, FOR I HAVE SEEN THESE INTRUDERS, THESE CHILDREN OF THE SHADOWS, I HAVE WATCHED THEIR FACES IN MY CRYSTALS OF VISION AND HEARD THEIR VOICES WHISPERING IN THE VOID BUT THEIR NAMES ELUDE ME.'

Zivran released their minds again, and after a considerable pause Kirin was able to reply.

'Didn't get that, sorry,' he said, his voice breaking.

'WHAT DO YOU MEAN, YOU DIDN'T GET THAT? YOU DARE MOCK ZIVRAN?'

'No, no, really, that's the last thing I want. Could you say it again? It's just . . . I'm not used to having conversations like this. Did you understand what he said, Maya?'

'Bits of it,' said Maya. 'No wait, I didn't get a word. Just say it all again, please. I'll try harder, I promise.'

They stared unflinchingly at each other and sounded very irritated when they spoke in chorus again.

'Never mind. Time is short, and I was never very good at all that God Talk. I know your faces. What are your names? Are you not the Lord and Lady of the Dark tower?'

'Well, yes and no,' said Kirin, expecting to be shattered into a million pieces. 'It's complicated.'

'You should not be here. How did you come here? Did you eat safat eggshells?'

'Yes.'

'Of course. Very interesting. I have always been fond of those who perform dangerous experiments, preferably on themselves. A shame They did not see you do it. Congratulations, nevertheless. You have done well. I am afraid I cannot allow you to meet My other guests, as your presence here would raise some difficult questions. A breach of etiquette, but you must remember you come uninvited. But you will not return empty-handed. You have amused Me, and must be rewarded. What do you desire?'

'We . . . did mean to ask for something,' said Maya. 'We learned about your Game, and what it would do to our world. We came to ask you to save us. To save our world.'

'What?'

'Or you could make us another one,' said Kirin. His stomach churned. 'If it's not too much trouble, please,' he added hurriedly.

'How did you learn about the Game?'

'That's . . . not important,' said Kirin. 'You asked us what we wanted, we said we wanted another world if you can't save this one. I know it sounds ridiculous; what makes it truly frightening is that you actually have the power to do this. We know about the trick you're playing on the other gods, and we understand you don't want to get caught. But it's not very pleasant for us down there, is it? We're all going to die, and we don't want to. You can play with this world if you want, but we'd be a lot happier if you moved us somewhere else first.'

'You dare meddle in the affairs of the Gods?'

'Well, yes, we do,' said Maya. 'If you're about to tell us no one's ever done this before, don't bother; we know. You thought you'd give people freedom to live their own lives, and you wanted to understand them better; this makes you a far better god than any other. It's an interesting experiment for you, but is that all it is? I think you *care* about us. I think you want us to grow, to learn, to be free. And we can never do that unless we survive your Game.'

Zivran was silent for a long while.

'What you ask for is impossible.'

'Why? Can't you create another world for us, exactly like this one, and move us there? Aren't you powerful enough?'

'Of course I am. It would take Me a week.'

'Well, then. What's stopping you?'

'If I removed the Pieces from the Game, the Players would not be pleased.'

'Then give them something else to play with,' said Kirin.

'It is not as simple as that. But I have promised you something, and Zivran keeps His promises, at least when He remembers He made them, so hear Me, and be gladdened; the next world I create will not be used for a Game. On that world, all life will be truly free. I will observe, and never interfere.'

'That doesn't help *us* very much. If you won't make a new world, stop this Game.'

'I CANNOT.'

'Very well. We'll stop it, then.'

'THAT, I AM AFRAID, IS IMPOSSIBLE. BUT I WILL REMEMBER YOU FONDLY. YOU HAVE TAUGHT ME A VALUABLE LESSON.'

'That's enough,' said Maya. 'If you don't save us, we'll drag you down with us. We're going to let the other gods know you cheated.'

'ARE YOU TRYING TO THREATEN ME?'

'I thought that was fairly obvious. You can kill us now if you want, but there are others who know. If we don't return, they'll stop the war. The gods will know they can't control their pieces, and they'll destroy you.'

'FOOLISH CHILD, IS THIS MY REWARD FOR ALLOWING THE PIECES TO MAKE THEIR OWN CHOICES? I AM A GOD, AND NOTHING YOU CAN DO OR SAY CAN HARM ME. I CAN DESTROY EVERYONE YOU KNOW IN THE BLINK OF AN EYE. I CAN TURN BACK TIME AND PREVENT YOUR VERY EXISTENCE.'

'But you won't,' said Kirin.

'WHY NOT, IF I MAY ASK?'

'Because then you'd have lost to us. Of course you are stronger than we are—you are, as you mentioned, a God. We know why you gods play games with your creations—it's because you like rules—you *need* rules. How can you test infinite abilities unless you place limitations on them? Yes, you could remove us, and no one else would know, but *you* would. And your great experiment, your game would have failed. *You* would have failed. And I suspect you'd rather die.'

'WELL ARGUED. UNFORTUNATELY, IF I GRANT YOUR WISHES, YOU WILL STILL HAVE DEFEATED A GOD. THAT IS NOT ALLOWED. THIS, INCIDENTALLY, IS ONE OF THE RULES THE GODS LOVE MOST.'

'But you're different!' cried Maya. 'You have to be!'

'I AM STILL A GOD. AS YOU KNOW, WE NEED RULES. I BEND SOME, I ADMIT, BUT I CAN*NOT* LOSE TO YOU. IT WOULD SET A REALLY BAD EXAMPLE. NOW, YOU MUST EXCUSE ME. THE WAR HAS REACHED THE DARK TOWER, AND IT SHOULD BE QUITE FASCINATING. YOU SHOULD LEAVE, TOO, AS YOU WILL, NO DOUBT, WISH TO BE INVOLVED. GOODBYE.'

'We're going to let the other gods know what you did. You won't get away with this.'

'NO ONE WILL BELIEVE YOU. GOODBYE.'

'But they might believe *me*,' whispered an old, dry voice, as the unwaba crawled out of Maya's clothes. 'Do not leave just yet, Zivran. It has been so long since we last met, and there is so much to discuss. My revenge, for a start.'

17

The Red Queen stood in her tent, staring into a mirror, watching her face change in the firelight. Her husband Aciram had told her she had to wear Maya's face to the battle, for political reasons; this had left her vaguely unsatisfied. She had worn Maya's face in public for a long time now, and it had begun to bore her. It was a pleasant enough face, but it had not given the Red Queen what she wanted; a voice in her head. A voice of her own. Any voice. Someone to talk to.

She watched her features melt and rearrange themselves into one beautiful face after another, hoping, as always, that one of them would really fit, that one would grow backwards and give her a person to belong to, to be. There was a time, she remembered, when she had been at least three people and had wished, day and night, for silence in her head, unimpeded control over her actions, clarity in her thoughts. Now she had all these, and was deafened by the silence.

Aciram knew she was unhappy, and tried his very best to please her. She hoped he thought he succeeded. But she could not be comforted with her doubtlessly rich life, or her days full of revelry; the hunt and arena did not thrill her, fine wine and food did not sate her, books and potions left her unmoved, and jesters and jugglers hired to amuse her now rested in dungeons or rakshas bellies. Aciram's passionate speeches and enthusiastic lovemaking amused her sometimes, and she responded with encouraging smiles and skilful love-play. Their long walks in Izakar's battlements and gardens soothed her, but she sought neither laughter nor peace. She had not expected to be married to Aciram in the first place; when she'd found out he was not Kirin he'd expected her to be enraged, but she had been pleased, and had rewarded his efforts at deception with a smile that had turned his heart inside out. She already knew all about Kirin, she'd explained later; Aciram was older, stronger and had seen so much more. Besides, she suspected she was a rakshasi now, and who better than Aciram to teach her how to be one? Some of the old training from her former life remained; try as she might, she could not persuade herself to eat human flesh, but the (cooked) feasting, the orgies and the new insights into ancient, wild magic were often diverting. She'd learnt so much and taught them so much about modern, refined magical techniques in return; much of the rakshas army's new scrolls of tactical spellbinding owed their existence to her. Rakshases were not as obsessed with history as mortals. The ravians cared deeply about their past, but each generation sought to rewrite history to fit their visions of the future; the rakshases never thought of collective futures, and even in their rivalries seemed more concerned about destroying their enemies utterly, taking away even their pasts. Perhaps it was because they were shapeshifters; Aciram had explained to her an aspect of rakshas philosophy she found most intriguing. When rakshases changed their skins, they saw themselves as reshaping not their own bodies, but the world around them. She had spent days pondering over this, and had then decided it was a waste of time.

Imokoi had fallen deeply and immediately in love with the Red Queen. And the Red Queen wished, from the bottom of her heart, that she cared for Imokoi in return. Or cared about anything. As things stood, she was in danger of getting bored, and for a being of her powers, boredom was dangerous. As the saying went, those whom the gods wish to see destroyed, they first make bored.

Perhaps it was just as well, she thought, conjuring up a blood-red sabre and waving it slowly in the air, that the first battle with the ravians would start at dawn. She remembered not liking ravians. Perhaps killing them in large numbers would satisfy her.

It would be interesting to find out.

She walked out of her tent into Danh-Gem's Wasteland, out of spell-wrought silence into a turbulent ocean of noise. It was night-time, but the sky was blood-red; the skyscraper rakshases had been at work. Scimitars of lightning thrust downwards from ominous, swirling maroon clouds, growling as they waited for morning, when the ground would turn red as well. Hot, dry winds whistled across Danh-Gem's Wasteland, across parched, cracked land thirsty for blood. Outside Aciram's tent, a ring of pashans stood, ever alert, stout spears looking like toothpicks in their stubby hands. Twelve werewolves, hand-picked by Alpha Laakon himself, prowled around the pashans, their eyes glowing red as they searched the shadows ceaselessly. They were looking for an assassin, a rogue werewolf who had come dangerously close to killing the Dark Lord. They did not know the name of this pack-traitor, this shadowy beast that had stalked the rakshas-lord for weeks, slaying his bodyguards ruthlessly and quietly, and had even entered Izakar one night and fought his way to the Dark Lord's private quarters, leaving a trail of bodies in his wake. The Red Queen, it was widely believed, was the one who had thwarted this assassination attempt; she had thrown this werewolf off the very top of Izakar. The assassin had, miraculously, survived the fall and disappeared. Before leaving, he had continued to behave in an uncivilized fashion; he had overcome a rakshas chieftain in single combat, dragged him out of the Dark Tower and tortured him, demanding to know where Kirin was, promising that he would spare his captive's life in exchange for this information. The rakshas had vanished and escaped to safety, and had then been executed for making up evidence; why would the werewolf have asked where Kirin was, when he had just met and attempted to murder him? The werewolf had not been seen since, but Alpha Laakon had promised the Dark Lord the would-be assassin's head.

The Red Queen found herself hoping the werewolf assassin would attack again tonight; she wanted to fight him, she had sensed he would be a worthy opponent. She had smelled great power within him when she had awoken that fateful night to find him standing by their bed in the Dark Tower, his human-form face stained with blood, his cold, piercing eyes strangely puzzled as he watched Aciram sleep. She had risen with a cry; the werewolf had leaped out of the bedroom window. There had been something very unusual about him, thought the Red Queen; when she had woken up, the first scent that had assailed her mind was not that of a werewolf at all. But she would only know what it was if she saw the assassin again, and until then, she was content to wait. It was something to look forward too, and anticipation might well be, she knew, more exciting than actual discovery. And there was so much to see around her, here, now, in Danh-Gem's Wasteland, where the armies of Imokoi and Asroye would meet again to continue an argument centuries in the making. She found the armies of the Dark Lord most interesting. How readily Aciram's soldiers sacrificed their lives for nothing! How easily they found meaning in the trivial and commonplace! Could they teach her to love causes, to care, to understand what she wanted?

She cast a chameleon spell on herself and slipped quietly past the guards. The werewolves looked up sharply as they sensed her presence, but saw only a faint shimmer in the air as she passed by.

To the west and north, the camp-fires of the asurs studded the earth, thousands of red tongues jeering at the hidden stars, squat, hairy figures cavorting around each fire, their shadows dancing their own dances on the cracked earth. The low braying of battle-conches and the insistent pounding of asur drums blended into one all-devouring song as the asurs celebrated what they were sure would be their last night on this world. Tonight each asur would tell his or her story, and that story would become part of the great song, would be carried to heaven on roads of smoke, so the asur's life would never be forgotten. Tomorrow deliverance would come; they would shed blood, rend flesh and impale themselves gloriously on cold ravian blades to honour their ancestors and their king. Human mercenaries from the Free States and battalions of Koli army deserters who had fled Pataal-e-Gurh and wanted to die guiltless had encamped on the outskirts of the asur camps; unable to sleep, they sat and watched the festivities, faces drawn, minds far away. Pits had been constructed near their camps for the pisacs, who had been kept hungry for days, chained and gagged to keep them from attacking the horses and war-beasts or ravaging the baggage trains; soon they would be released and would feed until they bloated up and exploded, and while they lived their magical auras would protect the asurs beside them. Well behind the asur camps, pashans stood in rows, in a sleeping forest of living stone. There also were encamped several battalions of Artaxerxian cavalry under the command of the Sultan's legitimate heir, the timid prince Dara, newly returned from expeditions to the far west; it was rumoured that the Sultan had sent him to Danh-Gem's Wasteland to die, and ease Omar the Terrible's ascension to the throne of Amurabad. Vanar heavy infantry, chiefly comprising heavily armoured gorilla-vanars from Vanarpuri, made up the final cohort of this army, apart from the rakshases, who had not yet arrived. They would teleport to the battlefield at dawn.

The ravian army had emerged from Vrihataranya, south of the Grey Mountains, and would reach Danh-Gem's Wasteland by daybreak. King Zibeb was clearly a master of strategy; even two days ago, Aciram had not been sure where the ravians would first meet his forces in the open, or when. Which was why Imokoi's forces had been divided; the vanars and the shadowsnatchers kept watch over the passes in the Grey Mountains to hold off any army that might attack from the ravian stronghold of Epsai. The ravians had all but eliminated the rakshas bases in Vrihataranya. The lords of the forest had fled westwards, to Imokoi, along with the vanars. Vanarpuri had fallen, and now lay ruined and empty, home only to corpses, jackals and the ghosts of Bali's dreams;

Angda would have to rebuild the vanar capital if the war ended well for her people, who were now refugees in the west, victims of their leaders' hubris. Battles raged every day in western Vrihataranya as the rakshases and vanars met and repelled ravian attacks from Epsai, but it had been known for a while now that the strongest ravian army was elsewhere. Scouts had reported sightings of ravians in the north, in Ventelot. Bjorkun and his Skuan raiders had taken a force of pashans and jinn to Imokoi's northern borders, to hold the ancient fort of Fusag against any army that sought to invade from the north. Whether a ravian army had already joined battle there, Aciram did not know; there had been no reports from the north for several days now.

The news of the ravian king's march to the Wasteland had gladdened Aciram, who was tired of fighting shadows. The Dark Lord's army had been assembled with frightening speed—a fraction of Imokoi's strength, but more than enough to give the ravians a very warm welcome to the Dark Lord's domain. Even if King Zibeb's army won the first battle and forced Aciram to retreat, the ravians' troubles would have only begun. Alpha Laakon and his werewolves waited in the Dark Tower, along with hordes of asurs, the mightiest of rakshases from Vrihataranya and the songscaper clans, and bands of ogres, kravyads, pazuzus, gargoyles, pashans and miscellaneous monsters. And south of the Dark Tower, north of the Wasteland, Omar the Terrible and his Artaxerxians, cavalry, infantry and sorcerers with jinn, lay in wait along with a company of knights from Ventelot. Omar was the pivot of Imokoi's defences; his army, fast and flexible, could ride south, west, or north to meet the ravian threat wherever it appeared. Aciram's army was the greatest the surface world had seen since the Age of Terror, even without dragons. And these armies were not all that stood between the ravians and Izakar; mile upon mile of rakshas-enchanted land, treacherous swamps and enchanted traps lay in wait for the invaders. And then, of course, there was the Dark Tower itself, dizzying, bristling with steel and sorcery, magnificent, heart-breaking, impregnable.

The Red Queen wandered through Danh-Gem's Wasteland, observing the frenzy around her with detached interest. Sometimes she changed shape and participated in dances and debates; sometimes she teleported from one fireside to another, enjoying the sensation of magical displacement, the feeling in-between disappearance and reappearance, that instant when her entire body was made of wind and fire, when the elements reshaped themselves to create a house for her spirit. As the night wore on, and she poured one mug after another of fiery asur liquor down her throat, she began to enjoy herself; she danced and chanted in the guise of a voluptuous female asur, enjoying the compliments and leers, her head spinning, her heart racing. Several doughty asur warriors made lewd suggestions, mostly based around the thesis 'It's our last chance, love,' and she rejected them all, laughing, and participated enthusiastically in the fights that broke out over her. The night became a blur; shrieks and hoarse yells, laughter and song, gut-burning drinks, thick hookahs that belched puffs of dense green smoke that tickled her throat and the corners of her brain, mushrooms that tasted like sunbursts, sweat and skin and hair and strong breath. Fires winked and danced inside her head; she saw strange visions, flashes of the past, ghosts of voices inside her head. She laughed, cried, danced, lost herself to the asur song. Cheered on by a garrison of danavs, she set a new all-Imokoi for single-night alcohol consumption, broke a lecherous lieutenant's arm, sang several raucous songs, was profusely sick, and collapsed in a tangled, happy, exhausted heap.

'Wake up, Your Majesty!' Rough hands shook her and she sat up with a start. A werewolf captain had woken her. She looked around, her vision clearing slowly; an army of asurs slowly appeared as the blobs of solid colour in her eyes melted away. They were clad in armour, bore an assortment of uncomfortably shiny weapons and were looking at her with a mixture of fear and amusement. Following their example, she looked at herself and flinched; she was wearing Maya's body, clad in a rag that would have barely covered an asur.

'What . . . time?' she asked, the words crawling slowly up her throat.

'Dark Lord Kirin has been looking for you for hours!' said the werewolf. 'Come with me!'

'Kirin . . . back?'

'Please get up, Your Highness. The ravian king approaches, and there are formalities that must be observed before we slaughter his people. As ruler of Imokoi, you must speak to the ravian king before the battle begins officially.'

'Eurgh.'

The werewolf captain threw his head back and howled; an answering howl came from Aciram's tent, and several werewolves emerged, racing towards the Red Queen. But before they could reach her, she disappeared, and materialized inside Aciram's tent, where the Dark Lord waited in his black and silver armour, wearing Kirin's face and looking very dashing.

'Where have you been?' growled Aciram. 'The bloody ravian king is waiting in the middle of the battlefield!'

'You should have gone without me,' said Red.

Aciram laughed. 'Wouldn't have brought you if I didn't need you there. Politics. Formal declaration of war. Trust you to go to a party the night before a battle. I was afraid that damned werewolf had killed you. No time to talk. Now wear something decent quickly.'

The Red Queen raised an arm and snapped her fingers, summoning her finest armour, a tough, light coat of magically reinforced steel that she'd crafted herself and coloured red and gold with Tentatron ink. She looked like a warrior princess who'd walked out of one of the racier legends. Aciram nodded in appreciation.

'No time to lose,' he said. 'We'll teleport to the chariot.'

He kissed her fervently, and they both vanished.

The Dark Lord's armies cheered themselves hoarse as their rulers appeared in their chariot. King Hooba of the asurs, the Dark Lord's charioteer, urged the horses forward. The Red Queen looked back, and her eyes widened as she saw her husband's creatures, assembled and ready for battle—a great wall of living creatures, armed to the teeth, stretching across the horizon, waiting for Aciram's signal, eager to surge forward and butcher anything in their path. Meadows of swords and lances rose in the air, saluting the monarchs as they sped across Danh-Gem's Wasteland towards the ravian army that stood silent and waiting before them. A few inexperienced asurs broke ranks and ran behind them, thinking, not unreasonably, that this would start the battle earlier; they fell dead, with arrows in their backs. The Dark Lord's orders were to be obeyed, whatever the cost.

Red shaded her eyes as she looked at the ravians. Ravian sorcerers had worked on the sky, dispelling the sorcerous clouds of the skyscraper rakshases. The sky above Aciram's army was still dark red and stormy; above the ravians, though, the skies had cleared, and the fierce morning sun shone down brightly on their silvery-white helms and mailshirts, on their lithe bodies and sparkling swords and spears, so that the whole ravian army seemed to glow. Red shook her head to clear the cobwebs from her eyes and looked closer, and with her keen rakshasi eyes she could see the faces of the ravian soldiers: strong, handsome faces, keen, intelligent, determined. There were men and women, fair and dark, old and young, and not a single ugly one as far as she could see.

'They look pretty good, don't they?' she said.

'They'll look even better sliced up,' said Aciram. 'Why the grimace, love?'

'Head hurts,' said the Red Queen. 'How are your asurs going to fight after last night?'

'Don't worry. Asurs fight much better with massive hangovers. Gives them that edge. You missed last night's tactical briefing, so just stay near me at all times. We'll protect each other.'

And having expressed these noble sentiments, the Dark Lord and Red Queen of Izakar rode forward to meet the ravians. And not just ravians, Red realized; while there were several thousand ravians on foot and horse in front of them, there were also humans. Chariots and elephants, swordsmen and cavalry from Avranti, bearing the signs of the Sun Throne, stood in front of the ravians on the left flank, and large numbers of thin, ragged, unarmed humans, no doubt mind-abducted from the Free States or the Vrihataranya tribes, stood in loosely arranged groups ahead of the Avrantics. Asur fodder, thought Red, and almost felt a twinge of real anger.

The centre and right flank of King Zibeb's army, however, were made up of ravians, and even at a distance, Red could see these were *proper* ravians; the kind of ravians who made you believe in the old stories, in tales of valour and sacrifice, nobility and chivalry. Champions and knights, heroes and warriors, shining like diamonds in the sunlight, ready to smite the darkness in front of them once and for all. And none shone brighter than King Zibeb, on a magnificent white charger, and his chief general, Froyan, who rode by his side with the standard of Asroye now raised again to strike terror in the hearts of Imokoi's monsters. As they urged their steeds forward and rode to meet the enemy, the sunlight followed them, illuminating every step their horses took on the scarred earth of Imokoi.

As the ravians drew closer, Red saw that Zibeb was a tall and handsome ravian, simply dressed in white, bearing a single, slender sword and no insignia except a thin circlet on his head that bore the emblem of his ravian clan. He was smiling broadly through perfect, even white teeth. Red hated him on sight.

The ravians halted their steeds and dismounted. Aciram and Red stepped down from the chariot. They walked forward until they stood face-to-face with Zibeb and Froyan. After a few seconds of traditional cold-staring, Aciram cleared his throat. All of Danh-Gem's Wasteland held its breath, waiting for the first word, the first stroke; above them, the gods smiled contentedly. These were the moments that made Games what they were. Would Maya do something impulsive? Would Froyan, who'd done nothing interesting so far, make himself useful? Would Zibeb, who seemed to have no respect for the traditions of wartime conduct, try and kill his most dangerous opponent before the battle began? Would Dark Lord Kirin yield? Would he make some outrageous demand? Would he challenge Zibeb to single combat?

Aciram bowed, and would have greeted his enemy, but it was King Zibeb who spoke first.

'Dark Lord Kirin,' he said, 'would you have the goodness to unhand my wife?'

BOOK SIX

1

The unwaba crawled briskly to the centre of the table, and shot defiant looks at Kirin and Maya. Twin beams of light emanated from their eyes, illuminating the unwaba and casting stark shadows across the small room, black figures that looked gigantic in confined space and filled the walls with heads whose shapes resembled neither Maya's nor Kirin's. The little chameleon shuffled and blinked, unable to directly meet Zivran's unyielding, blank stare. 'Well, Lord Zivran? I see from your silence that you have remembered me, and understood well the grave impact of my words,' he said.

Kirin and Maya looked at each other, seeing nothing but white light. Their brows clouded slowly, faces struggling to portray a confusion they did not feel.

'UNWABA?' said Zivran slowly. 'MY LOST LIZARD? IS IT REALLY YOU?'

'I am a chameleon,' said the unwaba stiffly. 'The oldest and wisest. Not a lizard. There is a difference.'

'UNWABA! BY THE ETERNALLY UNRAVELLING BEARD OF

ALAINMUR, THIS IS A PLEASANT SURPRISE! WHERE HAVE YOU BEEN ALL THESE YEARS? WE THOUGHT YOU WERE DEAD!'

'You did not think I was dead. You banished me and forgot me. There is a difference,' said the unwaba. 'But now I have returned, to demand reparation, payment and absolution, and to ensure you will never forget me again. Lift the veil of playful forgetfulness and look at me with your true eyes, Zivran. You will know me again, and what I want.'

Kirin and Maya clutched their throbbing heads and waited.

'AH,' said Zivran eventually. 'SO YOU WERE THE FLY IN MY OINTMENT, THE CHIPPED KEYSTONE, THE LEAFY ANKLE. THIS EXPLAINS A LOT.'

'I am not a fly. Or a construction error. Or a body part, with or without attached vegetation. What I am is—'

'THE UNWABA. I HAVE DECIDED TO REMEMBER. THEN ALL THIS IS YOUR DOING. YOU HAVE BROUGHT THESE DELUDED CHILDREN HERE, AND THUS LED THEM TO THEIR DOOM. YOUR PETULANCE IS UNDERSTANDABLE, MY FRIEND, BUT OCCURS AT AN UNFORTUNATE TIME.'

'It is an unfortunate time for all those who had placed their trust in you, Zivran. The creatures of the dying world, for example, among whose numbers I am proud to count myself.'

'THE DEATH OF THIS WORLD WILL GRIEVE ME MOST OF ALL, FOR NO ONE LOVES THIS WORLD AS MUCH AS I. IT IS A PART OF ME. YOU MUST UNDERSTAND THIS. I AM THIS WORLD'S CREATOR AND PRESERVER, AND I WILL DO ANYTHING I CAN TO ENSURE IT CONTINUES TO EXIST. WHY, THEN, DO YOU TREAT ME AS AN ENEMY?'

'Your words would be convincing, my lord, were I not omniscient. However, I am. And thus I am aware that matters have already progressed to a stage where saving this world is impossible. Even if I had not been fully aware of this as a result of my omniscience, the armies of the undead and the monstrous beings of rock and slime and shadow that lurk under the earth would have led me to suspect that you were being insincere when you spoke of the possibility of preserving it.'

'YOU SPEAK IN CIRCLES. YOU SUGGEST THAT I AM LYING? I, ZIVRAN?'

'Yes. This is because I know you are. Had I not known, I would have suspected that you had now convinced yourself that it would be enough to observe, to understand your errors as they are exposed and thus create a better world on your next attempt. And I would have been right. Speculation on this matter is rendered pointless by the fact that I am, as I might have mentioned before, omniscient, and am always right.'

'ENOUGH. I DID NOT WANT TO EMBARRASS YOU IN FRONT OF YOUR FOLLOWERS, BUT THIS IS TOO MUCH. YOU KNOW AS WELL AS I DO, UNWABA, THAT BEING A GOD—IF A LOWLY CREATURE SUCH AS YOU CAN BE CALLED A GOD—DOES NOT MEAN TRUE OMNISCIENCE. YOUR FOLLOWERS DO NOT KNOW OF S/HE . . .'S EDICTS, AND BLINDLY SWALLOW YOUR LIES. OMNISCIENT? LET ME REFRESH YOUR MEMORY. LONG BEFORE THESE WORLDS WERE MADE, WE GODS CHOSE TO SEPARATE, TO FORM SELVES, IDENTITIES, EGOS, IMPERFECTIONS—AND TO DISTINGUISH OURSELVES FROM THE INFINITE ONE, WE CHOSE TO FORGET. LONG BEFORE YOU WERE BORN, WE DECIDED THAT BEING INDIVIDUAL MEANT MORE TO US THAN KNOWING EVERYTHING—HOW COULD IT NOT, ONCE WE HAD TASTED THE DELICIOUS ELIXIRS OF DOUBT AND CHOICE AND CONFLICT AND BANISHED THE ENDLESS TEDIUM OF INFINITE CERTAINTY? HAS

YOUR TIME IN THE MORTAL REALM ADDLED YOUR MIND? HOW DARE YOU COME TO ME AND CLAIM TO BE TRULY ALL-KNOWING?'

'Very well. I will admit, being a god, that I might have forgotten that there were some things I do not know. Or perhaps I am in denial. It is irrelevant at this point. You rage, Zivran, but even in your rage you strike close to the truth. The mortal realm did change me. In the heavens, I had infinite physical power and a limited mind; down on your earth, however, along with this frail body, I found that my mind had expanded to a point that approached omniscience, albeit in a rather eccentric fashion. I was not lying when I confronted you; your reaction confirms that. But we digress, as gods tend to. Difficult decisions must now be made.'

'LIMITED PHYSICAL POWERS GAVE YOU INFINITE WISDOM BY LIMITING YOUR ABILITY TO FORGET? ARE YOU SURE? THIS IS VERY INTERESTING.'

'A shame, then, that we do not have time to discuss it. Stop trying to mislead me, Zivran; I have demands to make.'

'MAKE THEM.'

'I have always admired your many skills as a creator, and have realized that the errors you have never failed to introduce in your creations over the eons have been a part of your artistic and architectural process; a result of your inquisitive mind. You have often chosen to forget essential details, to see the effect of the flaws you introduce, to study them better, to make yourself work harder. I have spent years wondering whether, all those years ago, you deliberately slowed me down and made mankind mortal, just to see what happened. Whether you kept me among your creations for a reason, to let me watch over them; whether you knew all along that I would be here, now, forcing your hand, helping you save a world you intended to save all along. You are a god of a million faces, and mysterious beyond even divine comprehension. Is this Game just a part of some other scheme, some greater Plan? Are your friends, the gods who know the secret of the Game, helping you or are you letting them think they are? You are not the woolly-headed, eccentric god you pretend to be. Or are you?'

Eyes glittered like waking stars on Maya's face and Kirin's as Zivran smiled.

'I SEE NO REASON TO TELL YOU,' he said. 'MAKE YOUR DEMANDS.'

'You interrupted me in the process of making them; I will now continue. As I said, Zivran, I know this world is just one of many for you, a milestone on your road to a flawless world, or a flawless self, or whatever it is that you truly desire. Unfortunately, this world's denizens have only one world, and even a perfect future world is of no use to them. I do not know whether you care for your creations, and I never will. But you have wronged them, and you must pay. Make your children another world, and save them, for if the world must be destroyed, I will have it destroyed by the gods, and you with it.'

'DO NOT THREATEN ME, UNWABA. IT IS IMPUDENT AND UNWISE, AND I HAVE WARNED YOU BEFORE ABOUT THIS. I COULD DESTROY YOU MERELY BY WISHING IT.'

'But we both know you will not. A god's death cannot be hidden, not here, and your treachery will be revealed for all to see. Besides, we both know this will be an even more interesting experiment. Make them a new world, Zivran. Please.'

'AND YOU THINK THE OTHER GODS WILL NOT NOTICE IF EVERY LIVING CREATURE ON THIS WORLD DISAPPEARS?'

'You could explain it somehow. Leave the Players

something to play with. Keep the undead on this world. Their lives are over, and they can be broken and remade at will. The Game could continue for ever, with undying warriors perfectly subservient to the gods, ever willing to fight more battles, to try and capture again the most exhilarating moments of their lost lives. The Players will not care; they will have the entertainment they seek, an endless battle where the pieces can be rearranged in numbers, allegiances and even bodily structure as the Players please. And you will have a new secret world teeming with life and possibilities.'

'THAT IS, I MUST ADMIT, A VERY INTERESTING IDEA. AND WHAT WOULD I DO WITH THIS NEW SECRET WORLD?'

'You could hide it somewhere, or leave it in the hands of . . . someone you trust to take care of it.'

'AH. AS I SUSPECTED. YOU WANT IT FOR YOURSELF.'

'Yes and no. After all these years of exile, I think I deserve a little world of my own. But I do not seek to own this world; merely to live on it as a humble chameleon. The world would continue to be yours, of course.'

'BUT YOU WOULD HAVE YOUR REWARD, YOUR REVENGE AND YOUR VICTORY. YOU WOULD HAVE OUTWITTED ME. I CANNOT ALLOW THAT.'

'But I am a god, Zivran. Gods may temporarily defeat other gods; it is not impolite. Besides, we could both choose to believe that I was acting under instructions so secret that I did not know them myself, and you had planned this adventure all along.'

'YES, YOU ARE A GOD, IN THE HEAVENS, DECEIVING ANOTHER, AND ALL IS AS IT SHOULD BE. I SEE. ALL MOST INGENIOUS. IF ONLY YOU HAD SUGGESTED ALL THIS BEFORE THE GAME BEGAN. NOW, ALAS, IT IS TOO LATE. THE PLAYERS WILL WANT TO FINISH

THIS GAME. I HAVE ALREADY SPENT MORE TIME HERE WITH YOU THAN I SHOULD HAVE. I CANNOT HELP YOU.'

'Why not?'

'FOR A START, I MUST BE AT THE TABLE AT ALL TIMES. HOW CAN I BUILD A NEW WORLD, THEN?'

'I have already arranged for the gods to be distracted. A ship sails to meet you at the edge of the world, bearing wondrous gifts; its journey will be one worthy of song.'

'I SEE. AND WILL THE GODS BE DISTRACTED ENOUGH TO NOT NOTICE THAT EVERY LIVING CREATURE ON THIS WORLD HAS DISAPPEARED?'

'I already have a plan that will take care of that problem. Would you like to hear it?'

Zivran smiled, Maya's lips and Kirin's curling upwards, slightly twisted. 'OF COURSE I WOULD.'

The unwaba coughed and looked indignant. 'Well, that is extraordinary,' he said.

'WHAT?'

'I seem to have forgotten.'

The shadows in the room lengthened, filling the walls with starless blackness.

'YOU HAVE FORGOTTEN? HOW?' Zivran's voice was mocking.

'I do not know,' said the unwaba in genuine astonishment. 'How could I forget?'

'LET ME TELL YOU HOW, MY FRIEND. YOU ARE A GOD, IN THE HEAVENS, RETURNED FROM EXILE, AND NO LONGER SUBJECT TO THE PHYSICAL LIMITATIONS THAT AFFLICTED YOU DURING YOUR BANISHMENT. OR, IT APPEARS, THE OMNISCIENCE YOU CLAIM ACCOMPANIED THOSE VERY SAME LIMITATIONS. THIS MEANS, UNWABA, THAT YOU ARE READY TO MAKE A CHOICE.

'The love You felt for the world You lived in, the pain You must have endured over the eons, Your mad schemes of revenge . . . You can forget them all, if You so desire, and return to Your rightful place in the heavens as a true God by My side. You may even become a Player in the Game if that is Your will. Or, You may choose to expose My little trick to the Players, thus bringing about the destruction of the Game World and everyone on it, and My death, which will no doubt give You some measure of satisfaction.'

The unwaba stared at the shadow-walls, blinking and shivering.

'You would make me a true god again? Bring me back into the pantheon?'

'It is within My power to do so.'

'But I would be abandoning these children and their world.'

Pulled by invisible strings, Kirin and Maya shrugged.

'I had grown very fond of them,' quavered the unwaba.

'You will not remember them.'

'But how can you just let them all die, Zivran? Why can you not do as they ask, and let them live?' The unwaba's voice had changed. He sounded young and scared.

'I will do what I will do, and that is for Me to know. Have You chosen?'

'I have.'

'What is Your answer?'

'I wish to be a god, a good god, and join in the Game.'

'And this world You wished to save?'

'I will forget it.'

'Yes. I thought You would. Would You like Me to turn these two into stars as a reward for their courage,

AND FOR THE INTERESTING IDEAS THEY HAVE ALREADY GIVEN ME FOR MY NEXT WORLD? I WOULD OFFER CONSTELLATIONS, BUT THE PLAYERS WOULD NOTICE.'

'Do they have to die?'

'IT IS BUT A MATTER OF TIME.'

'Then as a last request from a former servant, Zivran, let them live. Let them return to the world and spend their last troubled days there.'

'ARE YOU SURE YOU WOULD NOT PREFER ME TO TURN THEM INTO SOMETHING SYMBOLIC? A TREE? WE COULD ALWAYS USE A NEW KIND OF TREE. OR A GIANT ROCK IN SOME OCEAN.'

'Let them be. Let them live. And let them remember the unwaba that was, that betrayed them before the end. And let them not trust in gods again.'

'I DO NOT THINK THERE IS MUCH DANGER OF THAT HAPPENING. VERY WELL. THEY MAY LIVE.'

'They will think all this was just a trick I played on them to bring me to you.'

'AND WHETHER THEY WILL BE RIGHT IS SOMETHING I NEED NOT KNOW, AND YOU WILL SOON NOT REMEMBER.'

'They will try and stop the Game.'

'LET THEM TRY. NO ONE WILL BELIEVE THEIR ACCOUNTS OF WHAT THEY HAVE SEEN AND HEARD HERE. WHEN THEY ATE THE EGGS OF THE SAFAT, THEY LOST THEIR MINDS.'

The lights died in Kirin's and Maya's eyes, and the room began to dissolve around them. The unwaba looked at them with what might have been an expression of infinite regret. It is difficult to read the face of a chameleon.

2

From the war journals of Eridon the ravian

—I write this in the middle of Danh-Gem's Wasteland, a stinking, foul place I should never have had to set foot on. King Zibeb renamed it the Fields of Hope Renewed after today's victory; there was an interminable council meeting where all our beloved heroes got to brag about how many rakshases they had gutted. I had my Young-Ravian-Hero-Just-*Thrilled*-To-Be-A-Part-Of-This face on, so they had no idea how much trouble I went through to conceal my disdain as I looked at their faces, so grave, so noble, so terribly annoying, and wondered if I could pass the time by tearing my head off and trying to balance it on my fingertips.

—I should really destroy this journal; if they find it, they will execute me on the spot. But I can't help myself; I do need someone to talk to since Agegi died, and I cannot trust anyone here.

—I am exhausted; I suppose battles tend to have that effect on those participating in them. Even though I spent most of my time on the field making sure I looked like a hero and then stepping back, usually to let Satorin or some other lout do the actual work, I feel more than a little fatigued. A warrior's life is so tiresome. The sweating, the persistent bodily odours, the endless shouting and jumping. I was simply not born for this.

—Or perhaps I was. Nenses the Seer told me my stars show I will rise to be a great hero, that I will be among those who topple the Dark Tower. Of course, what Lady Nenses really wants to See is more of me; she is just looking for a way to make Zibeb jealous. I don't blame her. We all expected him to marry her eventually, and his wedding to the human shocked everyone, or at least Nenses and me. Or is that Nenses and I? Us.

—My men are singing songs of hope and victory outside. For ravians, they are remarkably stupid. I suppose they will be very brave and resolute when asked to participate in the next stage of this war.

—I have to admit that I was very impressed by the sight of all Zibeb's champions united on the battlefield. This was, after all, my first real battle; teasing rakshases in the woods for Satorin to kill does not really count. Satorin did me great honour today, apparently: He said we could 'draw our swords together' for the next battle. I'm not entirely sure what that involves.

—I like Dark Lord Kirin. He kept Zibeb waiting for a really long time before turning up. The leaders of House Aegos claim he is half ravian, the son of Danh-Gem and Isara, which sounds like an outrageous lie. Or perhaps this Dark Lord slew Narak's son and assumed his form; whatever the truth is, everything about his manner and bearing screamed rakshas today. House Aegos will, of course, say anything to make Esmi look bad. Zibeb will regret this in time; his army is weakened considerably by the defection of the Esmi and Hanash leaders.

—Not that we are short of heroes. I am, I hear, one of them, and will have to work my way up a tediously long list. It is a good thing, however, that I am beginning my political career in a time of war, as many future opponents will be disposed of even without my direct intervention.

—A fairly large number of heroes, of course, are already accounted for. Myrdak, Peori and Behrim are dead, and so are Zibeb's Riders, slain by dragons over Kol. It is fitting that they met so dramatic an end; all their lives, the air around them had been distressingly full of exclamation marks. The archer Ikoche of Hanash, Peori's friend, had decided not to join her clan in exile, but must have changed her mind or been devoured by rakshases at some point, because she is no longer with us.

—I might as well make a list of the champions who rank higher than me at this point. If this journal is found and I lose my swollen head for treason, they might as well know what I, Eridon the Brave, Dashing Young Hope of New Asroye, thought of them. These, then, are New Asroye's most important names. I hope to scratch them out, one by one.

1. King Zibeb. House Aegos. Very, very clever. Completely ruthless. I do not know how he can be overthrown, and it will take me years, but there is no need to hurry. Perhaps the Dark Lord will do the honours for me.

2. Nenses the Seer. House Aegos. They say she outshines even Lady Isara of old, but then they also say, now, that Isara destroyed the old Dark Tower out of guilt. Be that as it may, Nenses is our most powerful mage. Watching her remove the red rakshas mist and bring in a new dawn was quite exciting. She has her eye on me already, and is lonely. This is an opportunity. She is still fiercely loyal to Zibeb, though. Let us see what can be done about that.

3. Satorin. House Akked, my own beloved house. Satorin the Invincible. Satorin the Lone Wolf. Satorin promised my father he would guard me all his life. He will make a useful ally, because he is easily the most skilled warrior we have. Some say he is better than Myrdak ever was and did not achieve that much prominence because he never sought power. More fool him, then. Still, he is discreet, reliable, and likes travelling too much to want a seat of power. And he loves me as the son he never had, the son he would have had if he had not spent so much of his time 'training' strong young ravian men in the arts of war.

4. Dalmaan, House Nergol, mage-priest of the Black Star, trickster, politician, strategist, rogue. Deadly on the battlefield and in the war councils. Has a sense of humour, and is not afraid to use it. If we lose this war, Dalmaan will find a way to escape, to rebuild the ravian nation and ensure its eventual victory. If I am ever to seize power, I will have to go through him; a sobering thought. I cannot risk his displeasure now, and he will suspect me if I let even a tiny part of my

ambition show. Dangerous. I am sure he will make a bid for power after this war. Perhaps I should help him.

—How fortunate we are to be long-lived! We can change allegiances whenever we want.

—The fact that I am much more handsome than Dalmaan does console me slightly.

5. Orro 'Earthshaker'. House Nergol. Dalmaan's cousin. They have nothing whatsoever in common. Orro is widely seen as Myrdak's successor as Zibeb's greatest champion on the field. He is fifth on my list, though, because he has no brain. This helps him tremendously on the battlefield, but renders him remarkably easy to manipulate outside it. Carries an enchanted warhammer that weighs more than I do. Uses it to shake the earth, and I wonder whether that has anything to do with his nickname. He is gruff and reticent in the beginning, but on closer acquaintance one might discover that he is also uncouth, violent and unhygienic. He is sometimes useful, though: I once teased a rakshas when Orro was nearby, and watched the resulting brawl from the relative safety of a tree. The rakshas was named Akab and was quite famous, as rakshases go. I was hoping he and Orro would eliminate each other and I could gain some fame out of the affair, but Orro rather pig-headedly refused to die even when the rakshas had torn half his face off. Instead, he reached inside Akab's chest, pulled out his heart and ate it. A charming sight. Satorin is the only one among us who has any chance of overcoming him in a fight. I have tried to put this theory to the test a few times, but Satorin has always stayed out of Orro's way.

—These five are the only relevant obstacles between me and the throne of New Asroye. There are others on the list, but mostly because it would be discourteous to exclude them.

6. Tekdash the healer. House Aegos. Coarse, jovial axeman, always ready with a quick, unfunny quip guaranteed to raise morale, and a quick, utterly humourless double-handed axe-swing guaranteed to lower enemy morale. Claims to save as many as he slays, which does not make much sense. There is much I could learn from him—he knows the herbs and power-stones of this land better than any other. He seems to be a genuinely pleasant fellow, but I will not hold that against him. If he survives this war, he may govern a province or two under my command.

7. Lord Degin. House Hanash. Sailor, swordsman and statesman, who chose to fight under the Aegos banner to avenge the death of his daughter, Peori. Trusted adviser to the king. He thinks I have a bright future, and has told me several times that his daughter had said she was fond of me. I am aware of this; Peori was *very* fond of me at least thrice a week during our first year at the Academy, before Myrdak came to teach us swordplay and distracted her.

8. Ashnen the Wise. House Akked. Veteran of many ages and countless wars, was among those who built the original Asroye and fought in all its wars. Universally respected and loved, and protected on the battlefield by Tekdash or Dalmaan. Loves me as a son or grandson. It is amazing that he is still alive; I give him two or three more battles at most. He drools in his sleep and breaks wind constantly.

9. General Froyan. House Akked. Why is King Zibeb's right hand so low on the list? Because he is stodgy and inconsequential, and owes his position to the fact that he

threatens no one. I see no reason to remove him from his post; he is an excellent administrator and has a very attractive daughter.

—I cannot be bothered to add more names to the list. I hope to have crossed out at least three names here by the time the Dark Tower falls.

—I suppose I should provide some form of record of today's battle for posterity's sake. King Zibeb said our victory marked the dawn of a New Age for Obiyalis. He also said this when he entered the portal, when he married the human Maya and when he captured the Skyriders. No doubt he will say it again when the Dark Tower falls.

—Speaking of Maya, she looked most fetching today in red armour. We were all looking at Zibeb with suitably sympathetic expressions when she appeared, and I am sure I was not the only one present who had to suppress a strong urge to guffaw. If I had had the misfortune to have 'fallen in love' with a woman who not only ran away an hour after our wedding but then consorted with my deadliest enemy, I would have encouraged my armies to capture her and then killed her in interesting ways. But King Zibeb, it seems, is prepared to live with Obiyalis with all its imperfections and seemed to have extended the same philosophy to his troubled bride. Queen Maya has officially been placed under some dark enchantment that makes her forget who she is.

—Looking back, I find I have not written about the royal wedding; I had not started this journal then, of course. I should note, however, that I was one of the last people to see our new queen before she escaped from Asroye, leaving the bodies of blameless soldiers and the poor dear king's broken heart behind her.

—I still do not know the story of their courtship; no one in New Asroye discusses it. From what little I know, it seems that the noble Myrdak had persuaded Lady Maya to come with him to Asroye, probably using a fine mixture of deception and violence, and had left her there before starting out on what would, luckily for all of us, be his final journey. Be that as it may, I had arrived in New Asroye on the day of the wedding itself, and had spent most of the day trying to buy dress robes of suitable magnificence; I had nothing to wear to a royal wedding, and neither did most of New Asroye's newly arrived nobles—no one had expected this wedding, of course, and it is safe to say that the happiest people in the city at the time were the tailors.

—The bride was demure and silent all through the ceremony, a fact that was appreciated by all present. I had heard that human women were vulgar and odorous; on meeting the Lady Maya I realized that was true, and inexplicably addictive. I myself have 'gone native' several times since then, taking care to leave no evidence.

—The grandeur of the occasion had overcome Maya slightly, I remember thinking; her face was gaunt and pale, and her eyes slightly clouded over. She swayed slightly as she stood at the altar. Perhaps the priests had placed some calming enchantments on her to ensure she did not embarrass the king in any way during the ceremony. Immediately after the exchange of vows and rings and the sealing of the marriage, she had asked to be excused; the wine, she said, was stronger than what she was accustomed to and her human body had reacted to it in unfortunate ways. I suspected immediately that something was afoot.

—Truth be told, I had no idea anything was afoot, because I was busy gnashing my teeth in appreciation at Zibeb's low cunning. Not only had he freed himself from the ordeal of waking up next to Nenses, but now humans, and specifically magicians, would no longer have any reason to oppose ravian rule. Not that they could have *prevented* it had they expressed violent opposition, but a lot of time and lives would be saved this way, which Zibeb seemed to see as a good thing.

—I realized in a while that my sense of general disquiet had been supplemented by a feeling of physical discomfort—a little nausea is common among those who are not used to portal travel—so I excused myself as well. On the way to the privy, I began to feel a sense of nearby danger that had nothing to do with my churning innards, so I walked faster, and as I opened the door to the central privy I saw a most interesting scenario. The two nurses who had been assigned to help Queen Maya in all matters feminine were sprawled out on the stone floor, their necks broken, their faces severely burned. There was a horrible stench of singed flesh and hair in the room. And the queen was nowhere to be seen.

—Sensing an escape attempt, and roundly delighted at this turn of events, I raced out of the privy, to see the queen perched in a most undignified manner on a windowsill at the far end of the corridor. Our eyes met, and she threw me an enraged, hurt, bewildered look I found most thrilling. She was probably trying to come up with some sort of foolish plan to injure me, but I stopped her with a wink and a finger to the lips, and pointed out a nearby door that would give her access to the stables. She was charmingly confused by this, and I took the opportunity to inform her that the price for my assistance would be a little queenly affection. She responded with fiery passion. In the form of a large and inconvenient ball of fire that narrowly missed me, and an air-based explosive spell that did not. When I recovered, I learned that she had killed at least three royal guards on her way out.

—I tried to catch her eye today; I was right in front on the right flank, and I think she saw me, but she didn't seem to recognize me. If Zibeb manages to win her back, things should be interesting. She didn't seem very responsive to him today, it must be said. When Zibeb asked Kirin to return his wife, the Dark Couple looked very disconcerted, but chose to deprive us of further entertainment by teleporting—a power that Maya seems to have acquired recently, and one that would have helped her considerably in New Asroye—and promptly beginning the battle.

—There were no dragons. I wonder why that is. Has Kol bought them? It is not that I particularly wanted to meet them on the battlefield, but this means that all those tedious weeks we spent devising psychic harpoons have gone to waste. Perhaps they await us at the Dark Tower, because Kirin clearly did not send his elite troops into battle today. But a force as mobile and effective as a dragon army should not be left idle at any stage. If the dragons do not turn up to fight us, however, our relief will greatly exceed our disappointment at not knowing why.

—King Zibeb had instructed us, in many interminable councils held in New Asroye and Vrihataranya, that it was essential that we conceal our tactics from the Dark Lord as long as possible. This left me somewhat puzzled, as I fail to see the point of developing better ways of fighting wars if we do not use them in wars. And Orro Earthshaker, of all people, voiced this concern. We had two hundred years' advantage over the rakshases when it came to fighting experience, Zibeb said, and he wanted to make sure we used our more advanced manouevres at times when we were sure their impact would be deadliest, so that the rakshases would not have any time to prepare counter-tactics. Fair enough. They were bound to know that we had at least one Ravian Star with us that could destroy the Dark Tower; what they could not imagine was that we had *seven*. Orro was in favour of using at least one Ravian Star at our first encounter, but the king and Froyan rejected his proposal, possibly on the grounds that it was Orro's idea, and Orro, lacking a brain, was in no position to have ideas.

—Zibeb's tactical brilliance did not stop there. He was actually open to the possibility that the rakshases might have spent a few minutes thinking up new battle plans over the last two centuries. The first encounter, he said, was our best chance to assess the extent of Kirin's tactical abilities, and that was why we had acquired the churls along the way, for the warriors of Imokoi to display their skills on. And here I was thinking they were just there to hang things on. General Froyan added that the first army we met would mostly consist of asurs and other dispensable fighters, and would be used, in turn, by the Dark Lord to assess our battle strategies. This was why we had fought the rakshases of Vrihataranya the old-fashioned way, and would not help our humans while they were butchered in Imokoi. Which meant that both sides were bringing large numbers of warriors to sacrifice in the hope of learning tactics they knew would not be revealed. Perhaps this would make sense if I were drunk.

—The battle began predictably enough. The asurs charged enthusiastically, and we sent in the churls to meet them. A rather ineffective move, because giant rakshases appeared out of nowhere between the churls and the asurs and proceeded to wreak havoc. I saw an elephant fly today. This world is quite delightful at times. We learned a lot about the enemy's battle plans; they plan to slaughter us.

—After this exchange of pleasantries, it was time for the real battle. I tried to stay as uninvolved as possible, but the rakshases appearing on the flanks, striking hard and then vanishing, seemed enthusiastic that I participate in the festivities, and I felt it would be rude to disappoint them. They were our hosts, in a manner of speaking. Meanwhile, our peerless tacticians had observed that the asurs, instead of charging us blindly in a massive tidal wave of bodies, split themselves up into small groups, moving in random patterns across the battlefield, attacking from several directions at once. Each group was made up of a mixture of danavs, both inexperienced *hnoobs* and veteran *leeths*, as well as a few lesser rakshases to provide magical support and prevent us from taking over their minds. How unsporting.

—Having spent some time admiring the enemy's tactics, we decided it was time to put an end to this nonsense. I sent a division of cavalry, horses held firmly in mind-riding control, charging into the asur companies, scattering them, giving our mages more chances to control asur minds. But the asurs had taken lessons in the art of attacking us; they never attacked one at a time, never gave us a chance to read the patterns in their movements and plan a series of sword-strokes that would parry their blows before they even made them. I saw this pattern everywhere; six or more asurs would leap at a ravian at the same time, each dragging a weapon or limb down as he fell dead, creating opportunities for at least one asur to land a telling blow. Some asurs even smeared themselves with a strange green poison-paste that stuck fast to ravian skin, slowing their victims down so that some other monster could attack unhindered. And they have at least one brilliant general—amidst all the chaos they managed to execute a nice pincer movement. We were surrounded within minutes, though there were at least twenty thousand of us. Despite all this, they were still asurs, of course, and no match for us. As the day wore on, we filled Danh-Gem's Wasteland with bodies, and then we killed some more, and made tombstones for them by breaking pashans. I use the term 'we' loosely; my main function was to provide moral support and stand attractively with one foot on the largest corpse available afterwards.

—As the battle wore on, the Dark Lord's stronger minions came to the fore, and the fighting grew more intense and less showy. After we had sent off two waves of asurs, a company of heavily armed gorilla-men and man-sized lesser rakshas attacked the mounted Nergol battalion on the left, forcing them inwards, and a band of grotesque creatures I could not identify met King Zibeb's swordsmen in the centre. There were goat-headed creatures, I learned later, called goborchends, who bore strange clubs called k'opalas, clubs that had mouths of their own, with sharp teeth and harsh screeching voices. Phiams, demonic beasts that cast spells that choke and strangle their victims, were advancing steadily on the right, and I was so engrossed in organizing their defeat that I was almost left out of the manouevres that eventually won the battle.

—When Zibeb saw that several massive rakshases, possibly members of Kirin's personal guard, had joined the battle and a vast number of men on horseback, possibly Artaxerxian, were getting into position for what might have been a decisive charge into the ravian centre, he prudently decided to call for the formation of a Spirit Trench. About an hour later than he should have, but no doubt he was distracted by the sight of his lovely bride slaughtering his men in a most efficient manner.

—As the steeds of the Artaxerxians began their charge, several ravian nobles, such as myself, began the construction of the Spirit Trench. It is difficult to describe the moves that create it; it is somewhat similar to the state we go into for Trance-duels, though there is a crucial difference. Unlike in Trance-duels, we remain on this plane, but our minds are somehow connected, and this increases manifold the effects of a spell cast by any of us.

Zibeb waited until the Artaxerxian horses were committed to the charge, and then we united our minds. Orro, eyes glowing white with power, began shaking uncontrollably as we focussed our destructive energies on him. When the horses were merely feet away, Orro leaped forward and struck the ground with all his might with his ice-mace.

The older rakshases must have been familiar with ravians' ability to rend the earth individually, but nothing could have prepared them for this. A huge furrow appeared in the earth as Orro struck it, as if some great bear-clawed god had gouged out some part of the world that annoyed him. The earth exploded upwards, emptying out a huge trench at least three hundred feet in length and a hundred across, and the charging Artaxerxians disappeared into it and were never seen again. They must have found this at least slightly unpleasant.

—With the loss of his cavalry, the Dark Lord's spirit broke and this day was ours. He vanished from the battlefield, taking nearly all his rakshases with him. We killed anything that was left behind and was not ours. Queen Maya left as well, which was disappointing, as she might have killed Dalmaan if given a little more time. It was a resounding victory by any standards—very few ravians were lost, and King Zibeb seemed pleased enough. Many well-worded congratulations were passed around and the more well-known ravian corpses were wailed over.

—We killed more asurs than anyone cares to count, and the monkey-men would have remembered our matchless valour, but cannot, because they are all dead. But rakshas casualties have been minimal, and they have seen how we fight. They outnumber us easily, and they are fiercer than any creatures I have seen on any other world. We have not even encountered Omar the Terrible, or Bjorkun the Skuan, or Angda, queen of the vanars, or the werewolves. Or the jinn, who are supposed to be unpredictable and very powerful. We have not met any of the rakshas generals in battle. Worst of all, all the ravian heroes on my list are still alive. The next battle will be more difficult, which is encouraging, but I think a rearguard position is what suits me, tactically speaking.

—A messenger has arrived with a secret summons from Dalmaan. This is most irregular. What secret does he wish to share? If he is plotting against the king, why would he want to talk to me? Perhaps he is looking for a young and gullible ally. Most interesting. I had several more interesting observations to make, but I suppose my deathless prose can wait a while.

(Eridon's war journal ends here. Contrary to the predictions of Nenses the Seer, he did not see the Dark Tower fall. He was charged with treason after his journals were discovered by Dalmaan's servants, and his present whereabouts are unknown.)

3

Kirin did not know whether he was asleep, awake, dreaming or even alive; all he knew was that he was wrapped in a dense blanket of darkness, silence and general dullness. He fought to control a sudden surge of panic, and succeeded without much effort. How many times in the last two years had he woken up with absolutely no idea where or how he was? The whole 'All is a blank. Again' situation had practically become a habit now. Under the circumstances, the only thing to do was wait until relevant information made itself available.

The last thing he remembered was Zivran's thunderous voice and Maya's face across the table, her eyes wide and horrified as the lights began to blur. That seemed long ago, and far away; something that had occurred in another lifetime, or in a dream, leaving only Zivran's words echoing faintly in his mind and the aftertaste of Zivran's voice burning a thick, slimy trail in his throat.

He tried to move, but could not. He tried to look around, to gain at least some sense of where he was, and failed. He knew he was not still in the heavens, and the safat-shell trance had worn off; then, he had felt light as air or fire, and had floated at will in infinite space. Now, he was locked in, weighed down, trapped, though he had no sensation of having a body at all, which made it difficult to investigate his condition further. Zivran had said something about their minds being lost; did that mean his mind was now stuck in some kind of hole for all eternity? That didn't make much sense, because if he was wandering around in some sort of cosmic void, there would definitely have been a better view.

He concentrated, searching for a sound, a hint of light, any sensation whatsoever. And his efforts were soon rewarded; a faint thumping sound in the distance slowly grew into a hearbeat, he began to feel faint contractions and see floating, colourful shapes, and realized he was back inside his own body. With this knowledge came surprise and wakefulness; he felt blood racing through his arteries, bringing warmth and life, felt his muscles move and flex, felt his nerves snap to attention in ever-widening arcs of awareness, heard the roar of air gushing into his lungs as he breathed, deeply, in relief and wonder. He'd never felt more alive; it was as if his body was a glove he was fitting into, a home he was reclaiming, and he marvelled at the complexity of its construction. His senses were beginning to return; already he could feel his skin begin to tingle, and hear the dull roar of the world outside. Soon an avalanche of sensation from the physical world beyond the borders of his body would smother this new acquaintance with the marvels within; he was beginning to wake up, and he felt a definite sense of regret. There was so much he would not remember. He felt relaxed, languorous, happy—more than happy, he felt euphoric, as if his whole body was glowing, as if a great weight had rolled off his shoulders.

Speaking of which, there was a weight on his shoulder. He opened his eyes slowly, not yet wholly awake.

Maya's head was next to his, her breath soft and warm on his neck. Her eyes were closed, and she looked as blissful as he felt. Kirin realized, with a sudden start, that their bodies were intertwined, draped comfortably around each other's on a blanket of leaves. He shut his eyes, trying to understand, to remember, to ask his body exactly what had happened while he'd been away, and opened them again, afraid that Maya would vanish, afraid that this was a dream, afraid that she would wake up, terrified that he would lose this moment.

But she was still there, nestled in his arms as comfortably as if she'd been doing it for years, and the sight of her stopped his heart. He held her close, wanting to touch all of her, wanting to drive away the darkness and see her, wanting her. He ran his fingers slowly down her back, feeling her skin respond to his touch, feeling desire run slow and surprise-filled through him.

'I'm not awake,' she murmured, and he sensed her smile.

'Good,' he said. 'Then you can't leave.'

'Why would I want to?'

She snapped her fingers softly, and a tiny ball of light appeared above Kirin's face. He blinked and turned his face, their lips brushing together. His eyes were half smiling, half anxious, drinking in the sight of her as if seeing her for the first time.

'Remind me to leave my body lying around with yours more often,' she said, grinning. 'It simplifies things.'

'Do you remember what happened?'

'No, but judging from how I *feel*'—she stretched, and snuggled up to him—'we made up for lost time. Very vigorously.'

'Did we . . .'

'Bits of us are stuck together, Kirin. What do you think?'

'Oh.'

'A masterly summation of events.'

'You're laughing at me.'

'Yes. Is that a problem?'

'It's just that—I've been dreaming about this, about you, ever since I met you. And we missed . . .'

At this Maya laughed, deep and soft, and kissed him. And Kirin was delighted to find out that the first remembered kiss was a perfectly acceptable substitute for the first kiss; that none of the most important moments of his life would ever come when he was prepared for them, and that he was happier than he had ever been before.

But then Maya broke the kiss and looked at him with an expression he could not fathom, and there was no trace of laughter on her face. The light-ball disappeared, but he had already seen that her eyes were glistening.

'Sorry,' she said. 'Unexpected and, well, unreasonable attack of maidenly reserve. This is complicated.'

'Very.'

'I mean, it's *you*, and I just love you terribly, but it's—and everything's so—you know?' She sniffed loudly and defiantly.

'I have no idea what you're talking about,' said Kirin. 'But if you don't kiss me again, immediately, I will be forced to take drastic action.'

She giggled and kissed him enthusiastically. 'You love me very much, don't you?'

'Yes, and you should give me a chance to say it from time to time.'

'Well, I did. Several years, and look what you did. It took direct intervention from a god to bring us together.'

'You know, all the time we spent apart trying to do what we thought was earth-shatteringly important—it just wasn't worth it. You're all I ever wanted in this world, and I was an utter fool not to have realized it when I should have.'

'What?'

'Nothing. I just needed to distract you and confuse you into compliance.'

And having thus laid bare his intentions, Kirin reached out for Maya and they made love again. And it was as beautiful and unexpected, ecstatic and passionate as it was always going to be. There was tension, and sweat, and relief, and comfort, and lust, and laughter, and madness and incredible bliss. And there was fumbling, and knocking of teeth, and grunts and unexpected strands of hair. There were embarrassing noises, flashes of pain and clashing limbs. There was love, and trust, and honesty, and they had each other. And for the moment they could have asked for nothing more.

* * *

Deerst Maya,

My sincerst regrds to you, and my respex to your esteemd fathr Mantric:

I must aplogis for my roodness in not being presnt when you returnd to the world outside. I was, at the time, somewat overcom by gelosy, rage and sorro, all of which had been groing and festering all throu the severl days you spent in the cave. This was, of corse, completly uncalld for givn my currnt state. These emoshns were eckos from my formr life, and I hope you will forgiv me.

Spikes, who has turnd out to be a frend I shud have made

while alive, told me the tale of your adventurs. You have survivd a jurney to the hevns and back. I am filled, as always, with admirashn. But the news Spikes gave me trubls me gretly; the gods have ronged us all, and the unwaba's betrayl is enuff to make me lose faith in everythng I once held sacrd. It fills me with despare to think how we have all been toyd with, to lern that the all-knoing unwaba, the arkitct of this Age, chose to do nothing to avert my death, that he used us all as his pupets with a heartlessnss well sooted to his cold-bloodd form.

I must also aplogis for the clumzness of this lettr, which you must attrebut to the fact that it is a work of diktashn. Spikes is riting it. My caligraffy is not what it used to be, givn the stifness of my fingrs. The fysicl appernce of this letter also leaves much to be desird; we had no papr or kwill, alas, and Spikes had to make do with the skin and bons of a passng tigr.

Enuff chit-chat, as you used to say.

Let me come to the crux of the mattr, then. My life, or un-life, call it what you will, has not turnd out as I hopd it wood, and I have decidd, after much delibrashun, to change its corse one last time. I have, to the best of my abilty, been a hero. I have always tried to conduct myself in a manner befiting the great honor bestod upon me in life and death, as a Prince of Avrnti, as a champion of Kol and as a herld of the Faro. I must confess this has led only to bitternss. I see now that my life was but a farce playd out to tickle the humors of waywrd gods, and the existens that was given to me after my mortl life endd was one of mear servitood. The story of my life, it now turns out, is but a crool jok. I nevr thout for myself as much as I shud have; I shud have been a troo leadr, but have always allowd myself to be led, and have errd not once but ofen in ways that would fill me with shame were I capabl of feelng that emoshn. I beleevd all my life that the gods were wachng over me, not nowing the terribl truth; they were. But peraps it is still not too late to make amnds.

On to more personl mattrs. I was your lovr, and you have now chosen anothr; I want you to feel neithr gilt nor regrt. I hope you find happinss with Kirin; a far cry from the days when I wachd him gelosly and secretly wantd to challeng him to a dool! I no he cares for you deeply, and I wish you a long and joyus life together. I will do what I can to ensur that you have a world to live this long and joyus life in; to that end I must now retrn to the army of the Scorpion Man, and try my very best to make its leadrs understnd how twistd the gods they serve truly are, and see if I can turn the tide of destruckshun, or at least delay it, to help the world and eez its passng even if I cannt save it. The unded must be made to understnd that they were creatd for idl amusmnt, by the same crool forces they had spent their lives worshiping. We—the unded, that is, not you and I—must do what we can to remind ourselvs—and the gods—who we were, who we coud have been had they not destroyd us.

In partng, let me say that it was an honor to have met you and lovd you. You were a consrt for a greatr hero than I, and I was lucky to have won your affecshn when I did. And I hope Kirin will gro one day to be worthy of you. If you remembr me, then remembr me as I was on our last nit togethr, befor fate turnd agnst me, befor you were takn away from me and I lost my way. Asvin lovd you until the end, but I can be Asvin no longr. The gods brok me and reforgd me, and it is time for me to becom the Cold Princ they creatd and give them a taste of the froots of their own powr.

Zivran wants to give the othr gods a spectacl. He shall have one. I will provid it.

I did not stay to say goodby; it woud have been dificlt to bear. I do not think we shall meet again; in fact, I hope we do not, for the path I have takn will leed me to doom and dangr. I hope you, too, will find a path worthy of you, and I hope, in my next life, to meet you and love you again. It is too late for me to enjoy the delits of this world, but I will do what I can to presrve them for your sake. Farewll.

In life, in deth, my once and futur love,

Yours,
Asvin/Pralay

* * *

Love was in the air. Amoebae extended quivering pseudopodia at each other, spiders spun intricate webs, peacocks danced, love-birds sang, flowers produced prodigious amounts of pollen and all nature was aglow. The sun shone jovially on Vrihataranya, smiling benevolently at everything except Spikes, who stood in waist-deep water in the middle of a stream, hunting fish that were swimming upstream to mate. This did not involve anything as primitive and undignified as moving his limbs in any way; he merely waited until a fish swam near him and skewered it with a single unsheathed spike. When a fair number of fish had accumulated on his body, he pulled them off, one by one, and tossed them at Kirin, who was sitting on the bank of the stream thinking romantic thoughts. Kirin slowed the flying fish down with his mind until they stopped in mid-air, and then dropped them neatly into a pile on a rock. Sunlight sparkled on the water and fish-blood made interesting patterns on the rock; it was a happy domestic scene.

The arrival of Maya, freshly bathed and looking terribly bright, broke up the solid male silence. She greeted Kirin with a kiss. Spikes, sensing an opportunity, sent an exceptionally squishy fish flying towards Kirin, but Maya turned it into a flower and caught it, and sent a fireball steaming into water near Spikes. Spikes snorted and returned to his fishing.

'What did Spikes say when you told him about us?' she asked Kirin.

'He had a lot to say,' said Kirin. 'He said "About time", "Good", and "Now don't make a mess of this". Even more significantly, he moved the corners of his mouth upwards by about a finger's width, which is more exuberant than he's ever allowed himself to be before. What can I say? It was emotional.'

Maya laughed and sat. 'Listen,' she said. 'All this is just lovely, but we have to talk about what happens now.'

'Fried fish,' said Kirin, adding another one to the pile.

'It's time to go, Kirin. The unwaba kept us out of things for long enough. We need to get back into the game.'

'Why?'

'What do you mean, why?'

'I mean the simple, standard Why? Why should we go anywhere near the game? I keep saying I'm not a hero, and then run off trying to be one. I've really had enough of quests and world-changing journeys. I've done my best, and achieved nothing. I'm not saying this to complain; I just think I've done enough, and now that I have a chance to be happy, I don't intend to let it go. And I need a holiday. We both do.'

Maya nodded. 'This life is almost perfect, Kirin, but it's selfish. The world still has to be saved.'

'Well, someone else can do it. Heroes turn up in situations like this, don't they? We should make room for them. I can think of far better ways to spend my time. Completely unselfish and extremely acrobatic ways.'

'Not good enough, Kirin. You can't quit now.'

'Says who? What do you suggest we do? Catch another safat and pay Zivran another visit? Put on mad prophet costumes and go tell people what the gods are doing and have them laugh in our faces and throw things at us? Turn up in the middle of a battle and ask them politely to stop? We're up against gods, Maya. They make worlds, turn time, touch their noses with their tongues, that sort of thing. What can we do?'

'Forget the world, then. We need to do something for ourselves. We just found each other. I don't know about you, but I want this to last. I want to be able to grow old beside you, while you stay young and firm. For this to happen, the world has to be saved. It's a reasonable request.'

Kirin shrugged and caught a fish. 'We had a plan. We tried. We failed. The unwaba made fools of us. There's a whole list of people who've sent us running around the world for nothing. How could we have believed that Zivran would take us seriously when we threatened to reveal what he did—and only ensure that our world would be destroyed? Anyway, now the world's going to end, and there's nothing we can do about it; it's out of our hands.'

'What do you want to do, then? Just stay here?'

'Well, let's put it this way. If the world was going to end soon, what would you want to do?'

Maya considered this for several minutes.

'Get very drunk and fool around with you,' she said finally.

'Now *that's* a reasonable request. I'd suggest Frags, but I think it's gone.'

'Who's going to save the world, then?'

'How would I know? Maybe Asvin is. Or your father. Or maybe some god will have a change of heart. I don't really care; they should feel free to save us all if they want to. But it won't be us. We'll be elsewhere, having a good time.'

'Where?'

'This is a bit sentimental.'

'I live for such moments.'

'I promised you I would go to Bolvudis with you. I'd like to keep that promise, even if it's years too late.'

Maya grinned. 'I suppose this has nothing to do with the possibility of beaches, sunsets, mermaids and exotic drinks?'

'Nothing at all. Your company is all I want.'

'I'd feel very guilty, Kirin.'

'You would learn to deal with it, given time.'

'I'm serious.'

'So am I. Compromise, then: Come with me until you know what needs to be done, and then you can change your mind.'

'I don't believe you're actually talking me into this.'

'Ravian mind control.'

'Spikes!' called Maya. 'Do you want to go to Bolvudis and wait for the end of the world?'

'Does it matter what I say or are we going there anyway?'

'We're going there anyway.'

'Yes, then.'

4

A slender crescent moon lit up the white limestone cliffs along the southern face of the island of Kah-Chuwa, the notorious pirate base south of Kol whose notorious pirate inhabitants terrorized the waters between Elaken in the west and Xi'en in the east. Beside one such cliff, pale grey in the moonlight, a little boat bobbed up and down on gently rolling waves. It was drawn by dolphins and surrounded by mer-people, floating with their heads and shoulders above water, their wild seaweed-encrusted hair waving in the warm, soft breeze. Two seagulls and a parrot sat on the boat's prow, and four people of very diverse shapes and sizes sat within it. A little distance away, a large barge drawn by a very solid-looking elephant-makara sat stolidly, water lapping musically on its sides.

'Mmfm?' inquired Telu-Yeti.

'Yes, we're here,' said the Dagger. 'Patience, Telu-Yeti.'

'She should have been here by now,' said Fujen. 'Something's wrong. Why did she bring the ship to Kah-Chuwa in the first place?'

'Perhaps we should go find the ship ourselves,' said Mantric. 'I'm tired of waiting, and I've heard there are pirates in these waters.' He chuckled to himself as the others glared.

'It's not like Orpi to be late,' said Fujen. 'She said she had the ship ready; the figurehead's been installed, the crew's been assembled. Are you sure that's exactly what she said, Pollux?'

'Indubitably,' said the parrot.

Jen shook her head. 'Even if she had a run-in with the Brethren of the Skull, she should have taken the ship to safety and sent someone here to meet us. Where is she?'

'She'll be here,' said the Dagger.

As if in answer, the sound of oars splashing made itself heard, and soon a longboat appeared around the cliff; in the distance, they could make out ten sailors manning oars, and one short and extremely curvaceous figure standing and peering at them in the moonlight.

'Baby-Duck!' called Jen, and there was laughter in the longboat far away. The standing woman blew Jen a kiss.

'Right,' said the Dagger. 'Disguises.'

'Why do we need disguises?' asked Mantric.

'Because men aren't allowed on board Fujen's ships.'

'What do you mean?'

'What I said. Wigs, Jen?'

'Yes,' said Fujen, dipping into a bag. 'Captain Blonde, Redbraid, or Long Joan Silky?'

'Captain Blonde,' said the Dagger quickly. Fujen fished out an outrageously curly blonde wig, and the Dagger donned it with a flourish.

'You, Mantric?' asked Fujen.

'I don't understand,' said Mantric. 'We can't save the world dressed as women!'

'Why not?' inquired Fujen, eyes narrowing. 'Women can't save the world?'

'That's not what I said,' snapped Mantric. 'We'd just look ridiculous dressed as women, is all.'

'I'm surprised you say that,' said the Dagger, grinning. 'You wear a nightdress all the time.'

'It's a spellbinder's robe, Amloki.'

'Same thing. You'll look very fetching in a gown. Try it; I quite enjoy the feeling myself.'

Mantric spluttered at him for a second, and then turned to Jen. 'Why aren't men allowed on your ships?' he asked.

'Bad luck,' said Jen.

'But I thought it was bad luck for pirates to have *women* on board.'

'It is. For other pirates. Very bad luck if we're on board. Now, they're almost here, so we can't chat. Orpi knows who you are, of course. The rest aren't very bright. Redbraid or Long Joan Silky?'

'Silky.'

Fujen threw Mantric a mop of straight black hair, and Mantric managed to pull it on his shining bald head just as Orpi's longboat came close enough for its passengers to see him clearly.

'I see where Maya gets her good looks,' said the Dagger blandly.

'Be quiet.'

'I apologize in advance for getting drunk later and trying to have my way with you.'

'Be quiet.'

'Do we have to pretend to be females as well?' asked Irik Seagull with some trepidation.

'Won't,' said Stivin laconically beside him.

'It's quite all right,' said Jen, beginning to giggle. 'You are, after all, gulls.'

'Mmfm!' said Telu-Yeti.

'What are you complaining about? You *are* a she-yeti, aren't you?'

'Mmfm.'

'Well, then.'

The longboat drew up beside them and Orpi leaped into Fujen's arms with a passionate 'Baby-Duck!' The sailors, who Mantric now saw were all women, cheered enthusiastically and wiped misty eyes. Orpi greeted Amlokini and Mantrica with warm hugs, and Mantric, like everyone who had ever met Orpi, was immediately entranced by her spectacularly large and appealing eyes.

'Why are you late, my love?' asked Fujen. 'And where is our ship? I want to see it!'

'It's *such* a lovely ship, Baby-Duck,' gushed Orpi. 'Terribly expensive, but worth every bit of it. And you should see the figurehead! Aishwarya really is the most beautiful duck in the world.'

'Well, where is the ship? What did you get, a trireme? A knaar?'

'Please, love,' shuddered Orpi. 'I wasn't going to throw that kind of money away on a rammer. We're going to the edge of the world—did you expect the girls to row all the way? I *spent* on this ship. None of that star-navigation nonsense; we have compasses, sextants . . . it's just a lovely, lovely ship. I thought for two whole days, and then I decided I wanted a carrack.'

'You got a carrack! That's brilliant! I've always wanted a carrack!'

'What is a carrack?' whispered Mantric to the Dagger.

'Our ship, apparently.'

'Well, it's more than just a carrack,' said Orpi, her eyes glowing with mischief.

'How?' asked Fujen.

'Guess.'

'All right, all right,' said Fujen, smiling indulgently. 'Four masts.'

'You know me so well, love. Go on.'

'High rounded stern. Forecastle, aftcastle. Let's see . . . stern with bowspit?'

'Of course.'

'Hmm. Lateen-rigged mizzenmast, mainmast and foremast, what, square-rigged?'

'You're so *clever*, Baby-Duck.'

'I can't understand a word,' whispered Mantric. 'Can you?'

'No,' whispered Amloki sternly. 'Now you know how everyone feels around you all the time.'

'I can see the ship if I close my eyes,' said Fujen. 'And it's a beauty, all right. Large square sails, wonderful propulsion, we reduce the sail size for storms. Smaller sails at bow and stern for better steering. And . . . oh gods . . . lateen sails for sailing across the wind?'

'Yes,' said Orpi, jumping in excitement. 'Yes, yes!'

'Oh, my love,' said Jen, sweeping her up in her arms, 'you *shouldn't* have.'

'Well, I didn't,' said Orpi.

Jen let go of her abruptly. 'What do you mean? You didn't get a ship?'

'Of course I got a ship. What do you think of me? You don't love me at all.'

'Don't sulk, Baby-Duck. Tell me everything.'

'Well, I got this ship. Everything you described, and a stable deck, and onagers to launch Psomedean Fire from as well. Sixteen of them.'

'Ooh, nice.'

'Yes. It was the finest ship in all Kah-Chuwa. Fast, elegant, deadly.'

'And then?'

'And then I decided I didn't like it. We're going to meet the gods, aren't we? It needed more.'

A huge smile spread slowly over Jen's face. 'What did you do?'

'Take a deep breath, my love,' said Orpi. 'You're going to need it.'

'What did you do, Orpi?'

'Lowered the forecastle. Elongated the hull. What does that mean?'

'Reduced wind resistance in front,' said Fujen breathlessly. 'Stability. It won't topple.'

'Gave it a square tuck stern. Changed the head; the snout now projects forward from the bows below the forecastle. Lateen sail on the third mast. Oaken keel, pine masts, carvel hull. What do you think?'

'It's perfect,' said Fujen. 'I love you.'

Orpi simpered. 'It's not perfect,' she said. 'I wanted to get vaman explosives for you, or even Xi'en fire-shots, but I didn't have time. I'm sorry.'

'You're sorry? You're *sorry*? Just wait till I get you alone on the lower decks. You'll be sorry then.'

'Ahem,' said Mantric, unable to restrain himself any longer.

'What is it?' snapped Fujen.

'I apologize for intruding,' said Mantric. 'But where *is* this ship?'

Jen turned to Orpi, who was suddenly engrossed in twirling a strand of hair.

'Well?' said Jen after a while.

'Don't be angry, love,' whispered Orpi. 'I couldn't bear it.'

'I'm not angry, Orpi,' said Jen. 'At least, not yet. Where is the ship?'

'I'm afraid I . . . sort of . . . lost it.'

'I see. And how did you achieve this sort of losing it?'

'I hate it when you talk to me like that. It's so . . . cold. It's as if you don't—'

'The ship, woman. Where is it?'

* * *

Orpi's plan had been very simple. There were only three shipwrights in the world capable of making the modifications the *Baby Duck* needed. Of these, only one could be found at short notice, and he lived in Port Kah-Chuwa. The pirates of Port Kah-Chuwa were sworn enemies of Fujen's, which made the whole operation very dangerous, but Orpi was a woman of steel, who sniffed at danger and looked at it sternly until it slank away, ashamed of itself. She had stolen into Port Kah-Chuwa, abducted the shipwright and inspired him, with a combination of charm and cutlass-prods, to finish work on the *Baby-Duck* in record time. As payment, she had promised to return him to Port Kah-Chuwa in one piece; he had initially thought this was a poor bargain, but Orpi had persuaded him otherwise, pointing out entirely reasonably that the other alternative was not being returned anywhere, and in several pieces. Orpi was a woman who kept her promises, and she had taken the shipwright home without incident. It was after that that things had gone wrong. Flushed with victory, Orpi had decided to stop by at Crossbones, Port Kah-Chuwa's most notorious tavern, for a drink or fifteen. She had forgotten one of the first things any pirate learned; no one went to Crossbones without losing something dear to them. The price for forgetfulness in Kah-Chuwa was high; in Orpi's case, one ship.

Some time before Orpi's daring incursion into enemy territory, several large and prosperous-looking galleys had weighed anchor at Port Kah-Chuwa; the first time in several hundred years that the island had received guests who were not pirates. These visitors were not seen as a threat to pirate power; they were fleeing the war in the north, and wanted to find uninhabited lands in the south to settle. They even spoke of attempting to cross the Vertical Sea, which proved that they were mad and endeared them further to their hosts. The pirates of Kah-Chuwa were always happy when their plunder came to them, thus sparing them a great deal of effort, and had given the newcomers a royal and rum-soaked welcome. Several days of drunken gambling later, the pirates were surprised to find that their guests were not only still alive, but had somehow managed to win the deeds to their hosts' ships; it turned out that all the pirates in Kah-Chuwa and their ships had been commandeered to protect the strangers' ships on their journey further southwards. The pirates had been forced to admire their new employers; the idea of hiring the very people who would have disrupted their voyage to protect them was one that appealed to the buccaneer mind. And there was no doubt that the strangers were all very charming, and incredibly good at dice. The strangest thing about the whole business, the pirates agreed, was that they did not resent this turn of events in any way, and were only even slightly dissatisfied because all their traditional methods of cheating at gambling tables had proved ineffective.

And thus it was that Orpi found herself deprived of her perfect new ship; she had lost it to a striking young woman in a wager, and Orpi always honoured her wagers. The *Baby Duck* was now docked at a pier in Port Kah-Chuwa, in the middle of a long line of ships whose owners were mortal enemies of Fujen's. And Fujen's crew, apart from the ten sailors who'd come with Orpi, was now occupied in loading provisions and cargo into the new ship, mostly supplies for the settlers' southward journey.

'Ravians,' said the Dagger as soon as Orpi finished her sad tale. 'Only ravians could come and cheat all the pirates of Kah-Chuwa. And only ravians could make them feel good about it.'

'They would have a certain command over dice,' agreed Mantric. 'But how did they influence the pirates' minds? Were there no magicians among you? No pet monsters, protective amulets, enchanted artefacts? What sort of pirate town is this?'

'I don't know how they did it,' sighed Orpi. 'What was most terrifying, when I think about it now, was how peaceful the tavern was—usually there are at least ten horrible piratey people trying to kill one another any time you walk in. But when I went in, everyone was just lining up to get cheated. And they were so calm. If I had not been ridiculously drunk and in the company of a very attractive stranger, I would have found it odd at the time.'

'I see,' said Jen.

'I love you, Baby-Duck.'

'Calm? Peaceful? That doesn't sound like the ravians I know,' said the Dagger. 'How many were there?'

'I don't know. There were lots of new people. But pirate cities are like that.'

'The ravians don't need protection from the pirates,' said the Dagger, rubbing his chin. 'They could have just taken anything they wanted from Kah-Chuwa and killed anyone who tried to stop them.'

'Perhaps their ships were too crowded and they needed more, or just wanted to travel more comfortably,' said Mantric. 'But I know what you mean; all the ravians I've met have tried to kill me, and have not wasted any time in conversation. This is rather mysterious. Still, the only way to find out is to go and see.'

'That settles it, then,' said the Dagger. 'We go to the port and get our ship back.'

'If they are ravians, as you suggest,' said Fujen, 'wouldn't it just be easier to get another ship? I love fighting—you know that—but if there are many of them . . . I want to meet the gods, and we can do that in any ship, really.'

'But I want *this* one. It's our ship, and another one wouldn't *feel* right,' said Orpi, pouting. 'I feel *terrible*, Baby-Duck.'

Jen patted her reassuringly. 'That settles it, then,' she said. 'Port Kah-Chuwa it is. Do you have spare disguises, love?'

'Of course I do. But not for the yeti.'

'The yeti would have been difficult to disguise anyway.'

Orpi called out to the women in the longboat, and they tossed a sack over. To Mantric's alarm, Orpi, Jen and the ten sailors then began to disrobe. The Dagger, on the other hand, leaned back and sighed contentedly.

'We have to pretend to be men when we enter Port Kah-Chuwa,' explained Jen, beginning to cheer up.

'Why?' asked Mantric piteously.

'Think about it, Mantrica,' said Amloki. 'Do you really want to walk around pirate-town looking like a *wench*?'

'No,' said Mantric with feeling, and reached for his wig.

'Don't!' hissed Jen, Amloki and Orpi in unison, and Mantric leaped into the air, startled.

'Wear these clothes,' said Jen loudly, handing him a shirt, breeches, a fat belt and very impractical boots. 'Don't worry about your face, we'll give you a beard and whiskers.'

'Very well,' muttered Mantric, and stood there, clothes in hand, concentrating very hard on the water as the others dressed.

'She's shy,' giggled Orpi. 'It's too sweet for words. Would you like some help with the pants, love?'

'No,' said Mantric firmly. He looked at the others. 'You don't look like men at all,' he said.

'Why? We have beards. Look, I even have an attachable mole,' said Fujen, sticking what looked like a tar-coated slug on her cheek.

'And my boots have little platforms on them,' trilled Orpi. 'We will be fine. Wait till you've seen us with our beards.'

'But your . . . but your,' Mantric struggled for a word and gave up, 'your *shape* is wrong.'

The Dagger laughed. 'Don't worry,' he said. 'We won't get caught.'

'Why? They'll be too drunk and mind-controlled to notice?'

'No. We'll get away with it because pirates have their own rules in these situations: you reward people for effort. Seeing through disguises, even terrible disguises, is bad form. Girls have been dressing up as boys and sneaking on board ships for centuries, mostly dreaming of a life of freedom and adventure; men have been dressing up as women and sneaking on board ships for even longer, with slightly different expectations.'

'So even if they know they won't catch them?'

'As long as Fujen's girls are dressed as men, they're safe. In places like Kah-Chuwa, everyone has secrets and dark histories; no one wants to know more about you than what you want to show them. You are whatever you've made the effort to look like. Any pirate would be willing to believe even that Spikes was a demure damsel, if he wore a wig and a dress. Imagine that.'

'No thank you. But that's not a bad way to be,' said Mantric, lost in thought. 'Other societies should try it too.'

'Yes,' said the Dagger. 'Now stop wasting our time, take off your dress and put on your beard, love.'

The finest ships of the pirate fleet were anchored at Port Kah-Chuwa, in a jumbled torch-lit clutter of knaar and junk and galley, trireme and longship and dhow, ships old and new from all over the world. Pirates raced to and fro all along the harbour, loading ships with large crates in an appallingly neat and organized fashion. Twelve large ships were tethered side by side along the widest pier, right in the centre of the harbour, and the *Baby Duck* lay right in the middle of the line. Even Mantric, who knew nothing about ships, had to admit that this was the most beautiful ship he had ever seen. Not that he had much time to compare it with the other ships, as Fujen led him, the Dagger, Orpi, their ten crew-women and Telu-Yeti in a complicated skulk around the pier, darting from one shadow to another, occasionally swaggering out in the open, mingling with the locals, saying 'Yo ho ho!', 'Shiver me timbers!' and 'Avast!' for verisimilitude. After a while, Fujen lost interest in this exercise. The pirates were clearly under ravian control, she said; no brawls had broken out since their arrival, and no one they had encountered thus far even smelled mildly of rum. Several of her sworn enemies had walked right by her without even drawing their cutlasses; the notorious Commandant Lienundschinker, who'd sworn to kill her the next time he saw her, actually stopped and wished her good evening.

They strolled over the connecting pier and over the plank that led into the *Baby Duck* without much further incident. Fujen's crew welcomed her enthusiastically, and she informed them that it did not matter that Orpi had lost the ship; they would not honour the bargain she had made, as she had been drunk at the time, and besides, were they not pirates? She ordered them to start preparing for a daring escape from the port (pausing to pick up Mantric's trunks from the makara-drawn barge on the way). The crew took this well; a young ravian who had been on the *Baby Duck* supervising the loading of crates did not, and called for help.

The pier was suddenly full of ravians, all carrying heroic-looking weapons. While Fujen and her crew drew their cutlasses and prepared to die nobly and pointlessly, Mantric took it upon himself to explain to the ravians that he was a powerful spellbinder, and had a yeti with him and was not afraid to use her. With Telu-Yeti by his side, he was capable of removing the ravians' influence from every human on the island, he said, which was an outrageous lie, but the false hair all over his head added a great deal of gravitas to it; while he had no doubt that the ravians could overcome the pirates in battle, he said, this would leave no one to steer their ships for them.

What happened next shocked both Mantric and the Dagger, who had expected the ravians to answer their threats with pirate deaths. But the ravians saw the value of what Mantric said and asked him not to start a riot, and offered to send their leader to negotiate terms with him. Mantric accepted this offer with grace, and soon the Dagger and he were playing host on the deck of the *Baby Duck* to one Lady Ikoche, of the ravian house Hanash, a tall, cheerful, soft-spoken ravian noble who overturned their carefully-lain strategies by being utterly likeable without the use of any ravian influence whatsoever.

'You must understand, my dear Mantric,' said Ikoche, 'that I would not have commandeered your ship if I had realized you were not from Kah-Chuwa, a fact that your pretty young friend conveniently forgot to mention. Some pirates from this island attacked our fleet a few days ago; we lost a few ships, and needed to replenish our stocks, and felt these pirates should pay. We did control a few minds in the process to save ourselves time and minimize casualties. But yes, we should not have, and I apologize.'

'This is most irregular,' said the Dagger. 'Since when did the ravians start apologizing for using their powers?'

Ikoche sighed. 'I see the war on the mainland has touched your lives,' she said, 'and filled you with hatred for my kind. But we are not all the same, my young friend. In fact, my presence here is proof enough of our differences. House Hanash and House Esmi sail the southern seas because New Asroye's gates are shut to us. We did not support their unjust war. We sought peace, and we failed. We sought an end to all that was wrong and cruel in the ravian way of life, and we failed. So we have left their city and now seek new homes for ourselves in the south.'

'And you need our ship to help you carry your things there. But—'

'I do not need your ship,' said Ikoche. 'You are free to go. It was a simple misunderstanding.'

'You would just let us go?'

'Of course. But there is a price you must pay.'

'I'm almost relieved to hear you say that. What must we do?' asked the Dagger.

'You must tell me your stories. I want to know everything about you; it will help me understand the world better,' said Ikoche.

After a long and pregnant pause, the Dagger stated stiffly that they were on a secret mission of earth-shattering importance.

'Where are you going?' asked Ikoche.

'To meet the gods,' said the Dagger.

She regarded them gravely. 'You jest.'

'We do not, actually,' said the Dagger. 'We're going to meet the gods, and give them a present.'

'We cannot tell you what it is, because it is supposed to be a surprise,' said Mantric. 'It will make the gods happier if they do not know just yet.'

'A noble ambition,' said Ikoche. 'And is there any motive behind this act beyond sheer generosity?'

'We're trying to prevent the end of the world,' said Mantric.

Ikoche took this in her stride with no hint of surprise. 'I see. Is there anything we can do to help?'

The Dagger gave her his most charming smile. 'Yes. If you see anyone trying to end the world, stop them. They'll probably listen to you.'

Ikoche smiled and bowed. 'Well, you have a ship worthy of the journey,' she said. 'What is it called?'

Mantric and the Dagger looked at Jen accusingly. 'The *Baby Duck*,' said Jen shamefacedly.

A tremor ran through Ikoche's jaw. 'An excellent name,' she said. 'But if you are going to seek the favour of the gods, should you not name it after one of them?'

'This ship was a birthday present for the woman I love,' said Jen. 'We cannot change the name, even to please the gods.'

'Well, thankfully, it is none of my business,' said Ikoche. 'But should you reconsider, I believe there is a goddess known as the Baby of Destiny. Perhaps that would be a better name for your ship; it would please the gods and make an adequate birthday present as well.'

'I think that is a wonderful idea,' said Mantric. 'The *Baby of Destiny* it is.'

'*Baby Duck*,' said Jen.

'*Baby of Destiny*. Consider the circumstances.'

'*Baby Duck*. Consider the figurehead.'

'I will take your leave now,' said Ikoche, kindly but firmly. She walked down the plank to the pier, hesitated, and then turned and smiled at them.

'I have spent several months in your world, and every day it has found new ways to fascinate me,' she said. 'I wish you well; take your ship and save the world, and think kindly of us ravians as you do so. We are not all terrible people, and if the ways of Esmi and Hanash prevail, perhaps one day we may even be friends. I wish I could come with you! But my people need me, and I must put thoughts of adventure aside. Good luck! I have no parting gift for you, save one.'

'The pleasure of your acquaintance was gift enough for us,' said the Dagger. 'Perhaps we shall meet again one day.'

'I look forward to it,' said Ikoche. 'Farewell! And though you leave me empty-handed, I have something for you to remember me by.'

'What is that?' asked Orpi breathily, smouldering at her.

'A name,' said Ikoche.

A brief while later, as the first light of dawn filled the sea and sky with magical shades of blue and green, the *Duck of Destiny* sailed majestically out of Port Kah-Chuwa, towards the edge of the world and the gods that sat around it. Fujen and Orpi stood on the foredeck, arms outstretched in the wind. Mantric inspected his secret hoard in the hold, Pollux explained literary theory to the Bolvudis Seagulls on the sails, and the Dagger ventured below decks to get to know Fujen's pirates better. If the end of the world was nigh, he thought, there was truly no time like the present.

5

Suitably sinister clouds roared and crackled in the sky, their edges glowing purple and orange as the Dark Lord's army gathered to do battle with King Zibeb's ravians. Visible now in the distance behind them, the Dark Tower loomed over the landscape, mocking all invaders. Asur drummers kept up a frantic beat, monstrous war-beasts bellowed and trumpeted, pashans thumped the earth in unison, horns rang out in discordant notes and a pleasant time was had by all.

The Dark Lord stood on a great jutting rock, surrounded by armed werewolves. He was fashionably dressed in magical obsidian armour, peering out with his fiery eyes through slits in his ornate horned war-helm, and his dark minions looked at him with love as they felt battle-frenzy coursing through their veins. The Red Queen stood by her lord's side, cold and impassive, showing no signs of elation or awe as she watched giant rakshases fidgeting impatiently and snarling at the countless asurs milling about their feet.

Angda, queen of vanars, stood in front of the children

of Vanarpuri on the left flank, her face full of fear and wonder as she peered into the distance, gripping her broadsword tightly as the ravians strode forward, singing songs in melodious voices, their weapons shining with holy light. Their presence illuminated the battlefield, and the sun blazed fiercely through clear skies above them as they walked fearlessly on savage, blood-choked earth. Behind Angda, gorilla-men swung maces and pounded their chests, and baboon–vanar archers cackled as they thanked their enemies for giving them good light to shoot in.

The ravians had broken through the rakshas illusions all over Imokoi with frightening speed. They had driven bands of captured asurs ahead of their forces and laughed coldly as their mindless heralds fell in rakshas traps, in concealed ravines and trenches full of spikes, on broken bridges and covered slime-pits. Led by Lady Nenses, the ravian mages had cast great spells they called Asroye Silence on the land around them, sending circles of green light pulsing around them, draining all magic in the region they covered; illusions melted away, leaving Imokoi bare and defenceless, ripping apart the façade of gloom and horror. Teams of ravian builders, supervised by Dalmaan, had built bridges and pathways using their minds, creating makeshift structures with stones, chunks of earth and asur corpses that their army could march over, while squads of battle-mages, led by Orro Earthshaker had flattened physical obstacles in the path of Zivran's army, cutting the earth in a straight line from Danh-Gem's Wasteland to the Dark Tower. Aciram had hoped that the ravians would need several more days to reach the lands near Izakar, which would have given his forces enough time to reach full strength; as things stood, the army which held its ground mostly comprised survivors from the introductory skirmish and reinforcements from the Dark Tower, mostly asurs and pashans. The crucial difference, of course, was that the rakshases were no longer interested in toying with their prey. Today would be a day for those who survived it to remember for the rest of their lives.

The Dark Lord had sent messages to his allies spread out over Imokoi summoning them to the battle; Bjorkun's Skuans had sent word of their approach from the north, and Omar the Terrible was expected to return any moment from a raid he had led to help the shadowsnatchers fight a ravian incursion in the east. Omar had left the men from Ventelot behind to aid the Dark Lord; heavily armoured knights soothed their fidgeting steeds to Aciram's right, and in front of a division of archers and a war-band of danavs, wielding a massive two-handed claymore, stood Laird MacGaffen, a hero from the highlands of North Ventelot. His face was painted blue and he looked very depressed; leading asurs into battle was never easy. On a recent training exercise, he'd given his asurs a rousing speech about freedom and pride, but they hadn't understood a word, because of his thick accent, and when he'd raised his kilt in a show of bare-buttocked defiance towards an imaginary enemy, the asurs had gotten the message entirely wrong. Laird MacGaffen had not been able to walk straight since then, and he had a lot of anger to work off.

King Zibeb reined in his charger and the ravians halted. The flags of the ravian houses were raised, and New Asroye's champions marshalled their troops, trying not to break into spasms of fear as they beheld the enemy; an endless sea of asurs, and great rakshases standing in their midst like trees in savannahs, silent stone-forests of pashans, roaring hordes of vanars. But the discipline of the New Asroye army was without parallel, and as the churl-commanders, on Lord Degin's orders, sent captured asurs and pashans trotting to the front of the ranks, and Zibeb called them to arms in a great voice, they rejoiced in the grim task before them. The heroes spoke in powerful voices, and their words were reassuring and invigorating, assured and fiery, and filled their steadfast followers with hope and pride. Any ravian's life was long, but even if they died young this day, immortality was theirs.

'Why are they settling down? Do they expect us to charge?' asked Red. 'Aren't we the defenders here?'

'They can go no further. They lack the courage,' said Aciram. 'We must be good hosts, and go out of our way to make them feel welcome.'

'What if we just stood here and stared at each other? That might be interesting.'

'Ask them, and see what they think of that idea,' said Aciram, gesturing at his roaring, stamping legions. He grew in size, and a hush fell over his troops.

The Dark Lord raised his hand, and a great ball of fire appeared around it. The warriors of Imokoi stared at him adoringly, waiting for him to inspire them even further.

'Speech,' said Aciram, and covered his ears to drown out the roar of applause.

'Archers ready!' called Angda, and the vanars bent their bows.

'What is she doing?' asked Red, smiling.

'It would seem fairly obvious,' said Aciram.

'I am surprised because she is not a man, and I had expected her to remember the tactics we spent so many hours discussing. Perhaps you should ask her to instruct her archers to put their bows aside.'

Aciram clapped his hand to his forehead. 'I beg your pardon. I had forgotten.'

'We cannot hit them with arrows. They will merely stop them and hurl them back at us. We have seen them do this before.'

'Yes, yes, I know.'

'We might as well ask our archers to shoot one another. It would save them effort and arrows.'

'I had a lot on my mind, dearest. I should have remembered.'

'The archers are only to shoot when they have captured a large number of our troops and are using them against us. They are not to shoot at ravians.'

Eyes blazing, Aciram ordered the archers to stand down.

'Should I go through the list of other tactics, in case you have forgotten those as well?'

Aciram groaned and glared. 'How long have we been married?'

There was a sudden gust of wind as a very large mass of air shifted to make room for the rakshasi Akarat, and Red flinched as her view of the battlefield was obscured by two massive blue pillars. Aciram looked up and bowed.

'We are honoured by your presence here, sister.'

'I have not come to exchange pleasantries with you, Dark Lord,' rumbled Akarat. 'My son is dead. I need blood.'

'It burns my heart to hear this news,' said Aciram. 'We have lost many we held dear, and today we shall be avenged.'

'Held dear? I did not like him,' said Akarat. 'But he was my son. Show me the ravian who killed him.'

'We do not know how Akab died, sister. It was in Vrihataranya, and he was alone.'

'But it was one of them?' Akarat gestured towards the cloud of dust that heralded the ravians.

'Yes.'

'Then I will kill them all.' She grew even greater in size, and the Dark Lord's soldiers stared at her in awe. Not wasting any more time, Akarat charged. Aciram hurriedly ordered the rest of his soldiers to do the same. A wall of massive fireballs lit up the sky as they sped towards Zibeb's army, and many found their fleeing targets. The ravians cracked the earth with their death-spells, striking deep furrows into Imokoi's skin and sending asur and pashan bodies flying into the sky. The armies met in a hurricane of dust and metal and flesh, and the battle began in earnest.

The first day of the battle, for both sides, was mostly about getting to know each other. The ravians introduced the rakshases to the Willspear, a formation where a few powerful ravians united minds and sent a psychic bolt into a mass of their enemies, breaking through magical defences and strong magic-user wills and taking over the minds of lesser beings; all over the battlefield, rakshases hit by the Willspear collapsed terrified and fled, leaving the asurs under their protection to the mercy of ravian churl-commanders. Aciram's army, in turn, demonstrated its newfound flexibility and organization, not succumbing to battle-frenzy, making each asur's life count. The Red Queen's lessons in modern Koli magic had been learnt well; the ravians reeled under expanding walls of flame, deadly scream-arrows, and illusory monsters. The only notable casualties were a popular ravian leader named Ashnen, who died of old age and a vanar mace knocking off his head, and a Ventelot chieftain named Sir Eyric the Well-read, whose armour was crushed by Lady Nenses and rolled into a ball with him still inside it. The battle did not stop at night; neither side even noticed when night fell. Some names had already begun to echo through the killing field; Dalmaan the wily, untouched by blade or spell even though he had spent all day fighting Vrihataranya rakshases. The half-ogre half-rakshas Arisirt, who had engaged King Zibeb in single combat for four hours despite losing one of his heads. Lady Nenses, who had not killed the Dark Lord's generals, primarily because they ran away when she approached. But no one had wreaked more havoc that day than the Red Queen, whose cold, calculated approach to mass slaughter put every ravian to shame. Willspears left her unmoved, and Spirit Trenches could not catch her. She seemed to delight in throwing herself in danger. Time after time, she appeared out of nowhere to rally asurs whose rakshas guardians had been slain, holding their wills together with the power of her own and allowing them to retreat to safety.

There was a lull in the battle at dawn, and King Zibeb summoned his advisers for a meeting on the chest of a fallen rakshas.

'My heart is heavy, your majesty,' said Lord Degin. 'If we do not finish them soon, Omar the Terrible and Bjorkun the Skuan will arrive to strengthen Kirin's forces, and I do not know if we can defeat rakshas and jinn united.'

'Have faith, Degin,' said Nenses. 'The gods smile upon us, and they will protect us. Kirin's beasts have many bodies, but very few heads; once they topple, Imokoi is ours.'

'What news of Satorin? Has he relented?' asked Zibeb.

'No, your majesty,' said Dalmaan. 'We spoke again but a few hours ago, and he says he will not fight. He thinks we conspired against his foster-son, young Eridon. He does not believe that one he loved so dearly could be capable of treason. I even showed him the young rascal's journal, but he was not convinced.'

'Then Satorin has betrayed us,' said Degin. 'He must be punished. Say the word, your majesty, and I will bring him to his knees.'

'Satorin would cut you in half,' snapped Orro. 'If he must be dealt with, I will have to do the dirty work, as always.'

'I will not have my greatest champions killing each other,' said Zibeb. 'Some other way must be found to bring him to the field. Who will he listen to?'

'I have heard,' murmured Dalmaan, 'that there is a young lad named Onkad in House Akked . . .'

'His pretty cousin,' said Nenses. 'Charming boy.'

'Cousin?' snorted Orro. 'Why, if those two are cousins, then—'

Zibeb raised a warning hand and Orro fell silent. 'Go on, Dalmaan,' said Zibeb.

'I wonder if you know, your majesty, that Onkad foolishly decided to fight today's battle in Satorin's armour, thinking it would inspire our troops.'

'Did he, now? I hope he survived. Satorin would be deeply grieved if anything happened to him. I hope you had nothing to do with this decision, Dalmaan.'

'Of course not, your majesty. In fact, I tried in vain to persuade him not to undertake so dangerous a venture.'

Nenses smiled. 'How did Onkad die?'

'Die? He is alive and well,' said Dalmaan. 'I last saw him on the right flank, sparring with the rakshasi Akarat. Should

I go and protect him, your majesty? He is not an experienced warrior, and these rakshases are rather dangerous.'

Zibeb thought for a while. 'Do so, good Dalmaan.'

'If anything were to go wrong, despite my best efforts . . . I fear I would not have the heart to inform Satorin.'

Tekdash the Healer, who had been listening to this exchange red-faced, could not contain himself any longer. 'All this is completely unnecessary,' he blurted. 'Satorin will fight when he is needed. Onkad is a fine young lad, a hero of the future. Killing him will be a base act, and unworthy of us.'

His fellow heroes turned towards him, shock and indignation drawn clearly on their faces.

'My dear Tekdash,' said Zibeb, in accents of horror, 'what on earth are you suggesting?'

On the second day of the battle, the fighting intensified. Manouevres and formations were thrown to the wind, and the ravians suffered because of this; the Dark Lord's forces were now fighting on instinct, and their attacks became almost impossible to predict and repel. Rakshases hurled themselves around the battlefield, striking and maiming and disappearing. Berserker vanars leaped high in the air in suicidal attacks, crushing their foes with their maces even as they impaled themselves on their swords. But the ravians rallied bravely, led by Satorin the Invincible; his rage was awesome and terrible to behold, and no rakshas could stand for long in his path. Each stroke of his blade took a life; in desperation, the Dark Lord sacrificed an entire legion of danavs to keep him at bay, drowning him in ever-growing mounds of asur corpses. The ravians suffered one terrible loss; Tekdash the

Healer, beloved son of New Asroye, was slain by the Dark Lord, crushed to death as he threw himself in the way of a Shatterstrike that would have killed King Zibeb.

The third day brought the rakshases hope. Help was at hand; Omar and Bjorkun were on their way, and soon the jinn would make their presence felt. This news reached the ravians, and they redoubled their efforts. Orro Earthshaker's mace struck terror into the very heart of Obiyalis, and his Spirit Trenches gouged out most of the Dark Lord's pashans. Satorin and the Red Queen duelled, and the battle stopped around them as asurs and ravians alike stood entranced by their sword-play. Satorin won the encounter after several hours of frantic combat, but did not kill the Red Queen. Instead, he tried to capture her and bring her to King Zibeb, and Arisirt the half-ogre sacrificed his own life to allow her to escape. But the day belonged to Akarat the rakshasi, who tore through the House Akked ranks, impervious to Willspear or sword-thrust, and ended her mad spree of destruction by picking up General Froyan and biting him in half.

'This battle has taught me several things about myself,' said the Red Queen to the Dark Lord that night.

'That you're the best damned fighter this world has ever seen?' asked Aciram.

'There is that, yes. More importantly, I now know what brings me pleasure.'

'This I would be most interested in knowing more about.'

'Power,' said Red simply. 'I like telling people what to do, and I like killing people. When I knew who I was, I wanted to rule the world. I have realized that I still do.'

'Well,' chuckled Aciram, 'you're in the right line of work.'

At noon on the fourth day, Akarat withstood a Spirit Trench without flinching and towered over the ravians who made it, tall as a hill, her skin covered in blood and earth.

'Let the one who killed my son step forward!' she roared.

The ravians parted ranks, and Orro stood at Akarat's feet, his great warhammer pulsing with white light.

'We do not know you, demoness, and any of us might have butchered your cub,' he said. 'But if he was your size, it must have been me.'

Akarat screamed and stamped a mighty foot, but Orro was deceptively quick; he dived, rolled and swung his hammer even as the earth shook with the weight of the rakshasi's strike. The hammer arced down in a white blur and hit her on the ankle, sending streams of white light coursing up her leg. Great bruises and burns tore across her skin. The ravians cheered, and Akarat fell heavily, but even as Orro raced up her leg, muscles bulging and taut, eyes burning and keen as he faced the moment that would make him a true legend, she disappeared in a puff of smoke, leaving the ravian hero flailing in mid-air; and then she reappeared a few feet away and swatted him with a giant hand, sending him soaring over the battlefield, still clutching his hammer. She vanished again, screeching in agony as her skin turned black, and reappeared in Orro's path, catching his legs and chest neatly as he fell. And then she twisted with all her might, wringing Orro like a used cloth, and his spine shattered in a series of earth-rending cracks. With his dying breath, Orro uttered a command, and the head of his hammer fell apart, revealing the source of its power: a Ravian Star. Akarat stared at the black sphere in horror for a second, and all time stood still, as she saw the lightning trapped inside it. She looked around her, at the other rakshases who'd rushed to her aid, at the ravians staring open-mouthed, at the Ravian Star falling endlessly earthwards. She considered vanishing, leaving her brethren to die, and thought about her son alone in Vrihataranya, about her lover shot in the back by ravian hunters. Then she caught the falling Star and stuffed it in her mouth. A thousand warriors exhaled, and every rakshas among them wept; Akarat trembled and roared, a shudder ran through her body, and she exploded in a shower of blood and flesh and bone. A sphere of while light radiated from her body, incinerating anything it touched, but Akarat's sacrifice had not been in vain; the Ravian Star would have destroyed most of both armies had it exploded outside her body.

And at dawn on the fifth day, unobstructed by clouds, a keen-eyed pisac loitering around the rear of the Dark Lord's army screeched in delight; the Red Queen, distracted by the noise, cast a far-vision spell and felt something distinctly approaching delight.

A lone rider stood on the horizon to the east, outlined by the first rays of the morning sun. His raised scimitar flashed and sparkled in the light as other riders, thousands of them, thundered up behind him. Omar the Terrible had arrived. The Artaxerxian cavalry began the long ride to the battlefield, and all the Dark Lord's forces raised a deafening cheer to the skies.

'You must not remain here, your majesty,' said Satorin. 'We will be caught between jinn and rakshas, and things will go ill. My men will hold their ground and cover your retreat. You should seek safety.'

Zibeb smiled. 'But then the Dark Lord would have won this battle, good Satorin,' he said. 'The gods are watching. No true ravian could even think of defeat this day.'

'There will be other days,' said Satorin quietly. 'Fall back! They are almost upon us.'

'This is but a test, my friend,' said Zibeb. 'You must have faith. Return to your men. They lose heart without you.'

'But the jinn . . .'

'Obey me.'

Satorin bowed, his brow clouded, and returned swiftly to the fray.

Something was wrong. The Red Queen cast her far-seeing eye on the Dark Tower. It was wreathed in smoke and flashes of orange flame. She looked higher, searching the skies, and saw three tiny specks approaching the battlefield. Crows. Aciram had sent them to the north with Bjorkun, and then all had been silent. Red was suddenly concerned; had an army of ravians overcome the Skuans and attacked the Dark Tower from the north?

She vanished, and teleported towards the birds. After several bursts of travel, she was far outside the battlefield, and able to see them clearly. Their wing-tips moved up and down in perfect unison; these were senior officers. But a second later, their military precision was thrown into disarray. One of the crows stopped in mid-air, its wings contorting horribly, and then its corpse arced earthwards. Seconds later, another one met the same fate. Red was watching this time, and she saw a faint shimmer in the air just before the second crow died; something almost invisible had killed the bird in mid-air. Red sent three powerful streaks of green fire soaring into the air. One of them, passing just behind the lone crow's tail, spluttered and exploded at it hit something, and there was a harsh, spine-chilling screech; at the same moment, the crow twisted and jerked in mid-air. One of its wings was now broken. It looked down, saw Red, and flew at her, while she kept up a steady stream of fireballs around it.

Lord Degin oversaw a strong Willspear and cheered with his men as it stunned two giant rakshases, leaving a battalion of asurs unprotected and dazed. He quickly filled their minds with hatred towards Artaxerxians and sent them loping off towards the cavalry. Omar's men now had spears in their hands, and were crouched low on their horses. The Artaxerxians split their forces; half the horsemen raced towards the Dark Lord's army's left flank, where Angda and her vanars were engaging a squad of House Nergol axemen, and the other half, led by Omar, veered towards the onrushing asurs. Degin cursed aloud as he saw Dalmaan and some House Nergol nobles, on horseback, racing to the head of the asur line. Trust Dalmaan to try and steal the glory. He looked around for a horse to capture, but fresh orders arrived right then from Zibeb, and he hurried to follow them, muttering under his breath.

The crow lost consciousness and hurtled towards the earth, but Red teleported quickly and caught it. As she cast a healing spell on it and felt its heart begin to flutter, she looked up, just in time to dive to the ground and avoid being sliced in half by the crow's mysterious assailant. And as she saw what it was, as it swooped up in the sky and circled around her, roaring challenges, dust in the air rushing with it and outlining its powerful muscles, she felt something akin to anger.

It was a jinn.

Omar and Dalmaan thundered towards each other, scimitar and sword flashing in the sun. And then they slowed down, and behind them, the Artaxerxian cavalry and the asurs, soothed by the House Nergol ravians, slowed down as well until they came to a standstill.

Omar and Dalmaan dismounted and approached each other slowly.

'There is so much evil in this world. So much hatred, so much betrayal,' said Dalmaan.

'Yes,' said Omar. 'Isn't it beautiful?'

They embraced.

The Artaxerxian cavalry sliced into the vanars on the left flank, the speed of their charge carrying them through several lines of stunned infantry. Angda's finest warriors died with spears in their backs, and the rakshases that fought by their side were brought to earth and trampled by charging horses before they had any time to react.

The Red Queen waited for the jinn to charge, and then shape-shifted into a small cat. As the jinn swept by her, she pierced its air-hide with her claws, and thought about fire. Flames blossomed inside the jinn's shape, and it soared into the air, screeching in agony as it was devoured from within, and dissolved in a puff of smoke. Red cast another healing spell on the crow and its eyes opened. 'Report,' she said.

All over the battlefield, shimmering shapes descended from the sky, gathering dust and smoke and blood-spray as they sped earthwards. The jinn charged into the rakshases; the force of the impact carried them right through their targets, leaving gaping holes in the rakshas' bodies. A hundred rakshases died in an instant, and the ravians surged forward. Nenses, Dalmaan and Zibeb sent out fresh instructions and explanations, and ravians everywhere cast their nets on vulnerable asurs, driving them into a frenzy, and the Dark Lord's army turned on itself.

'I am Commander Triple-Zero One, "Kraken". Take me to Dark Lord Kirin, please.' The crow was dying, despite Red's best efforts.

'Tell me what happened,' she said. 'You do not have any time.'

'We were sent to act as communications officers for the Fusag operation,' said Kraken. 'I noticed irregularities there immediately, and sent my officers to report them. They must have been intercepted on the way. I remained at Fusag with a few other officers, waiting for the opportune moment to effect a getaway. But we were watched at all times by jinn, and it was made clear to us that any attempt to report the goings-on at Fusag to the Dark Lord would have been rewarded with torture and death.'

'What *happened*?' asked Red.

'Bjorkun and Omar signed a secret treaty with the ravians at Fusag. They were promised dominion over the north and Imokoi and a brighter future for humans. Siege engines constructed in Fusag have been brought to the Dark Tower. While Omar and his men and jinn came to the battlefield to help the ravians, Bjorkun and the Skuans attempted to take over the Dark Tower from within. The rakshases of the Tower were attacked by jinn. I do not know what happened to them. It was terrible; the jinn swept out of the sky and started slaughtering rakshases and setting Izakar on fire. They threw the defenders from the battlements, broke the outer fortifications and hurled fire and stone on the denizens of the walled city. The rakshases fought back valiantly, and my officers and I escaped to bring this news to the Dark Lord.'

'Bjorkun controls the Dark Tower now?'

'I do not know. The werewolves, too, were taken unawares, but Alpha Laakon was rallying them when we left. The jinn were also used to slaughter the shadowsnatchers and vanars that stood guard over the passes to the east. Soon a ravian force from Epsai will join the king in Imokoi. All is lost. I have failed, and should be executed.'

'Yes. But we will execute you later. For now, tell as many rakshases as you can that they must return to the Tower. This battle means nothing now. If the Tower falls, we are finished.'

'Why did you not tell me?' roared Degin. 'I am a council member! I deserved to know!'

Zibeb patted him gently on the shoulder. 'Do not question your king,' he said. 'Look around and savour this moment, Degin. In this moment is Peori avenged. Good has triumped over evil.'

They looked around with satisfaction at the chaos that reigned over the battlefield. Jinn and rakshases hurled spells and weapons at each other, rakshases teleporting and shape-shifting, jinn looping and swirling. The Artaxerxian cavalry made merry among the asurs. And the ravians were everywhere, slaying at will, commanding asurs to attack one another, helping jinn overcome rakshases. The battle had turned into a rout.

'Thus is evil vanquished by the evil it contains within itself,' said Lady Nenses. 'It is time to destroy the Tower, Zibeb . . . your majesty.'

'Not yet,' said Zibeb. 'We will wait for the siege-engines from the north, and have these asurs build us some more. We will wait for the auxiliary force from Epsai, and give Izakar the siege it deserves. The Dark Lord knows he is defeated. It is only a matter of time before the Tower falls. But the jinn must be destroyed as well. Let them battle the rakshases as long as possible.'

Aciram heard the news, and his roar of anger echoed through the land. At his command, the rakshases begin to leave the field, abandoning the asurs, pashans and vanars. On the evening of the fifth day, the rakshases and Alpha Laakon's werewolves drove the jinn out of Izakar, and fought the Skuans in the streets; Bjorkun escaped, but most of his men did not. A shroud of smoke still covered the Dark Tower as its defenders began to repair the battlements, to prepare for the coming siege. The jinn had ravaged the city's food supplies and cast corpses in its water reserves, and as the Dark Lord stood on top of the Dark Tower and watched mighty siege-engines roll towards his ravaged city from the north, and the ravian army moving slowly, inexorably onwards from the south, he wept tears of rage. The Red Queen stood by his side, watching jinn circle in the air around the battlements, watching rakshas and werewolf generals barking orders at asurs far below. She showed no sign of any emotion whatsoever.

At dawn on the sixth day, Queen Angda, left alone on the field, surrendered. King Zibeb accepted her sword with grace, and then asked Lord Degin, chief churl-commander, to entertain their noble guest. Degin smiled, and said he had very definite plans for their entertainment. Soon after a splendid banquet, and a touching ceremony where the ravian heroes were rewarded for their valour, Angda found herself walking out alone into the open ground in front of Izakar's gates. Her tears flowed freely as her limbs moved of their own accord in a crude dance; she tore at her clothes and rolled around in the dirt like an animal. The ravians watched this performance and pronounced it deeply symbolic; it was decided by Zibeb's Council that Angda would dance until the Dark Tower fell. And as Aciram and Red watched the vanar queen's humiliation from above, and wondered whether to end it by killing her with magic, they knew that the Dark Tower had already fallen.

6

'Lights!'

Ulsive and Erious, the two imps in charge of the day's Muwi-vision, looked at each other and shook their heads. It was not worth pointing out to the director of this piece, Pygmy Lion the pashan, that the scene was taking place in bright daylight. Pashans, even artistic ones like Pygmy Lion, tended to get a little . . . rigid in their habits, and Pygmy Lion's directorial methods hailed back to the days when the Badshah of Bolvudis used to supervise Muwi-visions himself. The Golden Age of Bolvudis, as that period was called, was no doubt wonderful, thought Ulsive and Erious, but Muwi-vision had moved on since then. They rolled their eyes and shivered gently, hoping Pygmy Lion would get the message, and soon. They were on a tight schedule.

After a few minutes, Pygmy Lion said 'Oh.'

'Eye rolling,' said Ulsive.

Pygmy Lion cleared his throat and called, 'Chimaera!'

Nimbupani, Bolvudis's most reliable monster, lurched out from behind one of the evenly spaced trees of the Square

Forest. He looked most depressed; his mane and whiskers sagged, his tail drooped despondently, its forked tongue flickering in and out to denote snake despair (it was not known who the final audience would be and Pygmy Lion, despite his intellectual pretensions, longed for mass adulation).

'Action!'

Nimbupani walked from one tree to another, deep in thought as a hidden band struck up a soulful, mournful tune. A drum began to beat out a slow rhythm. Nimbupani walked around desolately for a while, and then, seeing Pygmy Lion gesticulating furiously behind the imps, raised his head and sang:

'Both my ends are cruel and carnivorous,
I'm up danger creek without a boat.
I'm looking at a future inside my own stomach,
Life's not easy if you're one-third goat.'

The drum-beat quickened, became a heartbeat, insistent, passionate, and a bevy of belly-dancers in costumes that were shiny when they were present, which was rarely, slithered in behind Nimbupani and undulated attractively, causing him to break into a reluctant smile. His heart was still laden with woe, however, and this became evident when he sang:

'A serpent-head tail works well with the ladies,
But mine breathes fire, and worse, wants to roast me!
The other day I asked it for a private little scratch,
And it bit me in the buttocks and then tried to toast me!'

The belly-dancers began to shimmy curvaceously. The beat quickened further, and Nimbupani began to dance, his lion-paws thumping to the beat, his goat-hooves tap-dancing eloquently. Imps emptied huge sacks full of lotus petals from the treetops. Nimbupani was beginning to come to terms with his sorrows, and was getting into the swing of things, which was inevitable, given one of the Rules:

It is Difficult to be Sad while Surrounded by Belly-Dancers.

Nimbupani sang, quite cheerily, given the lyrics:

'You think that's tough? You heard nothing yet, baby,
I asked my lion-head to watch my back,
I thought he'd scold the scary snake and save me,
But he chewed off my hooves for a midnight snack!'

He twirled and swirled with impressive panache, and then pranced effervescently into the grand finale:

'They get the lobsters, I get the indigestion!
Mating? Procreating? My chances are remote!
I want some lovers, I just get leftovers!
Life's not easy if you're one-third goat.'

As the drum-beats died down, Pygmy Lion yelled, 'And that's an eyeful!' and there was much applause. Nimbupani bowed, slightly embarrassed, and the imps buzzed off towards the coast. It was just another normal day in Bolvudis, but the Muwi-vision that Nimbupani had just lent his talents to was not one that could be called normal in any sense: Pygmy Lion's greatest masterpiece, *The Dark Lord Returns*, a Muwi-vision that would shake the foundations of the world if someone found a way to actually display it to the world before the world ended.

The Dark Lord Returns was an epic Muwi-vision in three parts, a stunning blend of pulse-pounding action, lip-locking romance, rib-tickling comedy, spine-chilling suspense and heart-warming family values, the most ambitious project ever undertaken in Bolvudis. It told the epic tale of the rise of Kirin, the Son of Danh-Gem (played by Karisman, a young lad noticed on the beaches of Bolvudis a day before the Muwi-vision began, and recruited because of his remarkable resemblance to the Dark Lord, as vouched for by a wandering one-armed minstrel who had come to Bolvudis after a rather unfortunate botched attempt to become Izakar's court musician). The Muwi-vision chronicled his world-changing life—his early days as a beggar-boy in the streets of Kol, when his only friend was the tough but lovable stray dog Motonrole (Chrysanthemum the Wonder Dog), his meeting with his true love, Rohinee, the woman who would later become the Red Queen (Quivering Fatima, eye-popping star of *Daughter of the Zombie Pirate*, the saga of a fallen woman with luscious lips, a heart of gold and a dysfunctional family), his journey to power and fame in a world full of perils (Nimbupani, Vutton the Giant Crocodile and others, friendly appearances), his duel with the evil ravian seductress and sorceress Chlamydomona (Maya, daughter of the Badshah of Bolvudis) and his death in the arms of his weeping mother-in-law (Pygmy Lion, cunningly disguised).

'Right, that's quite enough time wasted, next scene!' yelled Pygmy Lion. 'The Dark Lord meets Chrysanthemum the Wonder Dog in the vegetable market.'

'Someone ate the vegetables,' called a lowly assistant director. 'But the cannibal virgin sacrifice area is free. Will that do?'

'It will have to. Very well. The Dark Lord meets Chrysanthemum in the cannibal virgin sacrifice area. Bring me the cannibals. Speaking actors ready?'

'The Wonder Dog isn't,' called a lowly assistant director. 'He ran off a while ago. He seemed upset.'

'Go find him. Throw a few sticks at him; whatever it is, he'll come around,' said Pygmy Lion. 'Are the humans here? We need to get one more rehearsal in before we see this one. Hurry, people!'

'I'm here,' said Kirin.

'Wonderful,' said Pygmy Lion. 'Now, lights!'

* * *

Kirin and Maya lay on soft white sand, looking up at the stars. Night had fallen gently over Bolvudis, and the beach was empty; the makaras and mer-people Maya remembered from her previous visits to Bolvudis had left, and no one knew why. The sea was calm. Waves lapped quietly at their feet, and a breeze rustled through swaying palms behind them. Maya was sleepy; she had spent most of the day leaping around and fighting young Xi'en warriors, which was apparently what evil ravian seductress–sorceresses did to pass their time. But Kirin was wide awake; perfect, tranquil moments made him vaguely nervous, made him sure that disaster was lurking in some nearby shadow. But the only thing lurking in the vicinity was Spikes, fast asleep under a tree. Two gulls flirted with each other and chewy death on his shoulders.

'I wonder where my father is,' said Maya. 'Nimbupani said he'd sent messages to Bolvudis, and Irik and Stivin Seagull left a few days before we arrived with some boats loaded with trunks of equipment.'

'Saving the world, no doubt,' said Kirin. 'The unwaba tricked him too; I wish there was some way of warning him, some way of telling him to go home and have a good time.'

'We could go to Kol and try to find him,' said Maya. 'I haven't seen him for so long.'

Kirin turned towards her and kissed her. 'I was wondering when you'd tell me you wanted to leave,' he said. 'I didn't think you'd be happy here doing nothing.'

Maya sat up and shook sand off her back. 'I just feel guilty, Kirin. We're having too much fun. We're lying around in this perfect bubble, and the world's falling to pieces outside.'

'And you still think you can save it? Beat the gods, change history, be heroes?'

'No. But I don't like not trying. I understand why you feel we've done enough. But we haven't. I want to be here, with you, living this life; I've never enjoyed myself more. When we came here, I thought being near you, loving you, doing all the things I always wished I could with you—I thought it would be enough. But it isn't right.'

Kirin sighed and closed his eyes. 'I just wanted to live my own life for a while. Meeting Zivran showed me there's really nothing we can do, this whole thing is too big for us. They're gods. They will do as they please, and trying to stop them will only amuse them. Why try, when we have some chance of being happy, at least for a while? I thought being here with you would mean that my life would be . . . complete, in some way. Can't we stay for some more time? At least until we decide exactly what it is we plan to do?'

'But what if there's *something* we can do now, some solution we can find if we look for it? Shouldn't we at least try to find out? This feels like giving up.'

'That's because it *is* giving up. And it's not that difficult.

We're just accepting what's real. It's like knowing you're going to die some day, that people you love aren't going to be with you forever, that everything changes every minute of our lives. You can't fight these things or change them. Sometimes you just reach a point where all you can do is laugh at everything—I mean, if you look at all we've been through from the outside, it's really completely ridiculous—and then decide to make the best of what you have. Right now, I have you, and very little time. I don't want to run around chasing answers.'

'But we don't *know* that the world is going to end. The unwaba told us that, and the unwaba was lying. Asvin thought he was going to end it, and then he discovered he had no idea what he was doing—and now he plans to do what he can to save anything that needs saving. And there's still a war to stop, and Kol needs our help too. What if the gods don't see through Zivran's trick? What if they finish the Game and go away? What if they decide not to destroy the world?'

'Then we have nothing to worry about, and should enjoy our holiday.'

'I can't. I have to know I did what I could.'

'You have, and so have I. Besides, we can't go to Kol. We're the Dark Lord and his wife, remember? There's no going back to our old life now.'

'We'll find a way. We always have.'

'We'll find ways to throw ourselves in danger and achieve nothing, and if we survive, we'll wish we hadn't bothered. And then everything will end, and we'll feel really silly before we stop feeling anything at all.'

He looked at her again, and saw tears in her eyes. 'What is it?'

'I love you very much, but I have to go, Kirin. I can't stay here.'

'I don't want to leave.'

'You don't have to.'

Kirin said nothing. Maya leaned over and kissed him. Then she rose, and looked out over the sea, towards Kol, far away to the east.

'You can't go,' he said, not looking at her. 'What about *Dark Lord Returns*? They're all depending on you. There's a passionate lovemaking scene in a few days, after the bit where the Son of the Dark Lord wrestles the giant crocodile.'

Maya laughed. 'Get Spikes to play the seductress.'

'You're leaving me, and you're offering me Spikes to cuddle. And here I thought you loved me.'

Maya stopped laughing. 'Come with me, Kirin. Please. We can still win this.'

Kirin said nothing. Maya looked at him for a while in silence, and then began the long walk to their hut.

'What was that?'

She stopped, annoyed. 'Don't make this any more difficult, Kirin. I'll be back when I can. If I can.'

'No, I heard something. There was a light.' Kirin stood up, looking around.

There was another light. A flash of light, at Kirin's feet.

And then there was a baby.

Kirin and Maya both leaped backwards, yelling in horror. The baby looked at them cheerily.

'Ey. Mum-mum-mum,' it said, by way of introduction. It was an extraordinarily cheerful-looking baby, composed almost entirely of circles. Maya peered, delicately, and discovered it was a girl.

'What is this?' she demanded.

'It's a baby.'

'I know it's a baby, damn it. What is it doing here? Where did it come from?'

'What makes you think I know?'

They peered at the baby, and she peered back at them.

'Should we pick it up?' asked Kirin.

'Why?'

'Well, isn't that what you do with babies that appear out of nowhere?'

'What makes you think I know what to do with babies? Is it because I'm a woman?'

'Gog!' said the baby, sensing disharmony. She decided she didn't like it.

She began to cry, and Kirin and Maya stared at each other in absolute terror. The baby cried with venom. Her piercing wail shook the sky, and the Psomedean Ocean backed away slowly, and the palm-trees stopped swaying and would have shuffled embarrassedly if they'd had feet. The seagulls on Spikes's shoulder fluttered away, complaining loudly about the neighbourhood.

Spikes walked up to Kirin and Maya and looked at the baby, blinking slowly.

'How long have I been asleep?' he asked.

The baby continued to cry. Spikes picked her up and shook her gently, with the general air of a crocodile trying to snap a gazelle's neck, and the baby liked this. She cooed, and gurgled, and clutched one of Spikes's tusks with a tiny fist, and said 'Mamma.'

'Don't even think about it,' shuddered Spikes, and handed the baby to Kirin, who looked at her as if she might explode, and tried to hand her to Maya, but Maya, being a very intelligent woman, had backed out of range long ago.

'Well, enjoy your baby,' she said. 'I'm off to Kol.'

'I'm afraid you must remain here,' said a voice from the sand. An old, dry, whispery voice.

The unwaba strolled out from a hole in the sand. He had the grace to look sheepish.

'I can explain everything,' he said.

Kirin and Maya stared at him, each other, and the baby in turn for several seconds, opening and shutting their mouths.

'Explain *this*,' said Kirin finally, looking in horror at the small creature slobbering happily on his neck.

'That,' said the unwaba, 'is the Infinite Infant.'

Silence reigned for a while.

'Pray continue,' said Maya.

'The Infinite Infant, the Baby of Destiny, Future Wielder of the Thunderbolt of Universal Doom,' said the unwaba.

'Ah,' said Kirin. 'That explains everything.'

'Good,' said the unwaba. 'Now listen closely. Here is what you must do.'

'Can I stamp on him?' asked Spikes.

'Please do,' said Maya.

'I see. Humour. How droll. Please carry on wasting my time, I have so much to spare,' said the unwaba. 'The Infinite Infant, since you do not know, is one of the most powerful gods—goddesses, I should say—in existence. She will lead her own pantheon when she grows older, and will rule over all known gods. And since time is irrelevant where gods are concerned, it may well be said that she rules us now. I would advise you, therefore, not to drop her. Do you have any more questions?'

'I have several,' said Maya. 'First: Why is this baby here?'

'She is here because I brought her here,' said the unwaba crossly. 'I should have thought that was perfectly clear. I have kidnapped her.'

'You have *what*?'

'Kidnapped. It means abducted. Removed her in secret. With her consent, of course, because you don't do anything to the Baby of Destiny that the Baby of Destiny doesn't like. So one might argue it does not really amount to consensual abduction. It is, in fact, more like an elopement, or would have been, had I not been a chameleon and she an infant.'

'And why, may I ask, have you kidnapped her?'

'I should have thought that was perfectly clear,' said the unwaba, annoyed. Time spent away from him had clearly had deleterious effects on these children's minds. 'No? I have abducted her and brought her here to save the world. Which, you may remember if you tax your feeble minds considerably, is what we set out to do in the first place.'

'We haven't forgotten that little meeting we had with Zivran, or how you betrayed us,' said Kirin quietly. 'Do you seriously think there's any chance of us listening to you now?'

'You doubt me because you were not, at the time, aware of my rather ingenious plan.'

'The plan where you used us to return you to the heavens and then turned against us?'

'No. If you were listening as intently as you claim, you will remember that I was omniscient while on this world, and regained my ability to forget while in the heavens. I was, obviously, aware this would happen. I knew I would forget what I wanted when I met Zivran. Therefore, I took steps to ensure that I subsequently remembered what I had forgotten. By repeating to myself the simple mantra 'Precipitately

Purloin Infinite Infant', I overcame this problem. I was somewhat puzzled when I found myself repeating this to myself in the heavens without any idea as to why, but I decided to trust in myself—always a good choice—and did, in fact, pilfer the said child. Once that was done and I returned to this plane, I naturally regained my omniscience, and with it, my plan to save this world.'

Maya sighed. 'I've had enough of this,' she said. 'Squash him, Spikes.'

'What will we do with the baby?' asked Kirin.

'Leave it here. It's not our baby.'

'We can't do that. It's a baby.'

'When did you become so maternal? We'll give it to someone on the island. Quivering Fatima would like it.'

'Boog,' said the Baby of Destiny disapprovingly.

'This is my plan,' said the unwaba, completely unmoved by censure or threat. 'The other gods have not noticed the infant's departure yet, since those among them who are not completely fascinated by the Game are busy stealing, gambling, drinking or partaking in orgies. But Zivran will have noticed her absence, and mine, and will know we are here. He cannot allow this world to be destroyed while the Infinite Infant is on it.'

'Then are we safe?' asked Kirin.

'No. Over time, the other gods will find out, and then they will take the Infant and destroy this world as punishment,' said the unwaba. 'But Zivran and his allies, Stochastos and Petah-Petyi, will do what they can for now to ensure this world's survival. The Game is going very well—the war is most interesting, and Mantric has begun his journey to the end of the world, which should be interesting viewing. Since the gods are sufficiently distracted, Zivran will be able to begin the construction of a mirror-world, where he will place this world's living denizens if he so desires.'

'But if Zivran knows, won't he try and steal her back?'

'That is unlikely,' said the unwaba. 'To do so, he would have to break the rules of the Game, and that would be an admission of defeat. Besides, he will be aware of my demands as a kidnapper. I want to live on the new world, and I want to keep the Infinite Infant with me. The Infant will grow up on this new world and sustain it with her powers, and will learn to love its inhabitants. I will teach her to observe and nourish, and not interfere physically with the lives of her subjects unless absolutely necessary. This is something Zivran would find most desirable, as this is a direction of thought he wants all gods to consider, and the Infinite Infant will be very powerful in the eons to come. All the other gods, too, will be quite relieved if the Infant has a world of her own to grow up in; it makes the universe safer for them if the Baby of Destiny does not want the worlds they govern.'

'I'll pretend I understood all that,' said Kirin. 'Are you saying, then, that we've won? This world is safe?'

'Far from it. But there is real hope now. In a sense, it all depends on Mantric. If his gift satisfies the gods, Zivran might be able to move those still living in this world at the time, including myself and the Baby of Destiny, to the new one and persuade the other gods, and Mantric, that this was the blessing Mantric sought. If Mantric fails, however, we are all destroyed. He must give the gods exciting entertainment, allowing Zivran to finish the task of creating another world exactly like this one. And that is not all Mantric must do. He must offer the gods something when he meets them; it must be something that pleases them greatly, allowing Zivran to move us all to the new world.'

'What will my father offer the gods?' asked Maya.

'I cannot say. I have a confession to make; my omniscience is no longer perfect, though of course I still know more than you could in a thousand lifetimes. It will take me some time to remember how to remember all I forgot. Until then, Mantric's intentions are a mystery to me. Until the time of our departure for the heavens, however, I was perfectly aware of Mantric's plans.'

'Well, what did he plan to give them then?'

'Nothing. He had no ideas whatsoever.'

'That's encouraging,' said Maya.

'What *is* encouraging is that the gods have taken a great fancy to your father and his friend the khudran,' said the unwaba. 'While they may not intervene directly in the Game, Zivran has permitted them to exercise a certain amount of . . . influence over Mantric's journey. The gods will ensure their own entertainment by making Mantric's voyage very eventful. This is wonderful as far as we are concerned; it would be unreasonable to expect that they would find anything to sustain their interest if Mantric had been simply sailing towards them through a calm ocean. Given the immense significance and ambition of his quest, it is only just that it should be suitably . . . epic.'

'So they're going to throw a million obstacles in his path? That's wrong!' said Kirin. 'I thought the first rule of this Game was that the gods could *not* interfere!'

'The rules of all Games change. Like their creations, the gods tend to make up the rules as the Game unfolds.'

'Why pretend there are any rules, then?'

'Be sensible, Kirin. We speak of gods here. In the early days of the universe, when the gods began to Play, they soon realized that infinite knowledge led to the Players knowing all possible outcomes if the Rules were predetermined. This was deemed unexciting, and rightly so.'

'But you said that gods didn't know everything, that they forgot things on purpose!'

'That was one of the rules they made up as the Games unfolded. The system is not perfect. This is intentional.'

'I give up.'

'Klllg. Eeeee,' said the Infinite Infant.

'Yes, of course,' said the unwaba. 'The Infant, observing your despondence, has offered to create a new world for you herself, as she finds this one, and its inhabitants, namely you, interesting. However, that will not work; her powers will only be restored to her when she leaves this world, and then she will forget this world. Which brings me to the task that now lies before you.'

'Which I'm going to turn down right now,' said Maya. 'I do not trust you any longer, unwaba. Even if my father does please the gods with his offering and we escape to the new world, the one who stands to gain the most is you; you will have a world to run with no other gods watching and a very powerful goddess growing up under your control. And we would still have gods controlling our lives. I cannot accept this.'

'Your views on this matter are not relevant. Here is what you will do,' said the unwaba. 'The Infinite Infant, like me, is currently subject to the physical rules of this world. She is vulnerable and must be protected. If she is killed by anyone or anything on this world, the world will be destroyed. If she is taken back to the heavens, we lose everything, and the world will be destroyed. You must, therefore, take good care of the Baby of Destiny.'

Panic slowly enveloped their faces.

'But we don't know how to take care of babies,' said Kirin.

'Then you must learn,' said the unwaba. 'It is a skill that might be useful later on, if there is a later on. Maya, you will take her to your hut now and feed her.'

'Googaa,' said the Infinite Infant, pleased to hear this.

'I will do nothing of the sort,' said Maya. 'You cannot barge back into our lives like this and take over again. And I have no idea what to feed her. There's some rum in the hut, but that might not be a good idea.'

'If you want the world to be saved, this is what you must do,' said the unwaba. 'She must be kept safe, and I would advise you to be wary, because you are in great danger here. There is no escape for any of you; if you do not go out into the world and seek danger, it will invite itself home and find you. Now, Maya, return to your hut, and you, Spikes, must accompany her. Keep the Infant under supervision at all times.'

Kirin held the baby out towards Maya, who regarded her gravely and then shook her head.

'I'm sorry, but I simply cannot do this. I'm afraid of babies,' she said. She groaned as the baby gurgled and looked peaceful. Defeated, Maya held her arms out stiffly, and the Infinite Infant clambered on board. A warm, wet feeling trickled down her front. The Baby of Destiny had marked her territory. She snuggled up to Maya confidingly, her head bumping against Maya's chin, and grabbed her, indicating by the eloquent speech 'Boop' that she was now hungry.

'No!' said Maya.

The Baby of Destiny, sensing rebellion, began to cry, and Maya, muttering dark imprecations, stalked off with her.

Spikes looked for an escape route for a few seconds, and then shrugged and followed them.

'Now that we are alone, Kirin,' said the unwaba, 'I have two things to say that are for your ears alone.

'First, you are in great danger. I cannot see what it is, but it is strong, and fast, and it wants very badly to kill you. Protect yourself, and, more importantly, protect the Infant.

'Second, enjoy every moment of the remaining days of your life as much as you can. If we succeed in this mad venture, you will still have defeated the gods, and you will still have to pay the price.'

'Before you turned up, unwaba, I was happier than I had ever been before. You had to come along and ruin my holiday, didn't you?' said Kirin.

'On the contrary, I made it infinitely more pleasurable for you,' said the unwaba. 'I brought you hope that the world could be saved, largely through your efforts and very noble self-sacrifice, which must give you some satisfaction. Besides this, I have ensured that you will savour every moment of this holiday, by informing you that it is the last one you will ever have. You will now feel more alive than you have ever felt before.'

'Well, I don't. And I'm not saving the world, unwaba,' said Kirin. 'Mantric is. I'm just sitting around on the beach, minding my own business. Why kill me?'

'Mantric's story and yours are not inextricably interwoven,' said the unwaba. 'He, too, conspires against the gods and will almost certainly have to give up his life in the end. And as for you, you are behind all the events that now shake the world, in one way or another. A few days of inactivity between crimes against the gods mean nothing. Do you have any more questions?'

'Not really,' said Kirin.

'I knew that,' said the unwaba, and fell asleep.

* * *

Two days later, the team working around the clock to create the masterpiece that would be *The Dark Lord Returns* were horrified to find that one of the cast no longer had dates available. Vutton, the giant crocodile, floated into the bay, dead. Her eyes had been gouged out, and her lower jaw had been ripped open, and hung pink and limp, flapping to and fro as waves raced past her corpse. Her body was covered with claw wounds and what looked like wolf-bites, but that was ridiculous. There could not possibly have been a wolf in the Psomedean Ocean.

7

The ravian king drew his sword and pointed it at the unimaginatively named Black Gate, the tall, wide, intricately carved ebony entrance to the Dark Lord's city fortress, the only weak point in the ring of adamant obsidian that stood between the invaders from New Asroye and the city of Izakar.

'Choose your destiny,' he said in a low, thrilling voice.

'Flawless victory!' roared three thousand converted asur churls who'd recently been under the impression that they had come from Taklieph, their capital, to the aid of the besieged Dark Tower. 'Fight!'

'Excellent,' said Zibeb.

'Brutality! Animality! Fatality!' cried the asurs, getting into the spirit of things.

'Superb,' said Zibeb. 'Fight!'

The asurs raced to the gigantic battering ram Zibeb's army had created over the last week and, after much groaning and yelling and lashing of whips, hoisted it up. More asurs ran underneath it and lifted it further, filling up the space beneath it with their bodies. The massive pillar of wood and metal shook slightly as it rose, and then crashed thunderously to earth; hundreds of asurs died in the process, but for every asur that fell, two replacements trotted up enthusiastically, their minds afire with dreams of hope and redemption. It was unthinkable that so massive an object could be carried on the shoulders of beings as small as asurs, but ravian wills held it up, and ravian commands kept asur minds strong even as their bodies broke. On the next attempt, the battering ram rose, and stayed up, creaking loudly and wobbling slightly. The carpet of asurs below it tottered this way and that as they realized and immediately forgot, under the influence of the ravians, that they would never walk upright again.

The front of the ram (named Khanzab the Prayer-Breaker by Omar the Terrible) was shaped like a manticore's head; the tip was made of bronze and inlaid with death-spells and Willspears. Whips cracked, their wielders yelled tender words of encouraging invective, and the asurs began to walk, gathering speed, until they broke into a bow-legged run, carrying Khanzab towards the Black Gate.

Khanzab tottered on. On the battlements next to the Black Gate stood Katnadev, a songscaper rakshas chieftain, and Alpha Laakon, lord of the werewolves. They showed no signs of panic as they watched the massive battering ram gather speed slowly and move ever closer to the gate beside them.

'It looks like a big centipede, doesn't it?' said Katnadev conversationally. 'A big drunken centipede.'

Khanzab tottered on. Laakon looked behind him, at vanar and asur archers filling every inch of space of the battlements.

'Rain,' he said, and the archers cheered.

The sky darkened as thousands of arrows arced into the air and converged on Khanzab. There were no ravians to divert the arrows; the asurs were no longer under their influence, but unable to stop because of sheer momentum. The arrows landed, skewering hundreds of running asurs, quivering into the battering ram's surface, building a wall of obstacles in front of the advancing manticore's head.

Khanzab tottered on. And then faltered as the asurs under it tripped over the bodies of their comrades, and then the gigantic pillar crashed to earth, crushing all those who carried it. It slid along the ground for a while, mowing down forests of arrows, Willspears tearing the ground in front of it, a trail of flattened bodies in its wake, and came to a squelching stop in front of the Black Gate. Rakshases hurled fireballs at it until it exploded in a cloud of splinters.

Laakon yawned. 'This is boring,' he said.

'It looked like a caterpillar before we burst it,' said Katnadev. 'A big, hairy caterpillar. Do you know the ones I mean?'

'I'm going for a nap,' said Laakon.

'And that bunch of squashed asurs over there looks like a daffodil,' said Katnadev defiantly to Laakon's back.

The ravian siege of Izakar had lasted two weeks now. The first day had been very dramatic; the vanars had decided, after a few agonizing hours, not to let their queen undergo further humiliation and had swarmed over the battlements to rescue her; most had died within minutes, and then Aciram had succumbed to emotional blackmail and gone to rescue Angda himself. He'd simply appeared on the battlefield at night, disguised as Lord Degin, killed a few ravians, freed Angda's mind and brought her back. This daring deed had cheered the denizens of Izakar greatly, and they had come to realize over the next few days that even without Omar and Bjorkun, the Dark Tower was more than adequately defended.

The ravians had amassed an impressive assortment of siege equipment for the massive task that lay before them; nine concentric obsidian walls, each taller than the last, each fortified by sorcery, bristling with sleepless guardians and commanded by ferocious, well-organized generals. Ladders and siege hooks brought from the north by Bjorkun's Skuans lay waiting for a grand charge, but until the rakshases patrolling the walls could somehow be destroyed, there was no particular point in sending troops to scale the walls; as soon as they were in range, the rakshases sent expanding walls of fire roaring outwards, consuming everything in their path. The asurs and ravians constructed several huge siege towers and sent them rolling towards the city to little avail; large numbers of asurs marched in front of the towers to stop the flames with their bodies, but rakshas fires could not be put out easily. The Red Queen had taught the rakshas the spellbinders' flame-arts, and tower after tower collapsed, spilling the warriors within, in swirling torrents of blue and green flame.

Ravian catapults, mangonels and ballistae kept up a steady barrage of projectiles into Izakar; huge stones, bundles of corpses, balls of Psomedean fire. While many of their missiles caused significant damage, many others never reached the Dark Lord's city; powerful Vrihataranya rakshases stood on the battlements, turning the ravian projectiles into bales of hay or bouquets of roses; on one memorable occasion, Katnaran, a young rakshas from the western borders of the Great Forest, turned two burning Psomedean-fire bundles into statues of Zibeb and Nenses in compromising positions, winning considerable applause from the assembled defenders.

But while Izakar's walls were immensely strong, they were not unbreakable; on several occasions, powerful ravian Willspears shuddered into the outer wall and sent cracks running along its surface. But the songscaper rakshases, who had built these walls, were defending them with skill and experience, singing stones back into place, sealing walls and adding defensive reinforcements faster than the ravians could destroy them.

Both sides had taken massive losses in battle, and even with the Artaxerxian and Skuan reinforcements, Zibeb did not have enough men to completely surround the Dark Tower and bombard it from every direction. The attack was concentrated on the southern and eastern ends, but Zibeb ensured that the Dark Tower was encircled, and the Dark Lord's soldiers had no way of breaking through his defences unobserved, at least above ground. The ravians had laboured through several nights, building a wall around the Dark Tower. No ordinary wall, this—it was made of corpses from the battlefield, packed and piled into a gruesome line of circumvallation, watching their comrades ceaselessly with dead eyes. Occasionally, public-spirited rakshases in the Dark Tower would send huge fireballs arcing into the wall, giving their lord's servants what passed for a cremation. If the ravians had expected this technique to destroy enemy morale, the plan failed; the Dark Lord's marksmen seemed to derive a certain enjoyment from their reunion with old friends, and whiled away the long, tense hours between attacks by knocking off the corpses on top of the barricade to see if their friends lay underneath.

Even though the wall of corpses was well protected, it grew thinner every morning; the rakshases had nothing to do with this. Mysterious forces were at work. Green mists would seep out of the ground every night, and corpses would disappear in unguarded sections of the wall. Rumours of sightings of undead lych-lords floated through the ravian ranks, and did nothing to improve the general mood.

The Dark Lord's army was trapped inside Izakar, and appeared not to mind this too much. Occasionally, when food supplies fell short, the Dark Lord would send out a party of asurs, officially to break the siege but, for all practical purposes, to achieve more efficient food rationing. The ravians ran short of supplies first; tightened belts led to weakened control spells, which led to more asur rebellions. They tried digging under Izakar, only to find asur tunnels full of explosive traps, flooding mechanisms, and friendly and very hungry pisacs. The few ravians that did manage to penetrate the maze of asur tunnels ended up in the bellies of dungeon-master Ublyet's little pets or petrified by Zolaa the reluctant gorgon. Sneak attempts at sapping through the walls had not worked either; the walls seemed smooth and solid, but there were, at regular intervals, machicolations, murder-holes and arrow-slits concealed by illusions of stone, and sappers who managed to escape the notice of the rakshas sentries on the walls were met with boiling oil, arrows, miscellaneous household waste and lewd remarks, and were driven back time and time again.

King Zibeb had not anticipated having to wait so long; he had not expected the Dark Tower to respond so quickly and efficiently to the Artaxerxian betrayal. The first jinn attack had been remarkably successful, but the Dark Lord had hidden reserves; a hidden tributary of the river Abet had solved Izakar's water problems, and asurs from Taklieph had brought supplies of food through underground tunnels from the north and west. The Red Queen had rallied the forces of the Dark Tower against the jinn; gargoyles and pazuzus had battled them in the air, and asur blacksmiths, after extensive foraging through ancient halls full of plunder from Xi'en and two nights of intensive, magic-aided weaponcraft, had produced large quantities of jade-tipped arrows that burned holes in jinn spirit-skins and sent them screaming back to their controlling sorcerers. And three nights after Angda's rescue, the Red Queen, with Alpha Laakon and his werewolves, had launched a daring raid on the Artaxerxian camp, crossing the ravian lines through an underground tunnel and emerging amidst the sleeping Artaxerxian sorcerers. The jinn had lost their masters that night; it had been a furious battle, fought in just a few minutes. Like grey streaks of lightning, the werewolves had moved from tent to tent, shadowy death-dealers slashing, ripping, tearing; by the time the ravians and Omar's soldiers had come to the aid of the sorcerers, most of the werewolves had left, leaving a camp full of blood-soaked corpses and a collapsed tunnel behind them. Most of the freed jinn had disappeared; perhaps they were already back in the desert, hiding in the ever-shifting sands. A few jinn had remained on their own volition, out of sheer malice, to finish the carnage they had started. King Zibeb had ordered them to wait for his command before they attacked again. As a matter of principle, they had ignored him completely. Some of them still flew around Izakar, occasionally hurling themselves at defenders who caught their fancy, picking them up and hurling them to their deaths from great heights.

As the great battering ram Khanzab burst into tiny pieces, signalling beyond all doubt the failure of yet another plan, King Zibeb summoned his council to help him decide his next move. Lady Nenses was strongly in favour of using the six remaining Ravian Stars to bring down the Dark Tower, but Dalmaan insisted that the ravians' most powerful weapons should be held back until the vamans entered the fray; he had recently received word that the ravians' allies among the vamans had been captured and executed, which meant that vaman trouble was inevitable, and soon. Lady Nenses pointed out that this meant that the rakshases should be dealt with at once; a prolonged battle over Izakar would only give Kol and Bhoomi more time to rally their forces and come to the Dark Lord's aid. What better way to prevent this than with a little Ravian Star dropped on the Dark Tower, destroying the Dark Lord in a blaze of white fire just as Isara had two centuries ago?

At that very moment, the Dark Lord's war council, assembled in his private chamber, was interrupted by someone who had never before dared to climb the stairs to the upper levels of the Dark Tower: Ublyet the asur. It was evident that the dungeon-master was deeply troubled, and not just by the unaccustomed altitude.

'My little pretties,' he said, shuffling his feet. 'They gone.'

'Have your monsters been killed? Are there ravians in the dungeons?' asked the Red Queen.

'No, no. All tunnels full, pisacs doing fine, ravians ripped and rotting,' said Ublyet, looking most depressed. 'My pretty pretties vanished.'

Since no one knew exactly what Ublyet's pretties were, only that they were horrible monsters that tried to eat anyone foolish enough to enter the lower levels of the Izakar dungeons, this news did not cause the sort of inconsolable mass grief that Ublyet had evidently been expecting.

'I'm sure they will turn up,' said Aciram. 'Now if you don't mind, Ublyet, we have a battle to plan.'

Ublyet bowed miserably and shuffled out, only to burst in again a second later. 'They're here!' he yelled, leaping up and down in excitement.

'Your pretties are back? Good,' said Aciram. 'Leave us now, noble Ublyet.'

'No, no!' yelled Ublyet, spitting and rolling his eyes joyfully. 'Not lovely pretties! Heart still broken, but! Dragons are coming!'

Battle plans were thrown to the wind as the Dark Lord's council raced to the balcony, shoving one another aside like children. Was this possible? Could Ublyet be telling the truth? Had the dragons arrived to save the day?

Yes, yes and yes again. From the west, from the Mountains of Shadow, faster than the wind, lighting up the pale morning sky in the distance with gusts of wild fire, came the dragons, little bat-winged specks growing ever larger, and hope came with them, and thunderclouds followed. The Dark Tower echoed with cheers and roars as their shapes became clearer, fleet-winged Skuan fire-drakes and Xi'en serpent-worms slithering through the sky, speeding to the Dark Lord's aid. The Dark Lord's generals sped to the city to assemble their troops; the arrival of the dragons could not be greeted with anything less than a full-scale, all-out assault on the enemy. The ravians would be caught between earth and sky, and every life Imokoi had lost would be avenged. Drums and horns echoed insistent summons; the Dark Tower's time had come.

'It would seem,' said King Zibeb, studying the sky gravely, 'that we will have to use a Ravian Star.'

Lady Nenses smiled smugly, and Dalmaan stood and bowed.

'In light of the dragons' arrival, I withdraw my previous objections,' he said. 'Should we bother to vote?'

He looked around at the rest of the council, and said, 'No doubt Lady Nenses has already decided how best to get the Ravian Star to the Dark Tower. We have no air support after the unfortunate removal of the jinn, but she must have taken that into consideration.'

'I have,' said Nenses. 'I will cast a stability charm on a Star, and we will use a catapult to deliver it.'

'Why?' asked Omar. 'It might be intercepted at the wall. Much better to let a jinn drop it on the very top of the tower.'

'What jinn? And even if we had them, a jinn would not be able to deliver a Ravian Star,' said Satorin. 'It would explode on coming into something that is magical and not ravian.'

'Very well,' said Omar. 'I will drop it myself.'

'You intend to fly to the Tower?' asked Dalmaan.

'No,' said Omar in freezing accents. 'I will hold the Star, and the jinn will hold me.'

'An excellent idea, my dauntless human friend,' said Dalmaan. 'And if you had protected your sorcerers better, the jinn would still have been under their control, and this plan could have been carried out. Right now, there is a minor flaw in your plan; you have no jinn.'

'As it happens,' said Omar, 'I do have one jinn with me, and under my control. I have in my possession a lamp that was among the original five items needed to raise Danh-Gem from the dead. The jinn is sealed inside this lamp with a jade bead, and will obey my instructions even without the pentacles and amulets that my sorcerors needed to restrain their savage servants.'

He drew the lamp out from his robes and placed it on the table, smiling innocently at Dalmaan's blank face.

'It is settled, then,' said Zibeb. 'Give Omar the Star, Nenses. The rest of you, to arms! The dragons will be with us soon, and so will the rakshases. We must receive them graciously.'

As the other champions left Zibeb's tent, Lady Nenses looked doubtful. 'Perhaps I should drop the Star myself,' she said. 'Omar has been very useful, but this is too great a matter for him.' Omar's brow clouded, but he held his tongue and tried to pretend, as the ravians were, that he was not among those present.

'You will be needed on the battlefield. Remember, we will have dragons to fight, and you are our greatest mage,' said Dalmaan swiftly. 'Omar's humans can do without him.'

'But what if he fails?' asked Nenses.

'We have five more Ravian Stars, and several catapults,' said Zibeb. 'He will not fail. The Ravian Star, please.'

Lady Nenses drew out a black sphere from a bag on the floor. The stars inside it glittered and glowed as she handed it to Omar.

'Let us see this jinn of yours,' said Dalmaan. 'How do we know he will not turn rogue like the others?'

Omar smiled again, reached out with long, slender fingers and rubbed the side of his lamp gently. After a while, the lamp began to shake gently, but Omar did not remove the jade bead.

'Jinn of Al-Ugobi, slayer of the sands, hear me now!' he called. 'I will let you out of this lamp only if you promise to carry out for me, fully, promptly and diligently, three wishes of my choosing, at a time of my choosing, while also promising to obey no master but me until all my three wishes are fulfilled.'

'Not bad,' said Dalmaan with a smile.

The jinn, however, did not respond.

'Shake once for yes, and twice for no!' called Omar.

After a brief pause, the lamp shook once.

'You are shaking in response to the conditions I set out for you now regarding my three wishes, and not in response to anything said by any other person at any other time?' called Omar. This time, Dalmaan, Zibeb and Nenses all smiled appreciatively.

From the lamp there came a sound somewhere between a moan and groan. Then the lamp shook once.

'Excellent,' said Omar, and removed the jade bead. The jinn floated out, a shimmer in the air, its white eyes glowing as they found their place in its body. It looked around.

It was hungry.

'What are your wishes, Master?' it said.

'Carry me to the top of the Dark Tower, and stay there with me until I have dropped the Ravian Star on it. I will then give you further instructions.'

'As you wish, Master,' said the jinn.

The ravians stood in battle formation outside the Black Gate, weapons drawn, looking at the sky, their hearts pounding in time with the thunderous wing-beats of the dragons streaking towards them. In front of the ravians stood legions of asur churls. The Skuans and Artaxerxians held the flanks. Inside the Dark Tower, Aciram's forces filled the first three circles of the city; hordes of asurs, Angda and her vanars, and rakshases in human size waited for the Dark Lord's command. Laakon's werewolves, united and itching for their first taste of open battle, prowled the walls of the third circle, dressed in enchanted rakshas-hide armour, layered leathery skin-plates that would change shape with them.

The jinn soared skywards, holding Omar the Terrible by the shoulders. He clutched the Ravian Star close to his chest, afraid it would fall, afraid that something would happen to ruin this moment, his moment. He could not breathe; his heart was trying to climb out of his throat. Rakshases hurled fireballs at the jinn from the walls; the jinn dodged them without apparent effort. Omar had never flown before; nothing could have prepared him for the sight of armies far below like little ants in the sun, for the wind roaring in his ears, for the jinn's talons cutting into his body. His stomach rebelled and threatened to empty itself. His face froze in a mask of terror, and strange demonic visions clouded his eyes. But he was still Omar the Terrible, commander of Artaxerxia, and he mastered his struggling mind and body, concentrating only on the sphere in his hands.

Four pazuzus converged on the jinn, shrieking harshly. The jinn floated in mid-air, observing them calmly as they grew closer, scorpion tails twitching, fangs bared and gleaming.

'What are you waiting for?' yelled Omar. 'Protect me! Kill them!'

'As you wish, Master,' said the jinn.

A few seconds later, three dead pazuzus plummeted earthwards. The jinn held Omar in one hand, and held the fourth pazuzu in the other as it munched on its neck. It deposited Omar on top of the Dark Tower and hovered in the air, eating the pazuzu with much relish.

Omar stood on top of the Dark Tower, watching the world beneath him, listening to the roar of conch-shells, drums and horns far below as the Dark Lord's doomed army prepared for battle. This was where he belonged, he thought, with the world beneath him, waiting for him to decide its fate. He laughed, and held the Ravian Star aloft, rejoicing in the wind that whipped through the Dark Lord's banners around him, savouring the moment. They had five more! They could have won the war at any time of their choice, but had held back only to conserve their resources! Below him, grotesque stone gargoyles crawled slowly upwards, their jaws opening and slamming shut as they approached the intruder. Omar ignored them. He looked at the Dark Lord's army again, somewhat irked that no one significant had even noticed him. He would have liked to have stared into Kirin's desperate eyes as he dropped the Ravian Star on his beloved city. He would have liked to have had the whole world's eyes upon him as he showed them the peril of underestimating humans, of ignoring him. Omar the Terrible. King of the world. One day.

'Carry me into the air,' he said. 'If I drop this here, it will destroy us both.'

'As you wish, Master,' said the jinn. It dropped the half-eaten pazuzu on the nearest gargoyle, picked Omar up and soared high into the sky above the Dark Tower.

The dragons flew over the western walls of Izakar. At Aciram's signal, thirty pashans picked up chains and started pulling. Great gears ground, and the Black Gate creaked, shuddered and sang as it opened.

Omar stared at the dragons in disbelief. They had been so far away just a few seconds ago! They seemed to be heading straight for the Dark Tower, and appeared not to have noticed him. He would drop the Star when they reached the Tower, he decided; the ravians would marvel at their own wisdom in offering him their friendship.

'I have a question,' said the jinn.

'What?' asked Omar irritably, torn from his dreams of world domination.

'Why three?'

'Why three what?'

'Wishes. Why three?'

'I don't know. How does it matter?'

'It should matter to you,' said the jinn.

'Why?' asked Omar.

'You've spent them all.'

The jinn bit off Omar's head, thus effectively silencing him. It looked at the Ravian Star, black and shiny in his lifeless hands.

It then opened its mouth wide, and swallowed Omar whole.

There was a spectacular explosion. A blinding white sphere lit up the earth for a second, and then disappeared, and so did the tip of the Dark Tower. Danh-Gem's banners burned as they floated downwards and the gargoyles were shattered into tiny pebbles. The dragons felt the impact as they raced over the Tower; three Skuan drakes were thrown downwards, but they recovered, flapping their great wings, and reformed their line, screaming defiantly and sending sheets of flame gusting upwards.

'What was that?' asked the Red Queen, turning to Aciram, whose face had suddenly gone white.

'You'd wanted an open ceiling,' said the Dark Lord. 'I ordered it specially.'

The Black Gate was open. The two armies stared at each other for a few seconds.

'Charge,' said Aciram, matter-of-factly.

The Artaxerxians paid dearly for Omar's failure; Lord Degin sent them racing into the heart of the enemy, and there they met the werewolves. Horses and men were slashed to ribbons by the Pack, and even the rakshases paused and shuddered at the werewolves' ferocity. Not that the rakshases were being particularly gentle themselves; swelling to giant size, they trampled over asur, human and ravian alike, looking to end the battle swiftly and not let the dragons take all the glory.

The ravians fought with savage, controlled skill, each thrust taking a life, each smooth, seamless movement perfectly planned, perfectly executed, each charge a dance of metal and blood. But as the dragons reached the battle, even the bravest ravians looked up and trembled. There were more dragons here than even the veterans of the Great War had seen, more dragons than anyone knew existed, darkening the sky and shaking their earth with the pounding of their wings.

The ravians were, therefore, extremely pleased when the dragons did not attack them, but simply flew over the battle, showing no sign of even noticing it. Rakshas cheers turned into angry yells; Satorin led a charge that ended in the deaths of Katnadev and Katnaran, and Nenses sought out the Red

Queen. They duelled, with fire and light and will-thrust and illusion, showing no signs of fatigue as those around them were destroyed by their magical attacks. Lord Degin fell, crushed by leaping vanars. Angda ripped off his head and held it up for all to see, screaming and pounding her chest, and the vanars fought with new zeal, flying over the heads of their enemies, landing, striking and leaping again, avenging fallen Vanarpuri. And King Zibeb met the Dark Lord, and they roared in battle-frenzy as they clashed, for power, for victory, for the world.

At the head of the dragon army, Tjugari the Destroyer, fastest of the Skuan dragons, waited until he crossed the ravian army and then dipped, spreading his wings, and skimmed further southwards, searching the earth for a sign. Behind him, the dragons spread out, their shadows diverging as they streaked over the ground. Some flew on towards Danh-Gem's Wasteland, others rose higher in the air and circled. Messages flew between their minds, brief, precise signals that intensified into excited chatter as the earth below them began to shake. From the Dark Tower, both armies watched and wondered: What could possibly be so important that this battle, the battle to end all battles, did not even distract the dragons?

From the west, the Xi'en serpents raised the alarm; a thick mist was flowing in from the Mountains of Shadow, heading towards the Dark Tower and spreading every second; what it concealed they could not tell, but there was something in it, something that roared and hissed and chattered. They wanted to fly down and investigate, but Tjugari ordered them to wait; this was not what they were here for.

Finally, word arrived from Danh-Gem's Wasteland: huge cracks were spreading through the earth. It was time. Tjugari roared and breathed fire as he swept upwards and eastwards. Behind him, other dragons roared and swerved in magnificent manouevres, further and further away from Izakar. They did not have to travel long; the cracks in the earth sped northwards as they widened, towards the dragon army and the Dark Tower behind them. An hour passed; the battle raged on, and the dragons watched.

And then the earth split as massive heads burst through it, and the dragons screamed encouragement as Qianzai, Mother of Darkness shot out of the ground and took to the air. Twelve more eruptions, and her children followed her into the sky, leaving trenches in their wake. Qianzai was as beautiful and majestic as ever, but her body was covered with scars; some of her children shook uncontrollably as they rose, and the other dragons saw deep gashes on their bodies, as if claws the size of elephants had gouged out their flesh.

Tjugari flew up to Qianzai, saluting her with lowered wings and snout; she nodded curtly, her serpent body curling and twisting as she circled in the air.

The others? Where are they? asked Tjugari.

Dead, said Qianzai. *The deep-dwellers are coming. Do what you can.*

The ground heaved and shuddered, tremors spreading in ripples that washed over Imokoi, shaking even the Dark Tower some distance to the north.

Another dragon head burst out of the earth, a red Xi'en serpent. In the sky, the dragons cried out in dismay; her face was streaked with scars, and one of her eyes had been torn out of its socket. She heaved and strained, and pulled herself out of the ground, slowly, agonizing, each thrust displaying a fresh array of lacerations. But even as she gathered her breath for one final push that would free her from the grasping earth, her mouth twisted, and she slid back into the ground and disappeared, pulled in again by something underground.

In the terrible pause that followed her dying scream, every dragon heard Qianzai's voice, low and powerful, inspiring even in great weariness.

Dragonkind. Children of my heart. Hear me now, she cried. *You know why we are here. We are the keepers of the balance; order and chaos, fire and water, earth and sky. We are the guardians of the surface, the protectors of all who breathe upon it, their defenders against Above and Below. Today, the skin of the world breaks, and we alone can heal it. The forces of the underworld strike out in blind anger, and an answer from the heavens would destroy all that lives in-between. The three worlds have honoured us and hurt us, revered us and feared us. Today, we must show them why. Are you ready?*

And then the dragons heard a screeching laugh, and Tjugari the Destroyer's harsh voice.

And for those of you that didn't understand any of that, he said, *this is it. Bad things are coming. Burn them.*

In response, every dragon in the sky roared a mighty challenge, and bathed the cracked earth in a sea of fire. And then the earth burst open, and the creatures of the underworld stepped out in the sun.

They were beasts that defied description; shape-shifting masses of hatred encased in thick hides of skin and hair, chitin and mucus, shell and scale, fire and ice. Some were in the form of giant animals, great apes with crab's legs, mantises with millions of glistening tentacles, hill-sized boars with serpents for tails. They split the sky with their wordless challenges, roaring and screeching as they bathed in dragon-fire. Some spread vast slime-coated wings and soared upwards to meet their adversaries, others stomped and slithered northwards towards the Dark Tower, crushing the ground beneath them as if it were a thin layer of ice. Other creatures jumped out behind them, smaller monsters made of earth and dust and shifting piles of rock that staggered and jerked below the bodies of the larger monsters, sometimes disintegrating into swarming piles of rubble, and pale worms that fed on fire, growing larger as they foraged, obscene grubs that moved mindlessly through the Wasteland, coating it with oily, viscous fluids. No single will drove them; they struck in every direction, seeking only to destroy, paying heed to the dragons only when attacked, and then responding with insane fury in showers of venom and hurled clumps of earth. Some of the beasts succumbed to the rain of fire, burning horribly, crashing into the rest as their skins peeled off, revealing pink, glistening muscle beneath. But many of the creatures seemed immune to fire, and ignored the chaos around them, striding off in various directions, swinging their massive limbs. It was up to the dragons to herd them in, to attempt the task of driving them back into the earth. Several dragons pounced on the monsters, folding their wings and pouncing, landing on the beasts and fighting with claw and fang and tail-spike. But the beasts were stronger; they ignored their wounds as they tore into the dragons, tearing off their wings, bringing them to earth and stomping them to death. The dragons breathed fire, slashed out with tooth and claw and rose again, but the beasts were beginning to scatter and spread, heading off at random towards places unknown.

Zibeb leaned on his sword and looked at the madness around him, at fleeing rakshases and ravians, at asurs screeching in terror as the ground shifted and swallowed them, at ravians and pashans and humans who'd dropped their weapons and were simply staring, open-mouthed, at the creatures that advanced towards the Dark Tower.

'Come here and fight, you coward!' he cried. 'Let us end this!'

Aciram appeared behind him, swinging a great mace, but Zibeb was ready; he spun around, his sword hissing as he struck. He encountered only empty air as Aciram teleported mid-stroke, reappearing a short distance away. But the Dark Lord did not charge. Instead, he looked beyond Zibeb, at the monstrous beasts blundering towards Izakar, flailing their limbs uselessly as dragons above burned them.

'I don't know if you've noticed,' said Aciram, 'but the world seems to be ending.'

'We should hurry, then,' said Zibeb. 'It would be a tragedy if this ended inconclusively.'

A creature that looked like a giant squid with occasional elephant legs swept into the ravian rearguard, sending bodies flying with slow swings of its tentacles, and screams of horror echoed through the ranks of both armies as the combatants looked up and saw the twitching bodies of their comrades stuck to the beast.

The Red Queen appeared beside Aciram, her sword pointed at Zibeb.

'We should leave,' she said.

'Not without you, dear wife,' said Zibeb.

'Look at them, you fool,' she snapped. 'They're bigger than the Tower, and they're headed this way. The Tower itself is going to collapse any minute now. What are you fighting for?'

Zibeb sighed, and turned. His face tightened as he saw another underworld monster, a giant toad with a head that seemed to be made out of living shadow, leaping towards them. The beast sailed over both armies and landed in the city, flattening three city walls. An endless tongue shot out of the shadow-head, demolishing a guard tower. Rakshases and ravians milled around in confusion around the Black Gate, warriors looking not for combat but for survival in any form, escape from randomly slashing blades and falling stone, stray dragon-fire and spraying venom.

'If I had known your world was like this,' said Zibeb, 'I wouldn't have come.'

Aciram laughed. 'Truce?' he said.

'Never,' said Zibeb. 'But I think a tactical withdrawal seems in order. If any of us outlive this, rakshas, we will do this again. Or would you prefer peace?'

'Why should I seek peace? Victory will be ours in the end, ravian.'

'End? What makes you think this will ever end?'

Aciram bowed. 'Until the next time, then.'

'It has been an absolute pleasure,' said Zibeb, bowing in turn.

'Will you two stop trying to get the last word in and get the hells out of here, you ridiculous . . . *men*?' yelled Red, looking positively animated.

Both Aciram and Zibeb considered meaningful replies, but wisely chose instead to escape as a great tentacle came crashing into the ground where they stood.

After a few exhausting minutes, bugles and horns sang out, signalling retreat, but no one heard them in the clamour. They were unnecessary in any case; all those still alive were alive because they had already fled. The Dark Tower still stood, though the city around it had mostly been flattened; a monster seemed to have taken a fancy to it, and was rubbing its snout lovingly against the upper levels. To the east, an elephant-spider exploded in a blaze of white light as Lady Nenses used another Ravian Star. To the west, Bjorkun Skuan-lord tripped on a fallen asur's foot and cut himself in half on his battle-axe. By the northern outer wall, dungeon-master Ublyet capered and pranced in delight, yelling 'My pretties! My lovely little pretties!' until a burst of dragon-fire silenced him. The ravians raced eastwards, using Willspears and Spirit Trenches to slow down pursuing beasts; the vanars raced ahead of them, casting their armour aside as they fled. The werewolves raced westward for the valleys of the Mountains of Shadow, rakshases appearing and teleporting ahead occasionally in their midst. The humans and asurs fared worst of all, but then they had expected that when they had come to the Dark Tower, and were not particularly surprised.

Red and Aciram stood their ground by the Black Gate with a few Vrihataranya rakshases, unwilling to escape until they had at least made their present felt. As Red sliced off an intrusive tentacle and looked around for smaller creatures to pick on, she saw something that made her pause and blink with something approaching wonderment.

'Well, that's strange,' she said.

Beside her, Aciram detached a massive lobster claw from a howling beast that seemed to have plenty to spare, and turned violently towards her.

'Strange, did you say?' he roared. 'What could you possibly find *strange* about anything here, my love?'

'Look,' she said, pointing.

Aciram looked, as instructed, and saw a thick mist rolling in very fast from the south-west towards the Dark Tower, streaming across the land like a visiting ocean. Through the roar of the battlefield, he heard the sound of a thousand horns blowing as if from a great distance, and the rumble of what sounded like a great army.

A lone figure on horseback leaped out of the mist, and rode ahead of it. A human figure in black armour, on a grey steed with burning red eyes. A scythe glittered blue in his hand.

'To the death!' called the Cold Prince with no sense of irony whatsoever.

And then the mist lifted, and dragons, rakshases and monsters alike stopped and stared at a very strange sight indeed.

The undead had turned up uninvited, and they were looking to recruit.

'It's the end of the world,' said Aciram. 'Just like Duamu predicted.'

'Maybe you shouldn't have had him executed, then,' said the Red Queen.

'Maybe not.'

A whispering host of long-dead ancient heroes and warriors led the charge as they tore into the creatures from the underworld, blood and bone and dust swirling in their remembered shapes, reliving ancient battles with new enemies, calling out with sonorous voices in languages long dead. Skeleton warriors raced everywhere, waving ancient swords, stabbing and thrusting until they crunched to piles of bone under massive feet, and then rose and reassembled themselves. Ghouls, ghoulehs and legions of zombies staggered and stumbled towards slow-moving monsters, biting, tearing and clobbering, crazed with flesh-lust, unable to feel either pain or fear. Lych-lords summoned wave after wave of freshly dead warriors, and asurs, ravians, rakshases and pashans fought side by side under their command, bodies jerking as they cast off memories of life and grew accustomed to the invisible strings that now controlled them. Stone statues, human figures with the heads of cats, jackals, crocodiles and ibises, hammered and pounded ceaselessly on the rock-monsters, turning them into clouds of dust and pebbles. Pretas, jakyinis and moumras capered mindlessly about, falling upon stray enemies and sucking out their blood and spirits in an orgy of life-seeking hunger. The Marichelli grotesques wandered the field, striking blows when they could, assembling new creatures from scattered limbs and adding greatly to the general ugliness of the spectacle.

A black wave detached itself from the main force and swept westwards; spirit scarabs, swarming over anything in their path and reducing it to clean bone in seconds. Millions of tiny feet clattered over fallen armour and weapons and up the appendages of nearby monsters, biting through hide and muscle, bringing down behemoths a nibble at a time. At Tjugari's command, the dragons dispersed, and concentrated on rounding up roving monsters and guiding them with walls of shifting fire towards the Dark Tower, where the Four Horsemen and Erkila, Queen of the Damned, commanded the endless legions of the undead. There stood Tzimem, gold mask covered in slime as he toppled one great beast after another, cutting his way methodically through legs and tentacles until they fell, and then cutting his way out from under them if they fell on him. The heart in his hand pulsed louder than a dragon's wingbeat as it drank fresh blood from the mightiest beasts to ever walk the face of the earth. The Unnamed raced through the burning streets of Izakar, spreading mists of confusion and listlessness, her werecat Manslaughter, grown to the size of a lion, constantly by her side. The Muratorian, still uncomfortable on his horse of bone, stood at the Black Gate, mind-casting messages to the lych-lords, orchestrating the battle. And Erkila stood by his side, glowing white and beautiful, her black eyes shining with satisfaction as she beheld the carnage before her, occasionally stepping out in the form of a little kitten to overpower a monster that attracted her attention. But there was no doubt as to who led the undead in battle; it was the Cold Prince, who seemed to be everywhere at once, rallying his troops, taking on the fiercest of the monsters, leading the bravest charges.

The beasts of the underworld fought fiercely and well, crushing undead in their thousands, filling the earth with dead flesh and ichor, but there could be no victory against an army that responded to destruction with reassembly, that regarded decapitation as the acquisition of a new worldview. The battle lasted for three days, but its outcome was never in doubt. One by one, the monsters fell and were torn apart, and their diverse limbs added to their conquerors'.

And then the battle was over, and the dragons saluted the lords of the undead with fountains of fire and swept homewards, leaving the battlefield to the teeming host of the Great Pyramid. Innumerable bodies stood whispering and moaning, seeing the world through dry, immobile eyes, sensing life in the world around them, hungering to destroy it. They thronged towards the Dark Tower, towards their captains, and begged for more, begged to carry on with the slaughter, to turn the whole world, end the injustice of breath and warm skin and beating hearts. And Erkila heard their prayers, and turned towards the Cold Prince, saying nothing, but asking a thousand questions with her eyes.

'No,' said Pralay. 'Not yet. The creatures of the underworld are not defeated yet; we must first destroy them utterly, establish beyond doubt our sole right to end this world. We must delve beneath the earth, find their secret lairs and destroy them. When that is done, we will decide what is to be done with the rest of the world.'

Erkila smiled, and the Cold Prince knew she understood far more than he wanted her to, but she nodded, and issued her orders, and soon the undead host was gone. All save the Cold Prince; he dismounted and remained at the gate, silent and motionless, until the last zombie had lurched into a crack in the earth, and all was silent by the ruins of Izakar.

'Come out,' he said then.

The Red Queen and the Dark Lord materialized next to him. He gazed at their faces, and looked away.

'Your faces are known to me,' he said. 'I would urge you to change them if you can; these are not faces that bring me joy.'

The rulers of Imokoi changed their faces without question, donning the guises of ravians they had recently slain, and then Red stepped forward.

'Why did you remain?' asked Pralay. 'Why did you not flee with your rakshas brethren? This was no place for the living.'

'I stayed because I recognized you, and he stayed because he did not want to leave me here alone,' said Red.

'I have a question,' said Aciram, and cleared his throat.

'Ask,' said Pralay.

'Should I abandon the thought of rebuilding my kingdom? Would it be a waste of effort? What I really mean to ask is . . . have you and your . . . people set out to end the world?'

The Cold Prince turned towards Aciram, and the Dark Lord flinched. 'The undead army has been given the task of ending the world,' he said. 'But certain complications have arisen, and the battle you witnessed was part of our effort to resolve them. Certain forces have been seeking to end the world without the proper authorization, and the undead army, being, as it were, the official destroyer of this world, has no option but to eliminate these forces and establish its identity as the sole entity responsible for global demolition.'

'Does that mean you're ending the world or not?' asked Aciram. 'I apologize if this question is tiresome, but I have a certain vested interest in the matter.'

The Cold Prince sighed. 'I will strive to be more lucid,' he said. 'Yes, we will end the world, but only when we are sure it is the right time. We have been receiving confusing signals, and have decided to postpone world's end until we are sure the world needs to end. To that end, we will now go underground and continue our battle with the creatures of the underworld until we have destroyed them all.'

'In other words, you're trying to save the world,' said the Red Queen, walking up to the Cold Prince. 'This is your doing, isn't it, Asvin? You're trying to save us all.'

Pralay stepped back as if he had been stung. 'You know me?'

'It is you, Asvin, isn't it?'

The Cold Prince looked away. 'No,' he whispered. 'Not Asvin any more. How did you know? Do those faces bring their own memories?'

'No, Asvin,' said Red. 'You know me. Look at me closely.'

He looked into her eyes then, and saw who she was, saw her looking at him with those eyes under a waterfall in Shantavan, on a speeding vroomstick high above the streets of rain-drenched Kol, remembered waking up to find those eyes gazing into his, long ago, in another life.

'Rukmini?' he asked, confused.

'I was never Rukmini,' she said.

'I do not understand,' he said. 'But there is much I do not understand. Yours is not the first face that has drifted out of my memories into my sight. While I rode out on errands of my own, this world lost many of its finest; many have journeyed to the Great Pyramid before their time. I have been reunited with many I once knew. There are faces I have loved, faces I have fought; my oldest friends who betrayed me, rakshases who befriended me. Some come to me as bodies newly undead, drawn from the fields where they fell by my lych-lords. Others had their bodies taken away from them by the storms of war and come to me as restless spirits. Generals and kings, heroes and rogues. What are you, maiden? Are you undead, or rakshas?'

'Rakshas,' said Red. 'And the face I showed you is not mine, and belongs to someone who is alive, as far as I know. But it was the face I wore when we knew each other.'

'It does not matter any more,' he said sadly, looking away. 'You are alive, and that is good. I wish you long life, and every happiness.'

On a sudden whim, Red moved close to him, held his face in her hands and kissed him. His lips were cold and lifeless, and he stepped away after a while. Behind Red, Aciram's eyes glowed red, and his skin bulged. But Aciram did not even exist as far as Red was concerned; she was staring at the Cold Prince with a wonderstruck expression, and fat tears were rolling down her cheeks.

'I can feel again,' she said quietly.

Pralay laughed unpleasantly.

'Congratulations must be in order,' he said. 'I will take your leave now.'

'Take me with you,' she said.

'That is impossible.'

'We will meet again,' said Red. 'We have a world to rule, and many more wars to win.'

The Cold Prince mounted his horse and stared at her expressionlessly.

'If you look around you,' he said, 'you will see what happens when you try to rule the world. As for winning wars . . . if you have not yet learned that no one wins wars, you probably never will.'

He galloped off dramatically, a handsome, gallant and only slightly decomposed example of all that was good and pure in the world.

'Bloody hero,' said Aciram. 'Not win wars, forsooth. We're still standing, aren't we? And do you see any ravians anywhere?'

'He was right,' said Red. 'The world doesn't need to be ruled. It needs to be healed. It needs to be set right.'

'Be that as it may,' said Aciram, 'if you ever kiss anyone but me again, I will kill you.'

Red showed no sign of having heard him. She smiled to herself as she watched the Cold Prince race away. 'Of course, in order to set the world right, I will have to control it,' she said.

'And control it you shall,' said Aciram, putting an arm around her. 'Just give me and the lads a few days to get everything up and running.'

'Thank you for everything, Aciram,' she said, touching his cheek.

He guffawed loudly and pulled her to him. 'You want to thank me? You said you could feel again, didn't you?' he said.

'Yes,' she said. 'I know what I want now.'

'That's the best bit of news I've heard in a while. That will come in very handy when we celebrate our victory. And look, we are alone!'

Red disappeared.

8

The howling storm that had raged around the *Duck of Destiny* for four hours, threatening to engulf it with monstrous waves in various threatening shapes and sizes, disappeared as suddenly as it had arrived. The ocean's surface now resembled that of a table, and a few porpoises gambolled happily in the distance, adding insult to injury; puffy white clouds in the sky floated around sheepishly, pretending they had not been hurling lightning-bolts enthusiastically ship-wards a few seconds ago. The sun appeared, beaming guilelessly and cheerfully down at the drenched upper deck of the elegant carrack, and the Silver Dagger, drenched from head to toe, removed a small jellyfish from his left ear, threw it on the deck, stamped on it, and spoke for all the crew and passengers when he said, 'This is *completely* ridiculous.'

It wasn't so much the gales and towering waves that the Dagger was irritated by. Even the whirlpools and completely unnecessary clashing rocks he could have tolerated with a little effort. What got under his skin was the easy insouciance with which the gods threw obstacle after obstacle in the path of the *Duck*, and then restored things to normal moments after and pretended nothing of any consequence had happened. The Dagger wasn't asking for an easy voyage. All he was looking for was a little appreciation from time to time.

And then there were the signs and portents. Yes, the world was ending, but that had been established for a while, thought the Dagger. There was really no need to rub it in. There was a lack of finesse, of etiquette, there that upset the Dagger's refined sensibilities. A few signs of doom once every few days would have been quite enough. But the *Duck of Destiny* could not sail for even an hour without being accosted by some reminder of the onrushing all-consuming calamity. Pillars of fire in the distance, crew members succumbing to babbling fits, burning bushes that sizzled and hissed as they succumbed to nature's laws and sank under the waves, rains of fish and, unfathomably, gherkins, and that was not even counting the thunderous voices in the sky, the singing two-headed sea-cows, the illogical swarms of insects, the rude cloud formations . . . really, enough was enough. When he met the gods, thought the Dagger, he would give them a lesson or two in the art of subtlety.

Fujen, on the other hand, expressed no dissatisfaction over the bizarre and wondrous visions that manifested themselves regularly around the ship; if anything, they impressed and entertained her, and filled her with a sense of occasion and purpose. It was, after all, an honour to be singled out thus by the gods, though it was still difficult for her to believe that any of this was actually taking place, that she was really sailing to save the world. Her pirates were supremely thrilled as well, down to the last woman. They had spent most of their buccaneering careers deliberately avoiding the childish superstitions that made their male counterparts so susceptible to deception by anyone possessing an old bedsheet and an imagination, and saw these real wonders as a reward for all those years of scepticism.

Even when ghostly apparitions began to appear on the ship, proclaiming the doom of man in sepulchral voices, the pirates were amused rather than scared; they gave their visitors from the spirit realm nicknames and made up ribald jokes about them. What did worry Fujen and her crew, though, was that all their navigational instruments had gone berserk, and so had every means of telling the time. The sun and moon either hung in the sky far longer than they were supposed to or dipped and rose with manic speed; the stars were all out of place, and the wind changed direction every other minute. The *Duck of Destiny* sailed on in an ocean without time or location; many of the crew were not sure whether they were awake or dreaming, as days and nights froze or melted, and the sky and sea changed colour and form at will. Mantric had told Fujen this might happen, that the gods might toy with the ship, try to confuse them and awe them with pranks and spells. They were, after all, trying to affect the will of the gods; many would see this as hubris. These tests of will were, said Mantric, a good sign; they meant that the *Duck of Destiny* had the gods' attention. Besides, would it not be insulting to the gods if an audience with them were easily achieved? And why should the gods want to spend their infinitely precious time watching them sail through calm seas?

This also meant, of course, that every little thing the crew did incurred the risk of angering some god or the other, and that the gods themselves were vying for the crew's attention, in order to find more prominence in their story. It was vitally important, therefore, said Mantric, that all the gods be ignored equally, and in such a manner as not to annoy them. And so Fujen's pirates pretended not to understand when their shipmates spoke in strange voices, issuing divine commands; they pretended not to notice when clouds spelled out messages in the sky, or when attractive and attention-demanding naked nymphs emerged from the depths, telling their tales of woe, trying to divert the ship towards one quest or another. Sometimes, when the signs, portents or messengers in question were too loud or large to be ignored, Fujen and Orpi stood before them, observing them dispassionately, taking notes, conducting erudite discussions about the perfectly natural diversity in mid-ocean flora and fauna, taking care to mention how all of this was clearly of earthly origin and had nothing to do with any gods, and occasionally waving back politely at the sea-creatures that danced and leaped around the ship, until the gods gave up and tried something else.

When drama failed, the gods tried romance; amorous swans and clouds swooped down on the ship, hoping to start legendary god-child sagas. They met Stivin Seagull instead, and retired hurt.

Mantric very rarely played a part in Fujen's pirates' adventures with the gods and their creatures; this was because he spent most of his time below decks being mysterious. Three cabins on the lower hold had been sealed off and were for his use alone, and he spent his days in these rooms, working away on whatever present he intended to give the gods. No one else on the ship, not even Amloki, knew what was in those rooms. Mantric had refused to tell the Dagger what he had brought in those massive trunks from Bolvudis and Kol, because, he said, it was imperative that the gift be kept a secret from the gods until the opportune moment, and it was quite possible that the gods were looking through his eyes. Amloki's curiosity was threatening to overwhelm him, especially because the largest of Mantric's cabins clearly contained a living creature, something very fierce; it thumped and rattled chains and gnawed on wood ceaselessly and Mantric always had four or five pirates guard the entrance to his corridor whenever he went to feed it. Bertholamu the Berth Beast, as Fujen had affectionately named Mantric's hidden monster, spent its days pounding away at the walls and doors that kept the ship safe from it, and making spine-chilling quiet, wet sounds that made everyone that heard them think of ripped stomachs and exposed innards. The Dagger had tried once, out of general principles, to sneak into the room and see the monster for himself. To no avail; Mantric had placed strong magical wards on Bertholamu's door, and the Dagger had admitted later to himself that this had been a good idea; the Berth Beast, sensing company, had been completely quiet while the Dagger had tried to pick its lock, and this silence had been so intense and menacing that even Amloki's dauntless heart had trembled. What wild magical animal had Mantric brought for the gods? The Dagger thought of the chimaera in Bolvudis, the nundu that had almost killed them all in the Bleakwood, and hoped desperately that Mantric had any idea what he was doing.

'What are you doing, Mantric?' called the Dagger, pounding on Mantric's door.

'You can't come in,' yelled Mantric. 'I'm working. I must not be disturbed.'

'You need to come out for a bit,' said the Dagger. 'We need your help.'

'Can't it wait? I'm on the verge of an earth-moving discovery.'

'It can wait,' said the Dagger. 'You might notice that we have stopped moving.'

'Why?'

'Come and see.'

It was a whale. A huge, white, deeply unattractive whale, and it was lurking in front of the *Duck of Destiny*, moaning gently and bumping into the hull, causing the ship to shudder and lurch. The whale's back was covered with scars and deep gashes, and studded with harpoons joined to one another by a tangle of ropes, on which hung an interesting variety of dead human and plant life. Orpi and Jen stood on deck, watching it with interest, as Mantric and Amloki came running out, adjusting their wigs.

'What is that?' asked Mantric.

'It's a whale,' said Orpi helpfully.

'I can see it's a whale. What is it doing here? No, don't tell me. What do you want me to do?'

'Move it.'

Mantric glowered. He sent an angry blue fireball sputtering into the whale's hump, and it groaned and opened its mouth, displaying rows of rock-like teeth.

'Look at those corpses. This is no ordinary whale,' said Orpi. 'I think it's Hattima.'

'Don't be silly, Baby-Duck,' said Jen. 'Hattima's just a legend. Besides, if it were Hattima, the *Nurmi* and Captain Aguleb would be here, and there would be all sorts of trouble.'

'Ship ahoy!' yelled Irik Seagull from the crow's nest. 'Large trireme, heading straight at us!'

Jen blanched. 'It can't be,' she said. 'Not the *Nurmi*. It doesn't exist.'

In the distance, they could see the trireme, a black speck growing larger at an alarming rate.

'You tell them they don't exist, Jen,' said the Dagger. 'That should buy us some time.'

'We're in all sorts of trouble,' said Orpi. 'Man the onagers!' she called, and the decks were suddenly full of scurrying pirates.

'Perhaps someone could tell me what the hells you are talking about,' said Mantric as they raced across the *Duck of Destiny* towards the approaching trireme.

'The *Nurmi*,' said Orpi breathlessly. 'A great war-ship of the past, doomed to wander the seas for all time, bringing death and destruction with it.'

'Charming. Why?'

'Aguleb, a great pirate captain of a previous Age, swore that he would not rest in life or death until he had killed Hattima Timi the great whale, who had eaten his heart. But Hattima was cunning beyond all measure, and could not be caught. Aguleb hunts him still, searching the great seas around the world in the *Nurmi*, destroying anything that stands in his way. The great whale cannot be killed until Aguleb's heart is removed from its stomach. Unfortunately, any attempts on the part of adventurers to enter the whale's stomach and retrieve the heart have resulted in digestion.'

Mantric responded to this by collapsing spectacularly.

'I know it's not a nice story,' said Orpi reprovingly, 'but there's no need to faint.'

'Don't worry,' said the Dagger. 'He's sent the seagulls to spy on the ship. He's seeing through their eyes.'

Mantric began to stir and mumble.

'Even if it is this Captain Aguleb and that whale is the one he's hunting,' said the Dagger, 'I don't see what it has to do with us.'

'As long as we're between the whale and the *Nurmi*,' said Jen, 'it has plenty to do with us.'

Mantric sat bolt upright and his eyes opened wide.

'A black ship, hundreds of oars in three levels,' he said, wincing and rubbing his head. 'It moves fast, much faster than us. The undead walk its decks. Their flag is white on black; a horned skeleton driving a spear into a bleeding heart. Their captain has a skull for a head and a wooden leg. He's wearing an eyepatch, which doesn't make much sense.'

'It's Aguleb,' said Orpi. 'We're doomed, Baby-Duck!'

'We have the best ship in the world,' said Jen. 'And the best captain, though I say so myself. Now stand aside, ladies, and let me steer. We get out of the *Nurmi*'s way, and all's well.'

Jen took command of the wheel, barking out commands. Sails were raised and lowered, oars pushed and pulled. The *Duck of Destiny* twisted and turned in the ocean, but Hattima Timi the whale was wily and fast, and swam effortlessly alongside, always keeping the *Duck* between himself and the approaching trireme. They could see Aguleb's ship clearly now, a long, black knife cutting through the ocean, bare black masts looming like ribs over its undead decks. Skeletal undead pirates, dressed in rags, brandished rusty cutlasses and screamed wordlessly; jakyinis with seaweed dreadlocks swaggered about, cruel curved hooks in place of their hands glittering in the sun. Rotting sea-ghouls lurched in unison, raising a large catapult on the *Nurmi*'s foredeck. Each one of Jen's manouevres was matched easily by Aguleb's tiller-zombies; whale and carrack and trireme danced a fast-paced waltz in the ocean, their paths swerving and coverging.

'This is impossible,' said Jen, 'that ancient trireme can't possibly steer well enough to keep pace with our ship.'

'They don't know that,' said the Dagger. 'Onagers, Orpi!'

Orpi yelled out and five bolts of Psomedean fire arced towards the *Nurmi*. They all found their target, and Fujen's pirates cheered, but their yells of jubilation died a moment later. The *Nurmi* was burning but undeterred, and its crew did not seem in the least bit discouraged or damaged. If anything, they looked even more fearsome. The undead ship sped on towards the *Duck*, trailing fire like a comet. The battering ram on its prow was shaped like a dragon's skull, and an unearthly fire burned in its eyes.

Jen sent the wheel spinning, and the *Duck of Destiny* banked sharply to starboard. In desperation, Telu-Yeti sent four large harpoons shuddering into Hattima's side, but the whale had taken centuries of harpoons and survived; he swerved with the ship, watching it with a cunning eye. The Dagger stared at the crafty old whale in admiration, and could have sworn that he winked.

'A plan, if you please, Mantric,' called Jen. 'If they ram us, we're done.'

'I should have learned to swim,' said Mantric, shaking his head sadly. He knelt on the deck and raised his arms in the air. A blue light began to spread from his hands.

Captain Aguleb stepped forward and stood behind the *Nurmi*'s battering ram, his skull blazing, his cutlass high in the air. He spoke in a great voice that echoed across the sea.

'Know ye not the price, ye scurvy sunk-ship mice, of standing 'twixt Aguleb and his prey?' he roared. 'Fire shall not burn me, blade shall not turn me, think ye can spurn me today?'

'That's *awful*,' said the Dagger, looking at Jen, who shrugged, embarrassed.

'Traditional pirate,' she said. 'He's spent years rehearsing that, Amloki. Don't sneer.'

The dragon-skull battering ram streaked on towards the *Duck of Destiny*. On the *Nurmi*'s foredeck, the giant catapult creaked and snapped, sending its missiles flying towards the *Duck*. The missiles in question were jakyinis; several fell flailing in the ocean, but others flew into the carrack's sails, and slid downwards, ripping up the sails with their hook-hands. Fujen's pirates drew their cutlasses and charged, screaming challenges.

Mantric rose, and a stream of blue light sped from his hands into the water to the *Duck of Destiny*'s rear.

And a whale appeared there, bathed in blue light. It looked exactly like Hattima.

The *Nurmi* swerved sharply, sending several skeletal pirates flying overboard. Fujen and Orpi joined the melee on the *Duck*'s deck. Telu-Yeti was in the centre of the carnage, a terrifying sight as she scooped up one undead pirate after another and tossed them overboard.

Turning with impossible grace, the *Nurmi* swept past the *Duck*'s rear towards Mantric's whale illusion. The last few yards were covered in a blur; the battering ram sliced across the *Duck*'s rear, and there was an awful cracking sound as timber splintered and flew upwards. More undead leaped on to the *Duck*'s rear deck, huge, lumbering zombies that had once been Skuan raiders, giants bearing great battle-axes. But the *Nurmi* rushed on, past the *Duck of Destiny*, forgetting the insignificant mortals as it closed in on its real quarry. The real Hattima began to dive, intending to swim underneath the *Duck* and emerge on the other side, displaying himself to Aguleb out of sheer malice. His game would only end when he was the only living being in the water.

But the Silver Dagger dived off the *Duck of Destiny*, arms spread wide, dagger a dazzling arc of light, and landed neatly on the battle-scarred whale.

The undead Skuans rushed towards Mantric, who rose with alacrity and met them with a shower of green comets. Several fell off the deck, trailing flames, but the others rose and charged again.

The illusion-whale vanished just as the *Nurmi* charged into it, and the undead pirates screeched in unison, their rage tearing the skies apart. Aguleb roared to his tiller-zombies, and the *Nurmi* began to turn in an unnaturally small arc, even more undead falling off its sides.

The jakyinis disposed of, Fujen's crew sped back to deal with the Skuan zombies. Telu-Yeti led the charge, covered in undead muck; Fujen and Orpi stabbed and thrust in tandem by her side.

Its turn completed, the *Nurmi* set its course for the *Duck of Destiny*'s centre. There would be no turning aside this time; the mortals would soon join Aguleb's sailors in their eternal voyage around the earth, on the trail of the elusive Hattima.

But just then, with a great moan, Hattima Timi leaped out of the water, and a grappling hook snaked out and lodged itself on the *Duck of Destiny*'s mizzenmast. Living and undead turned in wonder and stared as the great whale soared through the air, and the Silver Dagger somersaulted in mid-air, caught a rope and swung down on the *Duck*'s deck, a nonchalant smile playing across his lips. Not one to stand and gloat until the battle was finished, he sent a volley of shuriken into the Skuan zombies, pinning them to masts and to each other, and then led a charge that ended, as it only ever could with the Silver Dagger leading it, in victory.

Hattima's landing, on the other hand, was not quite as satisfactory, as he crashed down on the *Nurmi*, squashing most of Aguleb's crew, and smashing the deck, and then wiggled in an undignified manner, jerked and fell back into the ocean. With at least thirty zombies twitching and stabbing on his back, he dived into the welcoming bosom of the ocean. Roaring in fury, Aguleb turned the crippled *Nurmi* again and set off in pursuit.

And the *Duck of Destiny* lay placidly again on the calm ocean, floating on gentle, lapping waves under the placid sun, its sails ripped, its rudder smashed, and several of its crew grievously wounded. Telu-Yeti showed her great skill then, cradling the wounded to her glowing heart until their bruises melted away and their bones creaked back into position.

'What did you do to that poor whale?' asked Jen.

The Dagger smirked as he kicked another zombie off into the water. 'There was an ancient Avrantic tantric pleasure-technique I learned back when I was a boy,' he said. 'It was called The Tickling of the Whale. Worked like a charm.'

'You have tickled whales before?' asked Orpi in wonder.

'No,' said the Dagger, looking mildly offended. 'But it turns out those Avrantic tantrics based their techniques on extensive scientific research. Excellent illusion, Mantric. You must do that at parties after we've saved the world.'

And then he fell on the deck, completely exhausted, and started to snore gently.

'What now?' asked Jen. 'The ship's crippled. Our only option seems to be getting on the longboats and heading home. And going mad and eating one another, I'm afraid.'

'Yes,' said Mantric. 'Which is quite a shame, really. I had such a nice surprise planned for the gods. Still, it is clear that they sent that whale and its pursuers after us, so perhaps they do not want it.'

Dark clouds gathered in the sky above them. Mantric ignored them.

'Perhaps we should have listened to them when they tried speaking to us earlier,' he said. 'But I was in such a hurry, you know. I couldn't wait to deliver the present. I might as well throw it into the ocean now. The rest of our journey will be so achingly slow and dull now.'

'What a waste,' said Jen, smiling slyly. 'But let me know when you're hungry. Orpi's grown a bit fleshy of late, and we can start with her.'

The clouds knotted overhead, coagulating into a solid black mass. It swirled and spun and began to take shape.

'Mmfm,' said Telu-Yeti.

And the clouds formed a shape. A duck's head. Its beak opened.

'QUACK,' said the *Duck of Destiny*'s figurehead, its eyes opening. It looked most surprised.

All over the ship, splinters of wood flew into the air as planks moved of their own volition, settling into a pattern that very slightly resembled overlapping feathers. Several of Fujen's pirates knelt and prayed.

And then the *Duck of Destiny* moved, slowly at first, wood and iron adjusting to the will that now commanded them, then picking up speed, swimming regally over the startled ocean. Its wooden head moaned and creaked as it looked from side to side in astonishment.

'Perhaps the gods want that present after all,' said Mantric, his eyes gleaming.

Orpi ran up to Jen and they kissed, and looked around in wonder, trying to find one part of this adventure that made sense, and failing utterly.

'Where are we going?' asked Mantric.

'I have no way of telling,' said Jen. 'Wherever the gods want us to go. You might have noticed that this ship is no longer under my command.'

'Land ahoy!' called Irik from the crow's nest. 'Archipelago!'

'That's impossible,' said Orpi. 'I don't know exactly where we are, but there are no islands in this part of the world. You'd have to sail east or west for several weeks.'

'And yet there are islands ahead of us, and our dear *Duck* has decided to take us there,' said Mantric. 'I am not surprised at all.'

'But how can islands just appear out of nowhere?' asked Jen.

Mantric smiled, and stared out to sea, at distant specks of land covered in mist. 'Someone must have made them up,' he said.

9

The great lakes of northern Vrihataranya had always been shrouded in mist and mystery. Magic lay thick and heavy in the air here, coiled around the creepers of ancient trees, seeping out of the ground, swirling in the waters of the rivers that emptied sluggishly into the lakes. Rakshases and vanars had terrible stories of the lands around the lakes; terrible demons of bone and blade that lurked in the shadows of the trees, giant tree-guardians that held sway over the valleys and hills by the lakes, devouring anything that sought to discover their secrets.

It was near these lakes that rakshases and ravians had fought fierce battles in the Age of Terror; the ravian capital, Asroye, was rumoured to be hidden somewhere in these terrible valleys. No one knew what secret paths the ravians used to evade the monstrous beasts that stalked these forests; among living rakshases, only Aciram knew, only Aciram had walked through those trails long ago with his cousin Danh-Gem. And Aciram would not speak of his adventures in north Vrihataranya; too much blood had been shed there, he would say. He had sought Asroye by the great lakes, and not found it; he did not intend to go back.

The westernmost of the lakes was encircled by two concentric rings of steep hills known among rakshases as the Demon's Jaws; countless rakshases had perished in the forest-covered valleys between the hill-rings in the Age of Terror. Some said the city of Asroye was built on a magical island in the middle of the lake encircled by the hills; others said the Hidden City lay far to the east, and the Demon's Jaws merely concealed a ravian fortress, similar to Epsai in the west. Three of Danh-Gem's brothers had died in this circle of terror, and even after the passing of the ravians, the valley had lain undisturbed for two hundred years.

But all that was merely history. Now, as the midday sun glared over the ancient valley and fought its endless daily battle with the impenetrable ocean of leaf and branch and creeper, something moved through the still, sullen air, whispering messages of disquiet to the slumbering trees.

I-Remember-You-When-You-Were-*So*-High, a handsome Infinite Umarwood princeling, chief custodian of the valley's secrets, tapped his neighbour I-Laugh-At-Your-Puny-Axe with the tip of an ancient branch and whispered, 'Oh, *dear*.'

The Umarwoods imploded with a soft *plop*, their massive boughs hurtling inwards into nothingness, millennia of knowledge vanishing in a shower of leaves and bark-dust.

Vrihataranya trembled.

And then a huge ring of trees, a circle cutting across the valley and touching both lines of hills, creaked in agony as they were sucked inwards, branches spiralling in crazed death-dances, birds soaring skywards and shrieking in fear. The earth shook to the sound of explosions, as tunnels opened up in the earth where the trees had stood, and huge clouds of earth and burning leaves filled the air. The Great Forest's denizens howled and shrieked and jabbered as they fled, as stabbing tongues of flame shot out of the ground and trees near the circle's borders splintered and exploded, and other trees were tossed into the air, their roots aflame. Ear-splitting crashes and pillars of smoke and flame rose into the sky, marking out a huge flaming jewel in the ring that was the Demon's Jaws. As the rain of ash, earth and burning branches settled in a sullen sizzle, thousands of vamans emerged, scurrying out of tunnels like ants, with axes in their hands and destruction in their hearts.

War-drums pounded and horns rang out. Mammoth armadrillos burst out through the tunnels, bombardiers yelling maniacally on their backs, flattening the earth under their mighty paws as they strode through the mangled forest. Sappers went to work, planting explosives, building trenches. Underground, squadrons of golems attacked mighty tree-roots, ripping and tearing their way inwards, and vaman logging machines puffed and steamed out of widened tunnels, removing wreckage and undergrowth, clearing paths, tearing aside broken pieces of the stunned forest. In just a few hours, the vamans slashed and burned out a ring wide enough for an army to stand in. And then the sappers and loggers moved aside, and Bhoomi's finest warriors marched out into the sun, rolling siege engines before them. Lines of bombardiers settled into trenches, fire-sticks pointing at unknown enemies. Catapults and ballistae were lined up behind the trenches. Armadrillo squadrons gathered in newly-made avenues, fidgeting, eager to charge. Heavily armoured vaman infantrymen thumped their axe-hafts into the ground in time with their martial chants. Bhoomi had arrived, and intended to stay a while.

On a hill to the west, three of Bhoomi's rulers sat on a giant tree-root, surrounded by a wide circle of patrolling Silverlode guards, watching their army shine in the sun below. Flaad Nagpo stroked his flowing white beard and chuckled.

'Damned funny if we came to the wrong place,' he said. 'Bhoomi's finest locked in a, whatsit, epic battle with tree insects.'

'Everything is going according to plan,' said Yin Stinpula, her eyes glittering. 'This is Asroye. It has to be.'

'New Asroye,' said Kuin Lizpula.

Flaad Nagpo made a rude noise. 'Same damned thing,' he snorted. 'Where are the bloody ravians?'

'I've explained this to you before, Flaad. They're not home,' said Kuin, her warm, matronly face lit up by a gentle smile. 'They've gone to topple Imokoi, or gone southwards to build new cities. They must have left a token force to defend their city. Not enough to take us on. If they charge, they'll have to reveal themselves. And their city, which means we destroy it. So they'll sit tight. Their best hope now is to wait and hope we can't break through the portal, and that their king and his army return in time to save them.'

'Then we should get on with it, shouldn't we?' said Flaad. 'We look damned silly, surrounding a bunch of trees.'

'Where are the demons of the Demon's Jaws?' asked Yin. 'This seems too easy. I don't like it. Something's wrong.'

Kuin laughed. 'If they arrive, they will be dealt with,' she said.

Nor Rispo walked up to them, his black armour coated with dust and leaves.

'Is the circle complete?' asked Yin. He nodded.

'Release the Furry Ones!' called Yin.

Mirrors flashed her orders across the trenches, and at four points around the circle, to the north, south, east and west, vamans sent red flares shooting into the sky. Golems rolled carts out of tunnels at the northern and eastern corners of the square formed by the flares; there were cages on these carts, and in each cage around fifty little round men chattered shrilly, their big, round black eyes shining in excitement, their colourful fur garish in the bright sunlight. The cage doors were rolled back, and the furry little men bounced out of the carts, squeaking in excitement. They looked around, blinking solemnly, swayed this way and that, and almost immediately turned in unison towards the centre of the circle, and started walking jerkily into the forest, pulled by invisible strings, singing silly songs strung together from nonsensical scraps of words.

'What are those things again?' asked Flaad, sticking a hairy finger into his left ear and twisting it vigorously.

Kuin sighed in exasperation. 'Do keep up, Flaad,' she said. 'The Furry Ones are drawn towards ravians. Our agents in the forest saved them from ravian hunters. They led us here. We're hoping they will lead us into Asroye, but even if they don't, they will help us know exactly where it is.'

'Why?'

Kuin shook her head. 'Watch,' she said.

The furry men giggled furiously as they bounced and capered through the undergrowth; they were flanked by lines of vamans bearing large shields, ready to form a phalanx at the first sign of danger. They did not have to wait long; about five minutes after the furry men began their caper into the circle, the leader of the northern group, a fat little purple creature, stopped as if he had run into an invisible barrier, squawked in astonishment, and then disappeared.

The vamans huddled together, their shields overlapping in turtle formation, as the rest of the furry men leaped forward and disappeared as well. From the centre of the shield-turtle, a flare streaked into the sky, bursting through the leaf-ceiling far above the vamans. Seconds later, another flare pierced the forest's roof from the east, as the Furry Ones disappeared there, too. And then answering flames shot up from the south and west; they had been found. A phalanx of vamans on the south side of the circle watched in astonishment as the purple Furry One from the north appeared in front of them, a blob of colour materializing out of nowhere, closely followed by the rest; as soon as they appeared, they stopped, blinked, squeaked and turned around, and jumped back the way they had come. In every direction, bemused vamans watched the strange little creatures appear, turn and disappear again, flickering in and out of sight, singing their strange songs, until messages came from their commanders, and the vamans cast nets, trapped the Furry Ones and dragged them back, kicking and squealing, to the trenches. Vaman engineers calculated the distance the Furry Ones had travelled, and once they announced their findings, a cheer ran through the ranks; all doubts could be put to rest. They had found New Asroye.

As the phalanxes retreated, the vaman catapults came into play; massive boulders crashed through the treetops as they soared towards the Hidden City. None of these found their mark; they, too, disappeared in mid-air, and reappeared in their line of travel, crashing to earth on the other end of the circle. But though the boulders caused no damage to the hidden ravian stronghold, they served the vamans well; as boulders flew in from every direction, the vamans drew their first maps of the Hidden City's outer walls. No counter-attack came from within the invisible walls; the ravians were evidently content to wait until the vamans found a way to actually strike them. Or perhaps they simply had no means of fighting back.

'Solid wall of portals all around the city, transport anything right through it, some tolerable illusion-work to make the city invisible,' said Nor Rispo. 'Ravians giving us architecture lessons. Hmph. Bhoomi could use defences like this.'

'That is all very well,' said Kuin, 'but how do we breach this wall? This must be why our predecessors could not find Asroye; the portals must extend underground as well, all around the city's foundations. Golems would just go through them without even realizing it, and carry on with their search, and they wouldn't even know that they had passed through the earthworks they sought.'

'We have the numbers now,' said Nor. 'Let the golems reach the portals underground, and dig deeper. We will tunnel until we can emerge from under the foundations of the city.'

Generals were summoned and orders issued. The vaman rulers sat in silence once again, watching their troops as the sun set.

'Earth praise the Furry Ones!' yelled Yin suddenly.

The others looked at her flushed face, and at one another, surprised and amused.

'You seem to be experiencing an attack of romanticism,' said Kuin.

'You know, at times like this I question our whole way of thinking,' said Yin. 'This is one of the turning points of vaman history, and you treat it like a resource management exercise. Look around you! We have found New Asroye and besieged it, it is only a matter of time before we capture it, and you sit here looking as if this were any other day. We should rejoice! We have surpassed our fathers, and ushered in the Age of Reason they could only dream of! This is a moment for fireworks, for wine and poetry!'

'No poetry. Gives me gas,' said Flaad.

Kuin patted Yin's shoulder reassuringly. 'I understand how you feel,' she said. 'I had expected my first surface campaign to be full of excitement as well, years before you were born, and I was rather disappointed when I discovered, after a glorious and meticulously planned victory, that I was . . . bored. It is the price we must pay for being efficient, for waiting for the perfect moment to strike. What we see today is, after all, merely the execution of the endgame; the real battle was fought in tactics a while ago. You cannot expect maximized excitement to occur concurrently with minimized risk.'

Yin nodded, but looked sad. 'It's all right,' she said. 'I suppose capturing the city once we break through the portal will be exciting enough. I don't know what's come over me, really. Maybe it's the magic in this forest. It makes me wish things weren't always so . . . mechanical.'

'Be grateful for easy victories when they come, Yin,' said Kuin. 'There will be plenty of excitement later. You think all this will end with the fall of Asroye? Far from it. The ravians will rise again. There will be other threats, new invaders, new enemies. I foresee very little sleep in the years to come.'

'Not to forget the fact that we're going to invade what's left of Imokoi and stop letting the humans pretend they run Kol,' said Flaad. 'And then there's Xi'en, Avranti, Artaxerxia. The north, the west, other worlds if we manage to make portals. Lots of new people to meet and conquer. That should be excitement enough, even for you.'

'I don't understand,' said Yin. 'You're joking . . . aren't you?'

Kuin cleared her throat nervously. 'Well, we should have mentioned it before,' she said. 'The thing is, the Slimy Ones invasion showed us that we can no longer pretend to be safe underground. Our sunworld policies will have to be . . . adjusted slightly. The plans are all in place. We really should discuss this later.'

Yin almost choked. 'You can't be serious! Nor, they're joking, aren't they?

'No,' said Nor. For the first time since Yin had met him, he smiled.

'We said we were going to bring about a bloody new Age,' said Flaad. 'What did you expect?'

'We were going to call it the Age of Reason,' said Yin. 'We were supposed to bring about lasting peace.'

'That's the plan.'

Kuin smiled reassuringly, and patted Yin's arm. 'It's been a tiring day for all of us,' she said. 'Get some sleep. You'll feel better in the morning.'

At dawn, the golems tore through the foundations of New Asroye, and the portals of the Hidden City were cast aside.

A beautiful city was revealed, a city of wood and stone and marble, of towers and arches and winding cobbled streets, of white domes and fluttering banners.

'Oh, that's so lovely,' said Kuin Lizpula.

Flaad Nagpo belched, possibly in agreement.

'Raze it to the ground,' said Nor Rispo.

And as the ravians rode out in a last desperate charge, and the vamans crushed them savagely, efficiently and mechanically, Yin Stinpula didn't feel better at all.

10

From *The Voyage of the Duck of Destiny*, by Telu-Yeti (a work in progress)

I

It's the end of the world, so send for the girls that know how to hold their rum,
We're Captain Fujen's Furies and we'll fight till doomsday come!
We sail with a smile from Turtle Isle to the shores of the Standing Sea,
Sing along to the song of the tarty tars of the *Duck of Destiny*!
Now, this little ditty is writ by a yeti and a pretty tidbit is she,
She may look slow, but her smile melts snow on the Mounts of Harmony.
Sold for a slave to a scurvy knave, but fearless Fujen freed her,
Now on the decks of the dauntless *Duck* she sings for her lovely leader.

II

So we sailed forth from pirate port to go and greet the gods,
To give them gifts so grand they'd understand that only sods
Would destroy this joyful world, its wild and wondrous creatures,
Its treetops tall, its fruits and all its fine geographical features.

At first, calm seas and gentle breeze; this placid, easy venture,
Wouldn't last, we knew, would fast turn into wild adventure.
But we feared not, cared not a jot, nor stumbled as we swaggered,
For we had mighty Mantric and the dashing Silver Dagger!

Heroes bold, they came from Kol, they filled us all with wonder,
Their eyes were bright, their breeches tight, our hearts they rent asunder,
Even though we all did know that men, they meant bad luck,
We owed them thanks, not walks on planks, for they had saved the *Duck*.

One fateful day the wind changed, danger reared its doleful head,
'Twas ancient ugly Aguleb and his crew of cruel undead!
Their souls they'd sold to demons old, they sailed to slay a whale,
They meant with dragon skull to ram our hull, and our hearts quailed.

Now gods, like seas and ships and shoes, are famous for being fickle,
We did not care, Dagger was there, and Dagger knew how to tickle,

The whale soon flew to the undead crew, spurred on by Dagger's finger,
With spell-bound fire and sword we slew the few that dared to linger.

The battle hurt our ship; we floated rudderless, despairing,
Was this discord a just reward for derring-do and daring?
A miracle we needed then, the gods were not found lacking,
The wooden bird, it shook and stirred! It was alive! And quacking!

Of no use now were oar and sail, or compass, wheel and mast
The gods themselves were guiding us, the *Duck* was gliding fast,
We looked ahead, some cried in dread, and others stared in silence,
Where had lain open sea but recently, there were now islands!

The sun was circling in the sky, the wind an endless howl,
The heavens loomed upon the doomed crew of the Fateful Fowl,
Time and tide had ceased to be, reason, space, diminished,
The gods had come to test us, should they best us, we were finished.

Then Fujen raised her cutlass. 'Gutless whelps!' she cried, 'Now hear me!
'I fear not death, nor dragon's breath, as long as you are near me!
'My dreadnought dears, my buccaneers, my anchors in rough weather,
'Conquer fear and doubt, sing out! We'll win if we're together!'

We dried our eyes and slapped our thighs, we yelled and yowled and roared,
We were on fire! We cried, inspired, 'Furies all on board!'
And then the *Duck*, it shook and stuck on a briny bar of sand,
Irik, our regal seagull, cried 'Ahoy! Look, ladies! Land!'

We leaped ashore, and leaped some more, and looked at all around us,
We looked for trouble, not for long, for trouble came and found us!
A hungry horde of cannibals! They fought hard but we fought harder,
We chopped and diced, we carved and sliced, and helped restock their larder.

We'd passed the test! We needed rest, but rest was not allowed us,
The *Duck* quacked; we ran back on board, afraid she'd leave without us.
Soon enough the *Duck* set off, towards another island,
With stately gait she swam the straits and steered us on to dry land.

And soon we were marooned again, left on the isle of Idrops,
Its name came from its master fierce, he was a fearsome Cyclops.
He trapped us in a cave and said he'd eat us by the dozen,
Mantric made us eye-patches and told him we were cousins.

The Cyclops winced, quite unconvinced, and moved to mince and mangle,
But Mantric cast illusion-blasts, and caused a merry tangle

Idrops gaped in human shape, we were a Cyclops clan,
'It wasn't me!' he gasped, aghast. 'It was the one-eyed man!'

From isle to isle we rode in style, from test to test we scurried,
From shore to shore we sang and swore, from beach to beach we hurried,
We solved so many riddles rare, won so many races,
Learned such fascinating facts, punched so many faces.

In Ages past the gods first cast these islands in the oceans,
To test the best of mariners, and cure them of the notion,
That they could beat the strangest creatures that the gods created,
Fair enough, but now, you see, these tests were quite outdated.

Piscibiscicla, an isle of warrior-women proud
Had an ancient, sacred law: Men were Not Allowed
Ships of men that met them then succumbed to their attacks,
But what were warrior-women to the pirates of the Quack?

They fell in love with Jen at once; she offered them employment,
They offered us their finest meats, much wine and much enjoyment;
We spoke for hours on food and flowers, on martial arts and dresses,
On legends and the lovely length of Amlokini's tresses!

On the isle of Mosmoro we met his monstrous beasts,
Pigs with wings and ruby rings, and goblin-turkey priests,

He thought we'd be distraught to see his twisted, strange creations,
He seemed surprised and beamed at our sincere congratulations.

We journeyed on, and met a tribe of nasty little boys
They'd formed an island empire, full of war-paint and sharp toys,
Their ways were rude, their weapons crude, they seemed to want us dead!
The Dagger smacked them silly, and then sent them off to bed.

Perhaps the toughest tests of all were on the isles of Aedens
One island full of luscious lads, and one of beauteous maidens,
Firm and lithe their flawless forms, guileless their pretty eyes,
We loved them with a sailor's love, and left them with a sigh.

On Cranial Isle a battle raged that shook the mighty trees,
Giant apes fought lizards great with brains the size of bees,
One such brute thought it astute to try abduct the Dagger
He's a wiser monkey now, though he walks with a stagger.

We found a lonely stranded man, his name was Livar-Gil,
For years he'd sought to build a yacht, return to hearth and till.
'Why go back, Gil?' we asked. 'Was not your old life rude and tough?'
We left him on the maidens' isle. He seemed content enough.

We duelled with young yamamba, snakes with white-haired epithelia,
We fought off giant mosquitoes on the isle of Anophelia,

We saw the fabled Aieou Isle, that sunken paradise,
Its marble kings had seaweed hair and ever-seeing eyes,

'Why carry on?' Jen asked Mantric. 'Why bother? What's the use?
'Why soldier on from dawn to dawn? Why take all this abuse?
'Why do gods make mortal men and then seek to destroy them?
'Why take the pains? Are they insane? Or do we just annoy them?'

'We are their spark, their works of art,' said Mantric, 'We're their muses,
'Each one of us a muddled mass that thrills, delights, confuses,
'Through us they see, they seek, they peek, they speak, they want, they wish,'
'Why kill us then?' 'I do not know. Look, a pretty fish!'

We saw the glittering diamondfish that swam with gem-fins westwards,
Heard the stirring songs of rocs as they rolled their eggs nest-wards,
What wonders we have seen! What scenes of hope and dread and glory!
What mysteries, histories, tapestries! What secrets, sagas, stories!

We chuckled and swashbuckled and the *Duck* held its head high,
But our hearts filled with dark despair each time we saw the sky,

For the midday sun, it shone right on, as if no time had passed
Between our tiff with Aguleb and the island we'd crossed last!

Had the mad gods stopped the world to watch us being clever?
Were we doomed to sail in vain from isle to isle forever?
Would we too turn undead, a crew of ill-famed pirate raiders,
And stalk the seas on killing sprees as Fujen's Isle Invaders?

The Dagger heard our worried words, and laughed as he told the crew,
If this was what gods desired, they hadn't thought things through!
For every day that the *Duck* stayed stuck, every fateful hour,
The gods would not destroy the world, and victory was ours!

'Cheer up!' said the dashing blade, 'And go and wash your necks!'
'If you feel muddled, come for a cuddle on the limpid lower deck!
'For if my weird is truly steered to an endless quest at sea,
'There's no place I'd rather grace than the *Duck of Destiny*!'

Through our cheers, our happy tears, our fears all veered away,
We drained our mugs with gluttonous glugs and the *Duck*, it steered away!
The gods, disarmed by Dagger's charm, granted us sweet rest,
The sun approved, and swiftly moved, and sailed towards the west.

The sea was calm and quiet that night, and bright the stars and moon,
We floated on, we sang till dawn, a change was coming soon,

At first light, we saw the strangest sight we'd ever seen,
The islands, they had disappeared as if they'd never been.

We'd passed the tests, we'd joked and jested through the churning waters,
On sea or land, none could withstand the daring *Duck*'s dear daughters!
A mist of mystery kissed the sea, a distant trumpet sounded,
We'd come to seek the Standing Sea and soon we found we'd found it!

A sheet of shimmering, glimmering, water stretched up to the sky,
Rainbows arced through mist-clouds dark and foam-walls mountain-high
Thunder growled, the Fateful Fowl had won against all odds,
We'd come to meet our destiny. We'd come to greet the gods.

III

So clap me in chains and slap me again and trap me in pits of spikes,
Beat me, eat me, stab me, grab me, do anything you likes,
But I'll never forget the joy I felt at the sight that met my eyes
When I saw that wonderful Vertical waterfall washing o'er the sky!
It's the end of the world, you sent for the girls that know how to hold their rum,
We're Captain Fujen's Furies and we're here, and doomsday's come!
We sailed with a smile from Turtle Isle to the shores of the Standing Sea,
Sing along to the song of the tarty tars of the *Duck of Destiny*!

11

The Chief Civilian stepped out rather gingerly on her new balcony, her pet amphisbaena coiled loosely around her neck. She regarded with a sceptical eye the pale moon that hung over her freshly reconstructed palace. Red Phoenix guards drifted by in the distance, circling the palace, watching magnificent vaman construction-cranes put their city back together. Central Kol's towers were growing steadily skywards, no longer a maze of creaking bridges and leaning towers and unexpected domes and corners. The vamans were rebuilding Kol to a new plan, bigger, broader and bolder than before. But was Kol's new heart *better*? Temat wondered. The city had told its own story through its towers before, each layer, each new style a testament to the efforts of a generation of ambitious architects and builders. Temat chastised herself immediately for thinking like an old person. The new towers were stronger, and safer, and much better organized. This was progress.

Roshin joined her on the balcony. 'They're reopening Frags tonight,' she said. 'Son of Frags, they're calling it. Do you want to go?'

Temat smiled. 'No, thank you. But you should go, and take the Sadori Sisters with you. I'll be perfectly safe—every self-respecting assassin will be there.'

'As you wish. One more thing. Arathognan is here. He says you wanted to see him,' said Roshin.

'I didn't. Take him to the Son of the Fragrant Underbelly with you, and make sure he has a good time. He has been working far too hard.'

'As you wish.' Roshin left, and the Civilian stood alone again, looking at the river Asa wind cold and grey through her new city.

In a small chamber in the labyrinth under the Civilian's palace, seven shadowy forms sat in a circle, their shapes flickering and shifting in the light of a single candle. Six of these figures were clad in grey cloaks, the seventh in a gown of shimmering violet.

'Tonight, a new Age dawns for Kol,' said Violet. 'Look around you, and be proud; you have been chosen to walk in the footsteps of giants.'

One of the grey-clad women cleared her throat nervously. 'You have honoured us greatly by summoning us here, Lady Violet, but what if Orange and Red are still alive? What if they return?'

'I have waited long enough,' said Violet, her voice trembling slightly. 'They have not come. And I do not think they ever will. The old Council was broken, and Kol broke with it; now Kol stands again, and must be protected. I loved my comrades dearly, but history cannot wait for them. And I cannot bear this burden alone.'

'You will not have to,' said one of the men. 'We are here, and we are ready. You stood alone in a time of great peril, and every shapeshifter in the world knows of you, and is proud that one such as you stands among us.'

Violet looked surprised and pleased. 'It is a time of great peril, yes, but it is also a time of hope, and of great opportunity. A new Kol is being wrought out of the ashes of the new, and with the Rainbow Council guiding it, it will rise once again to its former glory. We will usher in a new Age of peace and stability.'

'Yes,' said a shapeshifter, 'and we will guide the world's destiny.'

'Yes. Your enthusiasm is most touching. Then without further ado, let us begin the ceremony and give you your colours,' Violet said, smiling.

The woman who had spoken first cleared her throat again. 'Well, Lady Violet,' she said, 'we were just talking today afternoon—casually, you know—about how we were supposed to be the new Rainbow Council and all that, and how we'd wanted this day to come all our lives.'

'And as soon as you have sworn to obey the Rainbow Council's rules, and have accepted your colours, you will have achieved your heart's desire.'

'Yes, those rules. We talked about those rules, and swearing to obey them. There's the thing.'

'What?'

'We decided not to.'

The Civilian sensed someone behind her. She whirled around, her hand starting towards her concealed dagger. Ojanus, startled out of his slumbers by the sudden movement, rose and hissed malevolently.

It was Arathognan. He looked troubled.

'Are you all right?' he asked. 'I had a bad dream.'

The Civilian laughed. 'It'll take much more than a bad dream to harm me, Thog,' she said. 'What are you doing here?'

'You wanted to see me, my lady,' he said.

'Not at all,' said the Civilian. 'And I just asked Roshin to tell you that. Did she forget?'

'No,' said a voice behind them. Roshin's voice. A young woman walked on to the balcony, smiling, wearing Roshin's face.

'She thought she told him, but she didn't. She told me,' said the Red Queen.

Violet leaped up, her fingertips sprouting flame.

The shapeshifters laughed. 'Please, sit down, Lady Violet,' said one of the men. 'We mean you no harm at all. We respect and admire you far too much to even think of conspiring against you.'

Violet sat down, puzzled.

'First, allow me to introduce myself,' said the shapeshifter. 'My name is Bekrom.'

The others said their names in turn. The men were called Neskimas, Poulad and Pobrutho, and the women Latrina and Makanzi.

'I do not care what your names are,' said Violet, furious. 'Why do you have names? You cannot be part of the Rainbow Council if you have names!'

'Well, here's the thing,' said Makanzi pleasantly. 'We have names, and we like them, and so do all the other shapeshifters. And if the Rainbow Council doesn't like that . . . well, the Rainbow Council at this point is just you, isn't it? And there are six of us. We could vote, if you like.'

* * *

'Why are you drawing your sword?' Red asked Thog.

'Well, to defend the Chief Civilian and myself,' he said, confused.

'Well, don't. It's rude.' said Red firmly. 'If I wanted to kill you, I would have by now.'

Thog put his sword away, abashed.

Red turned to the Civilian, who was leaning against the railing, smiling faintly.

'I was wondering when we would meet,' said Temat. 'Are you the shapeshifter who went away with Asvin?'

'Yes. How did you know?'

'I didn't. But I do know that there are quite a few of you in the palace. And that you watch over me. And Ojanus seems most unperturbed by your presence, which indicates familiarity. I had always hoped to meet you. No doubt there is some matter of earth-shaking importance that brings you to me.'

Red considered this. 'Not really,' she said. 'I just dropped in for a chat. I've watched over you since you first came to the palace, and we've never spoken. Which is a shame, really, because I always liked you.'

'In that case, I am glad you changed your mind.'

'Yes. Of course, until a few days ago I thought I would kill you if we met, and take your place. But you'll be happy to know that I've changed my mind about that too.'

Thog gulped. 'Who are you?' he asked, reasonably.

'Hm. That's a tricky one,' she said. 'First I was one person, then two, then three, then two, then none at all, and then one, I think. Now—I don't know. I think I'm a lot of people. But I know who I'm going to be.'

The Civilian made an encouraging gesture. Red's face

changed into Rukmini's, and her expression changed to one of extreme fluffiness.

'I'm going to be Kol's next hero, or heroes,' said Red. 'As many as you like. I think that might be fun. I'd thought I wanted to rule the world and make everyone a slave, but then I was married to Aciram, who's pretending to be Kirin, and I was pretending to be Maya, see, and that was fun, because I got to kill lots of ravians in the war. But then the big monsters came out from underground, with the tentacles and slime and teeth, and all the zombies came out after them, and Asvin came with them, and he was a zombie too, and the world was ending, but Asvin stopped it. And I was really sad to see him, because I saw him die, you know, and I was happy too, because we were lovers before that, for four days, near the waterfall, when I was pretending to be Rukmini. And then I realized I could feel again, which was nice, and I thought I wanted to help people, you know? And make them feel nice too, because Asvin was doing that, though he didn't seem very happy, but I thought I would try it anyway. Never thought about that before, because it seemed soppy, but ruling the world was a bad idea, because it's just too much trouble, and asurs are smelly. So I'm going to be a hero, because it's easy, and it makes people happy, and the other shapeshifters will be angry and try to kill me, but they can't, because I'm the Red Queen and I'm more powerful than everybody, and I can help you run Kol so much better, too, because I already know everything about it and you, and I know so much more about the world that you don't know. Which is why I'm here. See?'

The Civilian smiled coldly.

'I'm sorry,' said Thog. 'I don't understand.'

'If we are to work together,' said the Civilian, 'you must not try these little tricks.'

Red's features loosened and shifted into Maya's. Her eyes narrowed and her voice deepened.

'So you're actually willing to listen. Good. I'll begin at the beginning,' said Red. 'So, there's this thing called the Rainbow Council . . .'

'After the Cravenstick disaster, we were all shaken. Our leaders had failed us, and were gone. We had to think for ourselves,' said Bekrom. 'We were no longer content to be phantoms in the city, hiding our powers. Questions we had never asked crawled up to the surface. We began assembling without your knowledge, asking one another why we were hiding, why we were pretending to be human. And we could find no answer.'

'Why were we hiding? Because the embracing of our egos is the first step to madness, to accepting our monstrous ancestry,' said Violet, her face pale. 'That is the first rule of being a shapeshifter.'

'You've been hiding in here too long, Violet,' said Neskimas. 'Centuries ago, your Council sat around and discovered that history was written by victors, and there was no real good or evil. And so pleased were you by these stunning discoveries that you never felt the need to make any more. Discover this, now: The world has changed. Rakshases aren't monsters any more. And they never were. If Kol and Imokoi can be allies, I see no reason why we should not use our powers in the open.'

'Because sooner or later, Kol and Imokoi will cease to be allies. And then humans will be our enemies. Kol will be thrown into chaos,' said Violet.

'See, there's that backward thinking again,' said Makanzi. 'At no point did we think that we wanted to be rakshases—nasty, ugly brutes. But surely you must acknowledge that it is no longer necessary for us to be ashamed of our ancestors. Kol has lived with our cousins, the spellbinders, long enough. And we all appear human in any case. What we decided was that it was time we made our presence felt.'

'And so you named yourselves?' asked Violet.

'Not yet. That happened after we saved Avranti from the ravians.'

'You saved what?'

'See, this is what happens when you don't get out of the palace. We went to war, wearing Icelosis's face. Two hundred shapeshifters broke ravian spells and saved countless Avrantic lives at Pataal-e-gurh, and helped the Durgans cleanse Avranti after that. The east is still in turmoil, but not because of the ravians; mostly just your average civil war. Succession and so forth. And that's not all. When the last ravian is driven out of the east and peace is restored, their new king will be a shapeshifter. Thus they will be delivered from ravians and war-mongering humans alike, and never again will Avranti march on Kol. Anyway, after we saw how well we'd done there, we got rather tired of Icelosis's face. And with our new faces came our new names.'

Violet leaned back, ashen-faced. 'What have you done? You have broken every shapeshifter decree!'

'That's all right,' said Bekrom. 'We're making new decrees.'

'And what then? World domination? More war?'

Neskimas shook his head, looking wounded. 'You wrong us, Violet,' he said. 'We have all taken vows that forbid making war on humans, on the weak. We intend to honour them. But we have seen what happens if you let them rule themselves, and try to help them from behind the scenes as you did. If we allow them to make war, when through our actions we might prevent their bickering and bring about long-lasting peace, is that not tantamount to encouraging their wars, even making war upon them? By ruling them wisely and kindly, we will help them. The Age of Peace and Stability you spoke of is no idle fantasy, Violet. We will bring it about. A shapeshifter on every throne from Xi'en to Artaxerxia. Harmony between kingdoms. Unity against ravians. Peace with our rakshas cousins. Protection against the vamans. We exchange countries every decade, to ensure none of us gets too attached to one particular piece of land. And best of all, no one knows, except us. The new Rainbow Council.'

Makanzi nodded enthusiastically. 'You see, Violet, the best thing about being a shapeshifter, especially one in Kol, is that we are not bound by the same regressive ties that join human to human, or vaman to vaman. We are mongrels, as diverse and accepting as Kol itself. We can become the vamans, or centaurs, or asurs we rule. We will unite all nations and stop all wars.'

'The only thing I heard there was you saying we would help humans by ruling them wisely and kindly,' said Violet. 'Do you know who you sound like? Ravians.'

Bekrom sighed. 'I wish we could have done things your way,' he said. 'But if it is indeed a new Age, if the world as you knew it has ended, the old ways must end with them.'

'You intend to kill me?' asked Violet matter-of-factly.

'Of course we do not intend to kill you,' snorted Neskimas. 'Why would we have wasted so much time explaining our plans to you, then?'

'I know this sudden change is difficult, Lady Violet,'

said Bekrom. 'But tell us, truly, is our plan not a good one? Will it not save more lives than it claims? Does it not give us a real chance of long-lasting peace?'

'I do not know,' said Violet. 'I will have to think about it.'

'And this is precisely why we are here,' said Makanzi. 'We need your brain. Before you ask, we're not zombies. But you are the oldest and wisest of us all, Lady Violet. We want you to rule Kol for us. From the labyrinth, if you so desire. Nothing needs to change for you. And do bear in mind that we could have carried out this entire plan without telling you. We're being honest only because we mean well.'

'Meaning well is never enough, child,' said Violet. 'This will end in tears and bloodshed.'

'Not for us,' said Neskimas.

'I suspect we are in agreement,' said Bekrom. 'This is just as well, as events were set in motion a fair while ago. One Rainbow Council member on the throne of every important nation. We will soon be set to strike in Avranti. Already our agents are travelling towards Artaxerxia, Imokoi and Xi'en, to prepare for our arrival. Bhoomi will prove more of a challenge, and I will take it up myself. Makanzi will help you govern Kol, Lady Violet. One way or another, with or without us, the plan goes ahead. Six thrones, one world. Are you with us?'

Violet spent a few minutes with her head buried in her hands. Then she looked up, and said, 'I will try. But you cannot harm Temat in any way.'

Bekrom looked grave. 'Temat's incompetence nearly destroyed Kol,' he said. 'Her life is therefore forfeit.'

'That's not true. There's nothing she could have done.'

Makanzi transformed into a perfect copy of the Chief Civilian. 'Well, you should have told us earlier,' she said. 'It's too late to stop the assassins now, and I can't allow all my practice to go to waste.'

'In that case,' said Violet, fighting to hold back tears, 'I cannot help you.'

She turned into a Xi'en warrior-woman in a violet robe.

'Before you strike, good Lady Violet,' said Bekrom, 'allow me to remind you that we now rule Kol, and harming us would be harming the throne. I believe your vow prevents this.'

All semblance of fight left Violet. 'I have nowhere to go,' she whispered. 'Kill me, then.'

'That would be terribly wasteful,' said Bekrom. 'Stay here, if you will. We have no desire to harm you in any way. Besides, your library needs tending. You have refused us; we encourage you to reconsider. We will ask you again.'

'I have to say, having considered everything, that that is the most remarkable story I have ever heard,' said the Chief Civilian.

'Thanks. It's all true,' said Red.

'Do you know Kirin and Maya's present whereabouts?'

'No. They fell out of the story a long while ago. They are probably dead, because otherwise they would have fought their way back in.'

'Let us hope they are still alive. I must also say that I am extremely annoyed to learn that I have been your puppet all these years.'

'Sorry about that. But your predecessors were, too. If it's any consolation, you were extremely difficult to manipulate.

And you have achieved more than any other living ruler in the world today. Only part of that owed anything to the Council's guidance.'

'You should have made your presence known to me long ago. There is much we could have achieved together.'

'The Council would never have allowed it. If they are listening, they are furious. They'll hide their heads in the sand for years, trying to decide what to do next.'

Five black-clad figures materialized around them. They were clad in Silver Phalanx ninja clothes, but no Silver Phalanx assassin could teleport.

'Is this your Council?' asked Temat.

'No,' said Red.

'Then we should be worried.'

'Yes.'

The newcomers ripped off their masks. They all wore the face of the shapeshifter Icelosis. Long, blackened daggers glistened in their hands. Ojanus coiled around the Civilian's neck, extended both his heads and bared his fangs.

'Lady Temat,' said one of the shapeshifters, 'you have failed in your duties as ruler of Kol. Your life is therefore forfeit.'

Temat ignored them and looked the sky. It was empty; the Red Phoenix guards had been removed. She sighed softly and looked at Red, smiling ruefully.

'Are they yours? Was this all a trick?'

'Well, it's my father's face,' said Red. 'But I have no idea who they are. Who are you?'

'Silence, human!' roared the shapeshifter. 'Lady Temat. Last words, if you please.'

Thog drew his sword. Red disappeared.

'Look out behind you,' said Temat.

The shapeshifter assassin looked puzzled at this, but

realized what she meant when Red appeared behind him and slit his throat.

The next few seconds were full of fireballs, slashes and shapeshifters flickering in and out of vision.

And then five bodies lay on the ground. Red appeared in front of Temat, looking pleased. Thog wiped his sword on his thigh. Ojanus hung limply around the Civilian's neck, both his heads slashed off. The Civilian stood still, looking out over the railing at the city she ruled and loved.

'That was fun,' said Red.

And then she noticed the red line across Lady Temat's throat.

The Chief Civilian turned and smiled. Then she slumped forward and fell on her knees before Red.

'Take care of the city,' she whispered. 'I tried.'

She fell dead.

Red cast healing spells, but it was too late. She was gone. Thog fell on his knees and wept bitterly. Alarm bells rang out far away, and Red could hear the sound of booted feet, running wildly in the distance. She looked at the Civilian's peaceful face, and up at the moon. She looked at Thog, and at Kol, and smiled.

'Can you keep a secret?' she asked.

'Yes,' said Thog.

'Good. Stand aside.'

Red sent a stream of green fire washing over Temat's body. Thog cried out in protest, but fell silent as he noticed Red's new face, stern and commanding, beautiful and cold, and her hair, long and steel-grey. Her clothes changed colour, and rearranged themselves into the Chief Civilian's robes.

'It looks like I'm going to have to rule the world after all,' said Red.

12

'Oweeyay,' said the Baby of Destiny with much solemnity.

'Yes, I know,' said Maya. 'But I'm reading. Play on your own until Fatima gets here.'

The Future Wielder of the Thunderbolt of Universal Doom bubbled mutinously, considered crying, and decided against it. Maya had recently sealed her mouth with Gum That Bubbles after three sleepless nights; she was clearly a woman with no heart at all. Instead, the Baby of Destiny tried low cunning; she sat up with much difficulty and concentrated on looking adorable. It was an unequal battle from the start; after a few seconds Maya succumbed to blackmail and social pressure, set her book aside and picked up the wobbling goddess, who accepted her affections graciously, saying 'Hoo!' and pulling a few clumps of Maya's hair out.

Bolvudis had clasped the Baby of Destiny to its heaving bosom, and a strange assortment of men, women and creatures lined up outside Maya's hut every day to coo over the bawling newcomer. This was fine as far as Maya was concerned; it allowed her and Kirin to escape their entirely unfair parental responsibilities and spend some time together. But given the baby's importance in the cosmic scheme of things, it was not safe to leave her alone with strangers, and even Spikes, though a wonderful nurse, needed to get away from her cradle once in a while and be randomly destructive to reassert his role in the universe. And so it was that Maya found herself sitting with the Future Wielder of the Thunderbolt of Universal Doom this pleasant afternoon, turning various objects into other objects, making flashing lights appear on the hut's walls, wishing she had Kirin's ability to juggle with his mind, and still trying hard to pretend that the Baby of Destiny had not captured all their heartstrings firmly in her tiny hands.

The unwaba had warned Kirin and Maya that the Infinite Infant was vulnerable on the mortal plane, and needed to be protected; that she was, for now, just an ordinary baby. The Infinite Infant, however, did not seem to be aware of this. Every now and then, she would forget she was no longer omniscient, and would start speaking in a grown-up voice when she thought no one was watching her. And she seemed to be able to eat almost anything, from insects to solid steel. On one memorable occasion, while Kirin had been sleeping open-mouthed, she had eaten her way right through the hut's wall, and had been found after a frantic search on Bolvudis's southern shore, trying to see if she could swallow the Psomedean Ocean.

But the Baby of Destiny was calm now, gurgling in amazement every time a little golden fish appeared above her head and disappeared with a *sploink*. And Maya found that she was laughing as well, and wondered if the Baby of

Destiny would remember her motley collection of nurses on the mad isle of Bolvudis when she ruled the galaxy.

After the fifty-first fish disappeared, the Infinite Infant fell asleep. Maya reached for her book, but there was a knock on the door.

'Fatima?' called Maya, remembering to put on a fashionably disgruntled expression.

The door, which had been bolted from the inside, swung open. Silhouetted against the light stood a man, naked except for a wolfskin loincloth. Maya stared at him appreciatively; he was an anatomist's dream, all well-defined and bulgy. Piercing blue eyes met hers, and she flinched at their intensity. Alarms suddenly rang out in her head; this was no prospective baby-cuddler. And then she noticed streaks of blood on the rippling muscles on his sweat-soaked arms, and fangs trying to burst out of his cruel, thin mouth, and she jumped up and leaped between the stranger and the Baby of Destiny.

'I am the Ursag,' he said. 'You have heard of me, and you know what I want.'

Every nerve in Maya's body was screaming at her, begging her to abandon the baby and leap out of the open window, but she smiled her friendliest smile at the Ursag.

'Hello, Ursag,' she said, 'or is that hello, *the* Ursag? It's good to meet you, but I'm afraid I have no idea who you are.'

The Ursag smirked, and his fangs glittered. 'Few meet me more than once, yet all have heard of me. I am he, the one from your nightmares. The silent shadow, the tireless hunter that stalks the night, slaying every evil thing it touches,' he said. 'Surely you have heard of the mysterious deaths all over this island over the last few days. My handiwork.'

'Well, that's nice,' said Maya. 'But sorry, I've been very busy, with the baby and everything. Is there anything I can help you with?'

A hint of doubt appeared in the Ursag's steely gaze. 'You are the Dark Lord's mistress, are you not?' he asked. 'Of course you are; I have been following you for days.'

'The Dark Lord's mistress? No, sorry. You need to take a right, run in a straight line for a month or two, stop at a big Dark Tower you'll find along the way, and then ask. Would you like some tea before you go?'

The Ursag's shoulders sagged. 'You are not the Dark Lord's mistress?'

'Would I be living in a hut if I were?'

'You have really never heard of me?'

'Not a word. But I'm sure lots of people have,' said Maya encouragingly. 'You seem nice.'

'I am not *nice*,' said the Ursag in a voice of ice. 'I am the Ursag, the most fearsome predator to walk this world or any other. And you are lying. The whole world knows of me. It must. Perhaps it is the word Ursag you are not familiar with. But you must know of the ravian werewolf, the only one of its kind, sent to slay raviankind's worst enemy, Kirin Kin-Traitor.'

'Why don't you just tell me your story and then I'll know,' said Maya, her knees threatening to give way.

'There is no point in my *telling* you my story,' he said. 'They had promised that they would ensure the whole world knew of me and the sacrifice I was making, in allowing myself to be merged with a monster. That bards in future Ages would sing of me, of my creation in the White Lady's tower of sorcery, of my escape from its burning ruins when the Dark Lord's forces ensured its secrets would stay lost forever, that there could be only one Ursag to hunt his enemy all across the world. That the Dark Lord himself would tremble every time someone whispered the name Ursag in the farthest corners of Obiyalis, and know his days were numbered!'

His eyes were glowing, almost white with fury now, and little specks of saliva flew out of his mouth. Maya looked outside, through the open door, wishing Kirin and Spikes would arrive. The Ursag thumped his chest as his voice grew louder, hoarser, angrier.

'I, the Ursag, have walked this wretched earth for untold days and stormed the heart of the Dark Tower itself. I, the Ursag, have looked into the eyes of the Dark Lord, and know that he is an imposter. I have leaped off the highest levels of the Dark Tower and lived. I have slain my way through north and south and tracked the real Kirin down to his island lair, a feat that required incredible skill, strength and patience . . . and you have not even heard of me? I am the Dark Lord's chief enemy! I am his nemesis! I am his story's bitter and meaning-laden end! Imokoi shivers at the rumour of my approach! How *dare* you not know me? What evil fate has befallen me?'

'Look at the bright side,' said Maya. 'That's a really nice loincloth.'

The Ursag began to growl, and the hut trembled. His face lengthened a little, and tiny red points flared up in his blue eyes.

'Don't do that. You'll wake the baby,' said Maya. 'Look, my sympathies and all that. I know what it feels like to wander all around the world for nothing. But I doubt your masters had any intention of making you famous. They thought you'd kill Kirin for them and they'd win the war. Then things got . . . complicated. Kirin had more important things to do, and he got a rakshas to impersonate him. And there was a new Dark Lord. You met him, right? You should go back and kill *him*. That's what'll help the ravians, you know, and make you really famous. Kirin's not even a part of this.'

'You lie. Kirin has fled here to escape the Ursag, the ravians' greatest hero. He spins his webs from afar, leaving his brave rakshas lieutenants to face Zibeb's righteous anger. But thanks to the Ursag's efforts, his secret now lies exposed. His fears have come true; he knew the Ursag would find him one day. He knew there could only be one winner in the long battle between Kirin and the Ursag. He knew how his story would end.'

'Kirin has no idea you exist,' said Maya, too exasperated to smile any more. 'If he'd been asked to name the villain he had to fight to save the day at the end of the story, it wouldn't have been you. Now, Myrdak, for instance—he knew how to make his presence felt, with the whole routine of threats, suspense and so forth. Didn't just come barging in like you did.'

'Had Myrdak known how to bring this story to an end sooner, I need never have existed. But the Dark Lord proved to be a better story-maker than Myrdak.'

'You're not listening. Kirin doesn't know how any stories end. This is because Kirin doesn't see his life, or anyone else's, or anything with real living people in it, as a *story*. You should try that, too. Then you won't get so upset when the other characters in your story, otherwise known as real people, don't behave the way you expect them to.'

'It is you that does not understand. We are all living out a great story. It has been twisted and perverted by Kirin and his evil minions, and it is my task to restore it and bring it to its rightful end.'

'Then turn a few pages ahead in your head, you fool, and you'll discover there is no rightful end. Things aren't going to clear up magically. There's no scene where everything's explained, and everyone's lives don't go back to being the way they were. There's no going back anywhere. And no one's happy ever after. Ever.'

'I will bandy words with you no longer, good lady. Kirin dies today.'

'Why? So you can go tell your king you've killed him? That'll make you really famous, killing a harmless man on a beach, and leaving the Dark Lord alive. What a fabulous end to the great Ursag's story. A murder on a little island, no witnesses, no audience, no glory at all. That, no doubt, is what people went through the whole trouble of turning you into a werewolf for.'

The Ursag took a deep breath and looked at Maya suspiciously.

'But they told me I had to kill Kirin,' he said. 'They said they would cure me only after I had killed Kirin. It is not just the story I care for. You cannot imagine the pain I feel as the monster's blood burns its way through my veins.'

'They told you what they did when they thought Kirin was the Dark Lord. You could go and kill him—I don't think he'd even fight you. But that wouldn't get you anywhere, since his death no longer helps your masters.'

'But kill him I must. It is not as if I have a choice.'

'You have several choices, actually. Would you like to hear them?'

The Ursag bristled, but looked curious. 'Yes,' he said finally.

Maya smiled again, and said 'For a start, you could go back to the Dark Tower and kill the person you were really meant to, in front of a large crowd, which is a good way to get famous. Better story, if that's what you want. Or you could try waiting for a bit. The world might end soon. And then working on building your legend will seem like such a waste of effort. Why fight? Hang around. Smoke some Muwi root. Walk around on the beach with us. Act a bit. We could always use a ravian werewolf in the Muwi-visions. Or—and this is a good one—go back and tell them you've killed Kirin. They'll never know you haven't. Kirin certainly has no intention of meeting the ravians and telling them otherwise.'

'And there is another path you have not mentioned,' said the Ursag. 'Kill Kirin, return to the Dark Tower, kill the imposter, and win immortality.'

Maya shrugged. 'You'll do what you have to. I was just trying to help. Which brings me to an interesting question. It has just occurred to me that you might not have come to meet me to find out what I thought you should do. And if you have indeed been following us for several days, you already know where Kirin is. Why, then, did you come to me first?'

'Because, dear lady, the story I have decided for the Dark Lord's death involves you. And your baby.'

Maya raised an eyebrow towards the heavens. 'Please tell me you're not planning to abduct us,' she said.

'I am indeed. This resolve was further strengthened by the information you recently gave me regarding Kirin's reluctance to fight. The Dark Lord's death must be suitably dramatic. For this, I will require your assistance.'

Maya laughed. 'That's a very bad idea.'

'You intend to try to resist? Please go ahead.'

'No,' said Maya. 'It's just that if you'd bothered to show up earlier, you would have known that abducting me is the silliest thing to do if you want to get Kirin to turn up. He's not a very good rescuer of damsels in distress. I should know. Besides, the two people who abducted me in the past died with swords right through them. One in the head, one in the heart. Do you really want to be the next?'

'In that case, prepare to die,' said the Ursag. 'When Kirin finds your scattered remains, and those of the baby, he will no doubt seek me out. He will find me soon enough.'

Maya laughed again. 'What is it now?' asked the Ursag, justifiably annoyed.

'Nothing,' said Maya. 'Just that if you harm this baby, the world will end. Seriously. And I will have spent my last precious minutes with you. I'm not sure why that's funny, but it is.'

'Just in case there is some truth in your words,' said the Ursag, coldly, 'I will spare the baby's life. Besides, it can look for revenge later, to avenge its mother's death. A good story. You, however, must now die.' He stepped closer to Maya, jaws lengthening.

'You work for the ravian king, don't you?' she asked.

'Of course.'

'Do you know he is my husband?'

The Ursag goggled. Maya observed, with great relief, that Spikes was some distance away and walking towards them.

'I'm telling the truth, you know,' she said. 'If you can track Kirin across countries and centuries, surely you can smell New Asroye on me, even though I bathe far more conscientiously. Perhaps you can even smell the wedding gifts. Where were you on the day?'

Over the Ursag's shoulder, she saw Spikes start and crouch into attack position.

'I do not understand,' said the Ursag. 'How is this possible?'

'They didn't tell the world about you, and they didn't tell you anything,' said Maya. 'I think you should give up now. In fact, as queen of the ravians, I order you to.'

Behind the Ursag, Spikes began a lopsided, slow, stealthy charge.

'No,' said the Ursag. 'I must kill Kirin. You are no ravian, and I will not take orders from you.'

He backed out of the hut and stood just outside the door. Maya smiled coldly, and raised her hands. Large fireballs appeared above her head.

'Well, you're not much of a ravian yourself, are you?' she inquired. 'Your danger sense is quite weak, for example.'

'If you are referring to the pashan charging up behind me while you childishly try to distract me with lights,' said the Ursag, 'I am perfectly aware of his presence.'

Spikes broke into a run. His claws were out, his head was down, and he looked terrifying.

'If I show no sign of alarm,' said the Ursag, 'it is because I do not consider him even slightly dangerous.'

Spikes leaped at the Ursag. Maya hurled her fireballs in the same instant, one on each side of the Ursag, to hit him if he dived to evade Spikes.

The Ursag spun around and rose majestically, one leg extended, and kicked Spikes's head in mid-air.

Maya screamed as Spikes flipped in mid-air and fell heavily, his body at an odd angle, as he landed with a heart-stopping crash. She sent a huge fireball into the Ursag's chest as he landed neatly on the ground.

The Ursag made no attempt to dodge her flaming missile. And showed no sign of even noticing the huge, ugly burn on his bare chest, or the smell of his sizzling flesh. He looked at

Maya and bared his fangs. On his chest, the burning circle melted away and healed almost instantly.

'After I have slain your lover,' he said, 'I will take you back to your husband. Stay here.'

He kicked Spikes savagely in the stomach, and the mighty pashan flew up and crashed to earth some distance away. Spikes showed no signs of pain, or indeed of any kind of feeling at all.

The Ursag shook all over. His eyes changed shape and colour, from piercing blue to fiery red. His body shifted jerkily to wolf form, grey hair sprouting in great slashes all over him. The change was clearly very painful; both ravian and wolf faces were twisted in anguish. But the transition was soon complete, and a huge wolf stood in front of Maya, who stared at him in terror, gaped wide-eyed at his enormous fangs, his lolling tongue, his rolling sinews. The Ursag sprang southwards, a grey comet streaking towards the beach where Kirin lay.

Kirin was lying on the beach watching boulders turn into sand when his ravian senses curdled up and began to throb. He sprang up, gasping at the intensity of the warning inside his head, and looked around. It did not take him long to identify the source of the danger.

A grey wolf streaked across the sand towards him, fangs bared. His blazing red eyes screamed murder, and his great paws cut deep grooves in the sand.

Kirin considered asking him why they couldn't all just get along, and then abandoned the idea as unsound. Instead, he reached for his Shadowknife.

He remembered with a groan that the Shadowknife was still with Spikes.

Who are you? Kirin thought, reaching towards the wolf with his mind.

The Ursag did not seem to be interested in introductions or pre-combat banter. He moved as smoothly and determinedly as a shark, tearing up the ground between him and his prey in great leaps. Kirin began to run, sending short bursts of ravian force skimming into the sand. They exploded upwards as they struck sand; the wolf evaded most of the bursts, and Kirin cried aloud in shock; only a ravian could have known exactly where he would strike. The wolf leaped in and out of fountains of sand, but now Kirin had predicted a few of his dodges, so other explosions threw him off his feet. Stinging walls of sand rushed over the wolf, followed by crackling ripples of flame. The wolf ignored all of these. Every time he fell, he shook himself vigorously, and began the chase again. The Ursag was trying to close Kirin down; Kirin sought, on the other hand, to keep a good distance between himself and his unknown assailant, to stay out of range of those razor-sharp fangs. Man and wolf circled on the lonely stretch of sand, neither gaining the advantage.

I think there's been some sort of misunderstanding, said Kirin.

I was born to kill you, said the Ursag. *I am invincible.*

Right.

And then the Ursag showed the full extent of his strength; he began to leap tirelessly at Kirin's throat, and neither spell nor force could deter him. Kirin managed to fend off a few lunges with his hands, losing blood in the process, but the werewolf wore him down; a few more cuts and Kirin would be laid bare for the sun to see. The Ursag was stronger than Kirin, and faster; he began to flicker between man and wolf shape as he struck. And strike he did, again and again; each punch left a huge, ugly bruise, each slash sent slowtime suspended showers of blood hovering in the salty air. Kirin parried blow after blow, but each thunderous strike drained him further and each evaded gut-ripping thrust cost him a few hours of breath.

Time slowed down. Kirin tried to strike a paralysing blow to the werewolf's neck, but the Ursag transformed into human shape and punched the ground. Time and sand flew up in every direction, and Kirin was knocked off his feet, on his back in the sand; a second later, a monstrous wolf form blotted out the sun as it hurtled down towards his throat. Kirin waited until the beast's muzzle was inches away from his face, and then pointed; a bolt of lightning shot out from his finger, plunging straight into the werewolf's chest, hurling the Ursag upwards and filling the air with the horrid stench of burning flesh. The Ursag twitched, shuddered, and transformed. Man-shaped he rose, and the look on his face filled Kirin with terror. There was a hole in his chest, and through it Kirin could hear the pounding of his enemy's heart.

'I don't want to kill you, or even fight you,' said Kirin thickly. 'I don't even know you. Whatever it is that this is about, it's not worth it. I don't want it. You can have it, just leave me alone.' He staggered a little. His head was spinning, and he felt like going to sleep. Strange shapes floated between him and his opponent; blood filled his eyes.

The Ursag laughed, a horrible, wet, blood-choked sound. 'Too late now,' he said. 'The story's gone too far. This is the part where you leave it. This is the moment you have dreaded since you first heard my name. You cannot flee any longer. Now I have defeated you. Immortality is mine.'

'I have never heard your name before. This is so completely pointless,' said Kirin. 'Please, stop.'

'I am unstoppable.'

'All right, then.'

The Ursag vaulted upwards, over Kirin, and landed on his feet behind him. Kirin turned fast, but the Ursag had already jumped again, and this time he kicked at Kirin's head as he leaped over him. Kirin tried to duck, but the Ursag's foot sliced his ear open, and he spun and fell on the sand. He tried to get up, but could not.

The Ursag's feet landed on the sand with a *thump* that echoed in Kirin's ears. 'I am stronger and faster than you could ever be,' he said. 'I was made to kill you. It is my destiny.'

He knelt, grabbed a fistful of Kirin's hair, and pulled him up. He let go, and Kirin slumped back on the sand again. The Ursag laughed aloud, and raised him again. 'Last words, Dark Lord,' he said.

Kirin lifted a quivering hand. The Ursag watched with interest.

And then Kirin sent a lightning-bolt through the Ursag's eye.

The Ursag was thrown back. A third of his head was missing, but incredibly he rose again, bellowing in rage, his single eye rolling madly. He staggered about on the sand, howling and tearing at his own flesh. Kirin lay back and watched wearily, too tired to do anything more.

Out of nowhere, a black net appeared, heading for the Ursag. The creature saw it, and tried to dive and roll out of its way, but the net moved faster, twisting and spreading as if alive, and it covered what was left of the Ursag's head. Kirin turned his head with great effort, and saw Maya running frantically towards him. The net thickened from the Ursag's head into a rope that ended on her fingers. It was the Shadowknife.

The Ursag roared, and tried to shift into wolf form, but the net held firm. And then Maya closed her eyes and concentrated, planting her feet firmly in the sand to steady herself as the Ursag thrashed and leaped. Great beads of sweat ran down her cheeks. The net tightened on the Ursag's head, and bit viciously inwards; there was a horrible squelching, crunching sound as the mesh solidified into a single point, and it rained tiny pieces of Ursag brain.

Maya threw the Shadowknife into the sand and ran to Kirin.

'Spikes?' he mumbled. 'Shadowknife? You?'

'Borrowed it for a while,' she said. 'Spikes is down. Alive, though. Yes, I know it's dangerous for mere humans, but there wasn't anything else.'

'You were better with it than I ever was,' he said in wonder.

'I have a more violent imagination than you do,' said Maya.

'That is why I love you,' said Kirin, grinning weakly.

'Yes, yes,' said Maya, casting a spell, trying not to show how terrified she was that he would die, because his wounds were many and deep. 'That's what they all say when they're saved from the ravian werewolves.'

'Who was that, anyway? Why did he try to kill me?'

'He said he was your greatest enemy. He had some long story as well. Tried to tell me, too.'

'Strange. And I never knew.'

'Yes,' said Maya, rubbing her nose. 'Now shut up and let me heal you.'

They kissed. Some distance away, behind a cluster of

palm trees, two imps named Aler and Unity buzzed away ecstatically, their eyes a blur.

'And that's an eyeful,' whispered Pygmy Lion reverently.

That night, Spikes, unable to sleep because of excruciating pain, was very irritated when he felt something crawling around on his left foot. He raised his right foot to squash whatever it was, when an old, dry voice spoke.

'Spikes,' said the unwaba, 'listen closely, for what I have to say is the most important thing you have ever heard.'

'I'm listening,' said Spikes.

'The end of the world is upon us. Mantric and the Dagger have reached the ocean's edge, and are about to meet the gods. If they succeed—if we are given a new world—there will be a price to pay. Mortals may not defeat the gods and live. One of your friends—Kirin or Maya—will have to die if the world is to survive.'

'Why?' asked Spikes.

'I just told you,' said the unwaba irritably. 'The gods command it. It is a fair price.'

'Why tell me?'

'Because you know them best, and so you will have to choose. Will Kirin live or Maya? Take your time, but make up your mind soon. I will ask you again tomorrow, if any of us still live.'

'Kirin,' said Spikes.

'Quick work,' said the unwaba. 'Very well. If the Dagger and Mantric save the world for us—probably sacrificing their own lives in the process—Maya will be offered to the gods. Agreed?'

Spikes said nothing.

'I know this is difficult for you,' said the unwaba. 'I will make it easier. I will take Kirin away for a few days. And you will take care of what must be done. Remember, it must be done if the world is to survive.'

'You are asking me to kill Maya,' said Spikes flatly.

'It will be easier than killing Kirin, will it not?' asked the unwaba. 'Do not fret about it overmuch. After all, there is every possibility that none of us will live to see the sunrise.'

13

The world stood still. The dauntless crew of the *Duck of Destiny* stood on the wooden bird's foredeck enveloped in clouds of fine mist, staring upwards in disbelief. In front of the *Duck*, the Vertical Sea stretched from ocean to sky, a shining, sparkling curtain of water, and strange shapes flickered and danced behind it. From east to west, as far as their eyes could see, the wall of water stretched, crowned by clouds and rainbows, the sound of falling water a dull roar rolling across the earth. There were voices in the water, mysterious musical voices speaking and singing in languages they did not understand. Eddies and currents of raw magic gurgled, churned and spun; little lights flashed by the *Duck*'s hull, and pale fumes of dense pure magic drifted skywards. The voyagers of the Fateful Fowl felt the weight of the sight of the gods, and were rooted where they stood, feeling naked and tiny before the powers around them.

Mantric had worn his finest robes, and stood calmly in the middle of the *Duck of Destiny*'s foredeck, his skin tingling and glowing a little because of the strength of the magical field around him. He looked younger, stronger, regal; a man worthy to be his world's ambassador. He was surrounded by the chests he'd brought from Kol and Bolvudis, the contents of which he'd so fiercely kept secret. Most of the chests were arranged in front of him, but two, the largest of the lot, he kept a little distance behind him, near the ship's wheel, where Fujen and the Dagger stood, with Orpi and Telu-Yeti. The rest of Fujen's crew stood behind their captain, shuffling uncomfortably, not daring to say anything.

The Dagger, a treat for the eyes under any circumstances but positively dazzling now in his smartest assassin's clothes, eyed the two large, man-high chests near him warily. The one on the right clearly contained the mysterious monster Mantric had been hiding from him all these days; it rattled and thumped from time to time. The beast within it was clearly not used to captivity and extremely resentful of its long and tiresome confinement. Occasionally it slammed against the chest so hard that cracks appeared on its side. Mantric seemed to be completely oblivious to his captive creature's escape attempts; he was busy just looking around him, gathering magic inside himself, experiencing more wild magic than any spellbinder had before.

The skies darkened and seemed to become solid above them, stars shining brilliantly in a bed of bright black. They looked up, and saw the gods, sitting in their dark chairs around the Vertical Sea.

If asked at that moment to describe exactly what they saw, no two people in the *Duck of Destiny*'s crew of adventurers could have given the same description; indeed, most of them would have been unable to even begin to put in words the incredible sensations they felt. Some saw human shapes filling the sky, shining like suns, beautiful benevolent faces old and young in radiant robes, the gods they'd always known existed, guiding their every step. Jewels the size of worlds adorned their many faces and bodies; some bore weapons in a multitude of arms. Others saw incredibly powerful, awe-inspiring, terrifying figures, shaped like humans or animals, a sky full of fangs and claws and eyes and horns and tails and mountainous sinews, creatures to bow before and worship, monsters to fear and love. Yet others saw only lights, great lights that stood or flickered, some intense and harsh, some gentle and inviting. A few saw nothing at all but stars, and strange ripples in endless darkness. Most of Fujen's crew fell on their knees, their minds blank, their eyes unseeing. Some prayed, others wept, others swooned, overcome.

The god who sat above the *Duck of Destiny* looked (to many of the *Duck*'s crew, though they would have differed on the number of his heads and limbs and the length of his long white beard) like an infinitely wise, immeasurable mighty father-guardian-king-magician-teacher-god. He now spoke and filled the heavens and earth with the sound of his voice, deep, rich, powerful, the first sound this world had heard.

'TRULY HAS IT BEEN SAID AND SUNG THAT TIME IS AS A RIVER, EVER FLOWING FROM AGE TO AGE, FROM WORLD TO WORLD, FROM PAST TO FUTURE, AND LIFE AND DEATH AND THE UNIVERSE ITSELF FLOW THROUGH ITS SWIRLING WATERS. AND THE GODS, THE ALL-KNOWING ONES, THE KEEPERS OF THE FLAME ETERNAL, STAND AS IMPERISHABLE ROCKS IN THE RIVER OF TIME, GUIDING ITS FLOW, CHARTING ITS COURSE, WEATHERING ITS IMPETUOUS REBELLIONS. YET IT MAY ALSO BE SAID OR SUNG THAT TIME IS AS A WHEEL, WITH THE GODS IN ITS CENTRE, WATCHING, RULING, LOVING, AS HEROES AND LOVERS AND EMPIRES AND WORLDS

RISE AND FALL AND RISE AGAIN. AND HERE IS YET ANOTHER TRUTH; THERE COME TIMES IN TIME WHEN THE GODS STOP THE RIVER, OR THE WHEEL, TO SEE, IN THEIR INFINITE WISDOM, WHETHER IT IS TIME FOR A CHANGE. FOR AN ENDING. FOR RIVERS AND WHEELS BOTH GATHER MUD IN THEIR ENDLESS JOURNEYS, AND IT FALLS TO THE GODS TO SMOOTHEN THE FLOW, TO BURN AWAY ALL THAT IS IMPURE AND UNCLEAN, TO SEEK PERFECTION IN ALL THINGS. YOU ARE HERE, TRAVELLERS, IN SUCH A TIME, TO SEEK AN AUDIENCE WITH THE GODS THEMSELVES, TO TURN THEIR ALL-SEEING EYES AWAY FROM THE UNIVERSE IN THEIR CARE TO ATTEND TO YOUR NOT WHOLLY INCONSEQUENTIAL NEEDS.'

Mantric smiled uncertainly. 'Hello,' he said.

'HELLO INDEED. DID YOU UNDERSTAND A WORD OF WHAT I JUST SAID?'

'Well, yes, I suppose . . . O gracious and omnipotent one,' said Mantric, trying gallantly to be religious. 'If my reply was unsuitable, forgive me. The scale of the occasion, um, petrifies my mortal tongue.'

'OH, STOP IT. YOU'RE NOT FOOLING ANYBODY. YOU MAY SPEAK PLAINLY, AND SO WILL I.'

'Thank the gods,' said Mantric, with infinite relief.

'YOU'RE WELCOME. NOW, LET US ATTEND TO THE BUSINESS AT HAND. YOU HAVE COME HERE TO ASK US TO SAVE YOUR WORLD.'

'Yes.'

'WHY SHOULD WE?'

'Amloki?' whispered Fujen.

'Shh,' said the Dagger severely.

'Don't shush me, man. We've got trouble.'

'I know. The last thing we should be doing now is drawing attention to ourselves.'

'Look,' said Fujen, pointing.

Amloki looked, and saw, to port and starboard, two large islands floating beside the *Duck of Destiny*, a short distance away. While recent events had rendered the unexplained appearance or disappearance of an island an entirely mundane occurence, the Dagger immediately understood the reason for Fujen's concern.

One of the islands, the one to the *Duck*'s left, seemed to be composed entirely of scales, each one the size of a full-grown elephant. The other one appeared to be a writhing mass of tentacles.

And both these islands were growing in size, rising through the waves.

'It's just a couple of islands,' whispered the Dagger reassuringly. 'Nothing to worry about it.'

'I'd worry about them less if they weren't *breathing*,' said Fujen.

'I wouldn't presume to tell the gods what they should or should not be doing,' said Mantric. 'We've just come here to beg, really.'

'A WISE ANSWER. YES, YOU HAVE COME TO BEG. AND THE MANNER OF YOUR COMING HAS AMUSED US GREATLY, YOUNG MANTRIC. YOU HAVE PASSED EVERY TEST WE HAVE THROWN AT YOU, AND WE ARE PLEASED. AND WHEN WE ARE PLEASED, WE ARE BENEVOLENT. NOW. SURELY A MAN OF YOUR WISDOM WOULD NOT HAVE COME TO THE GODS EMPTY-HANDED, ESPECIALLY WHEN THE FAVOUR YOU ASK OF US IS SO GREAT.'

'Not at all,' said Mantric. 'The first thing I thought when I planned this great journey to meet you, O big and mighty ones, was this: What gift should I bring them? What humble token of man's gratitude and worship could be worthy of the gods?'

He picked up the smallest of the chests near him.

'In this chest,' said Mantric, 'lie the most precious jewels in the world. Mostly gifts from the gods. Mortals have fought over these gems for ages; each one is priceless, both in gold and in centuries of bloodshed, intrigue and passion.'

He opened the chest, and his face lit up in the warm glow that emerged from it. Then he shut the chest and tossed it into the sea. The *Duck*'s crew watched, aghast, as priceless jewels, the finest of Kol's secret treasure chamber, sank into the depths of the Vertical Sea.

Mantric said, 'But what are jewels to the gods? You could just make more. Their only value to you is in the entertainment they provide as your creations kill one another over them. So it would be silly to return them to you. Let us leave them at the bottom of the sea, instead. Over time, you will no doubt push them back to the surface, in the bellies of fish that eat them. And the killing will begin again at some point in the future. If there is a future. These deaths, in your names, are my first gift to you.'

'INTERESTING. I HOPE, FOR YOUR SAKE, THAT YOU HAVE BROUGHT MORE GIFTS.'

'I have. I spent several sleepless nights wondering—what could gods want? Riches mean nothing to you. Power we can only give you through prayer and adoration, but if you're planning to finish us all off, clearly that's not very important to you either. I never really understood the idea of sacrificing monarchs or beautiful women, or even animals for that matter, to please you. If you wanted them dead, they'd be dead, wouldn't they? Of course, there must be some amusement in making people grieve after killing their loved ones to placate you. But there has been so much grief in the world of late, and so many untold thousands have died, and so many have lost the ones they love. If all that hasn't pleased you, then there's really not much I could offer to tip the balance.'

'DO YOU SEEK TO PRESERVE YOUR WORLD BY GIVING US AN ENDLESS LIST OF THINGS YOU HAVE NOT BROUGHT FOR US?'

'No. Most of these chests are full of strange and wonderful treasures—magical weapons, rare works of art, fine cloths, spices, books, all gifts from the Chief Civilian. I would have thrown them into the sea too, but they will spoil in water. My real gift for you is something else entirely.'

'It really is the end of the world,' whispered Fujen.

'Those islands are the end of the world?'

'When the end of the world comes, the leviathan rises. What we're looking at here is a kraken. *The* kraken.'

'That bit looks like a giant sea serpent. That other bit there looks like a giant squid. Which one is the kraken?'

'Does that really matter at this point?'

'But it can't be the kraken! The kraken is found in the north!'

'Well, perhaps it's here on holiday. I don't know.'

'Well, what do we do about it?'

'There really isn't much you can do about the kraken. The question is, what does it want to do with you?'

'My gift for you,' said Mantric, 'is a vision. A new idea. A dream. A story. What else could a man give his gods?'

'INTERESTING,' said Zivran. 'SHARE THIS VISION WITH US, THEN.'

'I do not know why gods make mortals imperfect; perhaps

this makes them interesting. I do not know. Such matters are above my understanding. But what I have learned, through my studies and my travels, is this: Man's duty is to serve and honour the gods, to give them stories worth remembering.' Mantric paused and took a deep breath, amazed anew by his ability to lie through his teeth, and thanked his stars for not making him a politician. 'But mortals are flawed and selfish, and do not follow the paths drawn out for them; their flaws make them stray, seek out new roads, twist and spoil the stories they should enact for the gods that made them. And when the gods run out of mercy, when their creations have strayed too far and their heroes and stories are not good enough, they destroy the worlds their children have corrupted and move on.'

'THIS IS CORRECT. YOUR UNDERSTANDING OF MATTERS DIVINE IS IMPRESSIVE. CARRY ON.'

'Thank you. But some of us spend our whole lives immersed in arcane studies, or struggling through battle after battle. For us, the gods' decision to end the world, no matter how justified, comes as a bitter end to our labours. If mortals are by their very nature doomed to displease the gods, every world is doomed. True heroes, men and women of legend who please the gods and preserve the world, do not come often; inevitably, dark times arrive, heralding the end. But surely the gods do not *enjoy* killing their own children, no matter how twisted they have become. The children, I mean, not the gods, of course.' Mantric gulped and continued.

'What if, I thought, a middle path could be found? What if we could find a way to show the gods stories of perfect mortals, fighting ceaselessly for justice, winning epic battles, loving against all odds with undying passion, conquering evil without and within, and being, in other words, really, really, ridiculously entertaining? And what if we could preserve these stories, so if the gods liked them, they could see them again and again? What if all the heroes of these stories would be truly immortal, bound to serve the gods forever? What if we could give the gods all the magnificent battles, the heroic quests, the soul-stirring romances, the heart-rending tragedies, the stomach-cramping comedies that would satisfy them, without needing to kill most of the world's denizens in the process? And that's not all. What if we could show the gods the stories of the *gods*? Show them their loves, their lives, their wars and journeys? Would that not be a gift to delight even gods?'

'IT WOULD INDEED. BUT MERELY WISHING FOR SOMETHING IS NOT A GIFT, MANTRIC.'

Mantric smiled. 'I am here to give you far more than a gift, O massive and scarily powerful entity,' he said. 'I give you a vision like no other. I give you . . . Muwi-vision!'

Mantric opened another chest with a flourish and hauled out an imp, a Picsquid and a sheaf of Muwi root.

'AS FAR AS I CAN SEE, YOU ARE OFFERING US TWO SMALL DEAD ANIMALS AND SOME FORM OF FLORAL LIFE.'

Mantric looked sheepish. 'Well, they do tend to die if taken far away from Bolvudis,' he said. 'But who better to resolve that problem than the gods themselves? If you would just bring these creatures back to life, O most godly one, I will show you something truly amazing.'

'THE RULES OF THE GAME FORBID OUR INTERFERENCE.'

'But surely you already broke those rules when you stopped time and put those islands in our way.'

'YOU WILL NOT QUESTION OUR DECISIONS, OR OUR INTERPRETATIONS OF OUR RULES, MANTRIC. WE ARE GODS.'

'I apologize. Well, then, allow us to return to Bolvudis, and I will demonstrate the magic of Muwi-vision there.'

'No, Mantric. We will not take you anywhere. You have disappointed Us. What would you show us in Bolvudis that We have not seen before? You seek to save the world with actors, with theatre? Besides, I have seen you at work in Bolvudis, and know full well that you have not even perfected your own discovery, this Muwivision. You still do not know how to move the images you have captured in your squids' ink to a medium where others can see them. Or have you discovered a way?

'No, I'm afraid not.'

'And you expected Us to solve this problem for you?'

'Well, the important thing is the idea, isn't it? You created the world, your divineness. This is merely a gap in the world that you could fill in a second.'

'True. It is also an unforgivable flaw in your gift to us. You travelled across the seas to the edge of the world for this, Mantric? We—I—expected so much more.'

And then there was a laugh inside Mantric's head, a jagged, mad laugh that convinced him he had lost his mind. This, he thought gravely, would probably be inconvenient.

'Amloki.'

'Yes.'

'Look.' Fujen nodded towards her right, towards the great island of slithering tentacles slowly approaching the *Duck of Destiny*. Some of the tentacles had left the main, writhing mass and now slithered slowly over the water's surface towards the ship's side. The Dagger saw huge, pink, moist suckers underneath them, and shuddered. On the left, the scale-covered island grew larger as well. More islands of scales appeared, in a line of humps sticking out the of water.

'Swords out, you think?' he inquired.

'We can't fight it,' she whispered. 'You'll have to think of something else. Can you . . . I don't know . . . tickle it?'

'You are seriously suggesting that I tickle a kraken?'

'I don't know. Whatever the appropriate position is for a kraken is.'

'I don't think there *are* any appropriate positions for krakens. Are you out of your mind? It's the bloody *kraken*.'

'Just checking. Swords out, you think?'

'Hell yes.'

Clever boy, said a voice inside Mantric's head. *You've done well. I'll handle it from here.*

Mantric considered protesting, but could not, because his tongue would not move. His body jerked convulsively, and his eyes rolled; he could see nothing but white light. Something had entered his body and was swiftly and efficiently usurping his control over it.

Calm down, my spluttering spellbinder, said Stochastos inside Mantric's head. *I'm on your side.*

Mantric choked, and would have doubled over, but something held him up. An instant later, he could see again, and hear, but when he spoke again, in his own voice, the words coming out of his mouth were not his.

'You misunderstood me, O gracious gods,' he said, noticing with admiration his body's new assured yet casual stance. 'The whole Muwi-vision idea was just an introductory speech. The real vision, the real gift, is something far, far bigger. An idea so vast in scale you'll be stunned to think that a mere mortal thought of it.'

'LET US HEAR IT THEN, MANTRIC.'

'You see, what I really want is the same thing you do. I want the end of the world.'

'WHAT?'

Stochastos leaned forward to be more persuasive, not noticing that Mantric's feet were now hovering a good two inches off the ground. 'What is the end of the world, really? To us, it's death, disaster and so on. But forget about us, we're most insignificant. What is the end of the world to *you*, O dangerous divines? Nothing more than a change of state. Old order crumbleth, new order rumbleth. A world enters a new Age, a new state, full of new ideas. Of course, you tend to take the "old order crumbles" thing a little too literally, but that's just the way you are.

'You're playing this Game with the world. And it's a fine game, nothing wrong with it. Not the nicest situation for us, because we're all dying, but you can't please everyone, can you? But I have an idea that can make your Game infinitely more satisfying.'

'I TIRE OF THIS, MANTRIC. TELL US WHAT YOUR IDEA IS, AND QUICKLY.'

'All right, then. Let's take my big idea—Muwi-vision—and marry it to yours—the Game. Imagine a GameWorld where the Game plays on endlessly and is seen by imps, mildly altered so they don't die when they're far away from Bolvudis and can roam all over the world. And they see everything, so you can see your favourite parts of the Game again in Muwi-vision whenever you want. But no one's acting—it's all real life. But every dramatic moment is made immortal, every story kept safe by Picsquids, and shown to you by some other creature you can invent. And you can control the Pieces perfectly—none of this viewing crystal nonsense. And that's just the beginning.

'What, I ask you, is the flaw in this plan? I'll tell you. Mortals. Living creatures. They're unpredictable. Unstable.

Whimsical. Worse, they die just as you're about to get to know them properly. Waste of all that training. And they don't seem to enjoy being controlled, even when it's good for them. The only solution to this is to eliminate them completely.'

'THIS IS WHAT YOU ASK OF THE GODS? I THOUGHT YOU WANTED TO SAVE LIVES.'

'Of course I do. I'll explain. The answer is zombies.'

'ZOMBIES?'

'Zombies. Easy to control. The rank and file have no will of their own, really. Even the leaders are extremely gullible. Detachable limbs, easy to rebuild in interesting new ways. The perfect renewable resource. So many people have died in these battles all over the world this year, and it's a simple matter to raise them all. Besides, the undead army has lots of really ancient undead heroes, people who remember what old-fashioned heroism is all about, people who were part of all the old legends and don't need to be taught anything. Imagine this: Legends relived. Heroes from different Ages pitted against one another. Former enemies fighting side by side. Perpetual war. Endless confusion. Endless entertainment. Huge armies with completely adjustable loyalties and none of the annoying defects of your average mortal. Unquestioning acceptance of traditional values and existing systems of power. Consider the possibilities. You tell them who they are, who they're fighting and why. And they *listen*. And cut one another up. We—you—stitch them together again, and give them a new story. They start again. They give you exactly what you want to see, or you blow them into little bits and they start again. They don't care—all they want is to feel alive, to feel anything. Everyone's happy. The Game gets so much better. And you can tell who *wins*—I don't know what you were planning to do with this one.

And everyone gets to be in Muwi-visions, too. Is this a good plan or a great plan?'

'You astound Us, Mantric! It is, indeed, a great plan. But what would We do with those who are still alive now? Destroy them all? This is your idea of saving your world? Is this what you want?'

'Well, that's the bit we get to after you decide whether or not you are satisfied with my gift.'

The kraken's tentacles reached the *Duck of Destiny*, and slithered up its sides, making horrible squelching noises. On board, they steadied their trembling hands and shaking swords and waited.

'We are satisfied. Your gift has pleased Us,' said Zivran, and there was a smile in his voice. 'You may ask Us for a boon.'

'Thank you so much, O puissant powers,' said Stochastos in Mantric's voice. 'My gratitude is infinite, as is your grace. My only desire is to help you remove the only flaw in this perfect new Game, this perfect new GameWorld. I speak, of course, of the living. Now, while it might be easiest for you to simply kill them, as one who stands guilty of being one of them, I must selfishly beg you to let the living live. We too are your children, and eager to be loved. We are proud to have been a part of your Game, but now we must leave it. Alive, preferably.'

'We must know how you know so much about Us, and Our Game.'

'Well, I have a little confession to make,' said Stochastos in Mantric's voice. 'You remember how I said you would find it amazing that I had thought of all this? With good reason. This wasn't my idea. No mortal could think of something this good, you see. My inspiration came from a goddess. The Infinite Infant.'

'WHAT? YOU KNOW WHERE THE BABY OF DESTINY IS? WHY DID SHE DISAPPEAR? WHERE IS SHE? TELL US AT ONCE?'

'I know she once appeared before me in a dream, O cosmic king, and that is all I know. But while she was there, she said a lot. A singularly loquacious infant, that one. Wherever she is, she has made a world for us, and wants you to allow us to live on it, and escape this one. It is her destiny to rule the pantheon one day, and she wants to govern a world whose people are not of great importance, who will not be missed overmuch if they are lost, to prepare her for this task. If you could place us on that world, O laudable lord, she would not have to seek another world to rule. She would not get in any other god's way, which is probably a good thing for everyone involved. She could toy with us happily, somewhere far away, in a secret corner of the galaxy, and let you play your perfect, completely subservient Game in peace.'

'HMM. MOVE EVERYTHING FROM THIS WORLD TO THAT ONE, YOU MEAN? HUMANS, RAVIANS, VAMANS, DRAGONS, COCONUTS?'

'Yes, O superb supreme being. One must never forget the coconuts.'

'WE MUST DISCUSS THIS, MANTRIC. YOU MUST WAIT.'

'It will be my pleasure.'

I have to leave now, I'm afraid, said Stochastos. *Pleasure meeting you. You had an interesting mind. But unless I attend that council and make a lot of trouble, they'll know something's wrong.*

Mantric swayed and almost fell as the chaos-lord left his body, the world flooding with strange colours before his eyes. *Had* an interesting mind? He would have thought about this some more, but lost consciousness and fell heavily on one of his useless treasure-chests.

'Are we winning?' asked Fujen as Mantric fell.

'I think so,' said the Dagger.

'Then why isn't the kraken going away?'

'Baby-Duck?' whispered Orpi.

'Yes, love?'

'Is this one kraken or two?'

'There is only one, Baby-Duck.'

Orpi pointed to the *Duck*'s rear. Fujen turned, and gasped. A huge serpent's head, each eye the size of the ship, had risen above the waves behind the *Duck*. To the right, on the island of tentacles, another mouth appeared, a squid's mouth, soft, cavernous and disgusting.

'Are the onagers ready to fire, my love?' asked Jen.

'Always, my love.'

'Then fire them, Baby-Duck.'

'THIS, THEN, IS THE WILL OF THE GODS,' said Zivran. 'YOU HAVE PLEASED AND AMUSED THE GODS, AND YOUR WISH SHALL BE GRANTED. THE LIVING SHALL BE SPARED AND GIVEN A NEW WORLD TO LIVE IN. THE WAYS OF THIS WORLD WILL END, BUT WE WILL NOT DESTROY IT; IT WILL BE USED TO BUILD A BETTER GAME. IT BEGINS NOW.'

Mantric remained rudely unconscious, but the rest of the crew whooped, cheered and hollered in joy, throwing hats and cutlasses into the air, unable to believe they had actually saved the day, and the world as well, and hoping someone would inform the kraken of this fact at some convenient point of time.

'HOWEVER,' said Zivran, and there was immediate silence on board the *Duck*, 'SEVERAL OF US FELT THAT YOUR GIFT TO US, WHILE VERY PLEASING IN EVERY OTHER SENSE, WAS INCOMPLETE, SINCE IT REQUIRES US TO ACTUALLY CREATE A NEW SPECIES BEFORE WE CAN EXTRACT THE MUWI-VISION IMAGES FROM THE PICSQUIDS' INK-SACS. NO DOUBT MANTRIC FELT THAT THIS MISSING ELEMENT ADDED A SENSE OF MYSTERY, THAT THE PUZZLE MADE IT MORE CHALLENGING AND INTERESTING FOR US. WE LOVED THIS IDEA, SO MUCH SO THAT WE DECIDED TO RETURN THE COMPLIMENT BY MAKING IT NECESSARY FOR YOU TO SOLVE A PUZZLE AS WELL BEFORE ENJOYING THE FRUITS OF YOUR LABOURS; HOW DOES ONE SURVIVE THE KRAKEN?'

The kraken thrust its heads out of the water, towering over the *Duck*, sending Fujen's pirates hearts racing. 'To arms!' cried Fujen, her voice quavering.

Zivran droned on smugly. 'WE THOUGHT YOUR STORY WOULD BE FAR BETTER IF YOU DIED NOBLY, SACRIFICING YOURSELVES TO SAVE YOUR WORLD. I OFFER YOU MY CONGRATULATIONS, CHILDREN. NO ONE HAS COME CLOSER TO OUTWITTING THE GODS THAN YOU DID TONIGHT. WE WILL REMEMBER YOU FONDLY ALWAYS. GOODBYE.'

The gods vanished.

Orpi opened the festivities, hurling a huge ball of Psomedean fire from an onager with deadly accuracy into the great serpent-head's eye. The ocean swelled, tilted and went berserk as the kraken's head crashed into the waves, and from the kraken's other mouth, in the heart of the island of tentacles, came a dreadful keening. The kraken raced towards the *Duck of Destiny* from every direction. Tentacles as thick as Vrihataranya's oldest trees rose into the sky and lashed down on the *Duck*, crushing and maiming and pulling with their hideous suckers. Fujen's crew fought back bravely with cutlasses and Psomedean fire, hacking and slashing and burning with everything they had, but without any real hope of victory. Every now and then, another brave pirate was dragged away, screaming, and the *Duck*'s figurehead squawked in agony as the kraken tried to squeeze the life out of her beautiful wooden beak.

The Dagger leaped to Mantric's side and shook him hard. Mantric stirred and mumbled something unintelligible.

'Telu-Yeti!' roared the Dagger. 'Heal him!'

But Telu-Yeti was busy being dragged away by a massive tentacle. Fujen ran up beside her and hacked at the slimy arm until it slithered away; Telu-Yeti rose immediately and charged at the kraken, screaming in monstrous battle-frenzy. She was clearly not in a very healing mood, thought the Dagger.

'Knew . . . they'd . . . turn . . .' mumbled Mantric. 'Open . . . trunk.' Then his eyes rolled horribly and he fainted again.

The Dagger ran back to the two trunks Mantric had left near him, somersaulting a few times to avoid a falling mast. The Berth Beast was still thumping away inside one of the trunks; the Dagger wondered whether or not to let it loose. Would it attack the kraken or the pirates?

There was certainly more kraken than pirate to go around, but it was too risky. He smashed the other trunk open and cried out in delight.

It was the Mirror of Icelosis. Mantric, bless his mad bald head, had remembered to bring an escape route, always the first item on the list of the discerning god-greeter. The Dagger dragged it out of the trunk and on to the middle of the deck, protecting it from the kraken with skilled thrusts of his sword, each slash chopping a tentacle, filling the deck with what looked like the largest collection of rotten fish in the world.

The Dagger put his hand on the mirror's smooth surface, expecting it to turn black and transform into a portal to Kol.

Nothing happened. The Dagger swore angrily; if he wasn't a hero, who was? He called Jen and Telu-Yeti to him. They raced back, ducking and rolling to avoid the kraken's monstrous limbs sweeping over the *Duck*, and they tried their luck as well, but the mirror remained obstinately silvery and clear; the portal did not open. Telu-Yeti even dragged Mantric to the mirror and placed his limp hand on it. Nothing at all.

'We have no heroes,' yelled the Dagger. 'He forgot the heroes! Get me a hero or we're all dead!'

Orpi raced up, her eyes flashing, covered in blood and slime. 'You're our last hope,' said Amloki. 'I know you're a hero, Orpi, put your hand on the mirror.' Orpi nodded, her face flushed, and touched the mirror. She gave it a look of such sternness that its heart, if it had one, broke into a thousand pieces, but to no avail. More tentacles appeared on the deck. The *Duck* began to rise and tilt slowly as the kraken rose under it.

Just as the Dagger was about to abandon the slowly sliding mirror and launch himself off the ship on to the kraken in a desperate attempt to find its heart and kill it, a tentacle slammed down on the Berth Beast's trunk, smashing it. The Berth Beast leaped out, landing lightly on the deck, looking for a fight, and everyone around him felt their spirits soar in joy and hope. The Dagger laughed aloud, realizing exactly why Mantric had kept the nature of the Beast hidden. Had they known the true nature of Mantric's protector, the gods might have been too scared to meet them. It was clear that Mantric had given more thought to returning home safely than to actually pleasing the gods; this raised the Dagger's already elevated opinion of his old friend to heavenly altitudes. He gazed adoringly at the monster that had cost him nights of sleep.

The Berth Beast's muscles were taut and lean. His eyes shone bright and fierce. His stride was the rolling, casual walk of a world-conquering emperor. His teeth were white and deadly. His ears were long, his nose was moist, and his name was Bunz.

Steel-Bunz.

Steel-Bunz raced across the *Duck*'s deck, nipping a tentacle here, dodging a falling beam there, until he reached the Mirror of Icelosis. He looked at it scornfully. Only a true hero could transform it into a portal, as used by the Seven Heroes of Kol? He touched it once with his whiskers, and immediately dark, inky clouds began to spread across its surface. Steel-Bunz looked at the mirror sharply, and the portal opened faster; the mirror seemed to shudder. The Dagger, almost crying with relief, dragged Mantric to the portal and pushed him through it, to Kol and safety.

Through the next few frantic minutes, the Dagger and Telu-Yeti stood by the Mirror of Icelosis, helping Fujen's crew cross, as Steel-Bunz took care of any tentacles that tried anything funny. Around them, the ocean and sky raged wildly, with waves taller than the *Duck* crashing against its sides. The kraken had already demolished the rear end of the *Duck*; now its wounded sea serpent head reared up over the figurehead, and snapped the living wood off with one ferocious bite. Its unimaginably vast, scaly tail swirled in the air high above the ship, snapping its remaining masts and rigging, ripping the remnants of its sails. But on the foredeck, Jen's pirates dived gratefully through Icelosis's mirror. Now only four of the *Duck*'s crew remained.

'Time to go, Jen,' said the Dagger, wiping his forehead, which seemed to have grown a crown of scales. 'We can tickle it before we leave, if you like.'

Fujen did not move or smile. She stood as if petrified, staring at the monstrous serpent-head chewing her beautiful figurehead.

'Thank you, Amloki,' said Fujen quietly. 'Thank you for bringing me on this adventure, from the bottom of my heart.'

'Thank me later,' said the Dagger. 'Is everyone through? Telu-Yeti! Move, move!'

Telu-Yeti stopped ripping suckers out of a tentacle, roared and raced towards the mirror, pausing occasionally to stomp on various slithering objects.

'I have sailed the seven seas, and seen many wonders,' said Fujen. 'But now, after this, I can truly say I lived a full life. That I meant something. That I stood for something greater than myself.'

'That's nice,' panted the Dagger, extracting himself from a sucker's sticky embrace with practiced ease. 'Now move, damn it!'

'I will not leave my ship,' said Fujen.

The Dagger paused, startled, and saw that Fujen's eyes were glowing white, and her body was unnaturally rigid.

'Well, technically, it's the Civilian's ship,' he said, but Fujen wasn't listening.

'The gods speak to me,' said Fujen in a strange, distant voice. 'They remind me that the captain goes down with the ship. That is how the story has to end.'

'Mmfm!' said Telu-Yeti beseechingly, but Fujen shook her head, walked forward and planted her feet firmly on deck, looking the rampaging kraken in its one good eye. She drew her cutlass in a touching gesture of mortal defiance and pointed it at the monster.

The Dagger pushed Telu-Yeti through the mirror. Steel-Bunz prowled ceaselessly at his feet, undaunted by the writhing mass of tentacles slithering towards them from every direction. The decks were completely covered now in slime and advancing suckers, bloated and obscene. A strange light shone down on Fujen. The Dagger, too, heard voices whispering inside his head. *You have fought well, little one,* they said. *It is time to rest now. Time to sleep. You are a doughty little warrior, but even you must eventually tire.*

The *Duck*'s deck cracked, and boards flew everywhere. Slimy fingers of doom rose though splintering wood. The kraken had coiled itself around the *Duck* now, and lifted it in mid-air. The mirror tottered, and would have fallen and broken, but the Dagger steadied it just in time.

Your journey ends here, said the gods. *You have pleased us. We will make you a star.*

The Silver Dagger considered the voices in his head. Then he laughed and made a very rude gesture skywards.

'Hey, Fujen,' he called. She looked at him dreamily. The kraken's head moved towards her, very slowly. A mouth the size of an island opened slowly, filling the air with noxious fumes.

'Nice knowing you,' said Amloki. 'Goodbye. Don't worry about Orpi, she's in good hands. Incredible hands, in fact.'

He winked lecherously. 'Or you could come along too,' he smirked, and leaped through the mirror.

Silvery streaks were beginning to appear on the mirror's surface. Steel-Bunz banished them with a quick snuffle. He looked inquiringly at Fujen, whose face was beginning to turn red. The light in her eyes had gone out, and she looked extremely indignant. She turned, as if waking from a dream, and saw the kraken's fangs inches from her face. She vaulted backwards acrobatically a second before its jaws snapped shut.

The kraken moaned and pulled, and the *Duck of Destiny* split in half. The mirror fell over and slid down towards a tentacle. Fujen picked up Steel-Bunz in one hand, tearing him off a sucker he was violating, and slid down the steeply sloping deck towards the mirror, cut off the tentacle that had gone through it, and slid through the mirror herself a second before another tentacle crashed down on it, picked it up and tossed it neatly into the kraken's gaping, slobbering squid-mouth.

* * *

Petah-Petyi's dice spins, sending sparks flying through space and time, and stops. She looks at their upturned faces. One million apiece. She smiles.

Zivran claps his hands and the world ends, in a great wave of magic that runs from the falling Vertical Sea and roars its way northwards and landwards, changing everything it touches forever, keeping everything it touches unchanged.

14

The unwaba clambered on to Kirin's face and he woke up with a start. Beside him, Maya stirred and mumbled.

'It is time,' said the unwaba.

'What time is it?' asked Kirin blearily.

'It is time for you to die, as per our agreement,' said the unwaba. 'The world has ended, and a new world has begun. The gods have been defeated. A price has to be paid.'

Kirin sat up. 'We're on another world now?'

'Yes. Far away from the Game. A drifting world, in a hidden space, out of the sight of the gods. Everything has changed.'

'Are you serious? The world ended? We were moved to the new one? What happened? I didn't feel anything.'

'Zivran was not aware that your feelings were an essential part of the process. The children of this world did not notice the shift; some had headaches, some strange dreams and others indigestion, but nothing significant enough to indicate the importance of the event that they had been a part of. If you want to be moved back to the old world to experience dislocation fully and be eaten by zombies, let me know. Maya will wake up if we speak further, so unless that is your will, we will have this discussion later. I will now wait outside while you say goodbye. Bring the Infinite Infant with you when you are done.'

The unwaba jumped off Kirin with surprising alacrity and waddled out of the hut.

A few minutes later, Kirin walked out of the hut, carrying the Baby of Destiny, his face completely expressionless apart from a certain tightness about the jaw.

'You did not say anything to her,' said the unwaba. 'Why?'

'That has nothing to do with you,' said Kirin. 'What do you want me to do?'

'You may choose the manner of your own death, as long as you do not suggest something clever, such as dying of old age eventually. How would you like to die?'

'I need to know how we were saved. And I would like some proof that this really is a new world.'

'Let us deal with your proof first. Do you see that tree over there?'

Kirin did.

'Now close your eyes and imagine you are standing under it.'

Kirin did. When he opened his eyes, he was standing under the tree.

'You are now able to teleport. Did you have this power in the old world?'

'No.'

'Well, then. The nature of magic itself has altered; every being in this world that uses magic will find their powers altered. You are no longer able to throw lightning from your finger, by the way, which reduces your options of ways to die by one. Is that proof enough for you?'

It was.

'Now, let us come to how the world was saved. An interesting story. When we went on our little trip to the heavens, you might have noticed that I stayed behind. Only to find myself embroiled in a most fascinating conspiracy; Zivran, Petah-Petyi, the Goddess of Chance, and Stochastos the chaos-lord, unlikeliest of allies, were all secretly trying to save the world, and found my well-planned arrival most useful. I brought the Baby of Destiny to this plane, telling you whatever you needed to hear, while Zivran created the new world—this world. Mantric and the Silver Dagger sailed to the edge of the Vertical Sea to meet the gods, and Zivran and Stochastos, working together and using Mantric as a mouthpiece, managed to whisk this world away right under the gods' noses, and the Baby of Destiny with it. A resounding victory in every way. And we agreed that should we ever be found out, you would be blamed for everything, and to eliminate any consequences, you would have to die to save the world. The happiest of endings, and the happiest of beginnings.'

'Zivran was on our side? He hid his feelings well.'

'Well, you could hardly expect him to share his true intentions with you. After all, you are all still lowly creations. Besides, he needed to test you constantly to see if you were worthy of his love. You did well, Kirin.'

'But all that didn't really matter, did it? In the end, the gods saved the world from other gods, and people who didn't know the world was supposed to end have no idea anything happened. And that's everyone except us, and we had nothing to do with it.'

'Not at all. You all ran around in a most wholesomely entertaining manner, and pleased us greatly. Besides, you took me where I needed to go, thus rendering yourselves extremely significant.'

'Still, it would have been better if the gods had lost to mortals.'

'That is precisely the sort of silly idea I would expect from you, and that is why I had to make sure you were inactive—or at least busy playing with that ravian dog—during the crucial final stages. The reason I made sure that it was actually Mantric and the Dagger who saved the world was that they were the only ones who could be trusted not to get swayed by their need to find themselves, or be true to their hearts, or fulfil some long-cherished dream, or any other equally foolish romantic notion. They got the job done, even if they were not heroes. In their place, you or Maya would have been drawn away from your journey by some silly personal errand, to help some unimportant nymph find her missing child or something equally ridiculous. Asvin would have sacrificed himself in some spectacular fashion, thinking his destruction would be enough to sway the gods. The reason I am such an excellent controller of world affairs was that I know how to pick the right person for the right task. And that is why this new world will do so well. Finally, a new world has both a rich history and a Divine Plan for the future.'

'There was no Divine Plan for the old world?'

'You want the truth? It was Zivran's world, Kirin. It is almost impossible to tell if Zivran has any idea what he is doing at any given point of time. The other gods had very definite plans for his world, though. The problem was not that there was *no* Divine Plan, but that as soon as the Game started, there were several, and any kind of consensus was almost impossible to achieve. This resulted, as it always does, in chaos, which led Zivran to wonder what life would be like for his creations in the complete absence of any guidance. Well, he is about to find out.'

'He is? But I thought you said this new world was hidden from the gods. Is Zivran still watching us?'

'No. The Infinite Infant has been given this world, and has made it invisible to other gods. But Zivran knows where the Infant is; well, he does not *know*, but he senses her presence, feels traces of her power from far away. She is the only link between this world and anything else.'

'What if another race like the ravians find the world and decide to invade it?'

'They will be destroyed, just as New Asroye has been destroyed by the vamans. This world is as resilient as its predecessor.'

Kirin took a while to absorb this. Visions of Asroye as he remembered it from his lost childhood floated before his eyes. He looked away, shaking his head.

'Since you do not seem to have anything to say, let me tell you a few things; I would like you to die as well-informed as possible,' said the unwaba. 'Let me tell you how a few stories will proceed. The ravians will have to sue for peace. They will have to become a woodland people, nomadic, mysterious, ever afraid, seeking allies to help them regain their former glory. They must not be allowed to create any more portals to other worlds; this could let the gods in. I will make sure the vamans, the rakshases and even the ravians see portal-building as an unforgivable crime. The rest of the world will have to get used to the fact that the ravians are here to stay, that they are a part of the world and have been since the first ravian arrived not long ago and was eaten by the Great Rakshas himself.

'What else might you be interested in knowing? Ah, Kol, the city you thought of as home until Qianzai scolded you soundly—Kol's future is uncertain. The Civilian, for all her weaknesses, held it together well and kept it under a measure of control. In the hands of the shapeshifter who now rules it, Kol will become greater than ever before, but more unstable as well; rakshases, shapeshifters, vamans and humans will all try to seize control from her shadowy hands. Her rule will end in violence; how and when and why I cannot see now.

'Great men and women have been lost forever, but their deeds live on, and will inspire others to rise to succeed them. This world has more than its fair share of greathearts and emperors in waiting; Aciram lives still, as does Zibeb, as do the four rulers of the vamans and the untested imperial houses of Xi'en. The Sultan of Artaxerxia has survived this war, against all odds. Rukmini of Durg has seen the world around her with new eyes, and will rise to greatness. And the wars birthed new legends and new heroes. The days ahead are full of doubt and promise. No one could ask for less or more.

'The world itself has changed and changed forever. The undead are gone; what will happen to those who die on this world I do not know. This is not the world as you knew it, which makes sense, since it is not the same world. Shifts of such significance cannot occur without certain errors; some living creatures have been left behind on the old world, and are lost to us. Other creatures have been spawned by the change; it is in these murky boundaries, beyond even my sight, that the future of this world will be defined. The nature of magic has changed, as you know, and the physical world has changed with it; some lands have shifted, others have disappeared, in places where magic held the elements together. More importantly, this world has no Vertical Sea; soon some brave explorer will discover the south and its denizens, and everything will change yet again. Exciting times, young Kirin. Interesting times. I am delighted to be here, and to know that all this is mine.'

'I thought this world belonged to the Baby of Destiny and you were just here to take care of her.'

'Of course. This world is hers. I merely rule it in her name until she comes of age.'

'I see.'

'Is there anything else you wish to learn?'

'Many things.'

'If you were thinking of prolonging your life with endless streams of questions, abandon the idea. I am so much cleverer than you.'

'That is true. But tell me, unwaba, how has this world changed you and your powers? Are you still omniscient?'

'No, alas. Zivran and the others decided it would be dangerous to allow me the whole range of godlike powers, given my proximity to the Infinite Infant in her, well, infancy. So I retain my physical limitations even on this world. But since my responsibilities now exceed those of most gods, I am now bound to forget. The future, I have to admit, is largely hidden from me, though I know most of it already, simply because of history's cyclical nature. My mastery over the past and present I retain.'

'Completely?'

'Almost completely.'

'Just as I feared.'

'What do you mean?'

'You don't know everything any more. What if this world is not as well hidden as you think? What if the ravians have made another portal somewhere?'

The unwaba looked both startled and confused, a difficult feat for a chameleon.

'You are right, Kirin, and I have made a mistake, which is almost an entirely new experience for me. Ignorance! Confusion! How annoying! How charming! The ravians did not have the blood they needed to create more portals, but the ravian portal at the Desolate Gard, where I met Maya, might still be open. Yes, we are not completely free yet. Zivran left a way in, the cunning old stoat.'

'In that case, I want go and make sure this portal is closed. I wish to seal this world's borders before I die.'

'That is an excellent idea, and I should have thought of it myself. Get the Baby of Destiny a basket or something, and summon your chariot. This will give us a chance to spend a few more days together, and you will be able to marvel at the vaman tunnels and the magnificence of Vrihataranya once again before you die. How pleasant for you.'

* * *

A large earthen bubble rose out of the floor of a vast cavern in the Desolate Gard, and a cluster of stalagmites that had rested in state on that particular part of the cave floor for centuries rose on it, and then splintered and scattered as the bubble popped open, and Kirin stepped out of the Chariot of Vul. The unwaba sat on his shoulder, looking bored, and the Baby of Destiny hovered behind them in a basket of reeds.

It took Kirin just a second to realize that something was terribly wrong in the Desolate Gard. The air was thick and heavy with dust and the stench of death. The cavern's walls were stained with blood, and in the distance he could see fallen bodies, human bodies, adults and children, their limbs splayed out at odd angles. He tensed, and cursed aloud when he realized that he had, as usual, forgotten to bring a weapon.

But Kirin was never defenceless; the shattered stalagmites rose in the air and began to revolve around them in elliptical orbits as Kirin walked westwards, guided by the unwaba towards the portal of the Desolate Gard, his footsteps echoing ominously. Falling water somewhere in the distance played a chorus of hollow, moist, sinister noises that did nothing to alleviate his growing sense of dread.

He passed through a few caverns, encountering no signs of life, passing several dead humans in various stages of decomposition and a few mangled animal carcasses. He could see, to the west, a glowing white light. 'The portal is open,' whispered the unwaba. 'My sight is clouded. I sense danger. Leave me and the Infant here, Kirin; I have no wish to share your death.'

Kirin ignored him and walked on. And then, to the west, he heard voices, shrill high voices that chilled his blood; he knew those voices, he had heard them before, sweet and musical, singing their strange songs as their owners ripped out chunks of his flesh with their charming little pointed teeth.

A little round red man appeared out of nowhere at the mouth of the cavern in front of him, squealing happily. More chubbies popped up beside him, their round eyes shining with excitement.

Kirin knocked them all out with well-aimed stalagmite fragments, and walked on.

'You were wise not to kill them,' said the unwaba, who seemed to have recovered his composure. 'They will offer you a painless, happy death after you close the portal.'

Kirin walked on without comment, efficiently meeting all further chubbies with flying rocks, until he reached the portal of the Desolate Gard. A massive dome of white light that rose out of a pit in the ground in a vast cavern, bordered by a hemispherical cage, bent iron bars as thick as a man's waist meeting in a silvery sphere on the roof of the cavern, a broken lock. He looked around, at the cavern's walls, which seemed to have been painted in blood and bright coloured fur.

'Some ravians evidently tried to escape, and were followed,' said the unwaba. 'Did they reach the other side of the portal, I wonder. It does not matter, really. Destroy the portal.'

But Kirin stood, motionless, in front of the ravian portal, and his mind was far away, an Age away, and his eyes saw not the Desolate Gard, but Asroye, wide, beautiful avenues, marble buildings covered under a spreading wave of light.

His musings were disturbed by a large bat that flew into his face, flapping its wings frantically. Kirin cast a transformation spell on it distractedly, intending to turn it into a mouse or anything less fluttery, and almost jumped out of his skin when the bat transformed into a large, muscular, mostly naked man. Kirin recognized his old friend Djongli, but a conversation of any kind was rendered impossible by Djongli running out of the cave, flapping his arms and squeaking excitedly. Not one to be troubled too much by such an everyday occurrence, Kirin shrugged, set the Infinite Infant's basket down on the cave floor and turned to the unwaba.

'What now?' he asked.

'Now you destroy the portal, your last great task,' said the unwaba. 'And then, with infinite regret, for I love you dearly, I watch you die and keep your promise to the gods.'

'I don't remember actually promising to die,' said Kirin. 'And I'm not sure Zivran even wants me dead. In fact, the only person who really stands to gain from my death, unwaba, is you.'

'Don't be ridiculous.' The unwaba jumped off Kirin's shoulder lightly, his old age and frailty showing no signs of bothering him.

'You want me dead because I know about you. Because my presence limits you, and your ability to control this world. I know your weaknesses. You wish to move on, whisper in the ears of people more interested in ruling, and killing and conquering, people who will not question you or argue with you, people who do not know how insignificant you were before the old gods, who do not know you are physically weak and not all-knowing as you claim. You have no intention of letting the Baby of Destiny rule anything, do you? You don't want anyone else to influence her.'

The unwaba chuckled. 'I could not have put it any better myself, Kirin.'

'You will fail,' said Kirin. 'My death means nothing. Maya and Spikes will stop you.'

'I instructed Spikes to kill Maya in your absence to ensure your survival,' said the unwaba. 'When I return, either Spikes or Maya will be dead, and the survivor will be a nervous wreck and an obedient slave.'

Fire flickered on Kirin's fingers.

'Don't be a fool. I cannot be killed,' said the unwaba. 'I am still a god. If I die, the other gods will know, and this world will be discovered and destroyed. Zivran can sense any event that might harm the Infant; the death of her guardian would, of course, count. Should any harm befall me or her, Zivran will come to our aid instantly and all your labours will be in vain. Calm yourself, Kirin! Do not make this any more difficult than it has to be.'

The fires on Kirin's fingers and in his eyes went out. 'You win, then,' he said simply.

'I know,' said the unwaba, with infinite malice. 'Now destroy the portal.'

'I have one more thing left to do before that,' said Kirin. 'I just had an idea; one of those rare ideas that are mine, and mine alone. Something I learned from the gods, in fact.'

'Indeed. And what have the gods taught you, young man?'

'That nothing is sacred, and there are no real rules,' said Kirin. 'The gods have taught me how to cheat.'

He picked the unwaba up and tossed him into the portal. The unwaba yelled in surprise and anger, and his tail wiggled furiously in mid-air as the light washed over him, covering him completely in brilliant white, and then he was gone.

Kirin raised his hand, and the Infinite Infant's basket rose and floated towards him.

'I'm sorry,' said Kirin, 'but I was really tired of having other people make up my mind for me. And now the only way I can set this world free is by sending you through the portal as well.'

'Ey-mum-mum-mum,' said the Baby of Destiny gravely.

'It was an honour to have met you. You're going to rule the gods one day, aren't you? Good luck. When you do, please try and keep even the lowliest of your creations happy. Try and be kind to everyone, especially the powerless.'

'Boop!'

Kirin moved his hand, and the basket began to float into the portal. But just as it was about to enter the dome of white light, Kirin hesitated. Even with the future of the world at stake, could he do this to an infant? What if the Baby of Destiny was too young to travel through portals? What would happen if she died?

And then he heard a woman's voice in his head, musical, powerful, amused.

Relax, she said. *I'll be fine. I'm the Baby of ****ing Destiny.*

Kirin nodded weakly, and the basket floated through the ravian portal into a world far away.

Kirin raised both his arms then, and the moongold spheres holding the portal together spun as they rose. He snapped his fingers, and they shattered into pieces, and the portal's light went out. Kirin stood in the darkness, exhausted but smiling. The world was free.

He swayed and would have fallen, but then heard the unwaba's voice again.

I instructed Spikes to kill Maya in your absence.

He knelt swiftly and summoned his chariot.

* * *

Kirin leaped out of his chariot and raced towards his hut, his heart pounding.

The hut was empty. Kirin stood at the door, feeling huge, ragged breaths burst out of his lungs, wondering wildly what to do next.

'You all right?'

Kirin snapped around. Spikes stood behind him. The pashan looked worried.

'Sit down,' said Spikes. 'Something happened while you were gone.'

'Where's Maya?' Kirin managed to ask.

There was a pause that stretched into centuries as Spikes rubbed his nose.

'I don't know. In the village, I expect. Listen. The imps and Picsquids are missing. Something's wrong,' said Spikes finally.

A huge knot dissolved in Kirin's heart, and he leaned against the wall and shut his eyes.

'You look ill,' said Spikes. 'Speaking of Maya, you really shouldn't run off without telling her. She's not very happy with you.'

Kirin laughed then, hysterically. 'Did the unwaba tell you to kill her?'

'Yes.'

'Why didn't you tell me?'

'Well, you were asleep. And then you were gone. Why are you laughing? Are you drunk?'

'No. I'm just glad you didn't do what he told you to.'

Spikes shrugged. 'Why would I kill Maya? I'm not stupid. And I'm not in the habit of taking life-changing decisions based on the advice of lizards in any case.'

'He was a chameleon, not a lizard,' grinned Kirin. 'There's a difference.'

In the middle of comforting a distraught, imp-less Pygmy Lion, Maya was surprised when Kirin appeared out of thin air beside her and swept her off her feet. She protested mildly when he hugged her hard enough to squeeze the life out of her, but seemed pleased enough.

'I think the unwaba knew what you'd do,' said Maya afterwards, as they lay side by side on the beach, sipping dangerous-looking red drinks out of coconut shells. 'I know you never liked him, but he was a sweet old thing.'

'That's very generous of you, given that he ordered your death and tried to get me to kill myself,' said Kirin.

Maya waved her hand dismissively. 'Why would he tell you what he could or couldn't do as this world's new guardian if he didn't want you to react in some way? He was testing you, and you passed. He wanted you to throw him through the portal. Think about it; this way, the unwaba gets his revenge on the gods that forgot him. He let a world get away, and now he's far away with the Baby of Destiny, and no one can touch him or blame him. Maybe he wasn't lying when he told us he loved this world and wanted it to be free. Maybe all this was his way of helping us escape the gods and the Game.'

'Thank you for trying to rob me of my one well-deserved moment of satisfaction. But yes, I suppose that's possible. We'll never know the truth,' said Kirin. 'And we should be used to that when there are gods involved; we can only see what they let us see. The worst part of all this is that everything that happened with the unwaba could be a lie, a joke. Maybe we aren't on a new world at all. Maybe they're still sitting around us, laughing, playing their Game. We have no way of finding out.'

'Well, I choose to believe we won the day, saved the world and defeated the gods,' said Maya. 'And now I can go back to believing that the gods don't exist, and that we were free all along, and ruled our own minds. It's easier, and makes me feel happier.'

'Even if we have escaped, if all this isn't a part of some even larger Game, they won't let us get away so easily,' said Kirin. 'It'll set a bad example. They'll hunt us. They'll find us again, one day. What happens then?'

'Another adventure. And that's the only way it could ever be. What were you expecting, a happy ending? Any ending is the end of the world, Kirin, even a happy one. If we didn't know that things were going to change, for better or worse, why would we want to go on? Now stop worrying.'

Kirin was not initially entirely convinced by this piece of wisdom, but when Maya took his clothes off in a no-nonsense sort of way, there was no question of any further argument.

* * *

'I have to leave,' said Spikes a few days later.

Kirin and Maya looked at him in blank astonishment.

'I was expecting some sort of reaction,' said Spikes. 'But this is better. I'll be off, then.'

'Wait!' cried Kirin. 'What do you mean, you have to leave?'

'None of the words are particularly difficult,' said Spikes. 'It's time for me to go to Imokoi. I am supposed to be the ruler of the pashans, you know. I can't stand here and watch you laze around until the end of time.'

Kirin and Maya stood up, brushing sand off their bodies. 'Do you want us to come with you?' asked Maya.

'No. That would mean trouble,' said Spikes. 'Besides, I will need some time alone. It's time for me to have children.'

'You're a girl?' Kirin gasped.

Spikes made a strange barking noise and Kirin and Maya stared in wonder. They had never seen Spikes *laugh* before.

'No. If you must know, it is time for me to find a suitable mate and assist her in the creation of an egg. If you're thinking about hugging me and weeping, don't,' said Spikes. 'We will probably meet again, though it's best not to make plans.'

'I won't know what to do without you,' said Kirin.

'You don't know what to do when I'm here either,' said Spikes kindly. 'But if you manage to get yourself into serious trouble—which you will—I might turn up.'

'I'll try and send a message to Imokoi when I plan to get into trouble,' said Kirin.

'Don't bother,' said Spikes. 'I will always know exactly where you are.'

Maya hugged Spikes and he patted her head awkwardly, trying not to crack it. 'I will miss you too,' he said. 'Now stop being sentimental.'

'Do you have to go right now?' asked Kirin. 'Stay for a while. We'll arrange some sort of large-scale debauchery in honour of our heroic deeds. A proper Spikes farewell feast.'

'No,' said Spikes simply. 'Goodbye, now.'

Seeing Kirin's face, he relented, stepped forward and gave him a quick hug. And then Spikes walked off down the beach, leaving deep grooves in the sand, pausing occasionally to eat a rare and beautiful insect.

Kirin and Maya watched Spikes until he was a small dot in the distance. And then Kirin sighed deeply and threw himself down on the sand, and Maya sat down next to him, a hand on his shoulder.

'Since we're feeling this way anyway, there's another conversation we need to have, Kirin.'

Kirin looked away. 'No,' he said. 'I'm asleep.'

'The holiday's over now,' Maya said. 'And it was lovely, but it's time for us to return to our lives.'

'You can never really go back, Maya. This *is* our life now,' said Kirin. 'And I can't find a single thing wrong with it.'

'If what the unwaba told you was true, Kol needs us more than ever,' said Maya. 'If the Civilian's dead, and the vamans are trying to take over—Kol is in danger, Kirin. My father's in danger.'

'Your father saved the world,' said Kirin. 'He's old enough to take care of himself now.'

'Kirin, I want you to come home with me. I'm not going to live as long as you are, and I want to spend all the time I can with you.'

Kirin looked away. 'Kol isn't my home. I don't belong anywhere. I'm not ravian or rakshas and I'm certainly not human. Besides, our faces—'

'That's just an excuse and you know it. We defeated the *gods*, Kirin. There's nothing we can't do.'

'Neither of us is going to live very long if we go back to Kol, Maya,' said Kirin. 'It's a miracle that we're both alive now. I don't want to spend the rest of my life solving other people's problems. We've done our bit. We've already helped save the world once. It's a new world now. Let it take care of itself.'

Maya stood up. 'We've already done this once, and that was bad enough. This can only end one way,' she said, her voice shaking. 'I suppose it's for the best. We were never going to settle down in happy domesticity anyway. Not with our way of living. It wouldn't have ended happily either. You'd have had to watch me grow old and die.'

'It would be easier to bear than life without you,' said Kirin. 'Please don't go. Why would you want to live the rest of your life doing what other people have taught you is right? Didn't the unwaba teach you how wrong that is? We have to find our own way, Maya.'

'We're descending into drama,' said Maya with a sudden smile. 'Listen to us! This isn't the end of anything.'

'We have all the time in the world, unless this world decides to end too,' said Kirin, lying bravely in turn.

'I'll come back and visit you from time to time, when I'm not too busy. You should drop in any time you can, too. All you need is a hood.'

Kirin laughed and agreed, and they told each other yet again how much in love they were, and how nothing could stand between them and eternal happiness, but they both knew something had ended right then.

Maya left the next morning for Kol. And as Kirin watched her sail away in a dolphin-drawn boat, waving until she disappeared into the morning mist, his heart was full of sorrow and joy. Because though he'd known they could never have lived happily ever after, at least they'd lived as happily as they could have, together, for a while.

Epilogue

The gods gather around the GameWorld, murmuring excitedly. The control crystals are thrown away, the new-fangled rules forgotten. Their faces are alight with excitement. Some cast spells on the north, beginning a fimbulwinter that will sweep across the earth. Others brew eternal summer in the south. Others pull on invisible ropes, and great snakes of metal and lava burst forth from the bowels of the earth. The sun and moon are extinguished, and three new ones of diverse shapes and sizes are set in their place. The world is changing every second; new mountains and islands strain and shudder, flames shoot across the sky and the seas boil. Great lizards of bone leap out from under the skin of the earth, cascading dust and mud.

The dead walk the earth, in armour new and ancient, and with each lurching step they honour the gods, with each feigned breath they grow stronger, and there is much rejoicing. Zivran presides over the board, all-seeing, all-knowing, a curious smile drifting across his noble features. He draws the gods' attention to a solitary figure standing in a charred forest. A Hero, no less.

A splendid young man, physically almost flawless apart from an ugly gash on his throat.

'What shall it be?' asks Zivran. 'Should he rescue a princess? Slay a dragon, or some other monster? Win a battle? Find treasure? Avenge his father? What do You desire?'

'All of them,' suggests a drunken mountain god. Zivran catches Stochastos's eye and tries not to laugh out loud.

'Very well,' says Zivran. 'Let Us Play.'

* * *

Asvin drew his sword and stared at it. Sunlight flashed along the blade as he held it close to his face and studied his reflection. The image he saw was handsome, radiant, perfect, bursting with vitality. Yet he could not shake off the suspicion that something was wrong; if he looked at his arms through the corner of his eyes, they seemed pale, slightly grey, a lot thinner than the robust brown, bulging sinews that presented themselves to a direct gaze.

He shook his head, trying to clear the cobwebs in his mind. Who on earth was Asvin? His name was Avi the Strong, and he was a wandering warrior who ground evil empires to dust under the rather worn soles of his trusty sandals. And now he was journeying west to the kingdom of Sapnani, to rescue the extremely voluptuous princess Bilasi from the clutches of her evil cousin, a shape-shifting sorceress named Erkila. No, not Erkila, where had that name come from? The sorceress Infitada. That was it. And after that he had to avenge his dead father Thoseus . . . no, that wasn't it. His dead father Empeg. And then he had to kill a few dragons, find a priceless jewel in a desert cave to which a mysterious beggar had given him a map. The beggar had looked strangely familiar—his name, he'd said, was the Grey Falcon. He'd said Fox at first, but it was Falcon. Storm a mysterious castle after that, drop in for a battle if there was time, and scale a tower to spend the night with another princess.

It would be a rather busy day. For an ordinary mortal. But not for Asvin. Avi. Not for Avi.

For he was a Hero. A Chosen One. A Person To Whom Things Happened.

Many Things.

'LIGHTS,' said a voice in the sky.

Another sun rose swiftly, filling the sky with rich shades of orange. There was a furious buzzing, and seven imps flew down from the sky, their eyes rolling in a blur as they flew around Asvin, capturing every movement as he walked on, slightly puzzled. The landscape seemed familiar, but that could not be; he had never come to Sapnani before in all his journeys across the world. But those hills to his right, like teeth biting into the sky, those ruined castles . . . he had seen them before. He was sure of it.

'WALK FASTER,' said the voice.

'Why?' asked Asvin.

'WHY? YOU ASK US WHY? BECAUSE YOU HAVE TO RESCUE BILASI THE BEAUTIFUL!'

'Why?' asked Asvin.

'BECAUSE WE SAY SO!'

'Who are you?' Asvin waved his sword at the imps, who flew buzzing angrily.

'IMPUDENCE!' roared the voice. Sixteen skeletal warriors stepped out from behind trees and charged at Asvin. He sliced them all up in under a minute. He looked up at the sky and shook his sword, and for a moment it felt as if the clouds above were watching him, and in their strange patterns he saw faces. It was the sort of thing that inspired fear, he thought, but he felt nothing at all.

One of the clouds darkened, and a bolt of lightning hit Asvin squarely in the chest. He staggered and fell, his limbs scattering in every direction.

'WHY, INDEED,' sniggered the voice. 'THAT SHOULD TEACH HIM OBEDIENCE. HERE, YOU! PUT HIM BACK TOGETHER, I QUITE LIKE HIM. BUT ZIVRAN, CAN I PLAY SOMEONE ELSE NOW?'

Avi the Strong stood up and drew his sword. He would have to hurry, he thought. If the gods were smiling on him, he would rescue Princess Bilasi today. He broke into a run, drawing closer and closer to Castle Sapnani. And soon he came to a bridge that ran over a slow and sluggish little river. On this bridge stood a man, slimmer and shorter than Avi, and in his hands was a long, curved scimitar. Imps buzzed around his head, watching him ceaselessly.

'None shall pass,' said the stranger. 'Who dares walk the wilds of Sapnani?'

'I. Avi,' said Avi.

'Die then, Foul Knave, at the hands of Buyashka!' cried Buyashka, who clearly had a marked and completely unjustified aversion to certain names, and charged at Avi, stabbing and slashing. But Avi was no mean swordsman; he parried and thrust, wounding the stranger several times, but strangely drawing very little blood.

As Asvin slashed and spun and executed a particularly neat thrust through his opponent's thigh, he thought, for a moment, that he could hear cheers and whistles far away. Puzzled, he paused, and Buyashka seized this opportunity to drive his scimitar through Asvin's heart. As he did so, he moved in close, his head next to Asvin's.

'My name is Omar,' he whispered.

Avi pushed him away, and hacked at his arm, but Buyashka swerved and struck again, moving in like a serpent.

'My name is Omar,' he whispered. 'What is yours?'

Avi leaped backwards, ducked, stepped in close and cut off one of Buyashka's arms with a mighty stroke. As the swordsman staggered back, Avi charged, roaring, and buried his sword in his opponent's throat.

'Asvin,' he whispered. And he twisted his sword, tearing Buyashka's head off, and before the head fell to the ground, Avi could have sworn it winked.

* * *

Kirin muttered the incantation and the sand began to ripple. He stood and watched the little dunes flow out in circles, humming a little tune, juggling three shells with his mind.

'Where are you going?' said a voice behind him. A familiar voice. His favourite voice in the whole world. A slow grin spread lazily over his face as he turned around.

'I was going to Kol,' he said. 'To see if anyone needed saving.'

'That's a pity,' said Maya. 'And here I had come back for a long spell of independent thinking, ideally with a slice of lemon.'

They stared at each other in slightly embarrassed silence for a while.

'I've just changed my mind,' declared Kirin. 'I'm going to wander around in my golem-drawn rickshaw, to see what the new world is like and have lots of deeply meaningless and completely selfish adventures instead of sitting on the beach and getting fat. Now, in case you're interested, in the spirit of scientific discovery, in finding interesting ways to save Kol and help all humanity that don't involve just rushing into danger and getting yourself killed, I have room to spare.'

'I could come for a bit,' offered Maya. 'At least until something more interesting comes along.'

* * *

Acknowledgements

For my mother Samita and my sister Sayoni, first readers, lifelines, best friends.

For Thomas and Diya at Penguin India for hope, faith, support and tolerance.

For my friends, for love, sustenance, wisdom and constant confirmation that the world is a strange place full of people more wonderful than any I could ever make up. This means you, Sanghamitra, Sunay, Stoob, Broto, Rukmini, Nidhi, Arjun, Antara, Soumee, Meenakshi, Nilanjana, Sarnath, Rehan, Josh, Arunava, Paul, Vijay, Rupanwita, Momo, Bini. And the rest of you useless loafers as well.

For my father Subrata, who spent his life working boring jobs so I would never have to. And for Shakti, golden girl, supreme-being manifestation and all-round star. Wish you were here.